# Bungalow 2

## Also by Danielle Steel

* Published outside the UK under the title PASSION'S PROMISE

For more information on Danielle Steel and her books, see her website at
www.daniellesteel.com

# DANIELLE STEEL

## Bungalow 2

## BANTAM PRESS

LONDON • TORONTO • SYDNEY • AUCKLAND • JOHANNESBURG

TRANSWORLD PUBLISHERS
61–63 Uxbridge Road, London W5 5SA
A Random House Group Company
www.booksattransworld.co.uk

First published in Great Britain
in 2007 by Bantam Press
an imprint of Transworld Publishers

A CIP catalogue record for this book
is available from the British Library.

ISBN 9780593053300 (cased)
9780593053386 (tpb)

Addresses for Random House Group Ltd companies outside the UK
can be found at: www.randomhouse.co.uk
The Random House Group Ltd Reg. No. 954009

The Random House Group Ltd makes every effort to ensure that the papers used
in its books are made from trees that have been legally sourced from well-managed
and credibly certified forests. Our paper procurement policy can be found at:
www.randomhouse.co.uk/paper.htm

Typeset in Charter ITC
Printed in the UK by CPI Mackays, Chatham, ME5 8TD

2 4 6 8 10 9 7 5 3 1

To Beatie, Trevor, Todd, Nick, Sam,

Victoria, Vanessa, Maxx, Zara,

my very wonderful children,

for years of putting up with my writing,

celebrating the victories,

and supporting me through life's challenges,

and defeats.

I am but a piece in the tapestry of our family,

You are my reason for being,

and together we form a precious whole,

complete because of, and thanks to, YOU.


I love you with all my heart,

Mom / d.s.

And when the movie ends,
life begins.

# Bungalow 2

# Chapter 1

It was a beautiful hot July day in Marin County, just across the Golden Gate Bridge from San Francisco, as Tanya Harris bustled around her kitchen, organizing her life. Her style was one of supreme order. She loved having everything tidy, in its proper place, and in control. She loved to plan, and therefore she rarely ran out of anything, or forgot to do anything. She enjoyed a predictably efficient life. She was small, lithe, in good shape, and didn't look her age, which was forty-two years old. Her husband, Peter, was forty-six. He was a litigator with a respected San Francisco law firm, and didn't mind the commute to Ross, across the bridge. Ross was a prosperous, safe, highly desirable suburban community. They had moved there from the city sixteen years before because the school system was excellent. It was said to be the best in Marin.

Tanya and Peter had three children. Jason was eighteen and was leaving for college at the end of August. He was going to UC Santa Barbara, and although he couldn't wait to go, Tanya was going to miss him terribly. And they had twin daughters, Megan and Molly, who had just turned seventeen.

Tanya had loved every moment of the last eighteen years, being a full-time mom to her kids. It suited her perfectly. She never found it burdensome or boring. The tedium of driving car pools had never seemed intolerable to her. Unlike mothers who complained of it, she loved being with her children, dropping them off, picking them up, taking them to Cub Scouts and Brownies, and she had been head of the parents' association of their school for several years. She took pride in doing things for them, and loved going to Jason's Little League and basketball games, and whatever the girls did as well. Jason had been varsity in high school, and was hoping to make either the basketball or tennis team at UCSB.

His two younger sisters, Megan and Molly, were fraternal twins, and were as different as night and day. Megan was small and blond like her mother. She had been an Olympic-caliber gymnast in her early teens, and only gave up national competitions when she found it was interfering with her work at school. Molly was tall, thin, and looked like Peter, with dark brown hair and endless legs. She was the only member of the family who had never played competitive sports. She was musical, artistic, loved taking photographs, and was a whimsical, independent soul. At seventeen, the twins were going into their senior year. Megan wanted to go to UC Berkeley like her mother, or maybe UCSB. Molly was thinking about going east, or to a college in California where she could follow artistic pursuits. She had been thinking seriously about USC in L.A., if she stayed out west. Although the twins were very close, they were both adamant about not going to the same school. They had been in the same school and class all through elementary and high school, and now they were both ready to go their own ways. Their parents thought it was a healthy attitude, and Peter was encouraging Molly to consider the Ivy League schools. Her grades were good enough, and he thought she'd do well in a high-powered academic atmosphere. She was considering Brown, where she could design her own curriculum in photography, or maybe film school at USC. All three of the Harris children had done exceptionally well in school.

Tanya was proud of her children, loved her husband, enjoyed her life, and had thrived in their twenty-year marriage. The years had flown by like minutes since she'd married Peter as soon as she'd graduated from college. He had just graduated from Stanford Law School, and joined the law firm where he still worked. And just about everything in their life had gone according to plan. There had been no major shocks or surprises, no disappointments in their marriage, no traumas with their kids as Jason, Megan, and Molly navigated through their teens. Tanya and Peter enjoyed spending a lot of time with all three of their children. They had no regrets, and were well aware of how fortunate they were. Tanya worked in a family homeless shelter in the city one day a week, and she took the girls with her whenever she could and their schedules allowed. They both had extracurricular pursuits, and did community service through school. Peter liked to tease Tanya about how boring they all were, and how predictable in their routines. Tanya took great pride in keeping it that way, for all of them. Everything about their life felt comfortable and safe.

Her childhood had not been quite as neat and clean, which was why she liked keeping their life so tidy. Some might have called her life with Peter overly sterile and controlled, but Tanya loved it that way, and so did he. Peter's own youth and adolescence had been very similar to the life he and Tanya had created for their children, a seemingly perfect world. In contrast, Tanya's childhood had been difficult and lonely, and frightening at times. Her father had been an alcoholic, and her parents had gotten divorced when she was three.

She had only seen her father a few times after the divorce, and he died when she was fourteen. Her mother had worked hard as a paralegal to keep her in the best schools. She had died shortly after the twins were born, and Tanya had no siblings. An only child of only children, her family consisted of Peter, Jason, and the twins. They were the hub of her world. She cherished every moment that she spent with them. Even after twenty years of marriage, she couldn't wait for Peter to come home at night. She loved telling him what she'd done that day, sharing stories about the children, and hearing about his day. She still found his cases and courtroom experiences fascinating after twenty years, and she liked sharing her own work with him as well. He was always enthusiastic and encouraging about what she did.

Tanya had been a freelance writer ever since she'd graduated from college, and through all the years of their marriage. She loved doing it because it fulfilled her, added to their income, and she worked at home, without interfering with their children. She led something of a double life as a result. Devoted mother, wife, and caregiver by day, and singularly determined freelance writer at night. Tanya always said that to her, writing was as essential as the air she breathed. Freelance writing had proven to be the perfect occupation for her, and the articles and stories she'd written had been well reviewed and warmly received over the years. Peter always said he was immensely proud of her, and appeared to be supportive of her work, although from time to time, he complained about her long work nights, and the late hours when she came to bed. But he appreciated the fact that it never interfered with her mothering or devotion to him. She was one of those rare, talented women who still put her family first, and always had.

Tanya's first book had been a series of essays, mostly about women's issues. It had been published by a small publisher in Marin in the late 1980s, and reviewed mostly by obscure feminist reviewers, who approved of her theories, topics, and ideas. Her book hadn't been rabidly feminist, but was aware and independent, and the sort of thing one would expect a young woman to write. Her second book, published on her fortieth birthday, two years earlier, and eighteen years after her first book, had been an anthology of short stories, published by a major publisher, and had had an exceptionally good review in *The New York Times Book Review*. She had been thrilled.

In between, she had been frequently published in literary magazines, and often in *The New Yorker*. She had published essays, articles, and short stories in a variety of magazines over the years. Her volume of work was consistent and prolific. When necessary, she slept little, and some nights not at all. Judging by the sales of her recent book of short stories, she had a loyal following both among average readers who enjoyed her work and among the literary elite. Several well-known and highly respected writers had written her letters of warm praise, and had commented favorably about her book in the press. As she was in all else, Tanya was meticulously conscientious about her work. She had managed to have a family, and still keep abreast of her work. For twenty years, she had set time aside every day to write. She was diligent and highly disciplined and the only time she took days off from her writing mornings was during school vacations, or when the children were home sick from school. In that case, they came first. Otherwise, nothing kept her from her work. In her hours away from Peter and the children, she was fanatical about her work. She let the phone go to voice mail, turned off her cell phone, and sat down to write every morning after her second cup of tea, once the kids had gone off to school.

She also enjoyed writing in a more commercial vein, which was the profitable side of it for them, something Peter respected as well. She did occasional articles for the local Marin papers, now and then for the *Chronicle,* on an editorial basis. She liked writing funny pieces, and had a knack with comedic work, in a wry, witty tone, and now and then she wrote pure slapstick when describing the life of a housewife and mother, and scenes with her kids. Peter thought it was what she did best, and she enjoyed doing it. She liked writing funny stuff.

The real money she'd made, compared to what she made on her articles and essays, was writing occasional scripts for soap operas on national TV. She had done quite a number of them over the years. They weren't high literary endeavors, and she had no pretensions about what she did. But they paid extremely well, and the shows she wrote for liked her work, and called her often. It wasn't work she was proud of, but she liked the money she made, and so did Peter. She usually wrote a dozen or so scripts a year. They had paid for her new Mercedes station wagon and a house they rented for a month at Lake Tahoe every year. Peter was always grateful for her help with tuition for their children. She had saved a nice little nest egg from her commercial writing work. She had cowritten a few miniseries, too, mostly before the market for miniseries and television movies had been impacted by reality TV. These days no one wanted miniseries or TV movies, and the only regular work she got for TV was on her soaps. Her agent called her about a script for a soap at least once a month, and sometimes more often. She knocked them out in a few days, working late at night while the rest of the family slept. Tanya was lucky that she needed very little sleep, much to her agent's delight. She had never made gigantic money for her work, but she had produced steadily for many years. She was in effect a housewife and writer with stamina and talent. It was a combination that worked well.

Over the years Tanya's freelance writing had been a steady, satisfying, and lucrative career, and as the kids got older, she had plans to write more. The only dream she had that hadn't been fulfilled yet was to write the screenplay for a feature film. She had persisted in pushing her agent about it, but to some extent her work in TV made her ineligible. There was very little, if any, crossover between television and feature films. It irritated her because she knew she had the skills to do movies, but so far nothing in that vein had come her way, and she was no longer sure it ever would. It was an opportunity she'd been waiting for, for twenty years. In the meantime, she was happy with the writing she did. And the system and schedule she juggled so successfully worked well for all of them. She'd had a steady flow of work during her entire career. It was something she did with her left hand, while she tended to her family with her right and met all their needs. Peter always said that she was an amazing woman, and a wonderful mother and wife. That meant far more to her than favorable literary reviews. Her family had been her first priority during all her years of marriage and motherhood. And as far as Tanya was concerned, she had done the right thing, even if it meant turning down an assignment now and then, although that was rare for her. Most of the time, she found a way to fit it in, and was proud of having done that for twenty years. She had never let Peter or her kids down, nor her work, or the people who paid her to do it.

She had just sat down at her computer with a cup of tea, and was looking over the draft for a short story she'd started the day before, when the phone rang, and she heard the answering machine pick it up. Jason had spent the night in San Francisco, the girls were out with friends, and Peter had long since left for work. He was preparing for a trial the following week. So she had a nice, peaceful morning to work, which was rare when the kids were out of school. She wrote far less in the summer than she did in the winter months. It was too distracting trying to write when the children were home on vacation, and around all the time. But she'd had an idea for a new short story that had been bugging her for days. She was wrestling with it, when she heard her agent leave a message on the phone, and strode rapidly across the kitchen to pick it up. She knew that all the soaps she wrote for were on hiatus, so it wasn't likely to be a request for a script for a soap. Maybe an article for a magazine, or a request from *The New Yorker.*

She answered the phone just before her agent hung up. The message he'd left was a request for her to call him. He was a long-established literary agent in New York, who had represented her for the past fifteen years. The agency also had an office in Hollywood, where they generated a very respectable amount of work for her, as much as in New York, sometimes more. She loved all the different aspects of her work, and had been dogged and persistent about pursuing her career through all the kids' years of growing up. They were proud of her, and once in a while watched her soaps, although they teased her a lot, and told her how "cheesy" they were. But they bragged about her to their friends. It was immensely important to her that Peter and her children respected what she did. And she liked knowing she did it well, without sacrificing her time with them. There was a sign on her office wall that said "What hath night to do with sleep?"

"I thought you might be writing," her agent said as she picked up. His name was Walter Drucker, and he went by Walt.

"I was," she said, hopping onto a high stool near the phone. The kitchen was the nerve center of the house, and she used it as an office. Her computer was set up in the corner, next to two file cabinets bulging with her work. "What's up? I'm working on a new short story. I think it may turn out to be part of a trilogy when it grows up." He admired her, and the fact that she was unfailingly professional and conscientious about everything she did. He knew how important her children were to her, but she still stayed on track with everything she wrote. She was very serious about her work, and everything she touched. It was a pleasure to deal with her. He never had to apologize for her missing a deadline, forgetting a story, going into rehab, or blowing a script. She was a writer to her core, and a good one. Tanya was a true professional. She had talent, energy, and drive. He liked her work, although usually he wasn't a short-story fan, but hers were good. They always had an interesting twist, a surprise. There was something very quirky and unusual about her work. Just when the reader expected it least, she came up with a stunning twist, turn, or ending. And he liked her funny stuff best. Sometimes she made him laugh till he cried.

"I've got work," he said, sounding vague and somewhat cryptic. She was still thinking about her story, and not entirely focused on what he'd said.

"Hmm . . . can't be a soap. They're on hiatus till next month, thank God. I haven't had a decent idea all month, till yesterday. I've been too busy with the kids, and we leave for Tahoe next week, where I am head chef, chauffeur, social secretary, and maid." Somehow she always ended up doing all the domestic work when they went to Tahoe, while everyone else swam, water-skied, and played. She had finally just accepted that it worked that way. The kids all brought friends, and no matter how much she begged, pleaded, or threatened them, no one ever helped. She was used to it by now. The older they got, the fewer chores they did. Peter wasn't much better. When he went to Tahoe, he liked to take it easy and relax, not do dishes, laundry, or make beds. She accepted it as one of the few downsides of her life. And she knew that if that was as bad as it got, she was lucky. Very, very lucky. And she took pride in taking care of them herself, and not hiring help. She was a perfectionist to her core, and taking care of her family, in every aspect, was a source of great pride to her. "What kind of work?" she asked, focusing finally on what he'd said.

"A script. Based on a book. It was a best-seller last year by Jane Barney. You know the one. *Mantra.* It was number one for about nine million weeks. Douglas Wayne just bought the book. They need a script."

"They do? Why me? Isn't she going to write the script?"

"Apparently not. She's never done one before, and she doesn't want to screw this up. She's got consultation rights, but she says she really doesn't want to write the screenplay. She's got too many commitments to her publisher, a new book coming out in the fall, and a book tour in September. She's not available, or interested in doing the script. And Douglas likes your work. Apparently he's addicted to one of your soaps. He says he wants to talk to you about it, he claims you've ruined many an afternoon while he got stuck in front of the TV. He thinks you made the show what it is. Whatever that is. I didn't tell him you write that stuff between car pools, or while your kids are asleep."

"Is this for TV?" she asked, assuming it was, though it seemed odd to her that Douglas Wayne was now producing for television. He was a movie producer, and she couldn't see him doing a TV movie, or even getting one on the air. In spite of how well known he was, the market for TV movies was nearly down to zero. They were a lot more interested these days in leaving random people on deserted islands, or having hidden cameras observe people cheating on each other. Or celebrity reality shows, like *The Osbournes,* which was the crème de la crème of TV fare. On another show, a friend's nephew had won fifty thousand dollars for having the lowest blood pressure when a live alligator was held squirming over his head. It was one way of making a living, but not hers. And reality TV had no need for scripts. "Since when is Douglas Wayne in television?" He was one of the biggest producers in Hollywood, and the woman who had written the book was a world-class writer. *Mantra* had been an extremely powerful and depressing novel, and had won the National Book Award for fiction.

"He's not in TV," Walt went on somewhat lackadaisically. The bigger the project, the more laid-back he appeared, not that he really was. But he sounded half asleep at the moment. At noon in New York. He was leaving for lunch any minute. He had a short work schedule in the office, and did a lot of his business over meals. Most of the time, he was at a restaurant when she called him, and always with the biggest names in the business—publishers, authors, producers, or stars. "This isn't television. It's a feature. A big one. They were looking for a big-name writer," which she wasn't. Respected, yes. Big name, no. Just solid and reliable and steady, as far as she was concerned. "He wants you instead. He loves your segments on the soaps, he says they're the best ones, and a cut way above the other writers who write for them. And he loves your funny stuff. Apparently he reads everything you publish in *The New Yorker.* He seems to be a big fan."

"I'm a big fan of his, too," Tanya said honestly. She had seen every movie he'd ever made. How could this be happening to her? she wondered. Douglas Wayne liked her work, and wanted her to do a screenplay for him? Holy shit! It was too good to be true.

"Well, now that we've established that you two love each other's work, let me tell you about his picture. Eighty-to-one-hundred-million-dollar budget. Three major stars. Academy Award–winning direction. No crazy location shots. The whole picture is being shot in L.A. Screen credit for you, obviously. They go into preproduction in September. The film starts shooting November fifth, and they're figuring on a five-month shooting schedule, barring unexpected disasters. And six or eight weeks postproduction after. With luck, and a decent script, which I know you're capable of, working for Douglas Wayne, you walk away with an Academy Award." He made it sound like her dream come true, or that of anyone who wrote for Hollywood. It didn't get better than this and they both knew it. It was what she had dreamed of all her life, and not yet achieved.

"And I just sit here, write my little script, and send it off to them? How sweet is that?" She was smiling from ear to ear. It was what she did with her screenplays for the soaps, and they ad-libbed them fairly liberally after that, but a lot of her material got used. She wrote scripts that worked for them, which made the producers she worked for constantly greedy for more. And the ratings ate up what she wrote, and skyrocketed. She was a sure thing.

"It's not quite as sweet as that." Walt laughed at her. "I forget you've never done a feature before. No, my love, you don't get to sit there and crank it out between car pools and taking your dog to the vet." He knew her life for the past fifteen years. He always found it amazing that she led such a normal life, and prided herself on being a housewife in Marin, while turning out some truly excellent work, on a surprisingly regular basis. He had a steady income stream from her, and she had stuck with it over the years. Hers was a very solid middle-of-the-road career, and she had better reviews than most, which was why Douglas Wayne had asked for her. Wayne had said that he wanted her at any price, which was incredible, considering she'd never written a screenplay before. But the quality of her work was top-notch. And never having written a screenplay for a feature film before, it was an amazing vote of confidence from Douglas Wayne to seek her out, and Tanya was immensely flattered.

"Douglas Wayne said he wanted someone fresh, who understood the book, and hadn't been a Hollywood hack for the last twenty years." Walt nearly fell out of his chair when he got the call, and she was about to now. "You've got to be in L.A. for this. You can probably go home on weekends most of the time, during pre and post anyway. They're offering to pay all your living expenses for the run of the film. A house or apartment if you want, or a bungalow at the Beverly Hills Hotel, and all expenses paid." He told her what they were offering to pay her for the screenplay then, and there was dead silence at her end.

"Is this a joke?" she asked, suspicious suddenly. He couldn't mean what he had just said. She hadn't made that much money in her entire career. It was more than Peter made in two years as a litigator, and he was a partner in a very important firm.

"It's not a joke," Walt said, smiling at his end. He was happy for her. She was a hell of a good writer, and he thought she could pull it off, even if it was new to her. She was talented and professional. The big question was going to be if she was willing to go to L.A. for nine months. But no one, in his opinion, could be so devoted to her husband and kids that she would turn down an offer like this one. It was a once-in-a-lifetime chance, and Tanya knew that, too. Never in her wildest dreams had she thought this could happen to her, and she had no idea what to do. She had given up the dream of writing a feature film, and contented herself with soaps, articles, short stories, and editorials, and now here it was, her dream was being handed to her on a silver platter. She nearly cried. "This is what you've been telling me you wanted for the last fifteen years. This is your chance to show your stuff. I know you can do it. Go for it, baby—you'll never get another offer like this. Wayne was considering three other screen-writers, one of them with two Academy Awards to his credit. But he wants someone new. He wants an answer this week, Tanya. If you don't take it, he wants to lock in one of the others pretty soon. I don't think you can afford to turn this down. If you're serious about what you've been doing for all these years, it will put you on the map for-ever. A deal like this turns a hobby into a major career."

"I don't write as a hobby," she said, sounding insulted.

"I know you don't. But I could never have dreamed up a better deal for you, or anyone for that matter. Tanya, this is it. It's the brass ring. Grab it, and run like hell." She wanted to say yes, who wouldn't, but there was no way she could. A year from now maybe, after the girls went off to college, but even then she couldn't just leave Peter and go to L.A. for nine months because she'd had an offer to do a screenplay. They were married, she loved him, she had re-sponsibilities to him, and a life she shared with him. And she had the twins at home for another year. She couldn't just dump everything and go to L.A. for all of their senior year. A month maybe, two at a stretch. But nine months—there was just no way.

"I can't do it," she said in a hoarse voice, raw with feeling and re-gret. "I can't, Walt. I still have kids at home." She sounded near tears. It was a lot to give up, but she knew she had to. There was no other choice, not for her. She had never taken her eye off the ball. And the ball for her was Peter and her kids.

"They're not kids," he said tersely. "They're grown-ups, for chris-sake. Jason's leaving for college, and Megan and Molly are women. They can take care of themselves during the week. You'll come home for weekends." He sounded determined not to let her pass this up.

"Can you guarantee that I'll get home every weekend?" She knew he couldn't. Not the way features worked, and he knew it, too. He'd be lying if he said he could. She didn't see how she could do it. Her kids needed her during the week. Who was going to cook for them, help with school projects, make sure they were managing their homework and schedules decently, and take care of them when they got sick? Not to mention boyfriends, social issues, applications to college, and their senior prom in the spring. After being with them constantly all their lives, now she would miss this final important year. And what about Peter? Who would take care of him? They were all used to having her around full-time, not pursuing her own life in L.A. It just wasn't her. She couldn't even imagine doing that to Peter after the girls left. That had never been their deal. Their deal was that she was a full-time wife and mom, and she did her work quietly on the side, in a way that didn't interfere with any of them, or her role as the person who took care of them.

There was a long pause at Walt's end. "No, I can't guarantee it," he said, sounding unhappy. "But you probably can get home most weekends."

"And if I can't? You'll come out and take care of my kids?"

"Tanya, for that kind of money you can hire a babysitter. Ten of them, if you want. They don't pay the big bucks for you to sit on your ass in Marin and mail them the scripts. They want you on deck while they make the film. It makes sense."

"I know it does. I just don't know how to make it work with my real life."

"This is your real life, too. It's real money. Real work. And one of the most important pictures made in Hollywood in the last ten years, and maybe the next ten, working with some of the biggest names in the business. If you want features, this is the one. Something like this won't come your way again."

"I know. I know." She sounded utterly miserable. It was a choice she never thought she'd have to make. And one that was unthinkable given the values she lived by. Family first, writing second. Way, way, way second, no matter how much she loved to write, or the money she made. Her first priority had always been Peter and their kids. Her work life was organized around them.

"Why don't you think about it, and talk to Peter? We can talk about it again tomorrow," Walt said calmly. He couldn't imagine that any sensible man was going to tell her to turn down that kind of money, and he was hoping her husband would tell her to grab the chance. How could he not? In Walt's world you just didn't turn down that kind of opportunity or money. He was an agent, not a shrink, after all. Tanya wasn't even sure she was going to tell Peter. She was feeling as though she should make the decision on her own, and turn it down. It was certainly flattering though, and exciting to think about. The offer was incredibly enticing.

"I'll call you tomorrow," she said sadly.

"Don't sound so depressed. This is the best thing that ever happened to you, Tanya."

"I know it is . . . I'm sorry . . . I just wasn't expecting something like this to come along, and it's a tough decision. My work has never interfered with my family before." And she didn't want it to start now. This was Molly and Megan's last year at home, and she didn't want to miss it. She would never forgive herself if she did. And they probably wouldn't either, not to mention Peter. It just wasn't fair to ask him to take care of the girls on his own, given the workload he was carrying himself at the office.

"I think you can manage it if you work it right. And think of the fun you'll have working on this movie," Walt encouraged her, to no avail.

"Yeah," she said wistfully, "it would be fun." And a beautiful piece of writing. Part of her was dying to do it. The other part knew she had to turn it down.

"Just think calmly about it, and don't make any rash decisions. Talk it over with Peter."

"I will," she said, hopping off the stool in her kitchen. She had a million errands to do that day. "I'll call you in the morning."

"I'll tell them I couldn't reach you, that you're out of town till to-morrow. And Tanya," he said kindly, "go easy on yourself. You're a hell of a writer, and the best wife and mother I know. The two jobs aren't mutually exclusive. Others do it. And your kids aren't babies anymore."

"I know." She smiled. "I just like to think they are sometimes. They'd probably manage fine without me. I'm almost obsolete now as it is." All three of her children had gotten very independent in their final years of high school. But she knew this was going to be an important year for the twins, and for her. It was the last of her full-time mother-ing before they left for college. She still needed to be around, or at least she thought she did, and she was sure Peter would agree. She couldn't imagine his being okay with her going to Hollywood, to work for an entire school year, the twins' last one at home. Going to Hollywood to write a screenplay was certainly a startling idea, and not what any of them had expected she'd ever do, least of all Tanya herself.

"Relax, and enjoy it. This is a real feather in your cap, the fact that a guy like Douglas Wayne wants you. Most writers would sell their kids for that in a hot minute." But Walt knew she wasn't like that. It was one of the things he liked about her. She was a nice woman, with good, wholesome family values. But now he was hoping she'd park them for a few months. "I'll wait to hear from you tomorrow. Good luck with Peter."

"Thanks," she said ruefully. But for Tanya, it wasn't just about what Peter expected of her, it was about the high standard she set for herself. A minute after she hung up, she was standing in her kitchen, looking thunderstruck. It was a lot for her to absorb, and a lot for her family to swallow.

She was standing still in the middle of the room, staring into space as she pondered it, as Jason walked into the kitchen, with two friends he'd brought back from the city.

"Are you okay, Mom?" He was a tall, handsome boy who had slipped unnoticed into manhood, with broad shoulders, a deep voice, her green eyes, and his father's dark hair. He was not only a gorgeous kid but even more important, he was a nice one. He had never given them any trouble. He was a good student and a star athlete. He was thinking of going to law school, like his father. "You looked kind of weird just standing there and staring out the window. Something wrong?"

"No. I was just thinking of everything I have to do today. What are you up to?" she asked with interest, while trying to force the movie offer out of her head.

"We were going to go over to Sally's house and hang out at the pool. Hard work for a summer morning, but someone has to do it." He laughed at his mother, and she stood on tiptoe to kiss him. She was going to miss him like crazy after September. She hated the fact that he was leaving. She had loved all those years when the children were little. The house was going to seem empty without him, and worse yet, the following year when all three of the kids were gone. She was clinging to their last moments together, which made it all the more impossible to consider Douglas Wayne's offer. How could she miss these last precious days with her children? She couldn't. She knew she'd never forgive herself if she missed them.

Jason and his friends left half an hour later, as Tanya bustled around her kitchen. She was so confused and distracted, she didn't know what she was doing. After they left, she sat down at her computer and answered a few e-mails. She couldn't think straight. She was staring blindly at the keyboard when the girls came home an hour later. They were chatting animatedly as they walked in and glanced over at their mother.

"Hi, Mom. What are you doing? You look like you're falling asleep at the computer. Writing?"

Tanya laughed at the question, and awoke out of her reverie, as she looked at them. The two girls looked so different, they didn't even seem related. It made it easier for them to be twins than if people had easily confused them.

"No, I usually try to stay awake while I'm writing." Her plans to work on the short story that morning had gone right out the window. "It's not easy, but I manage." She laughed, as they sat down at the kitchen table. Megan wanted to know if she could bring her boyfriend to Tahoe in August, which was a sensitive question. Tanya discouraged her children from bringing their romances on holiday vacations. There had been a few exceptions but as a rule she and Peter thought it was a bad idea.

"I think it might be nice if we just keep it family this time. Jason's not bringing anyone, and Molly isn't either," Tanya said sensibly.

"They don't mind. I asked them." Megan's eyes looked straight into her mother's. She was fearless. Molly was much shyer. And Tanya always preferred that they bring friends of the same sex on trips, instead of the boys and girls they were involved with. It was a lot simpler, and Tanya was conservative in a number of ways.

"I'll talk to your father about it." She was stalling for time on everything. All of a sudden she had too much to think of. Way too much. Walt had turned her whole morning upside down with his phone call. Her whole life, in fact. In a nice way, but it was upsetting.

"Is something wrong, Mom?" Molly asked. "You look weirded out about something." She had noticed the same thing as Jason. And Tanya was feeling weird. Walt's call had completely thrown her. He had put a lifelong dream in her hands, and she knew she had no choice but to turn it away. In her book, good mothers didn't leave their kids for senior year or any time. It was okay for kids to grow up and leave parents, but never the reverse. It reminded her too much of her father abandoning her.

"No, sweetheart, nothing's wrong. I was just working on a story."

"That's nice." She knew they were proud of her. It meant a lot to Tanya. The respect of her husband and children was important to her. She couldn't even imagine what they would think of the offer Walt had just made her on behalf of Douglas Wayne.

"Do you guys want lunch?"

"No, we're going out." The kids were meeting friends for lunch in Mill Valley.

Half an hour later they were gone, and Tanya sat staring into space in her kitchen again. For the first time, she felt as though she were being torn between two worlds, two lives, the people she loved and the work she had always enjoyed doing. She almost wished Walt had never called her. She felt stupid, but as she turned off her computer, she wiped away a tear that crept out of her eye. And then she went out to do errands. She was on her way home when Peter called her to say he'd be home late and not to make dinner for him. He was going to grab a sandwich at the office and eat at his desk.

"How has your day been?" he said, sounding affectionate but busy. "Mine's been crazy."

"Mine's been a little crazy, too," she said vaguely, upset that he wasn't coming home for dinner. She wanted to talk to him, and she knew he'd be exhausted after preparing for his trial. "How late do you think you'll be home?"

"I'll try to make it by ten. Sorry about dinner. I'm going to do as much work as I can with the other guys." She knew he was deep in preparation for a trial.

"That's fine."

"You okay? You sound distracted."

"Just busy. The usual. Nothing special."

"Kids okay?"

"They're all out. Megan wants to bring Ian to Tahoe. I told her I'd talk to you about it. I don't think it's such a great idea. They'll start fighting on the second day, and drive us all crazy." He laughed at the accurate description of his earlier trips with them. They had taken him skiing with them the previous winter, and he had left two days early after breaking up with Megan. They patched it up as soon as she got back to the city. She was known in the family for her turbulent love life. Molly hadn't had a serious romance yet. And Jason had dated the same girl all through high school and had just broken up with her during the early days of summer. Neither of them wanted a long distance romance when he was away at school.

"I'm okay either way about Ian," Peter commented. "But I don't care if you want to make me the heavy." He was always a good sport about it, and they presented a united front to their children, although like all kids, they made the usual efforts to divide and conquer in order to get what they wanted. Their attempts were almost always unsuccessful. Peter and Tanya had a powerful bond and usually shared the same opinions. It was rare for them to disagree about their children or anything else.

He had another call then, and told her he'd see her that night. It was always comforting talking to him. She loved their exchanges, their time together, the way they still cuddled up to each other at night. Nothing about their relationship to each other had become commonplace or was taken for granted. They had one of those rare marriages that had never been seriously challenged. And after twenty years, they were still in love with each other. As Tanya thought about it, she couldn't even imagine being without him. The idea of living in L.A. for nine months, alone five nights a week, was inconceivable. Just thinking about it now, she felt lonely. It didn't matter how much they offered her, or how important the movie was, her husband and children were more important to her. And as she pulled into their driveway, she knew she had made the decision. She wasn't even sad about it. Maybe a little disappointed, but there was no question in her mind, this was the life she wanted. She wasn't even sure she'd tell Peter about it. All she had to do now was call Walt in the morning and tell him to turn it down. It was flattering to have been asked, but she didn't want it. She already had everything she wanted. All she needed was Peter and their kids and the life they had.

# Chapter 2

As it turned out, despite the best of intentions, it was after eleven o'clock that night when Peter came home. He looked absolutely exhausted, and all he wanted to do was take a shower and get into bed. It didn't really matter to Tanya that they hadn't had a chance to talk that night. She had decided late that afternoon not to even tell him about the movie offer she'd had from Douglas Wayne. She had made up her mind to turn it down. She was already half asleep when Peter slipped into bed after his shower, and put his arms around her. She murmured contentedly with her eyes closed and smiled.

"... long day ..." she murmured sleepily, leaning back against him, and he pulled her closer. He smelled of soap and shampoo from his shower. He always smelled delicious to her, even when he woke up in the morning. She turned around in his arms then and kissed him, and he held her tight for a long moment. "... bad day?" she asked him softly.

"No, just long," he said, admiring her in the moonlight that was filtering into their room. "Sorry I was so late. Everything okay here?"

"Fine," she said sleepily, nestling happily in his arms. It was the place she liked best to be. She loved ending her days next to him, and waking up next to him in the morning. That had never changed over twenty years. "The kids are all out." It was summertime, and they spent every waking moment with their pals. She knew the girls were spending the night at a friend's again, and she knew Jason was responsible and a good driver. He rarely stayed out very late, and she felt comfortable going to bed and not waiting up for him. He had his cell phone on him at all times, and she knew she could always reach him. All three of their children were reasonable, and even in their teenage years they hadn't given their parents any serious problems.

Peter and Tanya cuddled close to each other, and five minutes later they were both asleep. Peter got up before she did the next day. She brushed her teeth while he was in the shower, and went downstairs in her nightgown to make him breakfast. She peeked into Jason's bedroom on the way, and saw that he was sleeping soundly. He wouldn't be up for several hours. She had breakfast on the table for Peter when he came downstairs, looking handsome in a gray summer suit, white shirt, and dark tie. She knew from what he was wearing that he must have a court appearance at some point that day. Otherwise he would have worn a sport shirt and khaki slacks, and sometimes even jeans, particularly on Fridays. He had a nice, clean, preppy look, similar to his style when he had met her. They made a handsome couple. She smiled at him as he walked in and sat down to cereal, poached eggs, coffee, toast, and a bowl of fruit. He liked eating a good breakfast, and she always got up to cook it for him, and for the children during the school year. She took pride in taking care of them. She liked to say it was her day job. Her writing career took a backseat to them.

"You must be going to court today," she commented as he glanced at the paper and nodded.

"Just a quick appearance to request a continuance on a minor matter. What are you up to today? Any interest in meeting me in town for dinner? We got most of our prep work done yesterday."

"Sounds good to me." She met him in the city for dinner at least once a week. Sometimes they went to the ballet or the symphony, but most of all she enjoyed spending quiet evenings with him at little restaurants they liked, or going away somewhere for a weekend together. It was an art form they had studied carefully, keeping romance alive in a twenty-year-old marriage with three kids. So far they had done well.

He glanced across the table at her as he finished his breakfast and studied her carefully. He knew her better than she knew herself.

"What are you not telling me?" As always, he stunned her with his unfailingly accurate perception. It would have amazed her except that he had been doing it for all the years they'd been together. He always seemed to know what she was thinking.

"That's a funny thing to say." She smiled at him, impressed by what he had just said. "What makes you think I'm not telling you something?" She never understood how he did it. But he always did.

"I don't know. I can just feel it. Something about the way you were looking at me, as though you had something to say and didn't want to say it. So what is it?"

"Nothing." He laughed as she said it, and so did she. She had just given herself away. It was just a matter of time before she told him. And she had told herself she wouldn't. She could never keep secrets from him, nor he from her. She knew him just as well as he knew her. "Oh shit . . . I wasn't going to tell you," she confessed, and then poured him a second cup of coffee, and herself another cup of tea. She rarely ate breakfast, just tea, and nibbled the leftovers on their plates. It was enough. "It's not that important."

"It must be, if you were going to keep it a secret. So what's up? Something about the kids?" It was usually that, some confession one of them had made to her in confidence. But she always told him anyway. He was good about keeping secrets, and she trusted his judgment, on all subjects. He was smart, and wise, and kind. And he almost never let her down.

She took a deep breath and a sip of her tea. For some reason, it was hard to tell him. It was easier telling him things about the kids. This was harder because it was about her. "I got a call from Walt yesterday." She stopped and waited for a moment before she went on, as he looked at her expectantly.

"And? Am I supposed to guess what he said?" He sat there patiently, and she laughed.

"Yeah, maybe you should." She looked nervous and felt strange telling him. The idea of her living in L.A. for nine months was so horrifying to her that she felt guilty even telling him about it, as though she had done something wrong, which she hadn't. She was planning to call Walt to decline as soon as Peter left for the office. She wanted to do it quickly and get it behind her. She felt threatened just knowing that the offer was still open, as though, just by making the proposal, Douglas Wayne had the power to kidnap her from her family and the life she loved. She knew it was silly, but that was how she felt. Maybe because she was afraid a part of her would want it, and that part of her had to be controlled. She knew it was up to her to do it. No one else could do it for her, not even Walt. Or Peter. "He called me with an offer," she finally went on. "It was very flattering, but not something I want to do." Peter wasn't sure he believed her when he looked into her eyes. There was nothing she could write that she'd want to turn down. He knew after twenty years with her that Tanya needed to write as much as she needed air. She was very discreet about it, but it was a deep fundamental need, and something she did well. He was very proud of her, and had a deep respect for her work.

"Another book of short stories?" She shook her head, and took another deep breath.

"Film. A feature. The producer likes my work. I guess he's addicted to soaps. Anyway, he called Walt. He was inquiring about having me do the script." She tried to be offhand about it, but Peter looked across the table at her with a look of amazement.

"He offered you the script of a feature film?" He looked as stunned as she had when she first heard it. "And you don't want it? What is it, a porno?" He couldn't imagine Tanya turning down any film but that. Writing the screenplay for a feature film had been her lifetime dream. She had been talking about it for years. There was no way she could decline.

"No," she laughed, "at least I don't think so. Maybe it was," she teased, and then grew serious again as she met his eyes. "I just can't."

"Why not? I can't think of a single reason for you to turn it down. What happened?" He knew there had to be more to it than she was saying.

"It doesn't work," she said sadly, trying not to be a brat about it. She didn't want him to feel badly that she was going to say no. It was a sacrifice she was more than willing to make. In fact, it would have been a sacrifice for her to stay in L.A. She didn't want to leave him or the girls.

"Why doesn't it work? Explain this to me." He was going nowhere until she told him, as he sat across the kitchen table from her and explored her with his eyes.

"I'd have to live in L.A. while they're filming. I could commute on weekends. I'm just not going to do that, we'd all be miserable, and I'm not going to be down there, while you and the girls are here. Besides, this is their last year at home."

"And it could be your last chance to do something you've wanted to do all your life." They both knew he was right.

"Even if it is, it's still the wrong one. I'm not going to sacrifice my family to work on a movie. It's not worth it."

"Why couldn't you commute on weekends? The girls are never here anyway. They're either out with their friends, or at sports after school. I can manage. We'll take turns doing the cooking, and you could come home on Friday nights. Maybe you could go back down early Monday morning. How bad would that be? And it would only be for a few months, right?" He was more than willing to do it, and listening to him brought tears to her eyes. He was always so good to her, and such a decent person. It would have been hard on all of them, and she didn't feel right doing it, even if he was generous enough to offer.

"Five months to shoot the film. Two for preproduction, and one or two for post. That's eight or nine months. The whole school year. That's too much to ask. Peter, I love you even more for offering to let me do it, but I can't."

"Maybe you can," he said slowly, thinking about it. He didn't want to deprive her of what she had always wanted most.

"How? It's not fair to you, I would miss you horrifically, and the girls would kill me. This is their senior year. I should be here, and I want to be."

"I would miss you, too," he said honestly, "but maybe the girls would have to suck it up for once. You're always here for them, ready to do everything they want. It might do them good to be a little more independent for a change, and me, too. Tanya, I don't want you to miss this. It might never come again. You can't pass it up." He looked so earnest and loving as he said it that she nearly cried.

"Yes, I can pass it up. I'm going to call Walt as soon as you leave for the office and turn it down." She said it quietly and firmly, convinced it was the right choice.

"I don't want you to. Tell him to wait. Let's talk to the girls first." He wanted to be sensible about it and make it a family decision, in her favor, if that was at all possible and the girls were willing to be magnanimous about it. He hoped they would be, for their mother's sake.

"They'll feel totally abandoned, and they'd be right. I'd basically be gone for their whole senior year, except on weekends. And once they start shooting the picture, who knows if I could get away every weekend? You hear horror stories about that. Nights, days, weekends, shooting schedules that get totally out of hand, and pictures that go off the charts on budget and time. It could take longer than they say."

"The budget's their problem, you're mine. I want us to work this out." She smiled as she looked at him, and then got up and came around the table to hug him. She put her arms around him and kissed him.

"You're wonderful and I love you . . . but trust me, it won't work."

"Don't be such a defeatist about it. Let's at least try to make it work. We'll talk to the girls tonight when we come home from dinner. Now I'm not just taking you out to dinner, we're going to celebrate." And then he thought of something. "How much did they offer?"

She smiled for a minute, still shocked herself by the offer, and then she told him. There was dead silence in the room for a minute, and then he whistled. "You'd better take it. We have three college tuitions to pay next year, and those are peanuts compared to that. That's pretty heady stuff. And you were going to turn that down?" She nodded. "For us?" She nodded again, her arms still around him. "Sweetheart, you're nuts. I'm sending you down there to work your ass off. Hell, maybe I should retire if you wind up with a booming career writing movies." She had made a decent living at writing so far, although the literary publications never paid much. But the soap operas had always been nice money. Douglas Wayne's feature film was better than nice, it was fantastic, and Peter was duly impressed by their offer.

"That and a bungalow at the Beverly Hills Hotel for the duration, or a house or an apartment, whatever I want. And all expenses paid while I'm there." She told him the names of the director and the stars, and he whistled again. It was more than a golden opportunity, it was a once-in-a-lifetime shot at the stars, and they both knew it. He didn't see how she could turn it down. He was afraid that if she did, she would regret it forever, and resent him and the children for it. It was too much to give up.

"You have to do it," he said, still holding her in his arms. "I won't let you turn this down. Maybe we should all move to L.A. for a year." He was kidding of course, but she wished they could. The fact was they couldn't, he had a solid career as a partner in his law firm, and the girls had a right to finish school where they'd grown up. If any-one went to L.A., it had to be Tanya, alone. And that was everything she didn't want, except for the excitement of doing it, having a dream come true, and the money, which seemed totally incredible to them both. She had never sacrificed her family for her career, and she wasn't about to start now.

"Don't be silly," she said, smiling wistfully at him. "It's just nice to know they wanted me to do the script."

"Let's see what the girls say tonight. Tell Walt you're thinking about it, and Tanya"—he looked down at her with loving eyes as he held her tight—"just so you know, I'm proud of you."

"Thank you for being so nice about it. I still can't believe they wanted me . . . Douglas Wayne . . . I have to admit, that's pretty cool."

"Very cool," he said, glancing at his watch. He was an hour late for work, but it had been important news. "Where do you want to go to dinner tonight?"

"Somewhere quiet where we can talk."

"How about Quince?" he suggested.

"Perfect." It was a small romantic restaurant in Pacific Heights, with terrific food.

"Take a cab in. I'll drive you home. We have a date."

He kissed her goodbye a few minutes later, and after he was gone, she sighed, stared at the phone, picked it up, and called Walt. She wasn't sure what to say to him. She thought the decision had been made the night before, but apparently it hadn't. She still couldn't see herself doing it, and when she told her agent that, he groaned.

"What can I do to convince you that you have no other choice?"

"Tell them to make the movie up here," she said, feeling pulled. Even Peter made it sound so feasible, but in her heart of hearts she knew it wasn't, no matter how good a sport Peter was. She had a feeling her daughters would see it the same way she did. This was hardly the year they wanted their mother leaving home.

"I hope Peter convinces you, Tanya. Hell, if your husband is okay with it, what are you worried about? He's not going to divorce you for going to L.A. for nine months."

"You never know," she said, laughing at him. She knew that wouldn't happen, but absence was never a good thing for a marriage.

Besides, she loved being with him. She could only imagine how miserable she'd be without him all week long for all those months.

"Call me tomorrow. I'll tell Doug I still haven't gotten hold of you. When I told him that yesterday, he said you were worth waiting for. He's got his heart set on your writing this script."

Tanya caught herself before she said "me too." She couldn't allow herself to get caught up in it, she knew. This was just a dream. A life-long dream, admittedly. But not one she could indulge.

She went to work on her short story after she hung up. Jason wandered into the kitchen at noon, and she made breakfast for him. They sat and chatted for a while, and the girls came home in the late afternoon. She didn't say anything to them about the offer. She wanted to discuss it further with their father first.

At six o'clock she dressed for dinner, and an hour later she took a cab into the city, thinking about the movie again. Suddenly, she felt sad at the idea of leaving home. She felt as though she were drifting downstream in a boat without oars, out of control. Peter was waiting at the restaurant when she got there, and they had a lovely dinner together. They both stayed off the subject of the movie offer until dessert. Peter said he'd been thinking about it, and he wanted her to do it. It was Friday night, and he wanted to have a family meeting about it the following morning.

"You have to make the decision, Tan. Even I can't tell you what to do. And you can't let them make it for you. They don't have that right. But you can ask them what they think."

"And what do you think?" She looked sorrowfully at him, feeling as though she were about to lose everyone and everything she loved. She knew that was silly, but it felt that way. There were tears in her eyes when she looked at her husband, and he reached across the table and took her hand in his.

"You know what I think, sweetheart. I know it's hard, but I think you have to do it. Not for the money, although God knows it's tempting and that would be reason enough to do it. But I think you have to because it's always been your dream. You have a shot at it. The girls will get used to it, even if it's an adjustment at first, and so will I. It's not forever, just a few months. You can't give up your dreams, Tanya. Not when they walk right through the front door and throw themselves into your lap. Something tells me this was meant to be. We can do it . . . *You* can do it. You have to do it. Never give up your dreams, Tan," he said softly, "not even for us."

"You're my dream," she said gently. "You have been since the day I met you." She held tightly to his hand. "I don't ever want to do anything to spoil that. Besides, I don't think I could stand being away from you five nights a week." They had an active sex life and were unusually close to each other, their lives interdependent and entwined for twenty years. She couldn't even imagine what a weekend marriage would be like. She just didn't think that a major Hollywood movie was worth sacrificing what they shared, even for nine months. Peter was far more open to the idea than she.

"You're not going to spoil anything, silly," he said, smiling at her, as the waiter put the check down next to him. They'd had a great dinner and an excellent bottle of wine. And as they left the restaurant, Tanya looked distracted. She was thinking about L.A., and how much she would miss him if he actually talked her into accepting. She couldn't imagine doing it. How could she leave a man like Peter, even five days a week? No movie script was worth it.

They dropped the bomb on the children the next day. Their reactions were not entirely what Peter and Tanya had expected, though some of it was predictable. Molly thought it was wonderful for her mom, and a major opportunity not to be missed. She promised to help take care of their dad if Tanya went. Jason thought it was totally cool and asked if he could stay with her and meet some of the actresses. Tanya pointed out that he was supposed to be going to college, studying during the week, and she would be home in Marin on weekends. But he wasn't in the least disturbed that she would be leaving his sisters alone with their dad for their senior year. Although Tanya was certain he would have had a total fit if she had done it for his senior year. He said their dad could take care of them. And Megan was livid. *Really* livid.

"How can you even think of doing something like that?" she shouted at her mother, with eyes blazing. The fierceness of her reaction took even Tanya by surprise.

"I'm not actually, Megan. I was planning to turn it down, but your father thought I should tell you, just to hear your reaction." They had certainly heard it in Megan's case, loud and clear.

"Are you both *crazy?* This is our last year home! What are we supposed to do for a mother, while you go hang out with movie stars in Hollywood?" She said it as though Tanya had suggested working for nine months in a brothel in Tijuana.

"I wouldn't be hanging out," Tanya said quietly, "I'd be working. It would have been a nice opportunity, if it had come a year later. But even then, I wouldn't want to leave your father."

"Don't you care about us at all? We need you here. Molly and I are applying to college this year. Who's supposed to help us with that if you're gone? Or don't you care, Mom?" There were tears in her eyes as Megan said it, and in Tanya's as she listened. It was a painful exchange, and Peter was quick to intervene.

"I'm not sure any of you know what an honor this is. Douglas Wayne is one of the biggest producers in the business." He listed all the stars then. Jason whistled, and reminded his mother he'd like to meet them all.

"I don't know them," his mother said somberly. "I don't know why we're doing this." There was no point upsetting the children with a family meeting. All it could do was worry them, in her opinion. And for what? Her decision had been made. She was staying home with them. In spite of that, Peter thought it was important that they know about the offer. But why? Megan had just said everything Tanya was afraid of hearing, and thought herself. If she accepted the offer, at least one of her children would hate her, and in time, maybe they all would. Jason certainly didn't seem upset. And Molly was always generous of heart and thought. Megan said in no uncertain terms that she would never forgive her mother if she went. Tanya believed her. Peter said she would get over it, and he would be there to help and take care of them while Tanya was out of town.

"I can't disrupt our family to this extent," she said grimly after their children left the room. "They'll never forgive me, and maybe after a while, you'll hate me, too," she said, looking worried. Jason had wished her luck and said he hoped she went. Molly had given her a big hug and said she was proud of her, and Megan stormed out and slammed the door. She slammed three more doors on the way to her room.

"No one's going to hate you, sweetheart," Peter said as he put an arm around her shoulders. "You may hate yourself though if you pass it up. I don't think you can count on this ever happening again, particularly if you turn this one down."

"I'm sure it won't," Tanya said calmly. "I don't need to do a feature. That was just a pipe dream years ago. I'm happy with my short stories and soaps." She made enough money to help Peter, and loved her work. She didn't need or want more than that. And Megan's reaction had told her all she needed to know.

"You're capable of better than soaps, Tan. Why not do it while you have the chance?"

"You heard Megan. I can't sacrifice her for a film. That's so wrong."

"She doesn't have a right to keep you from something that's important to you. And she'll be here with me. She'll get over it. She's not even going to notice if you're here. She's with her friends all the time. And you can help her with her college applications on weekends."

"Peter . . ." Tanya looked at him with wide eyes. "No. Don't push me. I appreciate what you tried to do, but even if they all thought it was wonderful, I couldn't do it. I can't leave them, and I won't leave you. I love you. Thank you," she said, as she stood up and put her arms around him, and he hugged her.

"You're going to hate being a Marin housewife after this. Every day you're going to think that you could have been there, working on a movie that will probably win an Academy Award. You can't let the kids make this decision, Tanya. You have to make it."

"I already did. I vote for staying home, and doing what I do now, with the people I love."

"We'll still love you if you go to L.A. I will. And even Megan will forgive you. She'll be very proud. We all will."

"No," Tanya said again, and meant it, as she and Peter looked at each other for a long time. "Sometimes you have to give up something you want, because it's the right thing to do for the people you love."

"I want you to do this," he said gently. "I know how important it could be for you. I don't want you to give that up, for me or the kids. It would be wrong. Very wrong. I'd never forgive myself if I kept you from this."

Tanya looked at him with frightened eyes. "What if it screws up our marriage? It might be even harder than we think," and she expected it to be very hard.

"Unless you fall in love with some handsome movie star, I can't see it screwing anything up between us, Tan. Can you? I'll just be sitting here waiting for you."

"I would miss you unbearably," she said, as a tear slid down her cheek. She felt like a kid being sent away to school, for their own good. She didn't want to leave him. She loved the idea of writing the script, but she was scared. She hadn't been out in the world on her own in twenty years.

"I'd miss you, too," Peter said honestly. "But sometimes, Tan, you have to be brave enough to grow. You have a right to do something like this, without it costing you anything. I wouldn't love you less for doing this. I would be very, very proud of you, and I'd love you more."

"I'm scared," she whispered, as she clung to him, and tears began to pour down her face. "And what if I can't do it? This isn't some silly daytime soap, this is the big leagues. What if I'm only a minor league player?"

"You're not, baby. I know that. And so do you, I hope. That's why I want you to do it. You need to spread your wings and fly. You've been preparing for this for so many years. Don't deprive yourself of it, for me or the kids. Go for it," he said, and kissed her hard. It was the greatest gift he could give to her, and as Tanya looked at him through her tears, she could see that there were tears in his eyes.

"I love you," she whispered to him as he held her, "so much . . . oh Peter . . . I'm so afraid . . ."

"Don't be, sweetheart. I'll be here waiting for you, and so will the kids . . . even Megan . . . we'll come down and visit you, and you'll be home on weekends. If you get stuck there, we'll come down. Or at least I will for sure. It'll be over before you know it, and you'll be glad you did it." It was the most generous gesture she had ever known.

"You're the most remarkable man in the world, Peter Harris. I love you so much . . ."

"Just remember that when movie stars start knocking on your door."

"They won't," she said, continuing to cry, "and I don't care if they do. I could never love anyone in the whole world as I do you."

"Me too," he said, holding her so tightly she could hardly breathe. "Will you do it, Tan? Hit a home run for the team." He pulled away so he could look into her eyes. Her eyes were terrified when they met his. She didn't say a word to him. All she did was nod, cry harder, and cling to him like a frightened child, afraid of leaving home.

# Chapter 3

They broke the news to the children at Lake Tahoe in August. The reactions were similar to what they had been previously. Molly was supportive and proud of her, Jason couldn't wait to visit her. And Megan didn't speak to her for the next three weeks. She told her in a venomous tone that she would never forgive her, and every time Tanya saw her, she was crying. Megan said it was the worst thing that had ever happened to her in her life. Her mother was abandoning her. A hundred times in the four weeks they were there, Tanya said she was going to call Walt and tell him she was backing out. But Peter wouldn't let her. He said that Megan would get over it, and it was good that she was venting. Tanya felt like a child abuser every time she looked at her, and cried nearly as often as Megan did.

It was a bittersweet time, Jason's last summer before college. His friends came and went, driving up from the city to stay with them. And every moment Tanya spent with him and his father seemed precious now. She had some wonderful long talks with Molly as they went on hikes. Megan avoided them, whenever their mother was around. She only started speaking to her again, and only out of dire necessity, in the last few days before they went home. They had a big family barbecue and invited friends on the last night.

Afterward she and Peter chatted as they cleaned up. She only had ten days left before she had to leave for L.A. Tanya had told Douglas Wayne that she couldn't come to L.A. until after she dropped her son off at school. She wanted to be there with Peter to settle him into his dorm. The girls were coming, too, and after that Peter would drive them home. Tanya was being met by a limo at the Santa Barbara Biltmore, and driven to L.A. Their tearful goodbyes would be there, if Megan didn't kill her first.

The last days before Tanya and Jason left were tough. She helped him pack his bags, and got everything ready for him for school. Laptop, bicycle, sound system, sheets, blankets, pillows, bedspread, photographs of the family, sports equipment, some things to hang on his walls, a desk lamp, and rug. She wasn't sure if she was more upset about dropping Jason off, or leaving them after that herself. She was taking far fewer things than she packed for him. She had no plans to do anything but work. She packed one hanging bag and a small suitcase, mostly with running shoes, sweatshirts, and jeans. She thought about it long and hard and finally took one pair of decent slacks, two cashmere sweaters, and a black cocktail dress, in case she had to go to some formal event with the cast. And she packed a million pictures of the kids in frames to put all over her bungalow at the Beverly Hills Hotel. She already knew she was going to be staying in Bungalow 2, her home for the next many months. It had two bedrooms so the kids could visit her, a small office, a living room, and a dining room, with a little pantry kitchen set up, although she couldn't imagine cooking for herself while she was there. It was going to be the first time she lived alone in twenty years. She couldn't even imagine it, and Peter teased that both of them were going off to school.

He hadn't wavered for a single second. He still insisted that it was going to be one of the greatest things that had ever happened to her. She wished she could agree. Right now all she could think about was how much she would miss her children and him. She would have backed out if she hadn't already signed the contract, and they hadn't sent the check. Her agent Walt had been ecstatic and couldn't believe she'd come to her senses. He had been sure she wouldn't do it, and he called Peter himself to tell him he was a hero for talking her into it and letting her go. Walt said he was a "mensch," and Tanya agreed, a man of strength, dignity, and integrity. He had put her best interests ahead of his own, and even their family's, and he had no doubt whatsoever that he and the children could manage. He had told Megan and Molly that again and again. Molly had promised to do everything she could to help, although she seemed more tearful lately, and stayed close to her mother, offering to help her, pack for her, and do errands with her. She couldn't get enough of Tanya suddenly, and Tanya was reminded of when Molly was little and they had been inseparable. Megan had always been more independent, and she said not a word to her mother as they drove down to Santa Barbara. She just sat staring out the window, looking like someone had died, while Molly held her sister's hand.

It nearly broke Tanya's heart to look at her family as they packed the van they'd rented, with Jason's things and her two small bags. She didn't need to take a lot, she was planning to come home every weekend. Their neighbor, Alice Weinberg, came to say goodbye to Tanya and Jason. She put her arms around Tanya and told her how envious she was of her, going to live in Hollywood to work on a script. They had been friends for sixteen years. Alice's husband had died two years before, of a heart attack on the tennis court, but she was doing fine. Both her children were in college, and she had opened an art gallery in Mill Valley. She said it gave some purpose to her life, but it was nothing like what Tanya was doing. Alice was tall and thin and dark like Molly, and the two women embraced before they left.

"Now call me and tell me who you meet down there!" Alice said through the open window as Peter started the well-packed van. There was barely room for all of them, and Tanya waved at Alice as they drove away. They had had many cups of tea in her kitchen since July, talking about her plans. Alice had said she'd keep an eye on the kids, although she wasn't home as much as she used to be. She was always meeting with artists and going to exhibits and art fairs to look for emerging artists and new work. She looked ten years younger than she had before her husband died. She had lost a lot of weight, had her eyes done, and streaked her hair. She was terrified of being on the dating market, and Tanya knew she had dated two young artists. She still missed Jim horribly, and she said there would never be anyone like him. He had been one of Peter's partners and only forty-seven when he died. Alice was forty-eight, just two years older than Peter, and six years older than Tanya, but she looked youthful and sympathetic as she waved and they drove away.

"Take care, Jason!" she shouted after them. "Don't forget to call James!" Her son was at UCSB, too, and her daughter was at Pepperdine in Malibu. Watching them leave reminded Alice of when her own kids had left for school. Melissa was a senior, and James was a sophomore this year. She had told Jason that James would show him the ropes. Jason had already e-mailed him and made contact, as he had with his roommate, who was a boy named George Michael Hughes from

Dallas, Texas. He had played lacrosse in high school, and was going to try out for the team at UCSB.

The drive to Santa Barbara was hot and crowded, with Jason's belongings piled up between them. The air-conditioning didn't work in the van, and Tanya didn't care, she was just happy to be with her kids. It took them eight hours to get there, with two stops for food. Jason had to be fed every few hours, but the girls didn't really care. Tanya couldn't eat. She was too upset about dropping Jason off at school, and knowing she was about to leave Peter and the girls. She felt as though she were losing all of them at once, although, as Megan pointed out to her when they got out in front of the Biltmore looking like Gypsies, they were losing her.

"I'll be home on weekends, Meg," Tanya reminded her again.

"Yeah, right. Whatever," Megan said to her mother, looking surly, and then walked away. She hadn't forgiven her yet, and maybe never would. Tanya was beginning to fear the next months would mark her for life, and her own guilt over it made her tolerate Megan's accusations to a degree she wouldn't have otherwise. It was a difficult weekend. Except for Jason. He was thrilled to be leaving for college.

They checked into the hotel, had dinner at a restaurant in town that night, and went to the Coral Casino across from the hotel the next morning for brunch. Jason didn't have to be at his dorm till two. And once they got him there, he instantly disappeared to look up friends, while Peter set up his computer and his sound system, and Tanya made his bed. She had to fight back tears while she did. Her little boy was leaving home . . . and worse yet, so was she.

It was a very strange feeling, not only for her but for the girls. They unpacked his duffel bag, and everything was set up for him by the time he turned up again, with James Weinberg in tow. As it turned out, James was living in the next dorm, and had already introduced Jason to half a dozen girls. He and his ex-girlfriend had had a tearful farewell before he left. It was the first time both of them would be free in four years, after dating all through high school. She was going to American University in Washington, D.C., and promised to stay in touch by e-mail. Jason was looking forward to his freedom after their long committed relationship, although he had missed her over the summer, but now everything was exciting and new. Tanya thought their break-up had been astonishingly mature for kids their age, and admired them both for how well they'd handled it, and how nice they'd been to each other even afterward.

"So how does it look?" Peter asked his son as they prepared to leave and looked around his dorm room. Tanya and the girls were prepared to hang around for a while, but it was obvious that Jason wanted them to leave. He had things to do, and orientation in twenty minutes, and a freshman barbecue to attend that night. He looked anything but heartbroken as they filed out of the dorm. He could hardly wait to embark on his new life.

He stood on the lawn outside his dorm and kissed them all goodbye. Both his sisters looked near tears. Peter gave him a powerful hug. And Tanya cried. She clung to Jason for a moment and told him to call her if he needed anything. She was only going to be an hour and a half away, five days of the week. She could run up to see him anytime, she reminded him, and he laughed.

"Don't worry, Mom, I'll be fine. I'll come down and see you soon."

"You can spend the night if you want," she said hopefully. She was going to miss him so much. He was the first of her babies to leave.

They lingered for a few minutes, and then he followed James and walked away. He was on his way. And then slowly Tanya walked Peter and the girls back to the van. Her limo had followed them from the hotel, and was waiting in the parking lot. Tanya didn't even know what to say. All she wanted to do was hold them, hug them, touch them. The emotions of seeing Jason go had almost been too much for her, and this was worse. She could hardly bear saying goodbye to the girls, and by the time Peter opened the door of the van, she was crying again.

"Come on, baby," he said gently, "he's going to be fine, and so are we." He put an arm around her and held her close to him, as both girls looked away. Their mother never cried, and she had done nothing but cry today, and for the past several weeks. The girls had contributed their share of tears, too.

"I hate this. I don't know why I let you talk me into it. I don't want to write a stupid script," she said, crying like a child, as Molly handed her a wad of tissues to blow her nose. She smiled at the tall, dark-haired twin. Boys had been checking out both girls since they'd arrived, and had been disappointed to find they weren't arriving freshmen. Megan thought it looked like a great school. Molly's first choice was now USC.

"You're going to be fine," Peter reassured her again. It was after four, and it was going to be at least midnight when they got home to Marin. Tanya had a much shorter drive to L.A., and all she wanted now was to go home with them. She was thinking about riding back with them, and flying down to L.A. early the next morning, but it would just prolong the agony, and she had an eight A.M. breakfast meeting with Douglas Wayne and the director the next day. She would have had to take a six A.M. flight, which seemed silly. She had no choice but to say goodbye to her husband and children now. Saying goodbye to Jason would have been more than enough. This was far too much. "Okay, girls," Peter said, turning to his daughters. "Say goodbye to your mom. We'd better get going." They walked her to her car, and the driver was waiting, looking bored. The limo sitting in the parking lot looked about a thousand feet long, and had colored lights and a couch inside.

"Erghk, that's awful," Megan said with disgust as she glanced in, and then at her mother. She didn't relent for a moment and hadn't in two months. And when Tanya reached out to hug her, Megan looked at her with hard eyes, and took a step back, to avoid her. It nearly broke her mother's heart, as Peter looked at her and shook his head.

"Say goodbye to your mom, Meg. Nicely," he said firmly. He wasn't going anywhere until she did. Reluctantly, she hugged her mother, as Tanya continued to cry. She was choking on small sobs as she hugged and kissed first Megan and then Molly. Molly held her tight, and started to cry herself.

"I'm going to miss you so much, Mom," she said, as the two clung to each other, and Peter patted their backs.

"Come on, guys, you're going to see each other on Friday. Mom will be home on Friday night," he reminded them both as Megan walked away. She had nothing to say to their mother. She had said it all during the course of the summer. Molly finally pulled away from her mother and wiped her eyes with a tearful smile.

"I'll see you Friday, Mommy," she said, sounding like a little girl again, although she didn't look like one. She was a beautiful young woman.

"Take care of yourself, sweetheart, and of Dad and Meg." Molly was the one who would, and she hoped Alice would look in on them. She was going to call her that night, and tell her she'd seen James, and remind her to check on Peter and the girls. Alice had promised to call Tanya the minute she thought anything was wrong with either of the girls, if they looked sick, or tired, or unhappy. She was a good mother, and had a nice way with kids, and Tanya knew that Molly and Megan trusted Alice and felt comfortable with her. They had practically grown up in her house, with Melissa and James, even though they were slightly older. Like Peter, Alice had reassured her the girls would be fine, and would adjust to her absence within days. Besides, she would be home on weekends—it wasn't like she was going away forever, or even very far. If anything happened, Alice had reminded her only the day before, she could hop on a plane and be home in less than two hours. Alice had promised to look in on them whenever she could, as much as they were willing to put up with. Once they got used to their mother being gone, she was sure the girls would be busy with their usual activities, and many friends. The girls shared a car so they could get to wherever they needed to go on their own. They were good, solid, sensible, wholesome kids. Alice had told her again and again that she didn't need to worry, but she knew Tanya would anyway.

Saying goodbye to the girls was hard, but it was worse saying goodbye to Peter. She clung to him like a motherless child, and he gently helped her into the limo, and teased her when he saw the colored lights inside that Megan had objected to. It was tacky, but he thought it was funny. "Maybe I should ride to L.A. with you, and let the girls drive home on their own," he said, teasing her. She smiled, and then he kissed her.

"I'm going to miss you so much tonight," she said softly. "Take care of yourself. I'll see you Friday."

"You'll be so busy you won't even miss me." he said, although in spite of himself, he looked sad, too, but he was glad she was doing this. He wanted it to be great for her, and had every intention of doing all he could to make it work for her.

"Call me when you get home," Tanya said softly.

"It'll be late"—closer to one than midnight now. Their goodbyes had taken a long time. She could hardly bear to let them go.

"I don't care. I'll worry till I hear from you." She wanted to know that they were home safe and sound. She didn't expect to get a lot of sleep that night without him. "I'll call you on your cell phone in the car."

"Why don't you relax, go for a swim, get a massage. Order room service. Hell, take advantage of what you've got. Before you know it, you'll be home cooking for us again. You're never going to want to come home to Marin, after the high life in Beverly Hills."

"You're my high life," she said sadly, sorry that she had agreed to write the script. All she could think of now was who wouldn't be in L.A. and what she'd be missing—her husband and children and the good times they shared.

"We'd better go." He could see that the girls were getting restless. Megan was fuming, and Molly looked sadder by the minute, and Tanya could see it, too. She kissed him one last time, and reached out to the girls. She and Molly kissed through the limo window, and Megan stared at her and turned away. There was sadness mixed with anger in her eyes, and a terrible look of betrayal, and then she got into the van. Molly climbed into the front seat next to her father, and all three of them waved as he started the van. Tanya sat watching them with tears rolling down her cheeks, and then with a wave, they rolled away. She kept waving to them from the window, and the limo followed Peter out of the parking lot. They drove toward the freeway side by side, and then Peter headed north, and the limo headed south. Tanya waved until they were out of sight, and then laid her head back against the seat and closed her eyes. She felt their absence like a physical pain, and then with a start she heard her cell phone ring. She found it in her handbag and answered it. She wondered if it was Jason, telling her he had forgotten something. She could turn back and get to the dorm in a few minutes if he needed help. She suddenly wondered if Peter had remembered to give him enough money, in case he needed cash. He had his first checking account, and a credit card. It was a first step into grown-up life. Responsibility had begun.

It wasn't Jason, it was Molly. "I love you, Mom," she said with her characteristic sweetness. She didn't want her mother to be sad, or her sister to be angry, or her father to be lonely. She always wanted to make things right for everyone. She was always quick to sacrifice herself. Tanya always said she was a lot like her father, although she had a sweetness all her own.

"I love you too, sweetheart," Tanya said softly. "Have a safe drive home."

"You, too, Mom." Tanya could hear the music blaring in the car and missed it. She would have felt foolish turning it on in the limo, particularly their kind of music, but she would have liked to. She was already lonely, traveling in solitary grandeur. She could no longer remember why she'd done this, or why it had seemed like a good idea to her, Walt, or Peter. It seemed stupid to her now. She was going to Hollywood to write a screenplay, where she would be alone and miserable for nearly a year, and at home in Ross she had the perfect life.

"I'll talk to you tomorrow," Tanya promised. "Give Meg and Dad my love, and a big squishy hug to you."

"You too, Mom," Molly said, and hung up, as Tanya sat in the limo, heading south. Thinking about them, she just stared out the window, too sad to cry.

# Chapter 4

I t was nearly seven o'clock in the evening as Tanya's limo drove up to the Beverly Hills Hotel, and stopped at the covered entrance. A doorman immediately appeared to take her bags, and greeted her with decorum as she emerged. Her blue jeans, T-shirt, and sandals seemed underdressed here somehow. There were beautiful girls who looked like models drifting by in shorts and high-heeled sandals, with perfect pedicures and masses of blond hair. Tanya was wearing hers in a braid, which made her feel oddly out of place, and embarrassingly plain. Her Marin Mom look seemed far too understated here. Even half-dressed in halter tops or see-through shirts, everyone looked glamorous and like a star to her. She looked and felt as though she had just crawled out of her backyard in Ross. And after the emotions of saying goodbye to Peter and her children, she felt like she'd been hit by a bus, or dragged through a bush backward, as the English said. It was an expression she loved using in her scripts for the soaps. It seemed so apt, and just how she felt now. Mugged. Sad. Lonely. Lost. Alone.

A bellman whisked her bags away, and gave her a claim check

to turn in at the desk. Once there, she stood cautiously behind a Japanese couple, and some people from New York, as what appeared to her to be Hollywood types wandered through the lobby. She was so distracted when it was her turn that she didn't even notice that the assistant manager at the front desk was waiting for her.

"Oh . . . sorry . . ." she apologized. She felt like a total tourist as she looked around. The lobby had been magnificently redone. She had had lunch here once or twice, when she came down for the day and met with the producers of her most lucrative soap.

"Will you be staying with us for long?" the young man asked, when she gave her name. She almost burst into tears when he asked.

"Nine months," she said, looking grim, "or something like that." He asked her for her name again, and then apologized instantly when he realized who she was.

"Of course, Miss Harris, I'm so sorry. I didn't realize it was you. We have Bungalow 2 waiting for you."

"Mrs. Harris," she corrected, looking bereft.

"Certainly. I'll make a note of that. Do you have a claim check for your bags?" She handed him the stub, and he came around the desk to take her to the bungalow. She didn't know why, but she dreaded seeing it. She didn't want to be there. All she wanted to do was go home. She felt like a kid who had been sent to camp. She wondered if Jason was feeling that way in his dorm room, but she suspected that he didn't. He was probably having a terrific time with the other kids. She felt like a new kid at school, too, probably far more than he did. She thought about him as she followed the assistant manager over a little walkway through a profusion of vegetation, and she found herself in front of the bungalow that was going to be her home until postproduction was over, whenever that was, at worst next June. Nine months away. An absolute eternity to her, without Peter and her children. Waiting nine months for her babies had been a lot more fun. Now she was going to have to give birth to a script.

She walked into the living room of the suite, and immediately noticed a vase of flowers nearly as tall as she was. She had never seen anything like it. There were roses, lilies, orchids, and gigantic flowers she didn't even recognize. It was the most beautiful arrangement she'd ever seen, and its exotic scent perfumed the room. The room itself looked newly done, in a soft blush pink, with comfortable furniture and an enormous TV. Beyond it she saw the dining room, and the little kitchen they'd promised her. And as soon as she saw her bedroom, she felt like a movie star, only to realize that the second one was bigger, with a gigantic king-size bed. It was done in the palest pink, with elegant furniture, and beyond it there was a spectacular pink-marble bathroom with a huge bathtub with Jacuzzi, and a stack of towels and a terrycloth robe with her initials on the pocket were waiting for her. There was a huge basket of lotions and cosmetics. A bottle of champagne was cooling in a silver bucket in the living room. There was a huge box of her favorite chocolates, as she wondered how they knew. And when she checked, the fridge was full of everything she loved to eat. It was as though her very own fairy godmother had been at work, and then she saw a letter on the desk. She opened it, and the handwriting was a strong male scrawl. It said, "Welcome home, Tanya. We've been waiting for you. See you at breakfast. Douglas." He had obviously somehow found out everything she liked, and then she realized he had probably talked to Walt, or maybe even Peter, or his secretary had. It was perfectly done. In the master bedroom, there was a cashmere bathrobe for her from Pratesi, with matching cashmere slippers in the perfect size, also a gift from Douglas. And much to her amazement there were silver frames with photographs of her children, and she realized for sure that they had talked to Peter, and even had him send pictures for them to frame. He hadn't said a word to spoil the surprise. They had done absolutely everything they could to make her feel at home, including a huge bowl of M&M's and Snickers bars, and a drawer full of pens and pencils and writing supplies, which was convenient. She'd been working on the script for two months, but she wanted to add some final touches to it that night before their meeting, assuming they'd want to discuss it. She was still looking around as her bags arrived and her cell phone rang at the same time. It was Peter, still on the drive home.

"So, how is it?" he asked with mischief in his voice.

"Did they call you? They must have." Even Walt didn't know her tastes this well. Only her husband and children did.

"Call me? They sent me a questionnaire. You can give blood with fewer questions than that. They wanted to know everything right down to your shoe size." He sounded pleased for her. He liked the idea that they were spoiling her. She deserved it, and he wanted this time to be special for her. He was handling it with love and grace.

"They gave me a cashmere robe and slippers, and M&M's, and all the makeup I use . . . holy shit!" She laughed. "They even got my perfume. And all the junk I like to eat." It was like a treasure hunt finding all the things they'd left for her. There was a satin nightie on the bed, with another matching robe, even a stack of books on the nightstand, by all the authors that she liked best. "I wish you were here," she said, sounding sad again, "and the kids. They would love it. I can't wait till you come down and see it."

"Anytime you want, sweetheart. Do you think they'll want my shoe size, too?" he teased her.

"They should. You're the real hero here. I wouldn't be here if it weren't for you."

"I'm glad they're treating you right. Life is going to seem very ple-
beian to you in Ross after all that. Maybe I'd better start buying you
chocolates and perfume, too, or you won't want to come home anymore." He sounded lonely. He missed her, even if he was happy for
her that good things were happening. The separation was hard for
him, too, even if he was a good sport about it, which he was.

"I wish I could come home right now," she said, looking around,
wandering from room to room with her cell phone in her hand. "I
would trade all this for Ross in a minute. And you don't have to get
me anything. All I ever need is you."

"Me too, sweetheart. Enjoy it. It's like being Cinderella for a
while."

"Yeah, but it feels weird. I can see how people get spoiled by this
though. It's all so unreal. All your favorite stuff all over the place,
champagne, chocolates, flowers. I guess that's how they treat movie
stars. My soaps never treated me like this. I was lucky they took me
to lunch a couple of times." She didn't need any of it, but it was kind
of fun discovering what they'd done. "How's the drive going?"

"Fine. The girls are asleep. I turned the music off, and no one
screamed." She laughed, envisioning the scene, with an ache in her
heart.

"Make sure you don't get sleepy, too. Maybe you should put the
radio back on, or something."

"Anything but that," he groaned. "The silence is so nice. I swear
they're all going to be deaf before they're twenty-one. I think I already am."

"Stop if you get tired, or ask one of the girls to drive."

"I'm fine, Tan. What are you going to do now?" He was trying to
imagine her in her new life. But she knew that even he couldn't visualize this. It was like something in a movie. She felt very glamorous

suddenly, even in her T-shirt and jeans, royally ensconced in the bungalow at the Beverly Hills Hotel.

"I don't know. Maybe take a bath, with a Jacuzzi, thank you very much." She laughed, and sounded like a kid, as she told him all about it. It was far more luxurious than their house in Ross. Their bathroom there was looking tired after sixteen years, and they kept talking about redoing it, but didn't. This one was brand-new and far more lavish than anything they would have done. "And then I'll try out my new robe and slippers, and order room service." She wasn't hungry, but some of this was fun, mostly the attention to detail, and the gifts were extravagant. She had just discovered a little silver box with her initials on it, with paper clips in her favorite sizes. They hadn't missed a thing. She loved the framed photographs of Peter and the children best. They made her feel at home. And she had brought half a dozen of her own. She arranged them in a group next to her bed, and on her desk, so she could see them in every room. "I can't wait till you come to visit. We can go to dinner at Spago or something, or just stay in bed here. Actually, that sounds like more fun." There was also an excellent restaurant at the hotel. But most of all she wanted to be in bed with him. They had made love only that morning, and it had been tender and wonderful, as always. It had been since the beginning. It just got better over the years. She loved the familiar comfort of their lovemaking. They had been together for half her life, and nearly half of his. "It's going to be like a honeymoon when you come here," she giggled.

"Sounds good to me. My life is definitely not going to be a honeymoon this week. Margarita is doing the girls' laundry, right?" Tanya had extended the housekeeper's hours once she knew she was leaving. And she was going to cook for them a few nights a week, too, when Peter couldn't, and leave them things in the freezer. The girls were good about organizing dinner, so she wasn't too worried, but sometimes they came home late from games and Peter came home too tired to eat most nights, let alone cook. The girls had promised to take care of him when that happened. Here she could have room service whenever she wanted. It suddenly made her feel spoiled and guilty. She really hadn't done anything to deserve this. It was an impressive way to start. "I'll call you when we get home," Peter promised, and Tanya went to run a bath when she hung up. She felt better than she had before, and for a minute or two it was actually fun. She felt like a totally spoiled kid. She would have loved to show the girls, and to take a bath with Peter in the giant tub. They loved doing that at home sometimes, and this one was huge.

She sat in the bath for over an hour, using perfumed bath salts, steaming peacefully, and then she got out, and put on her satin nightie and the cashmere robe. It was a soft dusty pink, and the matching slippers were a perfect fit. It was nine o'clock when she called room service, and ordered tea, although all her favorite brands of tea were in the kitchen. She ordered an omelette and a green salad, and settled down to eat in front of the TV. The service had been incredibly quick. And she discovered that they'd had TiVo installed for her. She turned it off after she finished dinner, and plugged in her computer on the desk. She wanted to check some notes she'd made that week for changes she was going to make on the script. She wanted to refresh her memory before the meeting the next day. It was after midnight when she stopped working on it. The script she'd written was in pretty good shape, and she'd already sent Douglas and the director several drafts, which they seemed to like. They had been very reasonable so far about what they expected from her.

After Tanya turned off her computer, she lay down on the bed. It was odd to think that this was going to be her home now for many months, but they had certainly made it as pleasant as they could for her. They had done everything imaginable and more to make it seem like a fairy tale. She turned the TV on again, while she waited for Peter and the girls to get home. She didn't want to go to sleep until she knew they were safe. She called him on his cell phone, and he was on the Golden Gate Bridge at twelve-thirty, less than half an hour from home. They had made good time, and the girls were awake. They said they'd had dinner at a drive-through McDonald's, which made her feel guilty for the luxury she was living in. She was relaxed and comfortable on the giant bed, wearing her new pink cashmere robe. She felt like a queen, or at least a princess, and she told Molly all about it when she talked to her. She asked to speak to Megan, too, but she was on her cell phone talking to friends and didn't want to put them on hold.

Tanya wondered how long it would be until Megan was back to normal with her again. The last two months had been an agony with Megan so angry at her, and so far she showed no sign of relenting. Peter was certain she would soon. Tanya was not so sure. Megan was able to hold a grudge forever, and more than willing to do so. Once she felt betrayed, she never forgave it. She had her own code of ethics, and high expectations based on the immense amount of time her mother had always spent with her. This sudden, unexpected change had come as a huge shock, and she hadn't taken it well. Her twin sister had accused her of behaving like a brat. But Tanya knew that underneath the outward hostility, Megan was scared and sad, so she easily forgave the unkindness of her daughter's words. As far as Megan was concerned, their mother had betrayed them. That was no small thing to Megan, nor to Tanya. She suspected it would be a long time before she was back in her daughter's good graces, if ever.

Tanya talked to Peter on his cell phone until they got to the house, and then he had to get off so he could help the girls carry in their things, and once again she felt guilty for not being there to help them. Peter insisted they could manage. He kissed her goodnight and promised to call her in the morning. She told him she would report to him about the meeting. She was planning to get up at six-thirty, and asked the operator to wake her. She turned the light off at one-thirty, and lay awake in the dark, wondering what her children were doing. She was sure the girls were in their bedrooms, and Peter was eating something before bedtime. She wished that she could be with them. It felt so strange to be in the room at the Beverly Hills Hotel, all by herself, in a brand-new satin nightgown. She felt as though she were shirking all her responsibilities and duties. She lay there for a long time that night, unable to fall asleep without Peter's arms around her. It had been ages since they'd spent a night without each other, it only happened very rarely when he traveled for the law firm. And even then, she occasionally went with him. This was a rare occurrence.

She fell asleep finally at three o'clock, with the TV on, and woke up with a start when the phone rang at six-thirty. It had been a short night, and she was tired. She had wanted some time to read parts of her script again, and to be wide awake before their breakfast meeting. She was meeting Douglas and the director in the Polo Lounge. She opted for a pair of black slacks and a T-shirt, sandals, and then put on a denim jacket before she left the room. She was dressed as one of her children would have, or as she would have in Marin, and she wondered if her girls would approve. She missed having them to consult with on what she was wearing. It was very basic. She wasn't an actress, she reminded herself. No one cared what she looked like. She was there to provide a script that sounded right, not for anyone to pay attention to her. What mattered was how good the script was, and she was confident that it was pretty good. She put her copy of it in an oversize Prada tote bag, and at the last minute put on a pair of tiny diamond earrings that Peter had given her for Christmas. She loved them and they seemed right to her in L.A., although she wouldn't have worn them to an eight A.M. meeting in Marin. And as soon as she walked into the dining room, she knew she had done the right thing, wearing the earrings. Without them, she would have felt even more out of place than she did. Looking around the room at the people dining there, she felt like a hick.

The room was full of important-looking men and beautiful women, several of them well known. There were dazzling-looking women having breakfast with each other, in pairs or small groups. Men dining with each other, and a few men with women, usually years younger. She noticed Sharon Osbourne having breakfast in a quiet corner with a younger woman. Both were expensively dressed, and wore large diamonds on their hands and ears. Barbara Walters was at a table having breakfast with three men. There were men and women from the entertainment industry scattered throughout the room, and at most of the tables, there were men conducting business and having meetings. For the most part, it looked like ideas, contracts, and money were being exchanged and changing hands. The smell of power hung heavy in the room. The Polo Lounge looked like a hotbed of success, and as soon as Tanya saw it, she felt noticeably underdressed. Barbara Walters was wearing a beige linen Chanel suit and pearls. Sharon Osbourne was wearing low-cut black. Most of the women had had face-lifts, the rest of them looked like ads for collagen and Botox. Tanya felt as though she had the only natural face in the room. She kept reminding herself that she was there because of the way she wrote, not how she looked. But it was daunting anyway to be in the midst of so many beautiful, exquisitely groomed women. Tanya felt unable to compete with that, or even try. All she could do was be herself.

Tanya told the maître d' whom she was meeting, and without pause, he walked her to a corner table. She recognized Douglas Wayne immediately, and as soon as she saw him, she recognized Max Blum, the director. He had five Academy Awards to his credit. Tanya nearly choked when he told her it would be an honor to be working with her, and that he loved her work. She discovered after she sat down that he had read everything she'd ever published in *The New Yorker,* right back to the beginning. He'd read most of her essays, and her book of short stories, and he'd been reviewing tapes of most of what she'd done on the soaps. He wanted to know everything he could about her work, her range, her style, her timing, her sense of humor and drama, and her point of view. And so far, he said, he liked everything he'd seen. There was no question in Max's mind, Douglas had been absolutely right in choosing her to do their script. As far as he was concerned, it was a stroke of genius to have made a deal with her. Douglas thought so, too.

Max and Douglas looked like opposites in every way, as they both stood up to greet Tanya as she approached their table. Max was small, round, and jolly, somewhere in his mid-sixties, and had had an illustrious career in Hollywood for forty years. He was hardly taller than Tanya, and he had a face like a friar, or an elf in a fairy tale. He was warm, friendly, and informal. He was wearing running shoes, with a T-shirt and jeans. The word one would have used to describe him was *cozy.* He was the kind of person you wanted to sit next to, hold hands with, and tell all your secrets to.

Douglas was an entirely different breed. What sprang to mind immediately when she saw him was that he looked like Gary Cooper in his middle years. Tanya knew from all she'd read of him that he was fifty-four years old. He was tall, lean, spare, had an angular face, piercing blue eyes, and gray hair, and the word that would have best described him was *cold*. He had eyes like steel. Max had warm brown eyes, a bald head, and a beard. Douglas had a thick well-cut mane of silvery-gray hair, and was impeccably neat. He was wearing perfectly pressed gray slacks and a blue shirt with a cashmere sweater over his shoulders, and when she happened to look down, Tanya noticed that he was wearing brown alligator loafers. Everything about Douglas spoke of style and money, but what one noticed most about him was that he exuded power. There was no question in anyone's mind, as one glanced at him, that he was a very important person. He looked as though he could have bought and sold the entire room. And as he looked her over, his eyes bored right through her. She was far more comfortable making idle chitchat with Max, who went out of his way to make her feel welcome. Douglas looked as though he were taking her apart and putting her back together piece by piece. It was an acutely uncomfortable feeling.

"You have very small feet" was the first thing Douglas said to her after she sat down, and she had no idea how he could see them, unless he had X-ray vision and was looking through the table. It never occurred to her that he had carefully studied the questionnaire that his secretary had had filled out by her husband and agent, in order to buy her welcome gifts. He had noticed her shoe size on the list, before they bought her the Pratesi robe and slippers. He was the one who had decided they should be pink. Douglas Wayne made all final decisions, even about the most minute details and trivial things. Nothing was trivial to Douglas. He had approved the satin night-gown and robe, too, also in pink. He had told them to get her something beautiful but not sexy. He knew from her agent and scuttlebutt around town that she was married and had kids, and Walt had finally admitted to him that she had nearly passed on this opportunity, in order to stay home and take care of her twin daughters. Walt had told him that Peter had helped her make the right decision, but it had been far from easy. She wasn't the kind of woman you sent a sexy nightgown to. She was the kind of woman you treated with respect and grace.

"Thank you for all the beautiful gifts," Tanya said, feeling timid. Both of them were such important men that she felt cowed and insignificant in their midst. "Everything fit," she said with a cautious smile.

"I'm glad to hear it." Heads would have rolled if it hadn't. But there was no way for Tanya to know that. It was hard to believe looking at Douglas that he was addicted to soaps, particularly the ones she wrote. She could far more easily imagine him hooked on more challenging fare. And she wondered how often people had told him he looked like Gary Cooper. She didn't know him well enough to comment on his looks, but the resemblance was striking. Max on the other hand was looking more and more to her like Happy in the Seven Dwarfs. And she was aware during their early moments of conversation that Douglas hadn't taken his eyes off her since she sat down. She felt as though she were being examined under a microscope, and in fact she was. Nothing escaped his sharp gaze, and it was only when they started to talk about the script that he relaxed and warmed up a little.

He suddenly became animated and excited, and as Tanya made comments about the script, and the changes she'd made, he laughed.

"I love it when you do funny, Tanya. I can always tell when you wrote the script on my favorite soap. If I start to laugh my head off, I know it had to be you." The script they were currently working on, and the movie they were about to shoot, didn't have a lot of leeway for funny, but she had slipped some in anyway, and they all agreed that it worked. She had done it in just the right doses, to add spice and warmth, which was the trademark of her work. Even when it was funny, it never failed to strike a poignant chord, and exude her natural warmth.

By the time they finished breakfast, she could see that Douglas had relaxed. She couldn't help wondering if he was shy. All the ice she had noticed when she joined them seemed to have melted. As Max said to a friend afterward, with a look of wonder, she had him eating out of the palm of her hand. Douglas looked totally entranced.

"You're a fascinating woman," he said, studying her intently again. "Your agent said you nearly didn't do the picture, because you didn't want to leave your husband and kids, which seemed nuts to me, and I thought you'd show up here, looking like Mother Earth, in Birkenstocks and braids. Instead, you're a totally sensible person." She was a pretty, youthful-looking woman, simply dressed. "You don't even look like you have kids, and you were smart enough to leave your husband and kids at home, and make the right decision for your career."

"Actually, I didn't," she confessed, slightly taken aback by his comments. Douglas didn't pull any punches, and said whatever he felt. Money and power allowed him to do that. "My agent told you the truth. I was going to turn it down. My husband made the decision before I did. He convinced me it was okay. He's at home, with our twins."

"Oh God, that's too domestic for me," Douglas said, and nearly winced, as Max smiled and nodded.

"How old are the twins?" Max asked with interest.

"Seventeen. They're girls. Fraternal twins. And I have a son who's eighteen and starting college today at UCSB." She beamed proudly as she said it.

"Nice," Max said, and approved visibly. "I have two daughters myself. They're thirty-two and thirty-five years old, and live in New York. One's an attorney and the other one is a shrink. They're both married, and I have three grandsons." He looked immensely pleased.

"Very nice," she returned the compliment to him, and then unconsciously they both turned to Douglas, who returned Tanya's questioning gaze. As he looked at her, he smiled.

"Don't look at me. I've never had kids. I've been married twice, no children. I don't even have a dog, and don't want one. I work too hard, and always have, to spend enough time with children. I suppose I admire whatever prompted you to almost stay home with your children instead of writing the screenplay. But I can't say I understand it. I think there's something noble about work. Think of all the people who are going to see our movie, how many lives you'll touch with what you put in the script, how many people will remember it one day." Tanya thought he had an inflated sense of his own importance, and theirs. One child seemed far more important to her than a thousand movies. One life. One human being on the planet to reach out to others. She never had a sense of importance about her work. It was just something she enjoyed doing, and that meant a lot to her at times. But her children meant so much more, and Peter. She felt sorry for Douglas if he didn't understand that. He lived for his work. Tanya had a sense that there was something missing in him, some vital human piece that hadn't been included. And yet she found him interesting. He was brilliant, and his mind was sharply honed. But she much preferred Max's innate softness. They were both interesting men, and she suspected it would be exciting working with them, although she hadn't figured out yet what made Douglas tick, and maybe never would. He appeared to be completely driven, there was a fire that burned in him that she didn't understand. You could see it in his eyes.

The three of them talked about the script for the next two hours, and Douglas explained to her what lay ahead, the changes he wanted her to make, the subtleties he still wanted included in the script. He had a fine sense of what it took to make an extraordinary movie. As she listened to him, she began to glimpse the workings of his mind. Douglas was the fire, and Max was far gentler, and tempered the producer's sharpness. Max brought humanity to the movie, Douglas brought a brilliant mind. There was something utterly fascinating about him.

They sat in the Polo Lounge talking about the script until nearly noon, and after that she went back to the bungalow and worked on what they'd said. Douglas had inspired her to take it to a deeper level. She tried to explain it to Peter when he called her, and she couldn't. But whatever he and Max had said to her made sense. She added some wonderful scenes to the script that day. She was still sitting at her desk at six, pleased with a good day's work.

She was surprised that night, as she lay on her bed, mindlessly watching the TiVo, when Douglas called. She told him about the work she'd done all afternoon, and he sounded pleased that she had gotten the drift so quickly. She had sensed, as much as heard, what they were saying, and absorbed it readily.

"It was a good meeting this morning. I think you've taken just the right amount of inspiration from the book, without going overboard. I can't wait to see what you've done today."

"I'll work on it some more tomorrow," she promised. She had been thinking of going back to it that night, but knew she was too tired. "If it's not too rough, I'll send it to you on Wednesday morning."

"Why don't you give it to me over lunch? How's Thursday?" She was startled by the invitation, but she had gotten the sense that morning that they were all going to be working closely. She felt totally at ease with Max, but she wasn't comfortable with Douglas yet. Max was easy. Douglas was as hard as steel, and cold as ice. And yet he was intriguing. Beneath the ice, she instinctively sensed something warmer, a human being behind the mind.

"Thursday would be fine," Tanya said, feeling slightly awkward. It was easier seeing him with Max, with whom she had more in common. Max was a warm friendly guy, he liked kids, as she did, and everything about him seemed open. Douglas was closed and sealed tight. The temptation was to try and find a way in to discover who he was. But Tanya didn't think anyone had scaled those walls in a long time, maybe ever. Douglas was guarded, and watching for intruders at the gates. She had sensed him observing her closely that morning, as though to find the weak places in her. Douglas was all about power and control and owning people. Tanya was very clear on that. Douglas had bought her services, but he didn't own her. She sensed that he would be dangerous to get close to, unlike Max, who had welcomed her with open arms. Douglas gave away as little as possible of himself.

"I'm giving a dinner for the cast at my place on Wednesday night," Douglas said then. She had the impression that he was feeling her out. She could sense him circling her, as though trying to assess her. "I'd like you to come. It's only for the major stars, of course, and the supporting cast." They were a glittering assortment working on this movie. Tanya was anxious to meet them—it would make writing for them easier, if she developed a sense of their style and rhythm. She knew who most of them were, but seeing them in the flesh would be exciting and fun. This was a whole new world for her. She was suddenly glad she'd brought the one black cocktail dress. She had nothing else to wear other than the black pants she'd worn today, and jeans. And given the way Douglas had looked that day, she suspected that dinner at his house would be dressy. "I'll send my car for you. You don't have to get dressed up. They'll all come in jeans."

"Thank you." She smiled. "You just solved a major fashion dilemma for me. I didn't bring much of a wardrobe. I figured I'd be working most of the time, and I'm planning to go home on weekends."

"I know," he laughed at her, slightly scornful, "to your husband and kids." He made it sound like something she should be embarrassed about, like a bad habit she had and ought to break. That's what it was to him, although he had admitted that he'd been married twice. But he clearly had an aversion to kids. He had looked nervous that morning when she and Max spoke of theirs.

"Are you really as normal as you pretend to be?" he said, trying to provoke her, which was a favorite game of his. "You're so much deeper than that. The kind of things you write, the way your mind works. I just can't see you in the role of suburban housewife, feeding breakfast to your kids." He was pressing her to see how she handled it, and what she did.

"That's what I do in real life," she said without apology. "I love it. I've spent the last twenty years that way, and I wouldn't have given up a minute with them for the world." She looked smug and happy as she said it. She knew she had done the right thing.

"Then why are you here?" he asked her bluntly, and waited to hear what she'd say. It was a reasonable question, and one she'd asked herself.

"This is a golden opportunity for me," she said honestly. "I didn't think I'd ever get a chance like this again. I wanted to write this script."

"And you left your husband and children to do it. So maybe you're not as bourgeois as you think." He was almost like the serpent in the Garden of Eden, trying to lure her away.

"Can't I be all of the above? Wife, mother, and writer? None of them are mutually exclusive." He pointedly ignored what she'd said.

"Do you feel guilty for being here, Tanya?" he asked with interest. He wanted to know more about her, and she was equally intrigued by him. Not in a sexual way, but he was an interesting person, a constant challenge. He darted forward and then moved away, sideways sometimes, almost like a snake.

"Sometimes I feel guilty," she admitted to him. "I did before I came here. I feel better, now that I'm working. Being in L.A. is starting to make sense."

"You'll feel even better once we start shooting. It's addictive, like a drug you'll have to have again. Once we finish the movie, you'll want more of it. We all do. That's what keeps us here. We can't stand it when the movie ends. I can feel it happening to you already, and we haven't even started." He touched a nerve in her somewhere, and she was frightened by what he said. What if he was right, and it was addictive, even for her? "You won't want to go back, Tanya, after it's over. You'll want someone to find you another picture. I think we're going to enjoy working together." He sounded like Rasputin, and she was sorry she had agreed to have lunch with him, or maybe he was just trying to test her, to find out how she was made.

"I'm expecting to enjoy it," she said sanely, "but I hope it's not as addictive as you say. I'm planning to go back to real life when this is over. I'm only on loan here, not for sale." She felt like she was sparring with a master, a dangerous sport for her. He was an Olympic-class manipulator, and she a rank amateur compared to him.

"We're all for sale," he said simply, "and this is real life for us, even though it looks like tinsel to others. That's why they call it Tinseltown. It's intoxicating. You'll see. You won't want to go back to your old life again." He sounded absolutely certain as he repeated it.

"Yes, I will. I have a husband and children waiting for me. This wouldn't be enough for me. But I know I'll learn a lot while I'm here. I'm grateful for the opportunity," she said firmly, sounding stubborn to him.

"Don't be grateful, Tanya. I didn't do you a favor bringing you here. Your work is very good. I like the way you view the world, your twists and turns, the quirky way you write about things. I like what happens in your mind." He had certainly understood her work, and done his homework. He had been reading her for years, and she felt as though he were trying to get inside her head. Scary stuff. Or maybe it was just a game he played to unnerve her. Perhaps life was a game to him, and nothing was real. She suspected that to Douglas, only movies were real, which was why he was so good at what he did. "I think we're going to enjoy working with each other," he said thoughtfully, as though savoring that concept. "You're an interesting woman, Tanya. I have a feeling you've played a role for all these years, the little suburban housewife with a husband and kids. I don't believe that's who you are. I don't think you even know who you are yet. I think you'll discover it while you're here." The way he said it sounded ominous to Tanya. It made her uneasy that he felt he could look right into her and assess her. It was none of his business to know what she was thinking, or even who she was.

"I think I have a good sense of who I am," she said quietly.

They were complete opposites. She was aware of that, too. He was glamorous and alluring, a symbol of the lure of Hollywood at its best and most enticing. She was innocence and a visitor from a life she loved and which he would have found totally boring. She wanted to become part of his world now, but only for a while, and without giving up her values or her soul. When the movie was over, like Dorothy in *The Wizard of Oz*, she wanted to go home. She wasn't going to let the temptations of Hollywood seduce her. She knew who she was. Her children's mother. Peter's wife. Douglas Wayne belonged to another world, but he was offering her an extraordinary opportunity to share his world for a while. She wanted to write the script for him, but not give up her real life or her soul. She wanted to learn everything he could teach her, and then go back to Marin. She was glad she would be going home on weekends, to her familiar surroundings, to breathe the clean air of her existence there. She didn't want just one life or the other. Now she wanted both.

"You think you know who you are," Douglas said, taunting her again. "I don't think you've even begun to discover who lives in your head. You'll find it out here, Tanya, in the months to come. This is a rite of passage for you, an initiation into the sacred rites and rituals of your new tribe. When you leave here," he said carefully, "we will be as much your family as they are. The danger is that if you fall in love with your life here, it will be hard for you to go back there again." What he said to her frightened her, and she didn't believe him. She knew where she belonged, and where her heart was. She was not confused about her allegiances to Peter and her children. And she was certain that she could work here without damaging her relationship to them. Douglas was not as convinced. He had seen Hollywood turn many heads before.

Tanya sensed, as she listened to him, that there was something faintly dangerous about him, and yet she knew he had no power over her. She was working for him. He didn't own her.

"Those are powerful words, Mr. Wayne," she said quietly, trying to put up a mental shield against the lures he was describing.

"This is a powerful place," he repeated quietly. She wondered if he was trying to frighten her. But in fact, he was only warning her of potential dangers and pitfalls, of which she was well aware.

"And you are a powerful man," she conceded. But neither he nor Hollywood would be enough to sway her, Tanya reassured herself. He was brilliant certainly, and a genius at what he did. But she was a solid woman. She was not a star-struck kid.

"Something tells me that we're very much alike," Douglas said, which seemed a strange thing to say to her.

"I don't think we are. In fact, I think we're night and day," she said. He was worldly, and she wasn't. He had power, and she had none. The life she led, and which she loved, was anathema to him. There was a purity and clarity to Tanya which challenged him, and drew him to her.

"Perhaps you're right," he said, pausing to think about it. "Maybe what I meant was complementary, not the same. Two halves of one whole. I've been fascinated by your writing for years, and I always knew we'd meet and work on something together one day. And now that time has come." She felt as though she were being pulled toward unfamiliar territory with him. And she was nervous about it, but excited, too. "I think I had a premonition about your work," he added. "I was drawn to it like a moth to flame." And her light was shining brighter than ever, now that she was here. He could hardly wait to start working with her. "You know what complementary means, don't you, Tanya? Two halves of one whole. They fit together seamlessly.

They add to one another, like spice. I think we could do that for each other in some way. I could add spice to your life, and you could add peace to mine. You strike me as a very peaceful person." It was the strangest thing anyone had ever said to her, and she felt instantly ill at ease when he said it. What did he want from her? Why was he saying those things? All she wanted to do was get off the phone and call Peter.

"I am a peaceful person," she said quietly. "What I want, and why I'm here, is to give you a seamless script. And all of us will work together to make this a very special movie," she said calmly, with an air of confidence she didn't feel. But she wanted to do the best job she possibly could.

"I have no doubt that you will, Tanya," he said confidently. "I knew it the moment you accepted my offer. But most important of all, with you writing the script, Tanya, I know it will be perfect." It was high praise coming from him.

"Thank you," she said seriously. "I hope the screenplay will live up to your expectations," she said formally but sincerely. There was something about him that made her uneasy and drew her to him at the same time. What she sensed most about him was that he was a man who always got what he wanted. That was the most intriguing piece about him. That and his relentless determination had made him who he was. And whatever else he was, Tanya could already see that Douglas Wayne was all about power and control. He had to have both at all times. And more than anything, she sensed that he always had to win. He wouldn't tolerate anything less. Douglas Wayne had to have complete, total, and utter control over everything he touched. And the one thing she was certain of was that no matter how important, powerful, or talented he was, he would never control her.

# Chapter 5

T he evening Tanya spent at Douglas Wayne's Bel Air house was as interesting, glamorous, and mysterious as he was. The house itself was an extraordinarily beautiful mansion. He had bought it years before, after his first important film, and added onto it several times since then, until it had become a vast sprawling estate, filled with elegantly appointed rooms crammed with exquisite antiques and priceless paintings. Douglas had magnificent taste, and Tanya was momentarily breathless when she walked into the living room and found herself staring at a well-known Monet painting of water lilies. The scene outside mirrored it, as members of the cast sat around the enormous swimming pool filled with gardenias and water lilies. The entire scene was lit by candles. There was an even more impressive Renoir in the second living room, two Mary Cassatts, and an important Flemish painting. The furniture was rich and masculine, an interesting combination of English, French, and Russian, with an exquisite Chinese screen in one corner, and a Chinese upright secretary next to it that looked like it belonged in a museum.

Tanya felt ridiculously out of place in jeans, although the others were similarly dressed. She recognized two of the stars instantly, Jean Amber and Ned Bright. Jean had already been in a dozen important Hollywood films, and had been nominated for three Oscars at the tender age of twenty-five. Her face was so perfect, she looked like a painting herself. She was laughing at something Max had said, wearing a gauzy see-through pale blue top over her jeans, and silver sandals with ankle straps and towering heels. Her skin-tight jeans looked painted onto her long, thin body. She was spectacular looking, and as Max introduced them, she smiled at Tanya. For just an instant, she reminded her of Molly. She had the same sweet innocent look, and long, shining ebony hair. The warmth in her eyes suggested that fame hadn't spoiled her yet, and she shook Tanya's hand with a warm grip.

"I loved your book. I gave it to my mom for her birthday. She loves short stories."

"Thank you." Tanya smiled warmly, trying not to be too impressed by her, but it was hard not to be. It was exciting to meet such an important star, not to mention working with her, and writing dialogue that she would bring to life. Tanya was touched by the reference to her book, and surprised that anyone so young would be moved by her work. Most young people liked short stories less than novels. "That's nice of you to say. I love your movies, and so do my daughters." She felt silly saying it, and Jean looked delighted. Everybody enjoyed praise.

"I'm excited to be working on a movie with you. I can't wait to see the script." They would be having meetings on it shortly, with all of the actors adding their notes to those of Max and Douglas and even her own. It was always a combined effort.

"I'm working hard," Tanya assured her. "It's an honor to write a script for you," she said, feeling awed, as two of the supporting actors wandered over. Jean didn't know either of them, and Max introduced them to Tanya and the star. He treated them all like his children, of whom he was very proud. It was as though on each movie set a new family was formed. Relationships were born, bonds were established, romances came and went, lifelong friendships began from time to time. A whole microcosm of life occurred, some of which lasted, much of which didn't, but for the moments of the making of the film, it all felt as though it would last forever and was real life. It was similar to the careful architecture of a magical house of cards that looked very similar to the Taj Mahal. Beautiful, delicate, breathtaking, enticing, and then when the movie ended, it was all swept away like sand, as they all dispersed to build sand castles again somewhere else. There was an incredible magic to it that fascinated Tanya. It all seemed so real as they stood there. They would work so hard together, create so much, believe so hard in what they were building and creating. And then when it was all captured on film, it would disappear in the mists and vanish, never to be seen again. And yet now, for this one moment in time, it was real to each of them. And then afterward, on film, their magic would be long remembered.

Tanya found being part of it incredibly exciting, and as she thought about it, watching people move around her with champagne glasses in their hands, laughing and talking, she remembered what Douglas had said to her on the phone, that it was addictive, and after she had been there for a while and tasted its temptations, she would want more. He had said she would never be able to go back to her old life again, that this would become her home. She didn't want that to be true, and yet she felt the lure of it as she stood there and watched them. She felt separate from them at first, but as Max continued to introduce her to people, mostly beautiful young stars, handsome men, and a few older ones, she began to feel comfortable in their midst. She was surprised at how easy it was to talk to them. It was such a dizzying exciting dance, she couldn't tell if what she felt was the thrill of anticipation, or the champagne. And all around them was the intoxicating scent of the lilies and gardenias. There were white orchids throughout the house, and some rare yellow and brown ones with long stems and tiny flowers in magnificent Chinese urns. And there was the distant sound of sensual music. The entire scene, from the art to the people, and even the oysters and caviar they were eating, was a sensual explosion.

Tanya was dying to go home and write about it. It felt like some form of glamorous initiation rite, as she stood silently admiring the people around her. She didn't hear Doug come up to her, and suddenly she saw him smiling at her, standing only inches away. She was wearing a white silk sweater, jeans, and low-heeled gold sandals with a matching purse, that she had bought that afternoon on her way back to the hotel. She had taken him at his word and worn jeans, and was glad she had, since the entire cast was wearing them. Doug was once again wearing an impeccable pair of gray flannel slacks with a perfect crease, an exquisite starched white shirt he'd had custom made in Paris, and black alligator loafers from Hermès.

"It doesn't get better than this, does it?" he asked her in a velvet tone. She felt Douglas more than heard him. She didn't know why yet, but every time she heard him or was near him, she felt simultaneously drawn to him and shut out, both attracted and repulsed. It was a strange kind of push-me-pull-you kind of response, as though you wanted to be close to him, yet knew you couldn't. He was like an Egyptian tomb full of dazzling riches with an ancient curse that kept you away.

He looked into Tanya's eyes and smiled at her in silence for a moment, admiring her, but enjoying saying nothing. He didn't need to. The way his eyes caressed her said it all. He talked to her in the soft undertone of someone who knew her well, yet he didn't. He didn't know her at all, except through her writing, which had already told him so much about her. She felt naked as she stood before him, and then he looked away. And this time she had no urge to run screaming from him. She told herself that nothing about him could control her or invade her. He couldn't take more than she gave, or so she thought. He was a man, not a magician. A producer. A person who bought stories, and brought scripts like hers to life on screen.

"Are you meeting people?" he asked, looking concerned. It seemed to matter to him a great deal that everyone enjoyed the evening, particularly Tanya, since she was a newcomer in their midst. She had met most of the cast, thanks to Max's warm attention, except Ned Bright, who had been constantly surrounded by a group of very pretty young women, who had all come with other men but gravitated instantly to him. He was currently Hollywood's hottest young male star, and it was easy to see why. He was charming and utterly gorgeous. And the girls around him had been giggling and laughing all night.

"I am," she said simply, looking into Douglas's eyes. She was determined not to be overly impressed by him, nor cowed. "I love your art, it's like visiting a museum," she said, noticing yet another famous painting spectacularly lit in a small living room off the pool she hadn't previously noticed. It was the music room, where he played the piano. He had studied to be a concert pianist as a child and young man, and he still played for his own enjoyment, and that of his close friends. She had been told that in his youth he had been thought to have immense talent.

"I hope it doesn't look like a museum, that would be very sad, like

seeing animals in the zoo instead of their natural habitat. I want people to feel comfortable with the art, and not afraid of it. One should
enjoy living with it as part of their experience, like a good friend, not
staring at it like a stranger. All my paintings are old friends." It was
an interesting way to view it, and as he said it, she found herself
looking at the smaller Monet in the music room. The way it was lit
brought it to life, and it almost seemed like a mirror image of the
pool, with people chatting happily all around it. The champagne that
was flowing lavishly was doing its job. People looked relaxed and
happy, and so did he. He seemed far more comfortable here, in his
own surroundings, than he had at the Polo Lounge at the hotel. He
looked graceful and gracious here, and totally in control of his own
world. Nothing escaped his notice, and he seemed to be keeping an
eye on everyone, and all the details of the evening. Max joined them
a few minutes later, as Douglas was telling Tanya about collecting
antiques in Europe. He said he had found some real treasures a few
months ago in Denmark and Holland, notably a fabulous Danish
desk, which he pointed out.

"It's a good thing we don't give these get-togethers at my place,"
Max said, laughing broadly. He still looked like an elf to Tanya, with his
round belly, bald head, and beard. He looked like one of Santa's
helpers, while Douglas looked like a movie star himself. Tanya had
heard that at one time Douglas had wanted to be an actor, but had
never tried it. He much preferred the powerful role of producer. He
controlled so much more that way, like the puppet master who brought
all the elements together. Max was more like the gentle Gepetto.

Douglas laughed too at Max's comment about doing these early
cast parties at his house. "It would be a little different," he conceded,
as Max explained to Tanya.

"I live in the Hollywood Hills in a house that looks like a barn and should probably be one. I have horse blankets on my couches, two-week-old fast food sitting around on the coffee table, and my ex-wife took my vacuum cleaner fourteen years ago when she left me. I haven't had time to get another one, I've been too busy. I've got my old movie posters on the walls. My finest antique is my TV. I've had it since nineteen-eighty. I paid a lot of money for it, the rest I got from Goodwill. It's a little different from Doug's house." All three of them laughed at what Max had said without regret or apology. He loved his house. He would have been acutely uncomfortable with a house like Douglas's, although he loved the art. "I've got to get another cleaning woman one of these days. My last one got deported, which was too bad, I really liked her. She was a great cook, and played a mean game of gin rummy. The dust balls are getting bigger than my dog." He went on to explain that he had a Great Dane named Harry who was his best friend. He promised Tanya she'd be meeting him on the set. He always came to work with him. He wore no collar or leash, so his tags wouldn't bother the sound man, and Max said he was perfectly trained. "He loves coming to work with me, the caterers always feed him. He gets depressed and loses a lot of weight between movies." He went on to say that the dog weighed close to two hundred pounds.

As they chatted, she was struck again by the differences between Max and Douglas. One was soft and warm and cozy, the other all hard edges and sharp corners, despite the highly polished veneer. Max looked like he'd bought his wardrobe at Goodwill, when he bought the furniture for his house. Douglas looked like the cover of GQ. It was fascinating for Tanya talking to them, and being with them. She wondered how much Douglas would be on the set, while they were making the movie. His biggest job was raising the money to make it, and keeping an eye on the budget. Max's job was getting the best possible performance out of the actors. And they both loved what they did. Tanya could hardly wait to get started on the film.

The food was served at nine o'clock at the pool, at several long buffet tables. There was one table entirely covered with sushi, from a popular Japanese restaurant. There was another table laden with lobsters, crabs, and oysters. And the third table offered exotic salads and traditional Mexican food. There was something for each taste, and the young male stars were heaping plates with food. Douglas introduced her to Ned Bright as he cruised past them, followed by four women. She noticed instantly how much he looked like her son, Jason.

"Hi," he said, looking happy and relaxed, apologizing for not shaking her hand. He was carrying two plates, one with sushi, the other with a ton of Mexican food on it. "Don't give me too many lines, I'm dyslexic," he said, laughing. She wondered if he really was, and she asked Max about it afterward. It might help her to know that.

"No, just lazy. He tells all screenwriters that. He's a really nice kid." He was the new face in Hollywood these days, and an absolute sensation. He was twenty-three and the male lead in the movie, opposite Jean Amber. He looked older than he was, closer to thirty, although he had played a blind sixteen-year-old boy in his last film, which had received lavish praise and had won him a Golden Globe. He also had a nice side career as a drummer and singer in a Hollywood band, made up of young stars. He was the lead singer. They'd just recently had a hit CD, and she knew all three of her kids would go crazy when she said she'd met him. Molly particularly nearly fainted when she heard it.

"Nice boy," Max reiterated, and Tanya agreed. You could see it. "His mother always visits him on the set, just to make sure we're treating him right and he's behaving. He just graduated from film school at USC. He says he wants to be a director, after he makes a few more movies. A lot of them think that but never do it. I have a feeling he will. I'd better watch my ass." Douglas and Tanya laughed.

The three of them found a table and three chairs to eat dinner together. Everyone had found somewhere to sit around the pool. The music on the sound system was soft and sexy, and seemed just right for the setting. Douglas was very sensitive to the right music, the right dinner, the perfect atmosphere for people to open up and get to know each other. Tanya was sitting on a chaise longue, and lay back after she finished eating. When she looked up, she saw the stars as Douglas watched her.

"You look beautiful, Tanya, and so relaxed and happy." She had pulled a pale blue cashmere shawl over her shoulders, and it was perfect with her eyes, draped softly around her. "You look like a Madonna," Douglas said, admiring her like a painting. "I love these days, before we start a film, when everything is beginning, when we have no idea what we'll capture yet, what magic will enthrall us. Once we start, our days are full of surprises, all of which are unknown right now. I love watching it unfold. It's like life, only better, because we control it." That was always an important element to him, Tanya could sense that. Control was essential to him.

Jean Amber walked over to talk to them, eating an ice cream sundae and a cookie. There had also been soufflés made to order, and baked Alaska. Max said the flames always made him want to toast marshmallows over it, but they didn't last long enough. He looked like the sort of person who would do that, unorthodox, funny, comfortable with himself. He was known to have a fondness for whoopee cushions, which he used on the set during breaks. He had an outrageous sense of humor, which Douglas didn't. Douglas was far more serious, and thought the sets should be kept quiet and in control, and lunch breaks spent with people studying their next scenes in the script. He was like the headmaster, and Max the funny, warm, outrageous teacher who had a profound affection for kids. To him, no matter how old they were, the actors were all his children, and they loved that about him. They treated him like a father, and respected him profoundly, both for his skill with his craft which was incomparable, and his kindness, which was equal to it. Douglas was far tougher and had to worry about insurance and budget. He kept his eye on the shooting schedule, and rode actors and directors when things were getting out of hand. His movies were so tightly run and meticulously budgeted, he never let them get out of control. Max did often. He loved spoiling his actors, and thought they deserved it for hard work and a job well done. He was all in favor of cast parties, particularly one like this. Douglas did a hell of a job on that score.

The party lasted till nearly one, as people who had worked together before found each other with delight and amazement at their good fortune to be working on the same film again. They were like kids at camp, happy to find camp friends from the previous summer. Or regulars on cruise ships, who were thrilled to find people they had sailed with before. It was all a matter of luck who you found working with you on a movie. Douglas and Max were particularly good at building casts with talented, compatible people who worked well together. They both felt this one would, and Tanya was a welcome addition. Everyone she had met that night was thrilled to have her among them, and several had read her book, which genuinely touched her. Several of them told her which were their favorite short stories in the anthology, so she knew they had really read it, and weren't just saying it to be polite.

The general atmosphere that evening was one of warmth and excitement. Everyone was happy about this film. It was a star-studded cast, and everyone knew Max's directing was flawless. They all agreed they were lucky to be there, on this cast, and luckier yet to have been invited to Douglas's house for dinner. Everything about Hollywood had a dream-come-true quality to it. It truly was the Magic Kingdom, and they were the chosen people, the luckiest of all to have risen to the top in Hollywood, and luckier still if they stayed there. But for now at least they were riding high. There were a handful of top Hollywood actors and actresses in the movie. And there were no important guest stars who'd be showing up later. Max liked a cohesive cast that worked together in harmony for the duration of the entire film. That created an atmosphere of benevolent cooperation, which only happened if the cast was together constantly and knew each other well. They really became a family then, and Tanya could already feel it. It was happening. Someone had sprinkled fairy dust on them. It was beginning. In fact, it had begun.

Max offered to drive her back to the Beverly Hills Hotel afterward. He didn't mind, and Tanya hadn't brought her limo. She had been given one for the duration of her stay, but she felt guilty keeping the driver sitting there all night, when all she was doing was going back and forth to the hotel. She had planned to take a cab, which she mentioned to Max, as he put a finger to his lips and silently scolded her.

"Don't say that. Douglas will take your car away. And why not keep it? You need it."

She said goodnight to Douglas after that, and thanked him for dinner and a lovely evening. She felt like a schoolgirl saying goodnight to the headmaster. He was in an animated conversation with Jean Amber, who was disagreeing with him vehemently, although good-humoredly, about something. She was telling him how wrong he was.

"Can I settle an argument for you two?" Max volunteered, always happy to help.

"Yes," Jean said staunchly. "I think Venice is much more beautiful than Florence or Rome. It's much more romantic."

"I don't go to Italy for romance," Douglas said, teasing her and loving it. He had no problem at all being surrounded by beautiful women. He had made a career of it. "I go for the art. The Uffizi is my idea of heaven. Florence wins hands down."

"The hotel we stayed in there was awful. I was stuck there for three weeks on location." She said it with the broad experience of a twenty-five-year-old, although one who had traveled widely, more than most, while making movies, but she saw little of the towns and cities where she worked. She never had time. They came to work on a movie, and left immediately after to go to another location. It was a very narrow focus on the world, but better than none. Tanya would have loved her kids to meet her, and hoped they would in time. She seemed like a lovely young woman, and she knew her children would be wildly impressed to meet her.

"I prefer Rome myself," Max offered, confusing the matter further. "Great coffeehouses, good pasta, lots of Japanese tourists, and nuns. You see more nuns in Rome, and I love the old habits. You don't see them anywhere else." Tanya laughed at his comments.

"I think nuns are scary," Jean commented. "I went to Catholic school when I was a kid, and hated it. I didn't see any nuns in Venice."

"Then clearly that's a point in its favor for you. I kissed some girl under the Bridge of Sighs when I was about twenty-one," Max added. "The gondolier scared the hell out of me when he said that meant we'd be together forever. She had bad skin and really bad buck teeth, I had just met her. I think that traumatized me for Venice.

It's amazing what colors your feeling about a city. I had a gallbladder attack in New Orleans once, and I've never wanted to go back since."

"I made a picture there, on location," Jean nodded sympathetically. "It sucked. Really humid. It screwed up my hair the whole time."

"I lost mine in Des Moines," Max said, rubbing his bald head, and they all laughed.

Tanya thanked Douglas for the evening then, and a few minutes later she and Max left. He drove her back to the hotel. She had had a surprisingly good time.

"So how are you liking Hollywood?" Max asked her conversationally. He liked her a lot. If she hadn't been married, he'd have put the make on her. But he had too much respect for the sanctity of marriage, and she didn't look the type to screw around. She was a nice woman, and he was looking forward to working with her. Like Douglas, he had great respect for her work, and Max liked her as a person.

"It's a little crazy, judging by some of the people I talked to tonight, but it's fun," Tanya answered him honestly. "I've been down here a lot for my soaps, but this is different." It had impressed her to meet so many big stars that night. She'd never done that before, except for the regulars on the soaps, who were minor celebrities in their own right. Though very minor in most cases. She had met the big guns tonight.

"It's definitely its own special little world. It's a very incestuous community, in the movie business anyway. Making a picture is like taking a cruise, it's a tiny little microcosm of the world, and has nothing to do with real life. People meet, instantly become friends, fall in love, have affairs, the movie ends, it's all over, and they move on to something else. It feels like real life for about five minutes, but it

isn't. You'll see when we start the movie. There'll be five hot romances starting in the first week. It's a crazy way to live, but at least
it's not boring." It certainly wasn't that. She had already noticed several of the young stars flirting that night, most noticeably Jean
Amber and Ned Bright, who were the film's two leads. They had been
eyeing each other all night, and chatted for a while. She had wondered about that.

"It must be hard to have a real relationship down here, given all
that, if you're in the movie business," she said, as they approached
the hotel.

"It is. Most people don't want one. They'd rather play around and
pretend they're having a real life. They're not, but most of them
never figure that out. They think they are. Like Douglas. I don't think
he's had a serious relationship since the Ice Age. He goes out with
women for a while, usually fairly important women, but I don't think
he ever lets anyone get close. It's not his style. He's all about power
and big business, and buying art, I guess. I don't think he's interested
in love. Some guys are just like that. Me, I'm still looking for the Holy
Grail," he said, smiling happily. Tanya really liked him. Everyone
seemed to. He had a huge heart, and it showed. "I never go out with
actresses. I want some nice woman who loves bald guys with beards,
and wants to rub my back at night. I went out with the same woman
for sixteen years, and we were perfect for each other. I don't think we
ever had a fight."

"So what happened?" Tanya asked, as they stopped under the
awning of the Beverly Hills Hotel, which was home for her now, although it didn't feel that way yet. She wondered if it ever would. She
still felt out of place here, and not fancy enough to be staying there.
She felt like a fraud, and surely not a star.

"She died," Max said quietly, still smiling. The memory of her still warmed his eyes. "Breast cancer. It was the shits. There'll never be anyone like her. She was the love of my life. I've gone out with some other women since. It's not the same. I'm okay. I get by." He smiled. "She was a writer, too. She wrote miniseries in the days when they were a big deal. We used to talk about getting married, but we never needed to. We felt like we already were married in our hearts. I still go on vacation with her kids every year, between pictures. They're great people. Two boys, both married. They live in Chicago. My kids love them, too. They remind me of her."

"She sounds like a nice woman," Tanya said, sounding sympathetic as they sat in his car and talked. He drove a beat-up old Honda, in spite of the big fees he made for directing movies. He had no need to show off. It wasn't his style, unlike Douglas, with his fabulous house and incredible art. She had been impressed. Anyone would have been. She'd never seen paintings of that caliber outside a museum.

"She was nice," Max said of his lost love. "So are you." He smiled at her. He liked who and what she was. The kind of person Tanya was was written all over her. He had liked her the moment they met, and even better tonight. She was genuine and solid, which was rare in Hollywood. "Your husband is a lucky guy."

"I'm a lucky woman," she said, smiling wistfully. She missed Peter a lot. They had lost the comfort of daily physical contact, the warmth they shared at night. It was a lot to lose. She was anxious to call him as soon as she got back to the room, although it was late. She had promised she would, even if she woke him up. She had talked to him and the girls before she went out. They were doing fine so far, and she was going home in two days. She could hardly wait. "My husband is a great guy."

"Good for you. I hope I meet him sometime. He should come down during the filming, and bring your kids."

"He will." She thanked Max for the ride and hopped out. And then she remembered her lunch with Douglas the following day. He was meeting her at the Polo Lounge, which was convenient for her. "Are you coming to lunch tomorrow?"

"No, I'm meeting with the cameramen, to discuss equipment with them." Max used a lot of complicated, unusual lenses to achieve the effects he was famous for, and he wanted to be sure he had them all on hand. "Douglas likes getting to know people individually. I'll catch up with you next week, when our meetings start. Have a nice week-end with your kids." He waved as she got out and he drove off, and she smiled on her way back to the bungalow. He was going to be great to work with. She wasn't as sure about Douglas. He still un-nerved her, although she had liked him better tonight. He had seemed less scary to her, viewed in his natural habitat, where he was visibly more at ease.

She called Peter as soon as she got back to her bungalow. He was half-asleep, but waiting for her call. It was nearly one-thirty.

"I'm sorry it's so late. It went on forever," she said, sounding breathless. She had run back to the room to call him.

"That's okay. How was it?" He yawned, and she could visualize him perfectly in their bed. It made her miss him even more.

"Fun. Weird. Interesting. Douglas Wayne has the most incredible art I've ever seen. Renoir, Monet. Amazing stuff. And the place was full of hot young stars. Jean Amber, Ned Bright." She named some others. "They're nice young kids. Molly and Megan would have loved it. I missed you. The director, Max Blum, is really nice, too. You'll like him. I told him about you tonight."

"God, you'll never want to come back to Ross after all that, Tanny . . . you're going to be way too glamorous for us." She didn't think he meant it, but she didn't like hearing it anyway. It was what

Douglas had predicted when he called her. And it was the last thing she wanted. She wanted no part of a Hollywood life. Just theirs, in Ross.

"Don't be a jerk. I couldn't care less about all that crap. They'd all die for a life like ours."

"Yeah, right," he laughed, sounding like their kids. "I don't think so. You're going to get spoiled down there, sweetheart."

"No, I'm not," she said, sounding sad. She had kicked off her sandals and was lying on the bed. "I miss you. I wish you were here."

"You'll be home in two days. I miss you, too. It's dead around here without you. I burned dinner tonight."

"I'll cook this weekend." She still felt guilty being there, and couldn't wait to come home to him and the girls. She'd been there for three days and it already felt like several lifetimes. It was going to be a long nine months. Very, very long. It had felt really strange to go out that night without him, but she had to, to meet the cast. It was a command performance for all of them at Douglas's house, although a very pleasant one for sure. But she would have enjoyed it more if Peter had been there. She never went out without him when he was out of town, which was rare. She had no desire for a social life of her own, especially down here. She had nothing in common with any of them. Especially Douglas Wayne. She could imagine going out for a hamburger with Max Blum, though. He seemed like he'd be a good friend, if there was such a thing down here, which she wasn't sure about yet. "I can't wait to see you. It's so weird being alone down here. I miss you and the girls so much." She hated sleeping without him, and had been restless and lonely for the past three nights. He was hating that part, too, and slept with a pillow in his arms for lack of her.

"We miss you, too," Peter said, yawning again. "I'd better get to sleep. I have to get the girls up in the morning. Meg's got swim practice at seven-thirty." He glanced at the clock. "I have to be up in four and a half hours." He groaned at the thought, but he hadn't wanted to go to sleep without talking to his wife. "I'll talk to you to-morrow. Sleep tight, baby . . . I miss you . . ."

"Me too," she said softly. "Night-night. Sweet dreams."

"You too," Peter said and hung up. Tanya lay on her bed in the bungalow, thinking about him and missing him. She went to brush her teeth then with a heavy heart. She could hardly wait to go home. And they were all wrong about her, she thought to herself. Peter, Douglas, predicting she was going to get spoiled down here and never want to go back to Ross. That was all she wanted. She missed her bed, she missed her husband, she missed her kids. She couldn't think of a single thing down here that could come close to that. She would have traded all the luxuries of her bungalow at that moment for a night in bed with Peter in Ross. For Tanya, then and always, there was no place like home.

# Chapter 6

Tanya met Douglas at the Polo Lounge at one o'clock the next day for lunch. She was wearing jeans and a pink sweater, and he looked as glamorous as ever in a well-cut khaki suit, blue shirt, yellow Hermès tie, and impeccable brown shoes. He always looked immaculate, and he was waiting for her when she arrived. He was drinking a Bloody Mary and chatting with a friend who had walked by. He introduced Tanya to him, and she was startled to realize it was Robert De Niro. They chatted for a few minutes, and then De Niro left. It would have been hard not to be impressed. But this was standard fare now. She wanted to tell Peter about it afterward, but she didn't want to hear any more from him, or anyone else, about how glamorous she was becoming, and what a hard time she'd have going back. That was all she wanted. Everything down here was unreal, and she didn't feel part of it. She had no desire to be. She just wanted to do her work, and go home. They were all wrong about how sophisticated and spoiled she was going to get. Tanya knew better. She knew herself well, and had her feet firmly planted on solid ground.

"Thank you for a lovely evening last night," she said to Douglas as she sat down. "It was fun meeting the cast. You have a beautiful house."

"I enjoy it," he said, smiling at her. "You have to come on my boat sometime. It's a lot of fun." It was a two-hundred-foot yacht. She had seen photographs of it at his house the night before. It looked huge to her. Her kids would have gone insane. "What do you do in the summer, Tanya? What did you do this year?" he asked, and she smiled. It was like a homework assignment in first grade. *My Summer Vacation, by Tanya Harris.* Her life was so much quieter than his, in every way. She loved it that way. She didn't need a yacht.

"We go to Tahoe in August. We rent a house there every year. The kids love it, and we have a good time together. Peter and I were talking about taking the kids to Europe next summer. We haven't been in years. It was too hard when the kids were small." She felt foolish saying things like that to him. He couldn't care less about what you did with kids when they were big or small. And a rented house in Tahoe must have sounded pathetic to him, compared to a two-hundred-foot yacht on the French Riviera. The absurdity of the comparison made her laugh, as she ordered an iced tea. She was planning to work that afternoon.

"I spend two months on the boat in the South of France every year," he said as though it were commonplace, which it was to him. "I go to Sardinia, too. It's great. And Corsica. Capri sometimes, Ibiza, Mallorca, Greece. If you take your kids over next summer, you'll have to come on the boat for a few days." He rarely extended invitations to people with children, although it was a long way off. But how much damage could they do in a few days? He suspected hers were probably civilized. She certainly was. He assumed her family was well behaved, and he knew they were college age. He never would have invited people with young children, he assumed they'd probably get seasick anyway if he had them on board for an extended time. A weekend would be fine.

"They'd love that. I can't wait to tell them I met Ned last night, and Jean. They're going to be very impressed with me."

"They should be." He smiled. "I am. A lot more than with Ned and Jean," although Tanya thought he had appeared to enjoy his conversation with her. Admittedly, Jean was a kid. She was spectacular looking but seemed young for her age. Actors seemed to lead sheltered lives in some ways. They lived in a tiny little bubble while making a movie, out of touch with the real world.

"They seem like kids," Tanya commented as he ordered another Bloody Mary.

"They are. All actors and actresses are children. They live in cocoons, protected from reality. It's always been that way. They play dress-up and have fun. Some of them work hard. But they have no idea how the rest of the world lives. They're used to having agents and producers baby them, and shield them, and cater to their every whim. They never really grow up. The bigger they are, the more unreal it is. You'll see when you work with them. They're incredibly immature."

"They can't all be that way," Tanya commented with interest. They were damning statements from him, but he knew the business well.

"No. But most are. They're narcissistic and spoiled, and all about themselves. That gets old very quickly. That's why I never go out with actresses. They're way too high maintenance for me." He looked into Tanya's eyes as he said it, and she looked away. Something about him made her uncomfortable. He always crossed some invisible boundary between them. He kept himself just out of reach, yet was always just a hair too intimate with her. Or more than a hair. Without moving an inch, he invaded her space.

They ordered lunch after that, and she asked him a number of questions about the picture, and the meetings they were having next week. She was planning on doing a final polish on the script that weekend, and there were some changes he wanted her to make. It all sounded fine to her. He was finding her easy to work with and entirely reasonable. She seemed to have very little ego about her work.

They had finished lunch by the time the conversation got personal again. It was always Douglas who brought it there. He was hungry to know more about her. He asked her about her childhood, her parents, when she had started writing. He wanted to know everything about her early life, what her dreams and disappointments were. She was surprised by the intimacy of his questions, and he volunteered nothing about himself, which didn't surprise her. He was a man who gave nothing away.

"It's all pretty ordinary," she said comfortably. "No tragedies, no dark secrets. No serious disappointments. I was sad when my parents died, of course. But Peter and I have been very happy for twenty years."

"That sounds pretty remarkable," Douglas said somewhat cynically.

"I guess it is these days," Tanya said pensively.

"It is, if it's true," he said, looking at her, and she was annoyed at the way he examined her, as though he didn't believe what she'd said, and would see the truth in her eyes.

"Is that so inconceivable to you, that people are happily married?" It seemed lucky but commonplace to her. They knew a lot of couples in Ross who had been happily married for twenty or thirty years. A lot of their friends were, although she and Peter seemed the most solid of all. And admittedly, some of their friends had gotten divorced over the years. But many of them had remarried, and were happily married again. She lived in a wholesome little world that seemed far from here. In Douglas's world, people rarely got married, and when they did, it was often for the wrong reasons, mostly for show, power, or material gain in some way. And he knew a lot of men married to trophy women. There were no trophy wives in Marin, certainly not among the people Tanya knew.

"Both of the women I married were huge mistakes," Douglas said conversationally. "One was a well-known actress, thirty years ago when I married her. We were both ridiculously young. I was twenty-four, just a kid starting out in the business. I wanted to be an actor then, too. I got over that very quickly. And I got over her very quickly, too. We were married less than a year. Thank God we never had kids."

"Is she a big star now?" Tanya asked out of idle curiosity. She wondered who it had been, but didn't dare ask. She knew he'd volunteer it if he wanted her to know.

"No." He smiled. "She never was. Pretty girl, though. She gave up acting, and married a guy from North Carolina. After she married him, I never heard from her again. I heard from a mutual friend she had four kids. She never wanted much out of life except a husband, children, and a picket fence. I think she got all three, but not from me. That wasn't my thing even then." Tanya believed that readily from everything he had said. And he still wasn't that type now. Tanya couldn't imagine him with children.

"The second one was more interesting. She was a rock star in the eighties. A huge talent, she could have had a hell of a career." He sounded almost wistful as he said it, and Tanya watched his eyes. She couldn't interpret what she saw there. Regret, pain, maybe grief, disappointment. That had obviously come to an end, too, since he wasn't married anymore, nor wanted to be.

"What happened to her? Did she quit the business, too?"

"No, she died in a plane crash when she was on tour. She went down with her whole band. The drummer flew the plane, and he wasn't much of a pilot. He could have been stoned. We were already divorced when she died. But I was sorry anyway. She was a sweet kid. You've probably heard her name." Tanya was impressed when he said it. She had loved listening to her music when she was in college, and still had some old tapes. She remembered when the plane went down. It made headlines at the time. She hadn't thought of her in years, and it was odd hearing of her now in such a personal way. She could see Douglas's sadness over her in his eyes. It humanized him to Tanya. There was a soft side to him after all.

"Why was she a mistake?" Tanya asked gently. She was turning the tables on him, asking him questions this time, curious about him, just as he was about her.

"We had nothing in common. And the music scene was crazy even then. She did a lot of drugs, although she said she wasn't hooked. She wasn't an addict, just a crazy, beautiful wild girl. She claimed she sang better when she was stoned. I'm not sure it was true. But she had one hell of a voice," he said, with a dreamy, distant look that made him look like a different person, somewhat softer and more human than he was today. Tanya wondered if she had been the love of his life, or if there was such a thing in his world. "We got divorced because we never saw each other. She was on tour nine or ten months a year. It didn't make much sense, and I was producing by then. She was a handicap for me. She got too much bad press over the way she behaved. Coke was pretty fashionable back then, or pretty common at any rate. She got arrested a few times. It didn't sit well with me." Nor had the men she cheated on him with, but he didn't say that to Tanya. "Those were crazy years, and she was a pretty outrageous girl.

I never liked being around drugs, and I still don't. It went with the territory for her. She wanted kids, too. I couldn't see myself having babies with her. I figured they'd all be drug addicts by the time they were six. That's really not my thing," he said again. "It never was. I was too busy trying to be successful, making a living. I produced my first movies then. Having a wife in rehab or jail wouldn't have done much for my career, although it happened to plenty of people back then. I was always scared to death she'd OD. But she never did."

"So you divorced her?" It sounded like a calculated move to Tanya. She had been bad for his career, so out she went. It was obvious what his priorities were. It sounded as though there had been more to it than that, but she didn't want to pry. It was intriguing, though. She wondered if that was why he was so closed, or if his sealed-off quality predated all that. She didn't have the impression Douglas had ever been warm or close to anyone, or if so, not in a very long time since his youth.

"Actually"—he smiled at Tanya—"she divorced me. She said I was an uptight, pretentious, arrogant, opportunistic prick. And all I cared about was money. And that was a quote. She was right, too." He said it without guilt or apology. He had said it many times about himself ever since. "Unfortunately, all those things she mentioned are a recipe for success. You have to be all of those things to get ahead in this business, and I was very determined to make some big films. She was a star in her own right. She didn't need help from me."

"Did that bother you?" Tanya asked, curious about what made him tick. He was a complex man.

"Yes, it did," he answered her question. "It bothered me that I had no control over anything she did. She didn't listen, she didn't ask for advice. She never told me what was happening with the band. Half of them had been in jail for drugs at the time. It didn't hurt her in her business, but it would have in mine. People who consort with druggies don't go far in any line of work, at least not in those days. Things were still a little more uptight twenty years ago. And in those days people still believed that coke wouldn't do you a lot of harm. We've learned a lot more about it since. I think sooner or later she would have either gotten badly addicted or wound up in jail. Maybe it's better that she died." It seemed a hard thing to say.

"Were you in love with her?" Tanya asked sympathetically. It was a sad story either way, and a waste of a young woman's life, and all those who had died with her. Tanya remembered it perfectly.

"Probably not," Douglas answered honestly. "I don't think I've ever been in love. It's not something that I missed. Most of the time"— he smiled ruefully—"I like deals better than girls. They're easier to manage."

"But not nearly as much fun," Tanya chided him.

"True. I have no idea why I married her, except I think I was impressed by her at the time. She was a knockout-looking girl with a hell of a voice. I still listen to her music sometimes," he confessed, and Tanya smiled at him. She hoped they were becoming friends.

"So do I," Tanya added. She knew she had put away tapes from her college days, and had kept a few out to listen to occasionally.

Douglas seemed depressed by the subject, by the end of lunch. He hadn't thought of his late second wife in a long time. It was kind of a tender memory to ponder now, except for all that had led up to the divorce. Afterward she had gone to jail twice for drugs, which was unthinkable for him. He was glad he was out of it then. He could still remember his feelings of outrage at the time. She had been a lost soul, though an extremely beautiful girl. He had loved showing her off when they were married. He said she had been the closest he had ever come to a trophy wife. He had never wanted another one since then. He was a man who functioned better on his own. And in later years he had little need for companionship, except for some entertainment in his bed now and then.

He never engaged in matters of the heart. His heart was never involved in his sexual endeavors. And when he wanted a woman on his arm, he chose carefully. He liked intelligent women who were interesting company, didn't outshine him, and looked well in the press with him. They were usually major, established stars, well-known writers, the occasional married politician, or even wives of his friends who were out of town. He was interested in companionship and suitable women, not fodder for the tabloids. His reputation was that of an important man who had made a mark on the world. His love life was of no interest, even and perhaps especially to him. He would have been content to take Tanya out with him, once he got to know her better, and had thought of it the other night at his dinner party. She was interesting, intelligent, and had a good sense of humor, and she was a pretty woman. She was the perfect profile of the kind of woman he liked having on his arm. And she sparred well with him, another plus to him. In a sense, he was auditioning her as a potential companion for social events, or even as a hostess at his dinner parties. He liked everything he had seen about her so far. And their working together for the next several months would make appearances in public together seem quite benign. He didn't like being gossiped about. And Tanya looked so respectable that that seemed completely unlikely. She was the kind of woman who drew praise, not criticism.

"What are you doing this weekend?" he asked casually as their lunch came to an end.

"Going home." She beamed. Her total delight at the prospect was evident, even to him, although he thought it somewhat silly. He didn't have a sentimental bone in his body.

"You really like all that Marin County housewife stuff, don't you?" he said, trying to shame her into admitting she didn't.

"Yes, I do," she said happily, "especially my husband and my kids. They're the best part. My whole life is about them."

"You're so much bigger than that, Tanya. You deserve a more exciting life than that." He looked sorry for her as he said it.

"I don't want excitement."

She had always loved the mundanities of her life with Peter, the everyday ordinary things that made their life seem normal and solid. The Hollywood life seemed false and shallow to her. There was nothing about it that she wanted, except the experience of writing a screenplay for a movie. Other than that, she had no interest in it. It seemed totally empty to her. And she felt sorry for the people who lived in it and thought there was something to it, like Douglas. As far as she was concerned, it had absolutely no substance or merit whatsoever. She suspected Douglas would have violently disagreed with her if she'd said it. She knew he loved the art scene, and was on the board of the Los Angeles County Museum. He had said he went to the theater whenever possible, and occasionally went to San Francisco for the ballet and symphony. He loved cultural pursuits and social events of all kinds. He even flew to Washington, D.C., for openings at the Kennedy Center, or to Lincoln Center and the Met in New York. He was a major figure in all four cities, and in Europe when he went there, which he did often. A life like hers would have bored him to extinction. She, on the other hand, loved it. She wouldn't have traded lives with him for anything in the world.

"Maybe after you've been in L.A. for a while, you'll look to broader horizons. I hope so, for your sake," he said, as they walked across the

Polo Lounge, and all heads turned as they recognized him and wondered who he was with. No one knew her, and it caused interest but not comment. She was a pretty woman of a reasonable age in jeans and a pink sweater, nothing more. But if she went out publicly with him, they would know who she was. Some women in L.A. would have killed for the opportunity. He liked the fact that it meant nothing to her. She wasn't trying to use him, and didn't seem the type anyway. He had guessed right on that score. There was nothing opportunistic about Tanya, in any way. She was a woman of integrity and dignity, with a fine mind and a lot of talent. She didn't need to trade on anyone to get ahead, and wouldn't have in any case.

She thanked him for lunch, and he wished her a good weekend. It had been more pleasant than she'd expected. He was good company, and hadn't gone over the line as often as she'd feared he would. In fact, he had been completely proper, and not as critical of her home life as he had been at first. He thought she was worthy of more interesting pursuits than those she engaged in, in Marin, but if that was what she wanted and how she enjoyed spending her time, it seemed foolish to him, but she didn't offend anyone. He knew her life would get bigger and more interesting once she'd been in L.A. for a while. He had the feeling as they walked into the lobby together that in time they could be friends. He liked the idea, and although she wasn't as sure about it as he was, it was conceivable to her as well. She just wanted to be careful not to encourage him in any way. There was a side of him that made her uncomfortable, and she knew the kind of profound disregard he had for the life she led. Family values were of no interest to him, children made him nervous, and he thought marriage vows only got in the way. Douglas liked people he could push around, or had some control over in some way. As long as she was aware of it, and kept her boundaries firm and her head clear, she was sure that they would get along very well. He wasn't the sort of man she wanted to let her guard down with. He was a business associate for now, and nothing more, and she wanted to keep it that way. And maybe in time, after they knew each other better, they would be friends. He had to earn her friendship first.

She worked on her computer for the rest of the afternoon, and had room service that night. Max called her to ask how it was going, and she discussed what she perceived as a few potential problems with him. He helped her solve them, and she liked the solutions he offered. She tried them and was pleased to find they worked. She was absolutely certain they were going to enjoy working together. She would have liked to go home that night, but Douglas had intimated that she should be on call in case they called for any meetings on Friday morning, but when they hadn't by noon, she took a cab to the airport.

She had let her car and driver go, and all she took was hand luggage. She took a one-thirty flight to San Francisco, and at three-twenty she walked into the house in Ross. No one was home, but she wanted to dance around the living room and sing. She was so happy to be home she could hardly stand it. She checked the fridge and cupboards and found them nearly empty. She went to Safeway, and bought food for the weekend and the following week, and was putting it away when the girls walked in and gave a shout when they saw her there. Even Megan looked happy for a minute and then grew quickly somber and went upstairs, remembering that she was supposed to be angry at her mother. But for a moment she had let it show that she was glad to see her, which pleased Tanya, and Molly was all over her like a puppy, hugging, kissing, standing close to her, and hugging her again.

"I really missed you this week," she admitted to her mother.

"So did I," Tanya said, with an arm around Molly's shoulders.

"How was it?" Molly asked with interest, dying to hear about it all.

"It was fine. I had dinner with Ned Bright and Jean Amber one night. He's mighty cute." She beamed at her daughter, so happy to see her.

"When can I meet him?" Molly looked excited at the prospect as her mother put the last of the groceries away.

"As soon as you come down to visit me. You can come watch them filming on the set. The director is really nice."

Molly went upstairs to call a friend and tell her about it a few minutes later. And Tanya was still tidying up the kitchen when Peter walked in. He knew she was coming home and had left the office early. As soon as he saw her, he spun her around in his arms and kissed her hungrily on the mouth, and then held her close to him. They were so happy to see each other. They went upstairs for an hour before dinner, and locked their door discreetly. It was the perfect homecoming, in every way.

Tanya cooked dinner for her family that night. She made their favorite pasta, and a big green salad, while Peter cooked steaks on the barbecue, and afterward they all sat around talking animatedly. She told them about the dinner at Douglas Wayne's house, and all the stars that had been there. Afterward the girls went out with friends, and she and Peter went quietly upstairs.

It was a normal Friday night, and she and Peter talked for hours, and cuddled. They made love again before they went to sleep. They had all survived her first week in L.A., and all was well in their world.

# Chapter 7

The weekend sped by too quickly for all of them. Tanya woke up depressed on Sunday morning, and Peter didn't look happy, either. She wasn't leaving till that night, but knowing she was going took the wind out of all of them all day. Megan's feelings finally erupted at lunchtime, and she got in an argument with her mother in the kitchen, over a T-shirt that had gotten ruined in the wash, which had nothing to do with anything. She was angry at her mother for going back to L.A. Knowing what was at the root of Megan's display of fury, Tanya tried not to lose her temper, and finally told her to behave.

"This isn't about the T-shirt, Meg," she said bluntly. "I don't like leaving, either. I'm trying to do the best I can."

"No, you're not," Megan accused her. "What you're doing is selfish and stupid. You didn't have to write the script for this movie. Face it, you're a lousy mother, Mom. You walked out on all of us so you could do it. You don't care about Dad or us. You're just thinking of yourself." Tanya stood dumbstruck for a long moment, and then tears came to her eyes as she looked at her daughter, and faced her accusations. It was hard to defend herself, and she wondered if Megan was right. Going to L.A. to write a screenplay was a very selfish thing to have done.

"I'm sorry you feel that way," Tanya said sadly. "I know this was a lousy year to do it, but this is when I got the offer, and I might never have gotten the chance again." She had hoped they'd understand it and forgive her, but maybe Megan wouldn't. She hadn't relented yet. They were standing there looking at each other, Megan glaring, and Tanya in dismay as Peter walked in. He had heard what Megan said, and had come in from the living room to tell Megan to apologize to her mother, and she wouldn't. She said she believed every word she had said. Without saying another word, she stomped upstairs. Tanya looked at Peter and started to cry, and he put his arms around her.

"She's just blowing off steam."

"I don't blame her. I would feel the same way she does, if my mother left me for senior year."

"You're home on the weekends. They're hardly here during the week anyway. They get home in time to eat, call their friends, and fall into bed. They don't really need you," he said, trying to reassure her, but she cried anyway. And she hated leaving him alone, too.

"They like knowing I'm here," she said, and blew her nose.

"So do I. But you're here on weekends. It's not forever. We did fine this week, and the movie will be over before you know it. Imagine if you win an Oscar, Tan . . . think about it. On a Douglas Wayne movie, it could happen." He had won at least a dozen of them. "What's he like, by the way?" Peter had been curious about him. And he knew he was a good-looking guy. He wondered if he was going to hit on Tanya. He hoped not. As a rule, Peter wasn't jealous. But Hollywood was heady stuff. In spite of that, he trusted her.

"He's weird. Selfish. Very closed, kind of shut down. He hates kids. He has a yacht. He has great art and a nice house. That's about all I know about him. That, and he was married to a rock star who died in a plane crash, after they were divorced. He's not exactly warm and fuzzy, but very smart. The one I really like is the director, Max Blum. He looks like Santa Claus, and he's really sweet. His girlfriend died of breast cancer, and he has a Great Dane named Harry."

"You really get the personal stuff, don't you?" Peter laughed. She had painted a very coherent portrait of them both. "It must be something about writers. People always tell you things they wouldn't tell me in a million years. And you don't even ask, they volunteer it." He had seen it happen a thousand times over the years. People always confided their deepest secrets to her. It amazed him.

"I must have a sympathetic face. Besides, I'm a mother, although I seem to be flunking that subject at the moment."

"No, you're not. Meg's tough." They both knew that about her. She demanded a lot of those she cared about, and was quick to criticize if anyone she loved fell short, even a friend. Molly was far more forgiving, and warmer. Megan had higher standards for herself and everyone else. Tanya always said her own mother had been like that, it was in the genes.

Tanya made lunch for everyone, and Megan didn't come downstairs. She said goodbye to her mother and went out. Tanya suspected that Megan didn't want to see her leave. People had different ways of saying goodbye. Goodbyes had always been hard for Megan. It was easier for her to get mad and stomp off than to feel sad or cry. And Molly clung to her till the last minute. They dropped her off at a friend's on their way to the airport, and she hugged her mother tight before getting out of the car.

"I love you. Have fun . . . say hi to Ned Bright for me. Tell him I love him . . . and I love you more . . ." She shouted back over her shoulder as she got out of the car and ran into her friend's house.

After that Tanya and Peter had some quiet time together, driving to the airport. It gave them a chance to talk about a case he was working on, the changes she'd made to the script, and just to sit in comfortable silence for a few minutes, enjoying each other's presence. They had made love more than usual that weekend, and Peter laughed about it before he dropped her off.

"Maybe this L.A. thing is good for our sex life." It was as though they were storing up each other's loving for the days they were apart. It helped. She was sad again when he kissed her at the airport. He couldn't come in past security, since he didn't have a boarding pass and wasn't traveling himself.

"I already miss you," she said, looking miserable, and he kissed her again. He was being an incredibly good sport about it.

"Me, too. See you Friday. Call me when you get in."

"I will. What are you doing for dinner?" Both girls were out, and she had forgotten to fix him something to put in the microwave.

"I told Alice I'd stop by. She checked on the girls this week a couple of times, and I told her I'd pick up some sushi and come over."

"Say hi for me. I was going to call her all weekend, and I never got to it. Tell her I'm sorry, and thanks for keeping an eye on the girls."

"She doesn't mind. I think she misses her own kids. It's less lonely for her if she drops by to see the girls on her way home. She only stays a few minutes. She's so busy with the gallery she's never there." Tanya was glad for her that she had it. It had been a hell of a blow for her when Jim died. She had been amazingly strong about it, but Tanya knew better than anyone how unhappy she was. The first year had been just awful, and Tanya had helped drag her through it. Now she was doing what she could to give back. It was a fair exchange between best friends. They had always been there for each other, and she was grateful for Alice's presence now.

Tanya ran back and kissed Peter again, and then rushed into the airport with her tote bag. She was the last one on the plane, and sat back against her seat and closed her eyes while she thought about the weekend. It had been wonderful being home with the girls and Peter. She hated to leave again.

She turned her cell phone off as they taxied down the runway, and she dozed as they lifted off. She slept all the way to L.A., and only woke up when they landed. It had been a busy, emotional weekend and she was tired, and drained by her argument with Meg. She wondered if she'd ever forgive her, or if things would ever be the same with them again. She hoped so. Megan was slow to forgive and could hold a grudge forever. Tanya was still thinking about her when she walked out of LAX and hailed a cab. She hadn't even told her driver she was coming in. She would have felt silly coming in from the airport in a limo. She felt strange availing herself of all the perks in her contract.

She was surprised to find that the bungalow looked comfortable and familiar when she walked in. She had brought a few more photographs from home, of Peter and the kids, and one of Alice with James and Jason. She had talked to Jason that weekend and he sounded happy. He was so busy in his new college life that he wasn't calling any of them. The girls had complained about it.

She called Peter the minute she sat down. She called on his cell phone, and he was still having dinner with Alice. Tanya talked to her, too, and it made her feel lonelier than ever knowing that they were together and she was alone. She wanted to be having sushi with them. Alice said it was no fun without her and they missed her. Tanya told Alice about the photograph of her she'd brought with her. And then they went back to their dinner, and Tanya turned on the TV. She felt strangely alone.

She took a bath in the enormous tub and turned on the Jacuzzi. It helped relax her. And afterward she turned on her computer, and worked on the script some more. She had a meeting the next day to discuss the producer and director's notes, and the following day they were meeting with the stars to do the same.

It was going to be a busy week assimilating everyone's notes and trying to incorporate them in the script somehow. She was looking forward to the process and to hearing their comments. She worked on it till nearly two A.M., and left a wake-up call for seven. She had to be at the studio on Monday morning at eight-thirty.

Tanya felt as though the phone rang the moment her head touched the pillow. She woke up with a start, and then lay back with a groan after her wake-up call. She missed Peter, so she called him. He was up and getting ready, and about to make breakfast for the girls. Hearing him made her feel guilty that he was there with them and she wasn't. They had a long road ahead of them, of breakfasts and dinners he'd have to make, and nights she wouldn't be there. A whole school year of them. She felt as though she were facing a prison sentence without them, as she and Peter chatted briefly before they started their day.

"I miss you so much," Tanya said sadly. "I feel like shit that you have to do all the work."

"You've been doing it for eighteen years, so what's the big deal if I do it for a few months." He sounded rushed but sweet.

"I think I married a saint," she said gratefully. He was being amazing.

"No, you married a guy who can never get eggs, juice, and cereal on the table simultaneously. I'm basically a dyslexic cook, so I gotta go. Play nice in the sandbox today."

"I hope they do, too." She was nervous about this first big meeting. They were going to get down to business, and maybe pull her work apart. She had no idea what they'd do or say. This was all new to her.

"You'll be fine. Don't take any shit from them. What I've read so far is great."

"Thanks, I'll call you when I get out of the meeting. Good luck with breakfast . . . and Peter . . ." There were tears in her eyes as she spoke to him. "I'm sorry I'm doing this. I feel like such a lousy wife and mom. You're a hero to let me do it." She still felt so guilty for being away, and leaving him all the domestic responsibilities she normally handled and had for nearly twenty years.

"You're the best wife I've got. And you're a star to me."

"You're the star, Peter," she said softly. She could hardly wait for the weekend so she could go home again.

"'Bye, be good . . . love you . . . ," he said, and rushed off the phone, as she went to brush her teeth and comb her hair.

She ordered breakfast from room service, a far cry from the hasty meal Peter had gobbled with the girls. Her driver and limo were waiting for her outside. And she was at the studio promptly at eight-thirty. Douglas hadn't arrived yet. Max Blum was already there.

"Good morning, Tanya. How was your weekend?" he said pleasantly, carrying a heavy briefcase that looked like it was about to explode as he set it down in the conference room where they had sent them. They had rented office space from one of the TV networks for the duration of the picture. Tanya had been assigned an office, too, but she'd told them she preferred to work at the hotel. It would be more peaceful and less distracting to write in the bungalow.

"Too short," Tanya said sadly. She was missing Peter and the kids more than ever today, after a taste of them over the weekend. "How was yours?"

"Not bad. I went to a couple of baseball games, read *The Wall Street Journal, Variety,* and *The New York Times,* and had several very intellectual conversations with my dog. We stayed up pretty late, so he was too tired to come to work today. It's a dog's life," he said as a secretary offered them both coffee, and they both declined. Max was carrying a Starbucks cappuccino, and Tanya had had enough tea at the hotel. As they chatted amiably, Douglas walked in, looking as always like the cover of *GQ.* He even smelled good, and had had a fresh haircut over the weekend. He always looked impeccable, even at that hour of the morning. Max looked rumpled, disheveled, his jeans were torn, his Birkenstocks were ancient and worn, his socks had a hole in them, and what little hair he had looked as though he had forgotten to comb it. He looked clean, but a total mess. Tanya was wearing jeans, sweatshirt, and running shoes and hadn't bothered to wear makeup. This was work.

They got down to the notes immediately. There were several scenes Douglas wanted changed, and one Max had a problem with. He said it moved too quickly, and showed none of the deep emotions of the actors in the scene. He wanted her to rewrite it to rip people's hearts out. "Make 'em bleed," as he put it. And as the morning progressed, she and Douglas got into an argument about one of the characters and the way Tanya had portrayed her. He said the character was boring, and he didn't bother to mince words. "I hate her," he said bluntly. "Everyone else will, too."

"She's supposed to be boring." Tanya defended her work heatedly on that point. "She's a fatally boring woman. I don't think I even mind if you hate her. She's not a nice person. She's tedious, a whiner, and she betrays her best friend. Why the hell would you love her?"

"I don't. But if she's got the balls to screw over her best friend, then she must have some personality in there somewhere. At least

give us some of that. You wrote her as though she's dead." He was almost insulting, and Tanya finally backed off. She would make some
changes to the character in question, but she didn't feel right doing
everything he said. In the end, Max stepped in and suggested a com-
promise solution. Still boring, not nice, but maybe a little more fire
and visible bitterness and jealousy, so the ultimate betrayal made
more sense. Tanya said she could live with that, and she was exhausted by the end of the meeting. It was nearly three o'clock by the
time they had gone over everyone's notes, and they hadn't stopped
for lunch. Douglas thought eating would be distracting. Tanya could
feel her blood sugar dropping and her spirits plummeting by the time
they walked out of the meeting.

"Good meeting, everyone," Douglas said cheerfully as they got up.
He was in great spirits, and Max had been nibbling some candy bars
and nuts he'd brought with him. He had worked on several movies
with Douglas and knew how he worked. Tanya didn't. She felt
drained, and her feelings were a little hurt by some of the things
Douglas had said. He had packed some tough punches and offered
no apology for it. His only interest was in making the best picture
possible, whatever it took, and no matter whose teeth he had to rat-
tle to get it. In this case, they had been hers. She wasn't used to his
style, or to having to justify her work to that extent and fight for it.
The producers of the soaps she wrote for were far more easygoing.

"You okay?" Max asked her as they left the building together.
Douglas had run out for an appointment, and they were all meeting
back there the next morning to meet with the stars as well. Tanya
was beginning to dread it. This was harder than she'd thought, and
she still didn't have a handle on what to do with the character
Douglas hated so much. She was going to work on it that afternoon

and night. It felt like preparing for an exam. His words had been fairly harsh.

"Yeah, I'm fine. Just tired. I didn't eat much breakfast. I started to fade about an hour ago."

"Always bring food when you take meetings with Douglas. He works like a maniac, and he never stops to eat. That's how he stays so thin. To him, lunch is purely a social event. If it's not on his calendar, he doesn't eat. People around him drop like flies," he teased.

"I'll know for tomorrow," she said, as he walked her to her limo.

"Oh no, tomorrow is different," he explained. "Tomorrow we've got stars. Stars have to be fed, on cue, and extremely expensive specially catered meals if possible. Directors and writers don't have to eat. You can beg something to eat from the actors' plates. Maybe they'll throw you some caviar or a chicken leg." He was exaggerating, of course, but not entirely. "It's always good to have an actor or two at a meeting. I try to request it. That way the rest of us get fed." She laughed as she listened. It was like being taught the ropes by an upperclassman at school. She was grateful for his help and good humor. "I'll bring Harry tomorrow, too. No one wants to feed an overweight director. They always feed a dog. He looks truly pathetic, and he whines a lot, and drools. I tried it once, the drooling thing, and they asked me to leave the room and threatened to report me to the union, so I just bring him instead." She laughed out loud at his comments, and he told her not to be discouraged about the rewrite or even Douglas's tough comments. It was standard operating procedure with him, on all movies. Some producers were a lot tougher than Douglas, and demanded rewrites constantly. She was wondering what kind of comments she'd get from the actors, and how carefully they'd actually read the script. The actors on the soaps she wrote for just went on stage and winged it. Everything they did here, for a feature film, was going to be a lot more precise.

She spent seven hours working on the script, addressing all of Douglas's comments, as well as Max's. She ordered scrambled eggs and a salad from room service, and at midnight she was still at work. She called Peter when she finished. She hadn't gotten to call the girls before that, the time just slipped by, and she knew they'd be asleep by then. He was still awake, reading, and waiting for her call. He suspected when he didn't hear from her that she might be writing, so he left her alone and waited to hear from her.

"So how was it?" he asked with interest. He figured she'd had a full day or she'd have called.

"I don't know." She was tired as she stretched out on her bed to talk to him. "Normal, I guess. Douglas hates one of my characters. I've been rewriting all her scenes all night. I think I've made her worse. He thinks she's too boring. We had a meeting until three o'clock, without stopping for breaks or food. I thought I was going to keel over by the time we finished. I've been working my ass off in the room ever since. And I don't think I've fixed it. We meet with the actors tomorrow for their notes."

"Sounds grueling," he said sympathetically, but he knew she had expected it. And she was a workhorse anyway. She never gave up on a problem till she fixed it, in writing or all else. It was one of the many things he admired about her.

"How was your day?" she asked, happy to hear him. She had missed him terribly all day, even when she was working. The week looked like a long stretch ahead. "I missed calling the girls. I was working and didn't see the time. I'll call them tomorrow."

"They were fine. Alice brought us lasagne, and her famous pound cake. We pigged out. I made the salad. I got off easy tonight." Which was a good thing, since he had had a long day himself, working with a new client on some tough problems that were surely going to wind up in litigation.

"Did Alice stay for dinner?" Tanya asked casually, and was surprised to hear she had. It was nice of her to bring them food, and she was grateful for it. But admittedly, Tanya had been there for her every second for months when her husband died. "I owe her big time after this. If she keeps it up, I'm going to have to cook for her for the next ten years."

"I have to admit, it was helpful. And she took Meg to her soccer game. Molly needed the car. Alice saved my life. I couldn't leave work in time, so I called her. She was just leaving the gallery and said it was fine." Tanya had done the same for her kids many times over the years, but she was grateful anyway. In some ways Alice helping them out assuaged her guilt, but in other ways it made it worse. She liked knowing that someone was picking up the slack for the girls, and helping Peter, but it also made her feel guiltier than ever for not being there to do it herself. She was just going to have to live with it for the duration. And at least Alice was there for them. More than anything it was a lifesaver for Peter, and Tanya was especially grateful for that. He couldn't do it all himself. He had too much to do at work.

They talked about other things after that, and then they both had to get off the phone, although Tanya would have liked to chat with him forever. They both had early meetings the next day, and needed to get some sleep so they had their wits about them. She promised to call him earlier the following night, and asked him to give her love to the girls. She felt almost like a stranger saying it to him. It was completely foreign to her to be away from her children and sending them her love. In her own mind more than his, she was supposed to be there to give it to them herself.

Tanya was back in the same conference room the next morning, and this time Max arrived with his dog, if you could call it that. Harry was closer to the size of a small horse, but he was very well behaved, and sat in the corner, with his gigantic head on his paws. He was so well trained that after people's initial surprise over his size, no one noticed him at all, until food appeared in the room, and then he sat up looking alert, whined loudly, and drooled profusely. Max gave him treats to eat, and everyone else gave him table scraps, and then he lay down again and went to sleep. Harry was an extremely polite dog. Tanya complimented Max on it halfway through the meeting.

"He's actually my roommate, not a dog," Max said with a grin. "He was in a commercial once. I put the money in the stock market, and he's done very well. He pays for his half of the rent. I think of him as more of a son." She could see that he did.

The meeting was long and arduous. Douglas ran it extremely well, with Max's help. And Tanya was very surprised at the copious notes the actors had made. Some were very sensible, which made good points, and others were totally disorganized and irrelevant, but for the most part they all had something to say, and something they wanted changed. The biggest problem was dialogue that didn't "feel like them," and then she had to work with them to find ways of saying the same thing in most cases, in ways they felt better with. It was a long tedious process, and Douglas got irritated with all of them more than once. His stress level seemed to be high in meetings, and he and Tanya got into another argument about a different scene involving the same character he hated and that they'd battled over the day before.

"Oh for chrissake, Tanya," he shouted at her, "stop defending the bitch. Just fucking change her!" Tanya was more than a little startled, and was silent for a while after that, while Max shot her encouraging glances. He could see that Douglas had upset her and hurt her feelings.

Douglas himself stopped to talk to her after the meeting, as the actors were filing out. It was nearly six o'clock, and there had been carts of food in and out of the room all day. She could see what Max had meant. Even scones, whipped cream, and strawberries at four o'clock, and a hell of a lot of sushi and tofu all day long.

After the meeting all the actors were heading for the gym, or for sessions with their trainers. Tanya just wanted to go back to the bungalow and collapse. She was beyond exhausted, from concentrating on what everyone had said all day, and trying to work with them on making changes in the script.

"I'm sorry I was a little rough on you today," Douglas said smoothly. He looked as though nothing had happened, but Tanya felt like she'd been hit by a bus and he could see it. "These meetings with the actors drive me nuts. They pick on every word and detail, and worry about how they sound when they say it. It's in their contract that they can request changes in the script, and I think they all feel they didn't do their job if they don't ask you to rewrite every scene for them. After a while I just want to strangle everyone. These meetings over the actors' notes always take forever. Anyway, sorry if you got the blunt end of my temper."

"It's okay," Tanya said easily. "I was tired, too. It's a lot of minutiae, and I'm trying to preserve the integrity of the script and keep everyone happy." It wasn't always easy, and he knew it. He had done this hundreds of times over the years, on dozens of scripts. "I've been working on the character you hate so much, and I don't think I've solved the problem yet, but I'm trying. I think the snag here is that she doesn't strike me as boring. I see all the undercurrents in her, all the hidden thoughts and intentions, so I get that she's not as boring as she looks. Or maybe I just identify with her, and I'm as boring as she is." Tanya laughed as she said it, and Douglas shook his head with a smile. Tanya was grateful he had stopped to talk to her to relieve the pressure. He had intimidated her considerably for the past several hours. It wasn't fun. This was better.

"That's not how I would describe you, Tanya. You're anything but, and I hope you know it."

"I'm just a housewife from Marin," she said honestly, and he laughed out loud.

"Try that on someone else. Helen Keller maybe. That housewife thing is the game you play or the mask you wear, I'm not sure which one yet. But I can tell you one thing I know for sure, it's not who you are. If it were, you wouldn't be here. Not for a hot minute."

"I'm a housewife on loan from my family to write a script," she tried again. He remained unconvinced.

"Bullshit. Not even close. I don't know who you fool with that one, Tanya, but it wouldn't be me. You're a sophisticated woman with a fascinating mind. Casting you as a housewife in Marin is about like putting an alien from another planet in a job at McDonald's. They may be able to do it, but why waste all that mind and talent?"

"It's not wasted on my kids." She didn't like what he said or how he perceived her. It bothered her. She was exactly what she said she was and how she appeared, and took pride in it. She loved being a mother and housewife and always had. She enjoyed her writing, too, especially now, and the challenge of it. But she had no desire to become a Hollywood person, and it sounded like that was what he was intimating, that she belonged there and not in Ross. And that was not what she wanted. She knew she would never do it, except this one time as a lark. After this she was going home and staying there. She had already made up her mind on that.

"The tides have turned, Tanya, whether you like it or not. You can't go back. It doesn't work. You've been here a week and you've already outgrown it. You did before you came. The day you made the decision to do the film, it was done, the die was cast." His saying that made chills run up and down her spine. It was as though he were saying that her way home had vanished, and she wanted reassurance that it had not. Every time Douglas said something like that, it made her want to run into Peter's arms. Being around Douglas, she felt like Bess with Crown in *Porgy and Bess*. What Douglas said was terrifying and mesmerizing at the same time. She wanted to go home. "You were very patient with all the actors today," he commended her. "They're an unruly lot."

"I thought Jean's comments were very good, in relation to her character. And Ned's made sense, too," Tanya said fairly, ignoring everything Douglas had said. She wasn't going to argue the point with him about whether she should be a housewife or not. He didn't get a vote, except for the duration of the film. After that, she didn't care what he thought. He had no power over her life, nor was he clairvoyant or a shrink. He was obsessed with Hollywood, and she was not. He was drunk on the power he had. She was learning that about him, even though he expressed it subtly at times, and showed his hand at others, depending on what worked best for him in the situation they were in. He was a pro to watch, like a tennis player at Wimbledon.

She went back to the hotel afterward, and worked on the script for hours that night. She managed to get some of the changes in. Others were harder to effect. She called Max several times the next day to discuss it with him, and he told her not to worry about some of it. Some of the changes and subtle alterations would happen on the set, farther down the road. Max was by far the mellowest person she was dealing with, and she appreciated his ever-calm perspective about everything. He was very easygoing, and supremely knowledgeable. It was a perfect combination, unlike Douglas, who exuded tension and an obsession with control, which she found difficult at times.

It was a busy week for her in L.A., and for Peter at the office. He was starting a trial the following week. And Tanya continued to meet with Max, Douglas, and the cast, and work on the script. Much to her chagrin, they scheduled meetings for all day Saturday that they said were important for her to attend, and on Thursday afternoon she had to call Peter and say she couldn't come home. She asked if he and the girls could come down instead.

"Damn, Tan . . . I wish we could. Molly has a big soccer game. I know Megan has plans. Some big deal she's going to in the city with John White, so she won't want to come. And I have so much work to take home this weekend, I'd be a nervous wreck, unless I was sitting in the room working the whole time. I don't think this is the right weekend."

"Mine looks like that, too," she said sadly. "I hate not seeing you and the girls. Maybe I should just fly up Friday and spend the night. I have to be back for a meeting on Saturday at nine A.M. Maybe I can take a six o'clock plane."

"That's crazy," he said sensibly. "You'd be exhausted. Just let it go. You'll be home next weekend." She hadn't expected them to schedule weekend meetings quite this quickly, although she had been warned it could happen. But not this soon. It depressed her that she couldn't go home, no matter how much work she had to do.

She called the girls and apologized to them herself that night.

Megan's phone was off, so she left a message on voice mail. Molly was in a rush and said it was fine. Tanya felt like hell, and Peter was on a conference call when she called him, and couldn't talk. Three strikes, you're out. She even called Jason after that, to see if he wanted to come to L.A. for the night, and he had a hot date and didn't want to come, although he thanked her for the thought and said he'd love to do it another time, just not that particular weekend.

She spent Friday and Saturday in meetings with Max, Douglas, and the cast, and individually with Jean to discuss the motivation of her character with her. Jean took her work very seriously, and wanted to get into the head and skin of the person she was playing. Tanya felt completely drained by Saturday night when she got back to the hotel at eight o'clock, and even more so when she found a message from Douglas, asking her to call him back. "Shit, what now?" she muttered to herself. She had seen a lot of him all week and had had enough. He was such a powerful persona that a little went a long way. But he was the producer of the film, so she had no choice. She called him back on his private line at home, which was the number he had given her to call. It was a compliment that he had. It made her a Hollywood insider instantly, not that she cared.

"Hi. I just got in and found your message," she said, trying to sound more cheerful than she felt. She missed Peter and the kids, and she knew that all of them were out. "What can I do for you?" she said, wanting to get off fast. She wanted to lie in the tub and soak. If it didn't seem so extravagant, she'd have asked for a massage. She'd earned it, but it seemed like a frivolous expense to her, and she didn't want to take advantage of her deal. A soak in the tub was enough.

"I figured you'd be upset about not getting home this weekend. I was wondering if you'd like to come hang out by the pool tomorrow and lie in the sun, if you do that." He laughed. She had a light tan, so he figured that she sat in the sun, either at home or in Tahoe. "Totally low-key. The Sunday *Times,* and no conversation if you don't want. It gets a little old being at a hotel." He was right, it did, but she wasn't sure she wanted to spend the day with him. He was her boss, after all. And she couldn't just lie there and ignore him, although she had to admit a day at his pool sounded appealing. Being at the hotel pool with all the starlets and models trying to pick up men was a little wearing, and she felt totally out of place not wearing a thong and six-inch-high heels. She felt like a country bumpkin next to them, although she'd treated herself to a pedicure earlier in the week, one night while she was working, and paid for it herself. It had made her feel better, and the manicurist had worked while she read her revisions on the script, so it didn't interfere with her work, and was a boost to her spirits. Every woman she saw in L.A. had perfect manicures, and she felt a little less out of place.

"That's a very kind offer," she said to Douglas. "I don't want to intrude on your Sunday though." She hesitated, not sure whether to decline or accept. She never felt totally at ease with him, unlike Max, who was becoming more and more like a big brother. Douglas was anything but that. He was a power broker, and always on the make in some way. It was stressful to be with him. She couldn't imagine him relaxing on a lazy Sunday or any other time.

"You won't intrude. We'll ignore each other. I never talk to anyone on Sundays. Bring whatever you want to read. I'll provide the pool and the food. And whatever you do, don't comb your hair or wear makeup." He had read her mind. She didn't want to get dressed up to come and see him. She couldn't imagine him sitting around with his hair sticking up though. Far from it. Max, yes. Douglas, never.

"I may take you at your word, if I come," she said cautiously. "It's been a long week. I'm tired."

"This is only the beginning, Tanya. Save your strength, you'll need it later. By January and February, you'll laugh at how easy these days were."

"Maybe I should go home and jump off the bridge now," she said, feeling daunted and slightly depressed. Not seeing Peter and her children made her feel even more down. And she was beginning to wonder if she was equal to the task.

"You'll be used to it by then. You'll take it in stride, believe me. And all you'll want when it's over is to do it again." He always sounded certain of that, because it was true for him.

"Why is it that I don't believe you when you say that?"

"Trust me. I know. Maybe we'll work on another picture together one day," he said, sounding confident and hopeful, as though it were a foregone conclusion. They hadn't even started this one yet. But everyone wanted to work on Douglas Wayne movies. Actors and writers begged to get hired for his films again and again. It was an almost sure way to get an Academy Award, which was what it was all about for the pros. It had a certain appeal to Tanya, too, but right now all she wanted to do was learn the ropes and survive it, not embarrass herself, and do a decent job. It had been a challenge for her all week, and she'd been discouraged more than once. "So, are you coming over tomorrow? How about eleven o'clock?"

She hesitated for a fraction of an instant and then gave in. It would have been too complicated to say no, so she didn't. "That would be fine. Thank you," she said politely.

"See you then, and don't forget. No makeup. And don't comb your hair if you don't want." Yeah, sure, she thought to herself, as Megan would have said. Whatever.

But the next day, she took him at his word, to some extent anyway. She wore her hair in a neat braid but didn't put on makeup. It felt good not to make any great effort, although she hadn't gotten particularly dressed up all week. No one did at the meetings, even the actors. But she had been more careful than she was now. She wore a faded T-shirt that was Molly's, flip-flops, and her oldest, most beaten-up jeans. She took a stack of papers she wanted to read, a book she'd been meaning to start for a year, and the *New York Times* crossword puzzle, which was one of her favorite pastimes. And she took a cab to his house. She had given her driver the day off, it was Sunday after all.

Douglas let her in himself, and noticed the cab as it pulled away. He was wearing an immaculate T-shirt and perfectly pressed jeans and black alligator sandals. He didn't have a hair out of place, and the house was remarkably quiet. There were no servants around, unlike the night she had come to dinner, when there had been armies of them everywhere waiting on the guests. The house was silent and peaceful, and he walked her out to the pool and invited her to sit down, lie down, or do whatever she wanted. He had a stack of newspapers for her on a table next to a chaise longue. And he disappeared a moment later.

He reappeared, and without asking if she wanted it, he put a drink in her hand. It was champagne and peach juice, a Bellini, one of her favorite drinks, although it was a little early for that, but it was mild.

"Thank you," she said with a surprised smile, and he put a finger to his lips with a serious look.

"Shhh!" he said sternly. "No talking. You came here to relax. We can talk later if you want." He settled into his own chair then on the other side of the pool. He read the paper for a while, and then let his chair down and lay in the sun after lathering sunblock on his face and arms. He never said another word to Tanya, and eventually she felt comfortable reading and doing her crossword puzzle, and sipping her Bellini. It was actually a lovely way to spend a Sunday, much to her surprise.

She had no idea if he was sleeping or not, but Douglas lay there without moving for a long time, and eventually she lay down and dozed in the sun. She could hear birds chirping and the sun was warm but not too hot. It was a beautiful September afternoon, and she felt totally relaxed. She was startled when later, she opened her eyes and saw him standing next to her, looking down with an easy smile. She felt as though she had been asleep for hours.

"Did I snore?" she asked sleepily, and he laughed. It was the first time she had ever felt relaxed with him. It was nice. And so was he, this time. It almost made her wonder if they could be friends. Before this she would have never thought it possible. She was seeing a different side of him.

"Loudly," he teased her in answer to her question. "First, you woke me up. Then the neighbors complained." She laughed at what he said. He set a plate down next to her, with sliced fruit and salad on it, and a little wedge of cheese with crackers. "I thought you might be hungry when you woke up." He was being incredibly attentive, and she had to admit, it was enjoyable. She was feeling lazy and spoiled. He was a wonderful host, and had done everything he said he would, including leaving her alone, and not even talking. He disappeared again then after that, and a moment later she heard him playing the piano in the music room off the pool. It had a glass wall that slid back, and after she ate, she got up and wandered into the room. He was playing a complicated Bach piece, and paid no attention to her. She sat and listened to him, amazed by his skill and talent, and finally he looked over at her.

"I always play on Sundays," he said with a happy smile. "It's the best part of my week. I really miss it when I don't." She remembered that he had trained as a concert pianist, and wondered why he hadn't pursued it. He had truly amazing talent. And he obviously loved it. "Do you play an instrument?" he asked with interest.

"Just my computer," she said with a shy smile. He was a most unusual man, with a wide range of abilities and interests.

"I built a piano once," he informed her as the piece came to an end. "It actually worked. I still have it. It's on the boat. It was a lot of fun to make."

"Is there anything you can't do?"

"Yes," he said, nodding emphatically. "Cook. Eating bores me. It seems like such a waste of time." It explained why he was so thin, and never stopped for lunch during meetings. "I do it just to stay alive. Some people treat it like a hobby. I can't stand that. I don't have the patience to sit at a dinner table for five hours, or to cook for twice as long. Aside from that, I don't play golf, although I can. That bores me, too. And I never play bridge, although I used to. People get nasty and petty about it. If I'm going to fight with someone or insult them, I'd rather do it about something I care about, not a hand of cards." What he said made sense and made her laugh.

"I feel that way about bridge, too. I played in college, and I haven't played since, for that reason. Do you play tennis?" she asked him for no particular reason, other than conversation, as he started another piece on the piano, which required less concentration than the first one.

"I do. I like squash better. It's faster." He was a man of little patience who moved at top speed in all things. He was an interesting person to study, and she thought about putting someone like him in a short story sometime. She could do amazing things with a character with so many facets.

"I've played squash, but I'm not great at it. My husband plays, too. I'm better at tennis."

"We'll play sometime," he said, as he focused on the music for a while and she enjoyed listening to him. Eventually, she went back to the pool to lie down so she didn't disturb him. He seemed to be lost in the piece. It was another hour before he stopped playing and wandered out.

"I loved listening to you play," she said with admiration, as he sat down in a chair near her. He looked energized and refreshed and his eyes were bright. Playing always did that to him. It was easy to see why he loved it. He was so good at it, and a real pleasure to listen to.

"Playing the piano feeds my soul," he said simply. "I couldn't live without it."

"I feel that way about writing," she confided in him.

"I can tell by the way you write," he said, looking at her. She looked comfortable and relaxed, which she wouldn't have thought possible when he invited her to spend the day at his pool. He had surprised her, and it had been a lovely, totally easy day. She felt restored. "That's why I always wanted to work with you, because I knew from reading you that you had that kind of passion and love for your work, just like I do with the piano. Most people don't have that. I knew you did from the first piece I read. It's a rare gift, for both of us." She nodded, flattered, and didn't comment. They sat in silence for a while, and then she looked at her watch. She was surprised to see it was five o'clock. She had been there for six hours and the time had flown by.

"I should go. If you call a cab, I'll go back to the hotel," she said, starting to gather up her things and put them back in her bag. He shook his head at the mention of the cab.

"I'll take you back." It wasn't far, but she didn't want to bother him. He had done enough. It had been a perfect day, and her grief and guilt over not seeing Peter and the children had vanished.

"I'll be fine in a cab," she insisted.

"I know you will. But I'm perfectly happy to drop you off." He walked inside to get his keys and a moment later emerged, as she stood up. He walked her into the garage, which was so immaculate it looked like an operating room, and opened the door of a silver Ferrari. She got in on the passenger side, as he started the car, and a moment later they were heading back to her hotel. They rode in comfortable silence, after the relaxing afternoon they had spent together. Although they had said little, she felt as though they had made friends. She had learned new things about him that afternoon that previously she hadn't even guessed, and loved listening to him play the piano. It had been the high point of her afternoon.

The Ferrari slid under the roof covering the driveway at the Beverly Hills Hotel, and he looked at her with a smile. "It was a great day, Tanya, wasn't it?"

"I loved it," she said honestly. "I feel like I had a vacation." It had been the next best thing to going home, which she hadn't expected at all, and surely not with him. She had always felt tense when he was around. Today she had even slept across the pool from him, and read for hours without talking. There were few people she could do that with, other than her husband. It was an odd thought.

"So did I. You're the perfect Sunday guest, other than the snoring of course," he teased her, and then laughed.

"Did I really snore?" She looked embarrassed, and he pretended to look mysterious.

"I won't tell. I'll turn you over next time. They say that works." She laughed, and didn't really care if she had, which was even more amazing. In a single afternoon, she had gotten comfortable with him. It was going to make working with him a lot nicer from now on, having seen this side of him. "Do you want to have dinner tonight?" he asked her casually. It was a spur-of-the-moment thought. "I was going to grab some Chinese takeout. We could eat it there, or I could bring it back to the hotel. We both have to eat, and it's not as dreary, having dinner with a friend. Any interest?" It sounded good to her. She'd been planning to order room service while working at her computer. Chinese takeout sounded like more fun.

"Sure. That would be nice. Why don't you bring it here?"

"Perfect. Seven-thirty? I have some calls to make, and I swim laps every night." He seemed to keep active and was very athletic. It explained how he stayed so trim and fit.

"Sounds fine to me," Tanya said easily.

"What do you like to eat?" he asked politely.

"Spring rolls, sweet and sour anything, beef, shrimp, whatever you like."

"I'll get an assortment of stuff," he promised. She thanked him, got out, and he sped off with a wave in the sleek silver car.

Tanya went in and showered, and checked her messages. There was a call from Jean Amber about the script. When Tanya called her back, she was out. She called Peter and the girls then. They had just come in from a baseball game. They were Giants fans, and had season tickets. They were all in a good mood, and no one seemed too upset that she hadn't come home. She was both relieved and saddened by it all at once.

"How was the game?" she asked with interest.

"Great! We won, in case you didn't watch it on TV," Peter told her, sounding jubilant.

"I didn't. I went to Douglas Wayne's house for the day."

"How was that?" Peter sounded surprised.

"Fine. Surprisingly easy. Good for work relations, I hope. He was very nice. We hardly said ten words to each other all day." She didn't tell him no one else was there. She was about to, but Molly got on the phone.

"Hi, Mom, great game. We missed you. We took Alice, to thank her for all the dinners she cooked for us. And Jason came home for the game."

"I thought he was busy," Tanya said, feeling left out suddenly. "I called him Thursday, and he said he had a hot date."

"She canceled, so he drove up to go to the game." It occurred to Tanya that he hadn't called her when the date got canceled. He went home to Ross instead to go to a baseball game. They'd all been there together, with Alice, and she was alone in L.A. "He drove back after the game. He'll be back in Santa Barbara tonight." It was still a weird feeling to know that her whole family had gone to a baseball game and had fun without her. She felt like a kid who didn't get invited to a birthday party. But she was working in L.A. It wasn't their fault, it was hers, and she could hardly expect them to stay home in her honor.

She talked to Megan after that, and she sounded fine. Alice got on the phone and said they were all doing well and they missed her, and so did she, and to get her ass home next weekend so they could gossip. Tanya laughed talking to her, and then talked to Peter again briefly. They were about to order pizza, standard Sunday-night fare. "I miss you," she reminded him, and he told her he missed her, too. She realized when she hung up that she hadn't mentioned she was having dinner with Douglas. There was nothing meaningful about it, she just liked telling Peter what she was doing, so he felt part of it. But she told herself it was so insignificant that she forgot.

She just had time to take a bath and change before Douglas

showed up with their dinner. She put on clean jeans and another T-shirt, and when she opened the door to the bungalow to him, she was in bare feet. She stepped aside, and he walked in.

"I know this bungalow. I stayed here once, when they were redoing my house. I like it," he said, looking around.

"It's very comfortable," she said easily. "It'll be fun when the kids come down." She took out plates in the kitchen, and they helped themselves from the five cartons he'd brought. He had gotten everything she liked, including something with lobster, and shrimp fried rice. They sat at her dining table, and made their way through the easy meal. "Thank you. That was perfect. You have definitely spoiled me today."

"I have to take care of my star writer." He smiled at her. "We can't have you getting homesick and pining away here, or running back to Marin." He was teasing her, but she didn't mind. "I thought I'd show you that we have Chinese takeout here, too." And then he remembered the fortune cookies and handed one to her. He groaned when he saw his. "Did you put this in here when I wasn't looking?" She shook her head, and he handed it to her to read.

"'A good friend will be good news today.'" She read it aloud and looked at him with a smile. "That's nice. It sounds about right."

"I always want them to be more exciting, but they never are. What's yours?" Douglas asked with an amused look.

She read it and raised an eyebrow as she did.

"What does it say?"

"'A job well done is its own reward.' Not too exciting, either. I like yours better."

"Me too." And then he smiled at her again. "Maybe you'll win an Oscar for the script." He hoped she would. And Best Picture for him. It was his goal. It always was.

"That's not what it says," she pointed out to him, and cleaned up the mess from their dinner.

"Next time we should write our own."

He helped her throw the empty cartons away, and a few minutes later he left. She thanked him for dinner, and he told her he'd had a great day. So had she. His fortune cookie was right. A good friend had been the good news of the day. For the first time since she'd met him, she felt like he could be. And what an interesting friend he was.

# Chapter 8

Tanya went home to Ross for the next two weekends, and she loved being with Peter and the kids. She had lunch with Alice one Saturday, and they chatted and gossiped about the people Tanya had met. Alice was as titillated by it as the girls.

"I'm surprised you even bother to come home anymore," Alice teased her. "It's mighty dull around here compared to all that."

"Don't be stupid," Tanya growled at her. "I'd much rather be here with Peter and the kids. It's all fantasyland down there. Nothing is real."

"Sounds real enough to me," Alice said with open admiration. She was happy for her friend that her career was going so well, and she was having this experience, and she assured her that her children were doing fine. She calmed all of Tanya's fears that they would never forgive her. Alice said that even Megan spoke of her with pride, which came as a surprise to her mother.

"She hardly talks to me anymore. She's been mad since last summer." Tanya was relieved by what Alice had just said. She was around the girls a lot more than Tanya was these days, and seemed to know their state of mind better, so Tanya trusted what she said.

"She's not as mad as she wants you to think. She's just punishing you for a while. Don't pay any attention to her, she'll back off." Tanya was pleased to hear it and mentioned it to Peter when she went home. He agreed.

"She's just putting you through hoops. She's been fine around here," he reassured her, and when Megan came home a little while later, Tanya smiled at her as though everything were fine between them. She asked Megan something inane about school, and Megan glared at her as though she had offended her again. She was even angrier when her mother suggested they start doing her college applications together. Megan said she wanted to do them with Alice, which was a slap in Tanya's face, which really hurt her. It was an indisputable rejection. "I'd like to at least look at them with you," her mother said gently, and Megan flatly refused to. "Maybe next time I come home," Tanya said hopefully, and Megan shrugged in answer.

"Whatever," she said and stomped upstairs, as Tanya's heart ached, and she tried not to let it upset her. At least Molly wanted to do hers with her mother, and had already shown Tanya several essays.

"I guess I haven't finished my hoops course yet," she said to Peter with a rueful look and he grinned.

The first weekend in October Tanya came home, as did Jason from UCSB, and they all went to the World Series. It was between the Giants and the Red Sox, and the games were terrific. The Giants were winning when she flew back to L.A. with Jason. She sent him back to Santa Barbara in her limo, which he thought was embarrassing but cool. The whole family truly enjoyed spending their time together.

And the second weekend in October, Peter and the girls flew to

L.A. and stayed at the bungalow with her. The girls loved it, and Jason came down on Saturday for the day. He stayed until after dinner.

Tanya and the girls went shopping on Melrose, and they all had lunch at Fred Segal's. She took them to some funny little shops she'd found, and they had a ball, while Peter and Jason lay around the pool, and Jason admired the women. They had dinner at Spago and ran into Jean Amber, whom the twins thought was gorgeous. She had given Tanya a big hug and made a fuss over Megan and Molly, and she flirted with Jason. He was blushing when she walked away. They were all overwhelmed at meeting her.

"I'll introduce you to Ned Bright the next time you come down, after we start the film," Tanya promised. Shortly after, another hot star walked in, and all three kids stared in disbelief. They went back to the hotel afterward, and had a drink at the bar, Cokes for the kids since they were minors, and several more stars walked in. Tanya didn't know them, but the kids recognized them. By the time the girls got back to the bungalow, they couldn't believe all the stars they'd seen. They were both squealing with excitement. Jason had just gone back to school in his mother's limo again.

"Wow, Mom, this is so cool!" Molly said with wide eyes, and for the first time in ages, Megan hugged her and was smiling, too.

"Thanks, Mom, for bringing us down here," Megan said generously. Alice was right. All was nearly forgiven. The weekend in L.A. had clinched it. They missed having her at home, but they had to admit, this was a lot of fun. They could hardly wait to do it again, and meet Ned Bright and the other stars.

The one who seemed less enthralled with it was Peter, who looked somewhat daunted when the girls disappeared into their room, giggling, and he and Tanya went to bed in theirs. He looked tired. It had been a long day, and he'd had a long week. They had settled a tough case.

"Are you okay, sweetheart?" she asked, rubbing his back when they got into bed.

"Just tired." The day hadn't been as much fun for him as it had been for his daughters, and he had hardly seen Tanya all day. She'd been busy shopping with the girls. And all the stars they'd seen didn't mean anything to him. He didn't know who most of them were, they were mostly actors and actresses who were cult figures to kids, not adults, although even he knew who Jean Amber was, and admitted readily that she was gorgeous. And she seemed to be crazy about Tanya. She acted like they were best friends. But only because they were working on a picture together now. It would all be forgotten in six months. Tanya had no illusions about that.

Peter looked at her as they lay in bed together, and Tanya was upset to see him look sad. "How are you ever going to come back to Ross after all this, Tan? We can't compete with your life here."

"You don't have to," she said quietly. "You win the contest hands down. This means nothing to me. It's just exciting to do the work. I don't give a damn about the life."

"You think that now," he said, looking at her. "You've only been here for six weeks. Wait till you've been here for a while. Look at how you're living. You have your own limo, you live at the Beverly Hills Hotel in your own bungalow, stars crawl all over you. This is heady stuff, Tan. It's addictive. Ross is going to look like Kansas to you in another six months." He looked seriously worried.

"Kansas is what I want," she said firmly. "I want us. I love our life. I couldn't live here on a bet. It would drive me nuts."

"I don't know, Cinderella. When the coach turns into a pumpkin again, it could be tough."

"I'm turning in my glass slippers the day we finish the film, and I'm coming home. And that's it. This was a one-time deal, not a way of life. I wouldn't trade what we have for anything in the world."

"Tell me that in seven months. I hope you still feel that way then." It upset her that he was thinking about it, and she was still sad after they made love. There was something subdued about him, as though he felt defeated, and unable to compete with her new life. His fear was exactly what Douglas had said, that her life in L.A. would be addictive and she would never want to go back. Alice had said it too the last time Tanya was in Ross. What were they all talking about? Didn't they get it? She wanted to go home when it was over, not stay here. That seemed like a very bad trade to her. But Peter acted as though he didn't believe her. He still looked unhappy, and he was quiet the next morning when they went to the Ivy for brunch.

The girls looked happy on the terrace, particularly when Leonardo Di Caprio sat at the next table and smiled at them. And Peter warmed up a little after they ate. Tanya sat close to him, held his hand, hugged him, and kissed him every chance she got. She couldn't get enough of him. She missed him so much when she was in L.A. But he didn't seem to believe that she preferred her old life. All she could do was prove it to him, when the movie ended and she went back. It annoyed her that everyone was so convinced she'd want to stay. She knew better than that, even if they didn't. And the only one she cared about thinking that was Peter. She didn't want him worrying about her falling in love with her so-called new life. It wasn't a new life in her mind, it was just a visit, a sabbatical she was taking in L.A., for the sake of her career. She had no other interest in it.

They went back to the hotel after lunch and hung out at the pool for a while. The girls swam while Peter and Tanya lay on lounge chairs and talked. He ordered a screwdriver, which was unusual for him, and Tanya was still worried about him. She had the feeling that he was panicked about her. The less he said, the more upset she felt.

"I'm coming home when this is all over, sweetheart. I don't like it here. I'm here to work, and that's it. I love our life in Marin."

"You think that now, Tan. But you'll be bored out of your mind there after this. And the girls will be gone next year. You'll have nothing to do."

"I'll have you," she said gently. "And our life. My writing. This isn't a life here, Peter. It's a joke. I just wanted the experience of doing a screenplay for a movie. You're the one who told me to do it." She reminded him of that, and he nodded, but he was sorry now he had. He was only just beginning to realize the risk he had taken. He looked worried all the time.

"It scares me now, Tan. For us. I just can't see you feeling the same about anything after this is over." He looked near tears as he said it, and she was shocked. She had never seen him look so shaken.

"How shallow do you think I am?" she asked unhappily. "Why do you think I come home on weekends? Because I love it there, and I love you. That's my home. This is my job."

"Okay," he said, taking a breath, wanting to believe her. He thought she meant what she was saying. He just didn't know how long she would feel like that. Sooner or later the life she was living here would get to her, he thought, and it would dawn on her that the world was her oyster, and her old life in Marin wasn't enough. He didn't want that to happen, but he couldn't imagine now that it wouldn't. He hadn't fully understood until then what her life would be like in L.A. while working on the movie. It was a lot more glamorous than he had thought. It was hard to compete with all that.

The girls got out of the pool and joined them then, and they couldn't pursue the conversation, which was just as well. They were going around in circles, and Tanya could see that Peter still wasn't convinced. Time would prove everything she was saying to him, but in the meantime he was a lot more worried now than he had been. She put her arms around him and held him close to her when they were back in her room in the bungalow.

"I love you, Peter," she said softly. "More than anything." He kissed her, and Tanya clung to him for a long moment. She didn't want him to go. The girls walked into the room then and reminded them that they had to leave for the airport soon. Tanya felt as though the weekend had reassured them and frightened Peter. She could see in his eyes that what he had seen there had disturbed him profoundly. He was quiet on the way to the airport, and looked distracted when he kissed her goodbye.

"I love you," she reminded him again.

"I love you, too, Tan," he said, smiling sadly. "Don't fall in love with it down here, I need you," he whispered. He looked so vulnerable it almost made her cry.

"I won't," she promised him. "You're all I want. I'll be home Friday." And she knew that this time, no matter what happened, she had to go home for the weekend. She wanted him to know that no matter what happened down here, who she met or what she saw, or how appealing they tried to make it, above all, and more important to her than anything, she was his wife.

# Chapter 9

Tanya went home, as promised, for the next two weekends, and Peter seemed to calm down. The fact that she came home every Friday night, as they had planned for her to do, seemed to reassure him. He admitted that the weekend in L.A. had unnerved him, but as soon as he saw her in Marin again, he felt sane. The life she led in L.A. wasn't one he wanted to be part of. And she continued to try to convince him that neither did she. All she wanted was the thrill of writing a feature film, and after that she was coming home. Life seemed almost normal again when she came up every weekend. She missed two important meetings to do it, but she said nothing about it to him. She told Douglas and Max that she just couldn't stay. She said she had to get home to her kids. They didn't like it, but as long as they hadn't started shooting yet, they were willing to let her go.

They started shooting on the first of November, and from then on her life was insane. They shot days, nights, location scenes, worked on soundstages they had rented, and sat in folding chairs on street corners during night shoots, while she worked frantically on the script to make changes. She was winging it a lot of the time. Jean proved to be difficult to work with, while Ned was a dream. She could never remember her lines, and wanted Tanya to adjust them for her. Tanya worked closely with Max on every scene, while Douglas came and went and observed frequently.

The first weekend after shooting started, she miraculously managed to go home. And if anything happened on the set, she promised to be available on the phone. She assured them she could make changes from there, and send them by e-mail. But for the next two weekends after that, there was no way she could go. Four scenes had to be rewritten, they were shooting out of sequence, and they were tackling some of the most difficult scenes in the film. Max promised her that she could take weekends off later, but for now he needed her right there. She had no choice. The girls were unhappy about it and Peter didn't sound pleased either, but he understood it, or said he did. He was starting a trial in a few weeks, and was buried at the office, too.

Tanya hadn't been home for two weeks when she got home for Thanksgiving, and she almost cried with relief when she walked in the front door. It was Wednesday afternoon, and Peter had just bought everything they needed for Thanksgiving. Her flight had been delayed for two hours due to bad weather, and she had been panicked she wouldn't get home. Jason was due home that night. He was driving up with friends. Alice's son James was driving up from Santa Barbara that weekend, too.

"God, am I glad to see you guys," Tanya said, as she set down her bag in the kitchen. "I thought they were going to cancel my flight." She felt as though she hadn't seen them in a million years, and it had only been two weeks. Peter looked thrilled to see her, and walked over to her to give her a hug.

"We're happy to see you, too," Peter said as the girls helped him unpack the groceries. He had bought everything Tanya had told him to. She was going to start cooking their turkey before dawn the next morning. It was huge.

Molly came over to hug her, and Tanya noticed instantly that Megan looked particularly grim and had red eyes. She looked so upset that Tanya didn't want to say anything to upset her. She gave her a kiss, and Megan didn't say anything. A few minutes later she disappeared.

"Did something happen?" Tanya asked Peter quietly, as they finished in the kitchen and went upstairs.

"I'm not sure. She went over to see Alice after school. She just walked in before you did. Molly and I bought the groceries without her. Maybe you should ask Alice. Megan doesn't tell me anything." Or her mother anymore, Tanya couldn't help thinking. A year before, that wouldn't have been the case, but things had changed since she started working in L.A. Now Alice was Megan's confidante, and Tanya was her absentee mother, who was no longer privy to her private griefs and joys. She hoped that would change again one day.

She and Peter talked quietly for a while, catching up. She told him about progress on the set, and the kind of pressure they were working under, dealing with crises and problems, and the usual insanity that seemed to be standard fare. It was interesting at least. And a little while later, Molly walked in and explained that Megan had broken up with her boyfriend. He had cheated on her with another girl. She said that Megan was next door talking to Alice about it, and as she said it, Tanya's heart sank. She felt as though she were losing her daughter to her best friend. She knew it was unreasonable to think that way, she was grateful to Alice for standing in for her, but it hurt her feelings that Megan no longer wanted to confide in her. It wasn't something you could demand, or even criticize her for, Tanya knew it was something she had to earn. Losing that was the price she was paying for not being around. She felt lucky that Molly still talked to her. And she felt stupid for it, but she felt suddenly jealous of Alice and the relationship she had with Megan. Tanya's loss had been Alice's gain. Megan didn't come home until dinnertime. Tanya had to call Alice and ask her to send her home.

"How is she?" Tanya asked her, sounding worried.

"Upset," Alice said gently, happy to hear from her friend. "She'll be okay. It's standard teenage stuff. He's a little shit, but they all are at that age. He just did it with her best friend, so it seems worse to her."

"With Maggie Arnold?" Tanya sounded horrified. Maggie had always been such a nice girl.

"No," Alice said, sounding very knowing. "With Donna Ebert. Megan and Maggie haven't been on good terms for months. They had a falling-out the first week of school." Tanya knew nothing anymore, which made her feel worse. And Alice knew it all. Tanya was completely out of the loop.

They had a quiet dinner in the kitchen that night, and the girls helped her set the dining room table for the next day. They took out the good crystal and china, and a tablecloth they used every year that had been Peter's grandmother's. Megan said nothing to her mother about the agonies she'd been going through. She just did what she had to do, and then went to her room. She treated Tanya like a stranger. She wasn't even angry at her. She just seemed distant and indifferent whenever Tanya tried to talk to her. She had completed half her college applications with Alice by then, without ever showing her mother a word.

"I'm fine, Mom," she said, brushing her off. They had lost whatever ground they had gained in L.A., and the weekends Tanya came home after that, when things were better. But in the weeks that

Tanya hadn't been able to come home, after the film started shooting, she had lost her connection with Megan again. Tanya felt unable to bridge the chasm between them, and Megan did nothing to help. She just stayed sealed off and at every opportunity went to her room. It made Tanya's heart ache, and she felt like a failure as a mother, despite Molly's constant reassurance that that wasn't the case. The difference between the two girls' reactions to her was extreme. It was a relief when Jason walked in after dropping off his friends, and went straight to the fridge. He kissed his mother on the way.

"Hi, Mom. I'm starving." She smiled at the familiar greeting, and offered to make him chili. He looked delighted at the suggestion, and sat down at the kitchen table with a glass of milk. It made Tanya feel useful to cook for him. He chatted with Molly about school, while Tanya emptied a can of chili into a pan and put it on the stove. Peter walked in, and there was a festive atmosphere in the room, as they all chatted with each other. A few minutes later Megan walked in.

She looked at her brother, and told him her news before she even said hello to him. "I broke up with Mike. He cheated on me with Donna." She still hadn't said a word about it to her mother. She shared her sorrows with everyone but her. Even the next-door neighbor had heard it first.

"That sucks," Jason said sympathetically. "He's a jerk. She'll dump him in a week."

"I don't want him back after that," she said, and talked to him about it while he ate. They were all in the kitchen together, but Tanya felt left out. She felt like an invisible person in her family now, whereas before everything had revolved around her. They had all needed her. And now they had learned too well to manage without her. She felt utterly useless, except to open a can of chili for her son and heat it on the stove. Other than that she served no useful purpose. She glanced over at Jason, and he was talking to Peter about his ranking on the tennis team, between bulletins from Megan about her love life. No one was talking to Tanya. She felt as though she didn't exist. Without even intending to, in most cases, they had shut her out.

She sat down at the kitchen table with them, and entered their conversations where she could. Eventually, Jason got up and put his dishes in the dishwasher. He left the kitchen with the girls, all three of them talking animatedly about ten things at once. They were a lively group. And then he glanced over his shoulder and called back to his mother.

"Thanks for the chili, Mom."

"Anytime," she called back, and looked over at Peter, still sitting there and watching her.

"You're so much more efficient than I am. I make a mess of the kitchen every night." He smiled at her, happy to have her home. It had been a long two weeks since he'd seen her last. But he knew how crazy it was for her on the set.

"It feels so good to be home," she said, smiling at him. "And weird, too," she admitted. "I feel like the kids don't even know who I am anymore. I know it's stupid, but it really bothers me that Megan tells Alice all about her love life, and she doesn't say a word to me. She used to tell me everything."

"She will again when you come home. They know you're busy, Tan. They don't want to bother you. You're making a movie. Alice has nothing else to do and she's right here. The gallery is fun for her, but it doesn't take up a lot of her time. She misses her kids, so she loves spending time with ours."

"I feel like I've been fired," she said sadly, as they walked slowly upstairs to their room. They could hear Jason and the girls in his room, laughing and talking. He had put his music on. The house had come alive again.

"You haven't been fired," Peter said gently as they closed their door. "You're just on leave. That's different. When you come home, they'll be all over you again. As much as they will with anyone now. They're all growing up." It was true, and that depressed her, too. She was suffering from empty-nest syndrome, and the worst of it was that she had left the nest first, or before the girls anyway. It defied the natural order of things. It was no wonder Megan resented her. Tanya didn't blame her a bit, and felt overwhelmed with guilt.

"I feel like such a lousy mother. Particularly with her leaning on Alice."

"She's a nice woman, Tan. She won't give her bad advice."

"I know that. That's not the point. The point is that I'm her mother, Alice isn't. I think Megan has forgotten that."

"No, she hasn't. She just needs someone to talk to around here. A woman. She doesn't talk to me about that stuff either."

"She could call me on my cell phone any time. Molly does. So do you."

"Give her a chance, Tan. She took it harder than the rest of us when you left. She's forgiven you. She just got out of the habit of talking to you." Tanya nodded. It was true. And it hurt like hell to hear the truth.

She felt like she had lost one of her kids. Molly had never wavered, and Jason still called her every few days to chat, when he had nothing better to do, or needed advice about school. In some ways, he was closer to her than to Peter. But Megan had disassociated herself from her mother almost completely. Tanya couldn't help wondering if the rift between them would ever repair. All she was good for now was to introduce her to movie stars. Other than that, she had almost no relationship with her daughter. Tanya couldn't believe how much it hurt. A lot. More than that. She felt as though she had lost a leg or an arm. And it had to be painful for Megan, too. She didn't even know how to broach the subject with her. Peter said to just give it time. But Tanya wasn't convinced that was the solution. She had lost her daughter to Alice. It wasn't Alice's fault, or even Megan's, it was her own.

"Try not to let it upset you," Peter told her kindly. "I think it will get better when you come home."

"That's months from now," Tanya said, looking depressed. "They've almost finished their college applications, and I wasn't even here to help them." She sounded mournful, and felt guilty yet again. She felt as though she were missing everything important. Romances, breakups, college applications, colds, and all the daily details of their lives that they now shared with Alice and Peter and rarely with her. It bothered her even more than she had feared it would.

"I've been working on their applications with them," Peter reassured her, "for the past two weekends. And I know Alice has, too. I think they're planning to finish them over Christmas vacation. You can give them a hand then, or some advice about their essays. But I think they're in good shape."

"Is there anything Alice doesn't do?" Tanya snapped, feeling grumpy, as Peter met her eyes. The separation was hard on all of them. They had known it would be from the start. It was just harder to live with than any of them had expected. Tanya had been afraid of this, that it would impact her relationship with her children, or with him. At least so far it hadn't with Peter, or even Molly. Megan was a direct casualty of the movie her mother was making. Tanya was afraid Megan would never forgive her.

"It's not Alice's fault," Peter chided her gently, as Tanya sat down on their bed with a sigh.

"I know it's not. I'm just frustrated. And I feel guilty. It's my fault, not anyone else's. Thanks for letting me whine." He was always a good sport, about everything. She knew just how lucky she was to have him. She never took him for granted. If it weren't for him, her Hollywood odyssey wouldn't have been possible at all, although she realized now that she was sorry she had done it. It was possible that the price tag was going to be too high, if it cost her her relationship with even one of her children. But it was too late to turn back now. They just had to go forward and make the best of it.

"You can whine to me anytime." Peter smiled at her, and sat down on the bed next to her to give her a hug. "What time are you getting up to cook the turkey?"

"Five o'clock," she said, sounding tired. She had been getting up earlier than that some days to be on the set, or staying up later. It was a crazy process and an insane way to live. She could see too why few people in the industry had healthy relationships or sound marriages. The lifestyle was just too strange, and precluded any kind of normalcy. And the temptations surrounding it were enormous. She had already seen several romances start on the set, even among people who were married to others. It was as though the people working on the movie forgot all other ties except to those they were working with at the time. It really was like setting sail on a cruise, or a trip to another planet. The only people who seemed to be real to them were those they saw every day. They forgot everything and everyone else, and lived in the tiny microcosm of their movie set. It hadn't happened to Tanya, and she knew it wouldn't, but she was fascinated, and somewhat horrified watching them.

"Wake me when you get up," Peter said. "I'll keep you company when you start the turkey, if you want."

Tanya looked at him and shook her head. "How did I ever get so

lucky?" she said, kissing him. "No, I'm not going to get you up. Are
you kidding? You need your sleep. But thank you for offering."

"You need your sleep, too. Besides, I enjoy hanging out with you."

"So do I, with you. It won't take me long. I'll come back to bed."

They went to bed shortly after, and Tanya cuddled up next to him
until she got up. He slept with his arms around her, as he always did,
and a peaceful look on his face. He was happy to have her home, as
happy as she was to be back. Despite her sense of failure and loss
with Megan, it felt wonderful to be home.

Tanya got up on schedule to put the turkey in the oven, did everything she had to do, and went back to bed for another four hours.
She slept as close to Peter as she could get, and when she woke up,
they were a tangle of sheets, blankets, legs, and arms. It was so much
nicer than sleeping alone in her bedroom in the bungalow in Beverly
Hills. She stretched, and smiled as she looked at him. It was the perfect beginning of their day.

"It's nice to have you home, Tan," he said happily. They made love
then, and got up shortly after that. Peter showered and dressed and
went downstairs. Tanya followed him down in her robe, to check on
things in the kitchen. She was surprised to see Megan sitting at the
kitchen table engrossed in a serious conversation with Alice, who
had made herself a cup of coffee. Alice looked totally at home in the
kitchen, and surprised when Tanya and Peter walked in. She had a
book next to her on the table, and looked at Peter with an easy grin.

"I brought you back your book. It was great. Funniest thing I ever
read . . . Happy Thanksgiving, by the way," she said to both of them,
but Tanya once again had the feeling of being an invisible person in
her own life. Almost as if she had died and come back as a ghost.
For a minute, she had the impression that Alice had looked right
through her.

"Can I make you breakfast?" Tanya offered, trying not to feel resentful or jealous of the deep conversation she and Megan were obviously having.

"No, thanks. I already ate. James and Melissa were up at the crack of dawn." Jason and Molly were still asleep. They had stayed up late. Only Megan was up, after a nasty phone conversation with her ex–best friend Donna early that morning that she had just told Alice about. Alice had come to the kitchen door with Peter's book, and was about to leave it there, when Megan saw her and asked her to come in. She told her all about her conversation with Donna after that. "That's a gorgeous turkey you've got in the oven, Tan," Alice said admiringly. "I couldn't find a decent one this year. They were all gone." She chatted amiably as Tanya poured Peter a cup of coffee, made tea for herself, and they sat down at the kitchen table with their daughter and neighbor. Peter asked her about the book, and Alice told him again how much she had loved it, and how funny she thought it was. He seemed pleased.

"I told you it was just your cup of tea. He wrote another one that's even funnier. I have to look for it. It's upstairs somewhere. I'll give it to you later," Peter said, with the comfortable tone of great familiarity.

Listening to him chat with Alice, Tanya wasn't sure a casual observer would have been able to figure out which of them he was married to, except that he had just made love to her. Barring that, he seemed equally comfortable with both women, and there was a tone of intimacy between him and Alice that suddenly unnerved her. She knew he wasn't sleeping with her, but he was certainly familiar and comfortable with her. Almost too much so, for Tanya's taste. They seemed to have gotten friendlier since Tanya left for L.A. She was in and out of the house constantly, checking on the girls, bringing all of them food, or had them over to dinner at her place. She had become more family than friend to the children, and even to Peter. And Tanya realized now that Alice's name came up in almost every conversation. She had either brought them something, done something for them, or gone somewhere with one or both of the girls. It was a huge help to Peter, but it also irked Tanya.

She sat looking at her now, and asked herself a question. She thought she knew the answer to it, but she wasn't quite as sure as she might have been before September. She decided to ask Peter later, and went on sitting at the kitchen table, listening to them, until Alice finally got up and left, and went back to her own house and children. Megan left the kitchen almost as soon as she did. There was a moment's silence in the kitchen after she went upstairs, as Tanya looked at Peter, hoping her fears were unfounded. She had never questioned him before, not even in her own mind. And she felt guilty about it now. This was all her fault, she knew, and no one else's. But Alice certainly seemed to have become comfortable in their house, and with Peter, far more than she ever had been before.

"I know this sounds crazy, and more than a little paranoid," Tanya said carefully, as she looked at him. They had made love less than an hour before, and everything seemed fine. But you never knew. People did stranger things. Maybe he got lonely without her, and he knew Alice had been looking for a man since Jim died. "But you're not having an affair with her, are you? I'm sorry to even ask you that, but it's beginning to feel like she's moved in." She had never been as evident in their lives before, no matter how close she and Tanya were. Alice had never been as close to Peter, and now she was.

"Don't be ridiculous," Peter said predictably. It was the appropriate answer, as he stood up to get himself another cup of coffee. Tanya was watching his face. "Whatever made you think that?"

"You guys see a lot of her during the week, and you're over at her house a lot. She's practically adopted Megan. I felt like I was walking into her kitchen just now when we walked in. I never felt that from her before. As though you and the kids belong to her, and not to me. Women are funny that way. They get possessive of the men they sleep with, and even their families." She looked troubled as she said it, and he shook his head.

"She's been a big help while you're away. But I don't think she has any illusions about me and the kids. She knows you're coming back." There was something about the way he said it that made Tanya feel uneasy.

"What does that mean? That she knows she has to give you back when I finish the movie, or that nothing is happening now?" There was an ever-so-subtle difference, a nuance that Tanya had picked up from him that she didn't like.

"I'm not sleeping with her. How's that for a simple answer?" Peter said succinctly, and then put his cup in the sink. He kept moving around. Tanya wasn't sure why, although the subject was uncomfortable for them both.

"Good. That's simple. I'm glad," she said, leaning over to kiss him on the mouth. "I'd be extremely upset if you did. Just so you're clear about that." He looked at her strangely then.

"What about you, Tan? Are you tempted in L.A.? Has anyone crossed your path that you'd want to have a quick fling with, or even a long one, for the duration of the movie? I know a lot of crazy stuff happens on movie sets, and you're a beautiful woman." She smiled at what he said, and didn't hesitate for a beat when she answered.

"No. Not for a minute. You're the only man for me. They all look like shit compared to you. I'm in love with you." Still. After twenty years. He looked pleased.

"I'm in love with you, too," he said softly. "Don't be mad at Alice. She's lonely, and she's nice to our kids."

"I just don't want her being overly nice to you. She acts like I don't exist when you're around," Tanya commented again.

"She's a good friend. I really appreciate her help. I couldn't manage without her sometimes. She keeps an eye on things when I can't get home early enough. And the girls like her a lot. They always did."

"I know. I like her, too. I just worry. It's hard being away five days a week." It had turned out to be much harder than either of them had thought it would be. After only two months it was rough. And Tanya was worried about missing weekends with them during the shoot. She was determined to get home as often as she could, but knew it wouldn't always be possible, as it hadn't been in the last two weeks. And she sure as hell didn't want him having an affair as a result. They both had to be strong. She was. And she could only assume he was, too, no matter how lonely Alice was, or how helpful with the girls. Tanya was getting strange vibes from her, and Alice had seemed slightly uncomfortable with her. Tanya had wondered if it was guilt. Apparently not. But she was glad she had asked, to clear the air. She was relieved by his response. She wasn't going to bring it up again. Once was enough.

She checked on the turkey again. It looked fine. And then she went upstairs to shower and dress. She heard Jason stirring in his room when she went up. It was nice to have him back. She smiled as she went back to her own room. It was an hour later when she came back downstairs, and by then Jason was in the kitchen, talking to his dad. She offered to cook him a light breakfast, she didn't want him spoiling his appetite for their turkey dinner, which they were planning to eat midafternoon. But he said he had already grazed adequately in the fridge. He had had cheesecake and leftover chili for breakfast. It was a perfect meal, in Jason's eyes.

At one-thirty they were all in the living room, dressed for Thanksgiving. And at two they sat down in the dining room. Peter carved the turkey, and they all agreed that the meal was better than usual this year. The turkey was one of the best they'd had. And as Tanya looked around the table at them, and said grace, as she did every year, she was grateful that they were together, that they loved each other, and that they had much to be thankful for again this year.

"Thank you for our family," she said softly before she said amen. And silently, she asked God to protect them in her absence.

# Chapter 10

L eaving home on the Sunday after Thanksgiving was one of the hardest things Tanya had done in a long time. She felt as though she had just gotten home and settled in, when it was time to leave them all again. She and Molly had had some delicious moments together, and it was so good to have Jason home again. And on Saturday afternoon Megan had finally told her everything that had happened with Mike. The confidences she shared, the obvious disappointment in her eyes, and the fact that she was opening up to her mother again nearly made Tanya cry. And she and Peter seemed closer than they had been in a long time. It had been a perfect holiday weekend. It nearly killed her to pack on Sunday afternoon, and go back to L.A. on Sunday night. She looked miserable when Peter drove her to the airport in a driving rain, and he looked equally unhappy.

"God, I hate to go back," she said, as they approached the airport. She wanted to tell him to turn around and go home and she'd quit the movie. She was really sorry now that she'd made the commitment. She felt that Peter and the girls really needed her at home. And she needed them just as much. "What do you think would happen if I quit?" She'd been thinking about it all weekend.

"They'd probably sue you, for what they've paid you so far, and damages to the movie. I don't think it's a great idea. Speaking as your lawyer, I'd have to advise against it." He smiled sadly at her, as he moved into the lane marked "departures." "As your husband, I have to admit I love the idea. I think you'd better listen to the lawyer, not the husband, on this one. I think they play hardball in the major leagues. You could pretty much kiss your ass and your writing career goodbye." It seemed like a small sacrifice to make, and almost worth it to her. "You don't want to get in a lawsuit, Tan. It would be a mess." She nodded and fought back tears. "We'll make it work. It won't be forever. Just another six months." It sounded like a life sentence to her, and to him as well. The movie seemed like a bad idea now. And her only choice was to bite the bullet, and get through it as best they could. Coming home was both easy and hard. It was nearly impossible to leave. Both girls had cried when she left, which nearly killed her. And Peter looked like someone had died, which was how she felt. What a huge mistake this had turned out to be. She didn't want to go back.

"The Christmas hiatus starts in three weeks, thank God. I'll be off for three weeks." It was the same three weeks as the kids' Christmas vacation, so at least she'd be around while they were out of school, and for a few days after. Only Jason's vacation was longer, but he was planning to go skiing with friends when she left. "I'll come home next weekend if I can."

"Maybe I can come down for a night if you can't. The girls can stay with Alice." Peter didn't want to leave them alone in the house.

"I'd love that," she said, as they pulled up to the curb. She had only hand luggage as always and nothing to check. "I'll let you know if I have to work next weekend."

"Just take care of yourself, Tan," he said, holding her tight. "Don't work too hard . . . and thank you for a wonderful Thanksgiving. We all loved it."

"Me too . . . I love you . . . ," she said, and he kissed her. There was an aura of desperation between the two of them. She had felt it when they made love that morning, as though they were both drowning, and being pulled away from each other by the currents.

"I love you, too. Call me when you get in." People behind them were honking and she had to get out. She stopped for a minute and looked at him, and then leaned back into the car to kiss him, as a traffic guard told him to hurry up and move on. He drove away a minute later, and she went inside with her bag.

They delayed the flight shortly after that. She left three hours late, and didn't get to the hotel until after one A.M. She called Peter from LAX when they landed. The weather had been awful on the flight, and it was raining in L.A., too. Everything about her return seemed depressing. She missed Peter and the girls already, and she was dreading going back to the set. She wanted to go home. She turned the key in the lock of the bungalow, and was surprised when she walked in. The night maid had left all the lights on, and soft music playing. Everything looked beautiful and warm and welcoming, and instead of like a lonely hotel room, she was surprised to find that it felt like home to her now, too. There was a bowl of fresh fruit on the coffee table, some pastries and cookies, and a bottle of champagne from the management. It was cozy and warm, and she sat down on the couch with a tired sigh. It had been an endless trip. And now that she was back, it didn't feel as bad as she had feared.

She walked into the bathroom, and the huge bathtub looked inviting. She put bath salts in and turned on the Jacuzzi, and sank into it five minutes later. She hadn't had dinner, and had a headache, and then she realized she could call room service and order anything she wanted. A club sandwich and a cup of tea sounded like a gift from heaven. When she got out of the tub, and put on her cashmere bathrobe, she called room service, and ten minutes later her sandwich and tea arrived. She smiled to herself, realizing that this wasn't quite the punishment she remembered. There were a few advantages at least, and some luxuries that made it tolerable. She turned on the TV while she ate, and watched an old Cary Grant movie, and then climbed into the bed, with perfectly pressed sheets. She missed having Peter's arms around her, but aside from that she spent a warm, comfortable night and felt rested when she woke up in the morning to a brilliantly sunny day. Sunlight was streaming into the room. And as she looked around, she felt surprisingly at home. This was her own private little world, separate from her family and home. It was so odd having two lives, one where she loved to live, with people she loved, and another where she worked. Maybe it wasn't as bad as she thought, she told herself, and she'd be home for vacation in three weeks. With luck, she'd get home that weekend, too. For a sudden instant, she felt almost schizophrenic about it, as though she were one person there, and a different one here. It was the first time she had felt that way.

She called Peter, and he was already on his way to work, fighting traffic on the bridge. He had left early that morning, and had a call holding on the other line. She said she'd call him that night when he got home, and told him she loved him before he clicked off. And then she got up and dressed for work.

There was the usual chaos on the set when she got there, and people seemed in good spirits after the four-day break over Thanksgiving. Max looked happy to see her, and even Harry wagged his tail when he saw her. It felt a little bit like coming home, just as it had when she walked into the bungalow the night before. She felt slightly guilty for what she was feeling. It wasn't nearly as bad as she remembered when she was in Ross with Peter and her children. She felt pulled now between two vastly disparate worlds. The good news was that she could have both. The confusing part was that it made her feel like two people, and she was momentarily unsure which one she was. The writer or the wife and mother. She was both. The wife and mother were what mattered most to her. But this wasn't bad either. She felt like a traitor, as she sat down in a chair next to Max and patted Harry. They both seemed like old friends now.

"So how was domestic bliss over Thanksgiving?" Max asked her, and she smiled.

"It was great. How was yours?"

"Probably not as blissful as yours, but not bad. Harry and I had turkey sandwiches and watched old movies on TV." His kids were in the East, and he didn't want to fly cross country for a few days, so he had stayed in L.A., but he was going to see them for Christmas.

"I nearly didn't come back," she admitted to him. "It was so nice being home with them."

"But you did, so at least we know you're not crazy. Douglas would have sued your ass from here to forever," Max said quietly.

"That's what Peter said."

"Smart man. Good lawyer. You'll see, the picture will be over before you know it. And then you'll want to do it again."

"That's what Douglas says. I don't think so. I like being home with Peter and the kids."

"Then maybe you won't do it again," Max said philosophically.

"That might be true in your case. You're saner than the rest of us, and you have something worth going home to. For a lot of people, this is all there is. And it screws up the rest of your life, so there's nothing to go home to. We're all trapped on a desert island and can't get off. You were smart to live the life you have till now. You're a tourist, Tanya. I don't think the movie business will ever be your life."

"I hope not. It's too crazy for me."

"That it is." He smiled, and then started giving orders to get people moving. They started shooting again half an hour later, once the lighting was set and the actors were ready.

They didn't finish till midnight, and Tanya called Peter from the set, so it didn't get too late for him. She had to walk away to call him, and spoke in a whisper. He said he'd had a good day and the girls were fine, and she told him what they'd been doing. It had been kind of a fun day. And then she had to get off and go back, Jean was having trouble with her lines again. She always did. Tanya had rewritten them a hundred times, and she still couldn't get them right. It was painstaking work.

It was one o'clock when she got back to the hotel, and two before she unwound and could get to sleep. The days were crushingly long. And she saw Douglas on the set the next day. He asked her how Thanksgiving had been, and she said it had been fine. He had flown to Aspen for three days to see friends. He had a very nice life.

He invited her to a party on Thursday night, as they had a short shooting schedule, and she hesitated. She didn't really want to go out. She wasn't in the mood. She was happy in her bungalow at night after work. Going to some fancy party with Douglas seemed like a lot of trouble, but he insisted.

"It'll do you good, Tanya. You can't work all the time. There is life after work."

"Not in my life." She smiled.

"Then there should be. You'll enjoy it. It's a screening of a new movie. It'll be a very casual evening, with some fun people. You'll be home by eleven." In the end, she agreed to go.

And he was right. It was fun. She met some of the biggest stars in Hollywood, two famous directors, and a rival producer who was one of Douglas's closest friends. It was a star-studded evening, and the film was great. The food was good, the people were pretty, and Douglas was great company. He introduced her to everyone, and saw to it that she had fun. And when he brought her back, to thank him she invited him in for a drink. He had champagne, while she had tea and thanked him for the evening.

"You need to do more of that, Tanya. You need to meet people here."

"Why? I'm doing a job, and then I'm going home. I don't need to make connections down here."

"You're still so sure you're going home?" He looked cynical about it again.

"Yes, I am."

"Very few people do. I could be wrong. You may be one of them. I don't know why, but I have the feeling you won't want to in the end. I think you know it, too. That's why you fight it so hard. Maybe you're afraid you won't want to go home."

"No," she said firmly. "I want to go home." She didn't tell him that she nearly hadn't come back after Thanksgiving.

"Is your marriage really that good?" he asked, a little more determined and daring, after the champagne.

"I think it is."

"Then you're a lucky woman, and your husband more fortunate still. I don't know any marriages like that. Most collapse like soufflés.

Particularly with the pressures of long distance, and all the temptations that Hollywood provides."

"Maybe that's why I want to go home. I love my husband, and our marriage. I don't want to screw it up for all this."

"Good lord," he said, with the look that made her think of Rasputin, or had in the beginning. She knew him better now, although he still had a wicked streak and loved to play devil's advocate. But he wasn't as dangerous as she first thought. He just looked it. "A virtuous woman. It says in the Bible that a virtuous woman is worth more than rubies. And surely a lot more rare. I've never had a virtuous woman," he said, pouring himself another glass of champagne.

"I'm sure you'd find it very dull," she teased him, and he laughed.

"I'm afraid you're right. Virtue is not my strong suit, Tanya. I don't think I'd be up to the challenge."

"You might surprise yourself, with the right one."

"I might," he conceded, and then looked at her intently and set down his glass. "You are a virtuous woman, Tanya. I actually admire that about you, much as I hate to admit it. Your husband really is a lucky man. I hope he knows it."

"He does." She smiled at him. It had been a nice compliment coming from him. He knew the difference. Virtuous women weren't his thing. He was a player, and always had been. But he respected her now that he had come to know her. And he enjoyed her company. He had had a very pleasant evening, and so had she. She felt no pressure from him anymore. Ever since the day they had spent at his pool, and eating Chinese takeout afterward, she had felt as though they were friends.

He got up a few minutes later, and she thanked him for taking her out.

"Anytime, my dear. It pains me to admit it, but I think you're a good influence on me. You remind me of what's important in life. Kindness, integrity, friendship, all those things that I usually find so boring. You never bore me, Tanya. On the contrary. I rise to the occasion, and have a much better time with you than a lot of other people I know." She was both flattered and touched.

"Thank you, Douglas."

"Goodnight, Tanya." He kissed her on both cheeks and left.

She went to call Peter. Douglas had been true to his word. It was eleven-thirty, and she was surprised when Peter's phone went to voice mail. She called him on the phone at the house instead of his cell phone, and Molly said he was next door with Alice. He was fixing a leak in her basement. She said it was flooding, and Alice needed help. Tanya didn't want to bother him there, and told Molly to have him call when he got in. Tanya lay down on her bed then to wait for his call, and fell asleep. She woke up with the lights on in the morning, and called him. The girls had just left for school, and she was due on the set in twenty minutes.

"Did you fix the leak?" she teased him. "You're a good neighbor to have."

"Yes, I am. She has about a foot of water in her basement. It's a hell of a mess. A pipe broke. I couldn't do much about it. We drank mojitos instead."

"What's a mojito?" Tanya sounded surprised. Peter was drinking more than he used to. She had noticed it in L.A. when he came down with the girls.

"I don't know. Some crazy Cuban drink. With mint. They taste good."

"Did you two get drunk?" She sounded worried, and he laughed.

"Of course not. It was just more fun than wading around her

basement, up to my knees in water. She wanted to try them out on me." Tanya had the same question in her mind that she'd had over Thanksgiving, but she didn't ask him again. She had said she wouldn't. And she didn't want to get paranoid. She had been out with Douglas the night before, and nothing had happened between them. There was no reason anything would have between Peter and Alice either. They were just making the best of a tough situation. It was hard being alone as a married person. And as Douglas said, you couldn't stay home every night. There were worse things than drinking mojitos with Alice, and she knew Peter wouldn't do any of them. She did wonder if Alice had a crush on him though. Peter was such an innocent, and such a straight shooter, he was liable not to notice if that were the case. Alice was barking up the wrong tree.

"I've got to get to the set. I just wanted to give you a kiss before you left. Have a nice day."

"You too. Talk to you later."

Tanya hurried to shower and dress and get to the set, and when she got there, they had just put out a small fire started by the lights. The fire department had come and Harry was barking frantically. It was more chaotic than usual, and nearly noon by the time they got the set lit right and started rolling. As a result they worked till nearly three A.M., and she couldn't get off the set to call Peter and the kids. It was one of those endless days that happen on movie sets. She fell into bed when she got home, and had to be up four hours later. It turned out to be a crazy week, and she couldn't get home that weekend or the next one. But the week after, their Christmas break started. By the time she got home, she hadn't seen Peter since Thanksgiving. It had been nearly three weeks. He was thrilled to see her when she walked in.

"I feel like I'm home from the wars," she said breathlessly as he picked her up and spun her around. She looked over his shoulder and saw Alice. She had walked in behind him and was looking at Tanya. "Hi, Alice," Tanya said, smiling at her.

"Welcome home," Alice said, and left a minute later.

"Is she okay?" Tanya asked, looking concerned.

"She's fine. Why?" Peter looked distracted, as he helped himself to a glass of water. He had just come from next door and looked happy to see her, as happy as Tanya was to see him.

"She looked upset."

"Did she? I didn't notice," he said vaguely, and then their eyes met. It was a point in time like two planets colliding, and exploding in midair. Tanya looked into his eyes and saw everything. This time she didn't need to ask the question. The answer had been in Alice's eyes, not his.

"Oh my God." Tanya felt as though the room were spinning around her. She looked at him, and she didn't want to know, but she did. "Oh my God . . . you're sleeping with her . . ." This time it was a statement, not a question. She didn't know how or when it had happened, but she knew it had. And still was. Tanya looked into his eyes again. "Are you in love with her?" He was a fool, but not a liar. He couldn't lie to her again. He set down his glass in the sink, turned to look at her, and said the only thing he could. It was the same thing he had said to Alice minutes before Tanya walked in.

"I don't know," he said, as his face went pale.

"Oh my God . . . " Tanya said again, as he walked out of the room.

# Chapter 11

The days over Christmas vacation were a nightmare for Peter and Tanya. At first he didn't want to talk about it with her, but there was no other choice. He owed her at least that much. Tanya was afraid to leave the house, she didn't want to run into Alice. Alice stayed clear of both of them, and made no appearances at the Harris house. Neither Peter nor Tanya wanted their children to know.

"What does this mean?" Tanya asked Peter finally, sitting in the kitchen, when all the children were out. They had gone to a Christmas party, and so far she and Peter were making an enormous effort to hide what was going on. She had been home for three days by then. Tanya felt as though her world had come to an end. With good reason. He had cheated on her with her best friend. It happened to others, but she had never really believed it could happen to them, despite her question to Peter about it over Thanksgiving. She had totally trusted him. Peter just wasn't that kind of man, or so she thought. But apparently, he was. He had hardly spoken to her since she'd been home. In three weeks, everything had changed. Tanya was looking at him across the table, her eyes filled with despair. His own misery was equally apparent. He felt as though he had murdered her. She had lost six pounds in three days, which was a lot on her tiny frame. And her eyes looked ravaged, they were two deep green holes with dark circles under them. He looked just as bad. No one had seen Alice since the day Tanya had gotten home, and their chance meeting in the kitchen, when suddenly it all came clear.

"I don't know what it means," he told Tanya honestly, hanging his head. He felt overwhelmed. "It just happened. I never even thought about it. I'd never been attracted to her. I think we just got used to being together while you were away. She's been a big help with the kids."

"And with you apparently," Tanya said grimly. "Did she put the make on you, or was this your idea?" She told herself she didn't want to know the details, and yet part of her did.

"It just happened, Tan. We went over for pizza. The girls came back here to do homework. I don't know . . . I was lonely . . . I was tired . . . we opened a bottle of wine, and the next thing I knew we were in bed." He looked sick, and so did she.

"And when was that exactly? While you were telling me how much you love me, and I was calling you every time I could get off the set? How long has this been going on?" It was a horrifying thought, whenever it had been. She wondered just how long she'd been a fool, and for how many weeks or months he'd been lying to her. She had suspected it over Thanksgiving, and told herself she was paranoid. So had he. Was he lying then? She wanted to know that at least. Just how big a liar was he?

"It was after Thanksgiving. Two weeks ago." He nearly choked on the words. And she had been gone for three. She hadn't been able to get home. The only thing she knew now for sure was what a colossal mistake it had been to go to L.A. to make the film. If it destroyed her marriage, she was never going to forgive herself, or him.

"Was it a one-time thing, or has it happened again?"

"It happened a couple of times," he said vaguely. "We're both lonely, I guess. She needs someone to take care of her." He sounded unspeakably sad, for all of them. Nothing would ever be the same. It was Tanya's worst fear. She had never expected this, neither from him nor from Alice. She couldn't conceive of doing it to them.

"I need someone to take care of me, too," Tanya said, as she burst into tears.

"No, you don't," he said, looking at her strangely. "You don't need me, Tan. You can move mountains, you always could. You're a strong woman, you have your own life and a career." She looked shocked at what he said.

"I'm making this movie because you told me I should. You said it was a once-in-a-lifetime opportunity and I shouldn't miss it. I didn't just go off to have a career. That's always been a low priority for me, and you know it. You and the kids always came first, and still do." He looked as though he didn't believe her, as they faced each other across the table. At that moment in time, the Grand Canyon was narrower than the gap between them.

"I don't think that's true anymore. Look at the life you lead down there. Face it, Tan, you're never going to want to come back here." He looked convinced.

"Don't you give me that shit, too. There's nothing about that life I want. That's not who I am. I wanted to work on the project, just once, for the hell of it. But that's all. Nothing's changed for me. My life is here."

"Whatever," he said, and sounded just like Meg. Tanya had an overwhelming urge to slap him, but restrained herself. It was obvious that he didn't believe anything she'd said. But she wasn't at fault. He was. She was working in L.A., but she wasn't sleeping with anyone. Only him.

"What are you going to do? What do you want, Peter?" she asked, and held her breath while he sat hunched over the table and stared first at her hands, then at her.

"I don't know. This is all very new. I didn't see it coming, and Alice didn't either," he said honestly. Tanya looked like a stranger to him now. He had never seen her this angry before. In truth, she was heartbroken, but it came out of her mouth as rage.

"I don't believe that," Tanya said angrily. "I think she went after you, and the kids. She saw her opportunity as soon as I left. She's been working Megan since last summer."

"She's not working her, she loves her." He defended Alice, which didn't sit well with her, and only made things worse.

"And what about you?" Tanya asked hoarsely as tears rolled down her cheeks. "Are you in love with her?"

"I don't know what I am, other than confused. I've never cheated on you once, Tan, in twenty years. I want you to know that."

"What difference does it make now?" she sobbed. He reached out to touch her hand, and she pulled it away.

"It makes a lot of difference to me," he said, looking anguished. "This would never have happened if you hadn't gone to L.A." It was so unfair to blame her now, but he did anyway. And privately, so did she.

"And now what am I supposed to do? I didn't want to go back after Thanksgiving, and you told me if I didn't I'd get sued."

"That's probably true." It was too late now anyway. The damage had been done, and he had decisions to make. They both did.

"What are you going to do now with Alice?" Tanya asked him, sounding panicked. "Is this a fling, or something more? You said you didn't know if you were in love with her. What does that mean?" She could hardly get the words out of her mouth, but she wanted to know. She had a right to, if he did.

"It means what I said. I don't know. I love her as a friend, and she's a wonderful woman. We have a great time with the kids, and we see things the same way. There are a lot of things I love about her, but I had never thought about this before. And I love you, too, Tan. I've meant it every time I said it. But I also can't see you living here any- more. You've outgrown your life here. You don't know it yet, but I saw it when I went to L.A. You're one of them now. Alice and I are much more alike. We have more in common now than you and I." His words were brutally painful and damning, as Tanya stared at him with wide eyes.

"How can you say that?" She looked horrified. "That's so unfair. I'm working on a movie. I'm writing it. I'm not in it, I'm not a star. I'm the same person I was when I left here three months ago. It's so un- fair of you to assume that I bought into all that bullshit and am never coming back here or I'd be unhappy if I did. That's not what I want. I want the life we always had. I really do love you, and I have not been fucking around in L.A. I wouldn't do that, nor would I want to," she said, looking hurt.

"It's hard for me to believe you'd ever want this life again," he said, looking mournful. It was his excuse for what he'd done.

"So what does that mean? You hire another wife before I even quit the job? What have you been doing, holding auditions, 'Housewife wanted, screenwriters need not apply'? What's wrong with you? And what's wrong with her? Whatever happened to decency, trust, and honor? She claims to be my best friend. What, does it suddenly make it okay to cheat on me, and betray me, just because I'm working on a movie in L.A.? With your encouragement, I might add." Her eyes blazed as she looked at him, but beyond the anger was grief. Peter didn't know what to say to her. He knew she was right, but it didn't change anything. They couldn't unring the bell. He was having an affair with Alice.

"What are you doing here, Peter? And what are you going to do now?"

"I don't know." He looked distraught as he said it. Alice had asked him the same question only that morning. In the blink of an eye, all three of their lives were a mess.

"Are you willing to stop seeing her, and try to put our marriage back together?" She looked at him long and hard, knowing she would never trust him again. And how would he avoid Alice, living right next door? The minute Tanya left for L.A., they'd be together again. She didn't trust either one of them anymore. This had been like a bolt of lightning that had struck her and their marriage. Where did you go from here? She wanted to know what Peter felt, if he even knew himself, which apparently he didn't. He was still too much in shock over what he had done, and the fact that Tanya had guessed it. It was like a tidal wave hitting their life.

"I don't know," he said again. And then he looked her in the eye. They both looked devastated. "I want our marriage back, Tan. I want to go back to the way things were, before you went to L.A. But I also want to figure out what I feel for Alice. There must be something there or it wouldn't have happened. I was lonely and tired of juggling everything myself, but I don't think that's why it happened. Maybe there was more to it than that. It wasn't just a mistake or a random fuck. I wish I could say it was, but I'm not sure that's the case. I owe it to all three of us to figure that out."

"And how do you propose to do that? Audition us in turn? Just how much leeway do you want here? You've just destroyed my life, both of you, my family, and everything I believe in. I trusted you . . . what am I supposed to do now?" she asked, sobbing openly. "What do you want?"

"I need some time to figure it out," he said hoarsely. They all did. And Alice had told him she was in love with him, and had been since her husband died. She just never thought there was a chance for them, and now she did. He had no idea what to do with that information either. He was drowning in his own confusion and what both women were saying to him.

"Do you want me to quit the film now? I will," Tanya offered and he shook his head.

"They'll sue our asses off, for your fees and damages. We don't need that headache on top of this. It'll just make a bigger mess. You have to finish the film." He looked grim.

"While you and Alice go on screwing here all week while I'm in L.A. at work. What do you think your children are going to think of this? You're not going to look like a hero to them."

"I know. I'm anything but. I get that. I feel like a complete asshole. Look, I fucked up. I slipped. I made a terrible mistake. I cheated on you. It happened. I can't take it back. But I also need to find out if it was a random mistake, or something more than that, that actually makes sense. I spend more time with her than I do with you now, Tan. We have more in common. We do the same things, have the same friends, want the same life. You're out in the stratosphere somewhere, doing something else. You wanted that. Be honest. Maybe all you wanted was the writing, but you got the whole ball of wax. You can't separate the two. The lifestyle comes with the work. You look mighty comfortable to me in that bungalow at the Beverly Hills

Hotel. I don't see you running out to rent a studio in some cheap neighborhood, or taking the bus instead of the limo they give you. I think you like all that, and why not? You're earning it. But I can't see you giving that up in six months. My guess is you'll want another film, and another one . . . you'll never want this life or me again."

"You have no right to make my decisions for me, or to tell me how I feel, or what I want. All I wanted was to come home at the end of it. And now you're telling me I can't, that there may not be a home, and someone else may have taken my place."

"It happens, Tan," he said sadly. "I didn't want this to happen either."

"But you did it anyway. I didn't. I had nothing to do with this, except that I took a job in another city for nine months. I come home every chance I get." She was begging him to be fair, but the situation wasn't. Just as life wasn't sometimes.

"It's not enough," Peter said honestly. "I need more than a wife who comes home a couple of weekends a month. I need someone here with me every day. The last three months nearly killed me. I can't take care of the girls, work, cook, take care of the house. I can't do it all," he said as he looked at her, and she looked angry again.

"Why not? I did. And I didn't cheat on you to relieve the stress, although I could have. I could be doing that in L.A., but I'm not." She was sure that several people would have been happy to oblige her. She would never have done that to Peter. But he and Alice had done it to her. It was a double loss, her husband and her best friend, which made it doubly depressing.

"Look, let's try to keep a lid on this over the holidays. Let's try to calm down, and figure out what we feel. We're all screwed up and freaked out. I'll try to sort this out by the time you go back to L.A. I'm sorry, Tan, I don't know what else to do or say. I just need some time to think. We all do. Maybe we'll all get sane."

"I'm sane," Tanya said, looking him squarely in the eye. She was deathly pale. "It's you two who went nuts. Or maybe I did when I signed on for the movie. But I didn't deserve this," she said, as tears filled her eyes again.

"No, you didn't. And I don't want to keep hurting you." Now that it was out in the open, it had to be cleaned up one way or the other. He had both women pulling on him now, in opposite directions, and he was completely confused himself. "I'd rather we not tell the kids until we figure out what we're doing, if that's okay with you." She thought about it for a minute and then nodded. They were fucked no matter what. There was no way their children weren't going to sense that something bad had happened. There would be inevitable stress between Peter and Tanya, and overnight Alice had become persona non grata in their house. That was going to be hard to explain. Their lies were going to have to be very creative over Christmas vacation. And whatever lies they told, their eyes told their own tale. Peter looked dead, and Tanya looked broken. Alice was hiding, and hysterical herself. She didn't want to be Peter's stand-in piece of ass while Tanya was away. She had told him that either he wanted an honest relationship with her, or it was over. She was relieved although embarrassed that Tanya had found out. But she said she had no remorse over what they'd done. She loved him, and Tanya finding out forced Peter to make up his mind about what he wanted and was doing, and step up to the plate. Alice had also told him that she was more than willing to sacrifice her friendship with Tanya for him. She loved him, and said she had for quite a while. It was yet another lightning bolt for him.

They were still sitting at the kitchen table when Megan and Molly walked in. They saw their parents and knew instantly that something had happened. Their mother looked devastated. They had never seen her look that way before, except when someone died. Their father got up, and took out the garbage. He needed some air.

"What happened?" Molly asked, looking at her mother, as Tanya put on a totally unconvincing happy face.

"Nothing. An old friend of mine from college died. I just heard the news, and I was talking to Dad about it. It made me sad, that's all," she said, wiping away tears again.

"I'm sorry, Mom. Can I do anything?" Tanya shook her head, unable to speak, as Peter walked back in. As her eyes met his, he looked as distraught as she did, and Megan saw it. A few minutes later the girls went upstairs, and Jason walked in. He saw it, too, and conferred with his sisters an hour later. Their parents' bedroom door was shut, which was unheard of in the afternoon. They knew something was wrong, but they couldn't figure out what. They could sense that it was serious. Megan was afraid her mother wanted a divorce and was moving to L.A.

"I don't think so," Molly said. "She'd never leave Dad, or us." She was sure of it.

"There won't be an 'us' next year," Megan reminded her. "And she left us this year. Believe me, she'd move. I think that's it. Poor Dad looked so upset." She didn't know what had happened, but she already felt sorry for him.

"Mom looked just as upset as he did," Jason pointed out to both of them. "I hope neither of them is sick." They had fully understood that it was a life-and-death matter, or close to it, and all three children were deeply disturbed. In their own room, Peter and Tanya were arguing again, as quietly as they could, so the children wouldn't hear them.

By that afternoon, a pall had come over the house. It felt like someone had died there, and the funereal atmosphere hung over them for days. Tanya finally went out and bought a Christmas tree with Jason, to put them in the Christmas spirit. But she ended up crying while she was decorating it, and Molly saw her. She tried to find out what had happened, but Tanya wouldn't say. Everyone walked on eggs for the rest of the holidays, particularly Tanya and Peter, but the children as well. Tanya saw Alice in the driveway once, and Tanya turned and walked away. And when Megan asked her mother why they hadn't invited Alice over for a drink even once since she was home, Tanya gave her vague excuses and said they were all too busy. Megan confronted her on it immediately.

"You're jealous of her, aren't you, Mom? Because we're all comfortable with her and she's like a second mother to us. Well, face it, if you had stuck around for senior year, she wouldn't be doing all this. She's doing it because you bagged on us," Megan said with the meanness and shortsightedness of youth. Tanya said nothing and hid her tears. But the same applied to Peter, she realized. If she hadn't gone to work in L.A., Alice wouldn't have been taking care of him either, or inviting him and the girls over for dinner several times a week. In other words, according to Megan, she had gotten what she deserved. Tanya wondered if it was true. But she had been in L.A. for four months, and lonely, too, and she hadn't cheated on Peter.

The atmosphere in the house stayed hostile and depressing all the way till Christmas Eve. They went to church together, as they always did. But this year they didn't join forces with Alice and her two children. They went separately. Only Megan complained about their not sitting with Alice, said she felt sorry for her, and she went to sit with her in church. Tanya spent the entire mass on her knees, with her hands covering her face, and tears running down her cheeks. Peter found himself staring at the two women during the service. The one begging him with her eyes to come and start a new life with her, the other mourning the old one. He had told Alice days before that he couldn't talk to her until he resolved this, it was too confusing, and now she looked panicked. The fallout from their brief affair had been like a tidal wave, and only seemed to be getting worse.

They barely made it through Christmas Day, and the children went skiing in Tahoe shortly after, and planned to spend New Year's Eve in the mountains. Tanya was sure they were relieved to get away. She was doing her best to cover up what was happening, but the masquerade was unconvincing, and by the time the kids left, she and Peter both looked as though they were ready for a nervous breakdown. And every time she couldn't account for his whereabouts, she was convinced he was with Alice. She no longer trusted him, and maybe never would again.

They chose not to acknowledge New Year's Eve at all, Tanya said she just couldn't. And they lay in bed and talked on New Year's morning. They had been in bed at ten o'clock the night before, but both looked as though they'd had no sleep. Tanya woke up feeling dead every morning, the moment she remembered what had happened. She no longer asked him what his plans were. She assumed that he would tell her when he knew.

They were lying side by side in bed, staring out the window. Tanya could see the corner of Alice's roof, and she lay looking at it in silence. Peter lay on his back and spoke to the ceiling.

"I'm going to end it with Alice," he said somberly. "I think that's the right thing to do." There was silence in the room. The right thing, as far as Tanya was concerned, was never to have done it. Ending it was the next-best thing.

"Is that what you want, Peter?" she asked softly. He nodded. "Do you think you can? Will she let you?" She knew better than anyone how tenacious Alice could be when she wanted something.

"She's being very reasonable. She says she's going to go away for a while. She has some things to do for the gallery in Europe. It'll give us a break. It's not like this has been going on forever." He sighed. He hated discussing it with Tanya, but he knew he had to. She had been waiting to hear his decision for over two weeks, and so had Alice. He had told her the previous afternoon and she agreed. She wasn't happy about it, but she said she understood, and if he ever changed his mind, to let her know. The door would always be open to him. That only made it harder for him. He knew he needed to close that door to save his marriage.

"And what happens when she comes back?" Tanya asked, looking worried.

"We keep our distance for a while, I guess, until things get normal again." But all three of them knew they never would. Tanya hadn't said anything to Alice, but she had no intention of ever speaking to her again. And she no longer trusted Peter when she went back to L.A. If not Alice, maybe now he would sleep with someone else. And once Alice came back from Europe, she had no faith in their ability to stay away from each other. It was a miserable situation for them all.

Tanya nodded in silence, and got up and showered. She couldn't throw her arms around Peter's neck and tell him she loved him. She didn't know what she felt anymore. Anger, rage, disappointment, fear, heartbreak, sorrow. She felt a multitude of emotions, none of them pleasant, and she wasn't even sure now if one of them was love. She hoped that in time their relationship would recover and bloom again, but she was no longer sure of anything. The situation had put up a wall between them. Peter made no attempt to scale the walls she'd built. He knew that could only happen with time, but it was a lonely place for him.

In the interest of repairing some of the damage, he invited her to dinner a few days before she went back to L.A. Alice had already left for Europe. And Jason had left for school that day. The vacation had been depressing, and incredibly stressful from beginning to end. Tanya agreed to go out with him, although she had little to say. They managed to limp their way through dinner, talking about the children, and as many inane topics as they could find. The evening wasn't fun for either of them, but they knew they had to start somewhere. They both carefully stayed off the subject of Alice. And in bed that night, Peter attempted to make overtures to her for the first time since she'd been home and had found out about his affair. But the moment he laid a gentle hand on her back, Tanya instantly stiffened. She turned away from him, and then back again, in the dark. There were tears in her eyes, but he couldn't see them. He could hear them in her voice.

"I'm sorry, Peter . . . I can't . . . not yet . . . ," she said softly.

"It's all right. I understand," he said, and turned away from her. He hadn't put his arms around her in weeks, or told her that he loved her, which was all she wanted. All their conversations had been about Alice. She hung between them still as surely as if she had been lying between them in their bed.

And as he lay with his back to her, Tanya lay with her head on her pillow, looking at him with wide eyes, and wondering if anything would ever be the same again.

# Chapter 12

Going back to L.A. was an even greater agony for Tanya this time. She hugged each of her children with tears in her eyes, and was so upset she couldn't even speak when she left. Even Megan looked somewhat sorry for her. Particularly since she had no female mentor now. She knew that Alice was going to be away for at least a month. She had called both girls to say goodbye. They didn't even know exactly where she had gone. The only one she had left her itinerary with was Peter, but he didn't share that information with anyone, and wasn't sure he wanted it himself. He didn't know if he trusted himself with it. After he wrote the numbers down, he thought better of it, tore the paper into little bits, and threw it away. He felt safer doing that, in case he weakened late one night, called her, and asked her to come home. He was determined to give her up, and was fairly certain that he could. As much as one knew anything in life, which he doubted more and more these days. It was hard knowing that Tanya no longer trusted him. She still looked devastated when he drove her to the airport and she put her arms around his neck.

"I still love you, Peter," she said sadly. They had never managed to make love before she left. Every time she thought about it, all she could think of was his betraying her with Alice. It was going to take her more time to recover from the shock and feel comfortable with him again.

"I love you too, Tan. I'm sorry all this happened." It had totally destroyed Christmas for all of them. No matter how hard they tried to hide it, their children had sensed easily that something was wrong. Both Peter and Tanya refused to discuss it, which only seemed to make things worse, and worried their children more.

"I hope it gets better soon," Tanya said sadly.

"So do I," he said honestly. He wanted their marriage to work again. He just wasn't sure how much damage had been done. Clearly, a lot.

"I'll be home on Friday, if I can." And if she couldn't, she wondered to herself, what would happen then? Who would he sleep with? Where would Alice be? Would he find someone else? Tanya no longer felt safe. For twenty years she had trusted him totally. Now she trusted nothing and no one, and least of all him. It was a terrible feeling, and he could see it in her eyes. Every time she looked at him, he felt the white heat of reproach, and the weight of her aching heart. It was a lot to live with, and they were both relieved to be spending some time apart. The last three weeks had been too much. She hated to leave him and the girls, but she was glad to go back to L.A. For once, he was right. It broke her heart, but all she wanted was to escape.

She got back to her bungalow at eight o'clock that night, and this time even her cheery little rooms at the Beverly Hills Hotel looked depressing to her. She wanted to be home again, and yet she didn't. She wanted to be in Ross with him, the way it had been before. She wondered if it would ever be that way again. And now that she was back in L.A., in the bungalow, she was lonelier than ever, and missed Jason and the girls. She missed everything and everyone, and even herself. She felt as though she had lost herself in the last three weeks. The only thing she hadn't lost were her children, but she even felt out of touch with them. She didn't call Peter that night, and he didn't call her either. The silence was deafening in Bungalow 2. She didn't even bother to put on music. She just curled up in bed, asked for a wake-up call, and cried herself to sleep. In some ways it was a relief. She didn't have to worry about Peter lying next to her, and wonder what he was thinking, or if he had heard from Alice. Tanya felt as though she couldn't stem the tides. She didn't know if his promise to end the affair was sincere, or if he could live up to it. She had no idea what to believe. She had trusted him before, and her peaceful little world had come crashing down like a house of cards in the past three weeks.

She was relieved to get back to the set the next day, despite the early wake-up call. Max was the first one she saw, sharing a bagel with Harry. The dog wagged his tail the minute he saw Tanya, and she patted him with a tired smile.

"Welcome back," Max said, smiling at her. It took him less than a second to see the shards of her heart in her eyes. She looked awful and had lost about ten pounds. He pretended not to notice. "How were the holidays?"

"Great," she said in a flat voice. "How was New York?"

"Ice cold and snowy, but it was fun. I think I'm too old for grandchildren. Only young people should have grandchildren. They wore me out." She smiled, as Douglas appeared with a stack of notes. Their last script changes were being distributed in a new shade of pastel colors. It was hard to keep track of the changes anymore, there had been so many.

"Welcome back to Hollywood," he said, with a raised eyebrow.

"Wonderful time in Marin?" he asked sarcastically. If so, she didn't look it. She was suddenly too thin. "You look like you haven't eaten since you left." Thank you, Douglas. Never one to mince words, or hide what he thought.

"I had the flu." She covered her tracks, and she doubted he believed her.

"That's too bad. Welcome back to work," he said, and moved on. He stayed on the set all morning to see how things were going. They had some tough scenes to shoot, but for once Jean Amber remembered her lines. She looked blissful, and word had gotten out that she had spent the holidays in St. Bart's with Ned Bright. They both looked very happy, and the energy between them was electric in every scene.

"Ahhh, young love," Max said with a grin as he walked off the set at lunchtime, having yelled "Cut! And print," which meant he liked the last shot. He glanced over at Tanya, and realized that she looked even worse than he had first thought. He had never seen a human so pale. "Are you okay? If you're still sick, you don't have to come to work. We can call you at the hotel."

"No, I'm fine. Just tired."

"You lost a hell of a lot of weight." He looked worried about her, and she was touched.

"Yeah, I guess," she said vaguely, and pretended to concentrate on the script, as tears swam in her eyes. She didn't intend him to, but he saw them, and they spilled down her cheeks, as he quietly handed her a tissue.

"Looks like you had a fabulous time," he said softly, as Harry watched the exchange with a puzzled look. Even he knew something was wrong.

"Yeah, really terrific." She blew her nose and laughed through her tears, and then wiped her eyes. "Some vacations are less fun than others. This one wasn't so great."

"This one must have been a lulu," Max said dryly. "What did he do? Lock you in the dungeon and refuse to feed you? You know, there are 800 numbers you can call for that. I think the last one I called was 1–800-D-I-V-O-R-C-E. It worked really well. They sent out a rescue truck and took the bitch away. Keep the number in mind in case he tries it again. Take your cell phone into the dungeon with you." As he said it, she cried harder, and he handed her more tissues.

"It wasn't quite as bad as that." And then she thought about it for a minute and was honest with herself. "Actually, it was worse. The whole damn vacation sucked, to tell the truth." It felt good to say it to him.

"Sometimes holidays are like that. Mine usually are. It was nice this year spending it with my kids. Usually I volunteer in a soup kitchen or something. It makes me feel better to see people less fortunate than I, I realize I'm not so bad off. Maybe you should do something like that." She nodded. "I'm sorry, Tanya," he said in a soft, sympathetic voice, which only made her cry more. "Should I call a plumber? I think you have a busted pipe. You've sprung a hell of a leak there." She was crying rivers, and he made her laugh again.

"I'm sorry. I'm a mess. I've been worse since I got back to L.A. Everything was so tense, and I had to put on a good front for the kids. Here, all I've done is cry since I got back last night."

"As long as it helps. Big problems? Or small ones?"

"Big," she said, looking him in the eye. Her eyes looked like bottomless pools of green pain. He hated to see it.

"Anything I can do to help?" She shook her head. "I figured. Maybe time will work it out."

"Maybe." If Peter was telling the truth, and Alice stayed away for long enough. And if she could get home on weekends. If not, God only knew what would happen, particularly once Alice got back. She didn't trust either of them anymore, and suspected she never would again, which was no way to be married. She looked at Max miserably and decided to confide in him. She hadn't told a soul since her discovery of Peter's affair. Her only confidants before that had been Peter and Alice. And she couldn't tell her kids. "I found out the day I got back to Marin, he had an affair with my best friend." Her agony was in her eyes, as Max winced.

"Shit. That's nasty stuff. Did you walk in on them? I hope not."

"No. I saw it in his eyes. I suspected it on Thanksgiving, but I don't think it had happened yet. Maybe I felt it coming."

"Women are amazing about that. They always sense it. Guys never know for shit until it bites them on the ass. Women *know*. I hate that about them. You can never get away with anything. And then what happened?"

"We spent three awful weeks torturing each other. She went to Europe. And he says he won't start it again when she gets back. He claims it's over."

"Do you believe him?" Max was flattered by her confidence. She trusted him, and valued his advice.

She shook her head in answer to his question. "Not anymore. And maybe never again. I'm afraid he'll go back to her when she gets home. He thinks I'll never come back from L.A. That I've got it under my skin, which is so unfair. He won't listen no matter what I say."

"That's an excuse, Tan. If he wanted to make it work with you, he wouldn't care if you'd been a belly dancer in a harem, or had an affair with the King of England, or Donald Trump. Bottom line, if he wants to make it work, he would tell you to get your ass home when this is over, and forget Hollywood. Maybe he wants out. Or he's scared, or feels inadequate with you. Is she young?"

"No." Tanya shook her head. "She's six years older than I am, two years older than him."

"Then it must be love. No one goes after a woman two years older unless it is." Max looked impressed.

"They're a lot alike, that's why I loved them both. She screwed me over totally. I think she went after him. She's been a widow for two years. And I'm gone all the time, as he pointed out. My kids think of her as an aunt. She gets along better with one of my daughters than I do. I think she was working it, and wanted him. My leaving to do this film is the best thing that ever happened to her. Shit luck for me." He nodded, looking sympathetic.

"What does he say?"

"That he ended it."

"Does he say he loves her?"

"He says he doesn't know."

"I hate guys like that," Max said, looking annoyed. "Either he loves her or he doesn't. How the hell can he not know?"

"He says he loves me, too," she said, blowing her nose again. "I'm not sure I even believe that anymore." Tanya felt as though her whole life had been destroyed, and she looked it. And in fact, it had. Max felt very sorry for her. She was such a nice woman, and had talked about her husband so much, and how much she loved him. He knew it must be an awful blow for her. And a fatal blow to her marriage, too.

"I believe that he loves you, Tanya," Max said thoughtfully, stroking his beard. He always did that when he was thinking. "I mean, what guy wouldn't? He'd have to be deaf, dumb, and blind not to. And I also believe that he's confused. And probably loves you both, which is really pathetic of him, but it does happen. Men get mixed up a lot that way. That's why they have mistresses and wives."

"Then what do they do?" she asked, feeling like a child as she listened to him.

"Depends on the guy. Some marry the mistress, some stay with the wife. He could be right about one thing, you know. You could outgrow him down here. I didn't think that would happen, and I figured you'd go scurrying back. But you never know, maybe you'll do another picture. Or maybe you'll dump his sorry ass if he dicks you around." She smiled at what Max said.

"I'd still go home. I have no reason to stay here."

"You could have a hell of a career in movies, if you wanted to. You did a great job with this screenplay. You're going to get a lot of offers after this picture is released. You'll have your pick if you want."

"I don't. I like the life I had."

"Then fight for it. Keep a leash on him. Go home. Kick his ass. Don't put up with any shit. And make him pay for what he just did. That's what my wives did to me when I got out of line."

"And what did you do?" Tanya asked with interest.

"I divorced them as fast as I could. But my mistresses were always younger and cuter and a lot more fun." They both laughed at his response. "In your case, if this guy has any brains, he'll hang on to you. If that's what you want, I hope he does. Has he ever done this before?" She shook her head. She did believe that. "Good. Then he's a virgin. He may never do it again. It could have been a one-time mistake. A slip. Just keep an eye on this woman, and don't believe a word either of them says. Trust your instincts, you'll never go wrong."

"That's how I figured it out. I knew it the minute I saw them."

"Good girl. Hang in. It may turn out okay. I'm sorry you had such a rough time." She shrugged.

"Yeah. Me too. Thank you for listening." As she said it, the dog barked and they both laughed again.

"He agrees with everything I say. He's a very smart dog."

"And you're a very smart man, and a good friend," she said as she leaned over and kissed his cheek, and Douglas walked by again.

"What are you two getting so cozy about?" He looked intrigued.

"She just proposed to me," Max explained. "I told her she'd have to buy me. Six cows and a herd of goats, and a new Bentley. We were just concluding the negotiations. She's giving me a tough time about the goats. The Bentley was easy." Douglas grinned, and Tanya laughed. She felt better after talking to Max.

"It looked pretty good to me this morning. What do you think?" Douglas asked him, and Max said he was pleased. The romance between Jean and Ned was working well for them. It had improved her performance immeasurably. It was a common thing. A lot of actors and actresses got involved during the shooting of a film. Kind of like shipboard romance. And when they docked, it was over. A few stuck, but most didn't. The cast was betting that this one wouldn't. Jean had a reputation for changing men like her shoes. And she had a lot of shoes. So did Ned. They were cut from the same cloth.

Douglas turned to Tanya then. "Do you want to grab something to eat tonight after we finish shooting? I want to talk to you about some changes in the script." Tanya was tired, but she didn't think she should turn him down. Meetings with Douglas were command performances, even if they came in the guise of dinner.

"Sure, if I can look like this." She didn't have the energy to go back to the hotel and change.

"You look fine," he said, seeming not to notice. "We can go out for sushi or Chinese. I won't take long. I know you've been sick." He had no reason to doubt it, she was very pale and had lost a lot of weight. She had no intention of telling him the truth.

They finished around eight o'clock that night. Douglas drove her to his favorite sushi bar, and she had her limo follow. He said he was going out afterward. Tanya was exhausted by the time they sat down to eat.

The changes he wanted to talk to her about were minimal. She was surprised he had wanted to do it over dinner. He said he wanted to catch up.

"So how was Christmas? Great with your kids?" he asked as they divided up the sushi and put it on their plates. He liked all the same ones she did.

"Yes, great," she said, trying to convince herself, and forget what the vacation had really been like. "It was actually nice to come back to work today." He watched her eyes as she said it, and saw something there.

"Why is it that I get the feeling there's trouble on the home front and you're lying to me? Tell me to mind my own business, if I'm too far off base." She didn't want to confide in him, but she didn't have the energy to lie either. Maybe it didn't make any difference anymore.

"I'm not lying. I just don't want to talk about it," she admitted to him. "To be honest, the holidays sucked."

"That's too bad," he said softly. "I was hoping I was wrong." She wasn't sure if she believed him. He was such an advocate of her buying into the whole L.A. scene. But when he saw the devastation in her eyes, he felt sorry for her. "Serious stuff?"

"Maybe. Time will tell," she said cryptically, and he nodded.

"I'm sorry, Tanya. I know how much your home life means to you. I assume it was a problem with your husband, not the kids."

"Yes, it was. First time. It was kind of a shock."

"It always is. No matter who you are. Trust issues. Relationships aren't easy, whether you're married or not." He smiled at her over the last of their dinner. "That's why I avoid them at all costs. It's easier being a free agent, and keeping things light." There was nothing light about her life, or her marriage, or the way she felt about Peter, and Douglas knew that. "I know that's not your style."

"No, it's not," she said with a sad smile. "I think coming down here put us to the test. It's a lot to ask to be gone for nine months, and only home for occasional weekends. It's been hard on Peter, and my girls. It's a shame it didn't happen next year. But it still would have been hard on him."

"Maybe it will strengthen the marriage," Douglas said as he paid the check. He didn't look as though he believed what he was saying, or even that he cared. Tanya was a foreign breed to him. He was fascinated by her, but he didn't really understand the value of the life she led, or why she wanted it so much. It sounded fatally boring and mundane to him. "Or maybe you'll find that you've outgrown each other," he said carefully, "or that you've outgrown him."

"I don't think that's the case," Tanya said quietly. "I think this is just hard." Harder yet now that Peter had added Alice to the mix. "We'll deal with it," she said, and wished she was convinced. She was quiet as they left the restaurant, and stood on the sidewalk for a minute, discussing the script again, and then Douglas looked down at her gently.

"I'm sorry you're going through a hard time, Tanya." This time he looked as though he meant it. He could see how upset she was, and he felt sorry for her. She was a nice person, and she looked genuinely pained. "It happens to us all. If I can do anything for you, let me know."

"I'd like to really try to get home for weekends for a while, without letting down anyone here."

"I'll do what I can," he said, and then got into his car as she got into her limo. He roared off in the Ferrari, and she went back to the hotel. She felt lonely when she walked into her bungalow. She missed Peter, and called him on his cell. He picked it up right away, as though he were waiting for her call.

"Oh . . . hi . . . ," he said, as though he was surprised that it was her, and her heart sank.

"Who did you think it was?" She was instantly suspicious now.

"I don't know . . . you, I guess. I was just talking to the girls." She wondered if he had been expecting a call from Alice, or even someone else. She hated how she felt about him now. She distrusted his every word. "How was your day?"

"Long. We were on the set till eight. I just talked to Douglas about the script over sushi. They keep wanting more changes." She was going to stay home in the morning to do the work he wanted. The next three months until they finished the film looked like an endless stretch of road ahead of her. And two months of postproduction made it seem like an eternity until she could be home full-time again. She had no idea if their marriage would hold up to the strain. She was beginning to doubt it. She felt sick when she thought of the months ahead, and what Peter and Alice had done. She had never expected this to happen. She had thought they were solidly married forever, and now everything was up in the air. Even though Peter had agreed to end the affair with Alice, Tanya was terrified the damage he had done was too great. "How was your day?" She tried to sound normal when she talked to him, but nothing felt right anymore. They felt awkward with each other, and her voice was filled with pain.

"Long, too, but it was okay." And then his voice softened. "I miss

you, even though everything's a mess right now. I'm sorry, Tan. I'm
sorry I fucked it all up." He sounded near tears as he said it. He had
gone back to their room and was sitting on the bed talking to her. He
was lonely, and she was, too.

"Hopefully, we'll fix it." Her voice was gentle. "I miss you too. I
love you." And then she had an idea. "Do you want to come down
one night this week, for the night?" They needed something like that.
A little romance in their lives, to strengthen the bond again.

"I don't think I can," he said, sounding depressed. "I have meetings
all week, and I don't want to leave the girls." And now Alice wasn't
next door to keep an eye on them, or help them if they had a
problem.

"They could stay with friends," Tanya suggested.

"I'll see. Maybe next week. This week is a killer."

"It was just a thought."

"It was a nice thought."

"I'll try to get home this weekend. I promise. I said something
about it to Douglas, that I really need to get home. I hope they don't
schedule any meetings on Saturday. Even if they do, I'll come home
right after." She thought it was important to be home for the moment, to try and shore up the damage that had been done.

As it turned out, there were no weekend meetings that week. She
didn't know if Douglas had done that for her, or they didn't need
them. But she got out promptly on Friday afternoon, and was in Ross
by dinnertime. Peter looked pleased to see her, and the girls were delighted to see their mom, and then went out with friends. She and
Peter went to a little Italian restaurant they liked in Marin for a late
dinner, and things felt almost normal when they came home. The
week had done them good. The dust was starting to settle. They
didn't make love that night, but for the first time in weeks they cud-

dled, and then finally the next morning they made love for the first time since his affair with Alice. It was sad but sweet, and there was a gentle, bittersweet quality to it, as though they were both reaching out and trying to find each other again. She had to force herself not to think that he had done the same things with Alice. She didn't let herself think about it, as she lay in his arms afterward and closed her eyes. He was afraid to ask her what she was thinking. He just wanted things to be all right between them again. He hoped they would be. All he could do was try to repair the damage he had done.

Tanya opened her eyes and looked at him. There was a small, sad smile on her lips. "I love you, Peter."

"Me too," he said, and kissed her gently on the mouth. "I love you, Tan . . . I'm so sorry." She nodded, trying not to think that his *I love you* sounded like *goodbye*.

# Chapter 13

Tanya made it home for three weekends in a row in January, and things started to feel normal with Peter again. She knew he was trying to make amends, and she was relieved to see week after week that Alice hadn't come back. It helped. She never wanted to see her again, which was of course impossible, since she lived next door. But the longer she stayed away, to break the spell, the better chance Tanya and Peter had to regain their marriage.

The fourth weekend she couldn't come home, but Peter said it was fine. He was preparing for a trial, the girls had plans, and the weather had been terrible all week. More than likely her flight would have gotten canceled or delayed. There had been storms up and down the state, and he said Tanya was better off in L.A. She had a lot of work to do, too. More script changes, and they were doing location shots for the next few weeks that were going to be difficult. They were estimating that the picture would end in six or seven weeks. She could hardly wait. She would be home then for two weeks, and then back to work on postproduction with the editors and Max. She had been in L.A. for five months by then, with roughly four more to

go, maybe less. She felt as though she had given blood for this picture. Or maybe worse, her marriage. But things were slowly improv-
ing with Peter. Their three weekends together had helped them a lot,
and Tanya was grateful she'd been able to get home.

At the end of the following week, she got a nasty case of flu, or
food poisoning, and couldn't get home either. It was another week
before she got home, which coincidentally was Valentine's Day. She
had bought Peter a red tie with hearts on it, and a box of his favorite
candy, and cute nightgowns for the girls and some T-shirts from Fred
Segal's. She was carrying all of it in a shopping bag, when she got
out of the cab in front of their house. She had wanted to surprise
Peter, so she hadn't called him, and as she got out of the cab, she saw
him coming out of Alice's house, and he had his arm around her
waist. They were laughing when he looked up and saw Tanya staring
at them. Tanya stood still for a moment, and then with her head
down, she hurried into the house. She was standing in the kitchen,
shaking, when Peter found her. He looked frightened.

"I see Alice is back," Tanya said as she looked at him. She made no
accusations, but they had looked totally at ease with each other, and
she had noticed that Alice had a new hairdo. "When did she come
home?"

"About ten days ago," he said, sounding solemn. He knew what
Tanya thought. It hadn't happened yet, but they had spent some time
together and talked about what had happened two months before.
They were both still trying to understand it, and figure out what it
meant, if it had been an accident or something more important for
either of them.

"Alice looks good," Tanya said in a flat voice, wanting to ask if he
had already slept with her, but she didn't dare. He could hear the
question without her voicing it. It was obvious what she thought.

"Nothing's happened, Tan. She's sick," he said with a serious expression. "She had a check-up when she got back, and they found a lump in her breast. She had a lumpectomy last week, and they're starting radiation in a few weeks." He sounded worried, and Tanya looked into his eyes.

"I'm sorry to hear it. Does that change things for us again?" she wanted to know. She didn't want to ride this seesaw with him. Once was enough. He shook his head.

"I just feel sorry for her," he said honestly. Tanya knew that was dangerous for them, but there was nothing she could do to stop it. Whatever he felt for Alice was between them, and if Tanya lost him to her now, she knew it was inevitable. Maybe it had nothing to do with her being in L.A. She couldn't tie him up forever. If he wanted out, he would find the way. Tanya felt defeated as she looked at him across the kitchen. She suddenly felt as though she had lost again. "I'm not going to do anything stupid, Tan," he said gently. She nodded with tears in her eyes, picked up her things, and went upstairs. But in a flash, with Alice's return, everything had changed. She could feel it, or maybe all she felt was fear, both her own and Peter's.

He took her to dinner the following night for Valentine's Day, and she gave him his present. He wore the tie to dinner, and he gave her a cashmere sweater. She loved it, but she was anxious all weekend. Knowing Alice was next door again was like having the devil come to visit. Tanya wasn't sure how to win. If that was what Peter wanted, she knew there was no way to stop him, or to change the course of fate. The girls were happy Alice was back, although they could sense that something had happened between their friend and their mother. Neither woman talked about it, both avoided the subject, and both refused to look them in the eye whenever they asked questions. Alice just said they needed a break. And Tanya said nothing. But it was obvious that Tanya didn't even want to hear her name.

When Peter took Tanya to the airport on Sunday night, she was quiet and looked strained. He finally brought the subject up himself. "I'm not going to let anything happen, Tan. Alice and I talked about it. She knows I don't want to do anything to jeopardize our marriage. Why don't you trust that, and go back to L.A. in peace?"

"Why is it that the only thing that comes to mind is 'the road to hell is paved with good intentions'?" she said with a small, wry smile, and Peter laughed. It was certainly apt.

"Trust me." She had trusted both of them before, and was well aware of what had happened. It was hard to trust them in such close proximity again. It was asking an awful lot of her. "You can put a tracking device on me, if you like. Or an alarm." He was trying to lighten the moment, and Tanya smiled ruefully at him.

"What about a chip in your teeth?"

"Anything you want. I told her I'd take her to radiation treatments if she needs me to, when she starts them in a few weeks. But I'm not going to do anything more than that, I promise." Tanya's heart sank at what he had just said.

"Why can't she get someone else to take her? She has lots of friends." Alice was a gregarious woman whom everyone liked, and people had always been drawn to her, like a magnet.

"If she can manage without me, she will. She said everyone is busy."

"So are you," Tanya pointed out. "She's going to get her hooks in you again," Tanya said with a look of anguish and despair. There seemed to be no way to keep them away from each other, and Alice needing help from him was exactly the kind of thing Tanya was afraid of and wanted to avoid. It was a perfect way to start their affair again. Sympathy, compassion, concern, pity. Tanya knew just how Peter worked, and so did their friend.

"Don't worry, Tan. It'll be fine," he said, looking confident, as they drove into the airport, and a moment later they were at the curb.

Tanya looked at him with worried eyes, and felt a wave of terror engulf her. "I'm scared," she said softly to him.

"Don't be. She's exactly what she used to be. A friend. The rest was a mistake." Tanya nodded, and kissed him goodbye. A moment later she was on the sidewalk carrying her bag, and turned to wave. He waved back, smiled, and drove away. And as Tanya walked into the airport, she felt panic eat at her again. She thought about it all the way to L.A. on the plane and when she got back to the hotel. She had no idea what to do to protect Peter from Alice and finally realized she couldn't. It was up to him.

She called him on his cell phone shortly after, and it went to voice mail. By the time he called her back at eleven o'clock that night, she was so anxious she was feeling sick. She didn't want to ask him where he'd been, but she could guess.

"How was your evening?" she said instead. She had left a stupid message on his cell, and he knew what she was asking him.

"I went to a movie with the girls. We just got back." She felt an instant wave of relief, followed by a second wave of fear. "Did Alice go with you?" She hated herself for asking, but had to know. She hated knowing she was back. It was a nightmare having her so close.

"No, she didn't. We didn't ask her."

"I'm sorry, Peter." She felt like someone she'd never been before, someone she didn't want to be. But she had no choice. Fear was in control.

"It's okay. I understand. How was your flight?"

"Fine. I miss you." They were almost back where they had been before his brief affair with Alice. Her being back now stirred the pot again, and ugly things were coming up. Mostly panic and resentment, and the anger Tanya felt at having been betrayed by both of them. It still seemed fresh.

"I miss you, too. Get some sleep. I'll call you tomorrow." She lay in bed for hours that night, wondering if he had sneaked next door, or if Alice was in her bed. It was becoming an obsession, and she hated herself for it. She knew he didn't like it either. Who would? But it was his own fault. Peter and Alice had created a mess that now all three of them had to live with. And Tanya was the innocent bystander in it all. She hated her role of unwitting victim, betrayed wife.

The picture heated up for the next month. They were nearing the end, and in the final frenzy of trying to get all the shots right, there was no way for Tanya to get home. They were in production meetings day and night, and she rewrote the script a thousand times. Even Max looked exhausted. It was the third week of March when Max held up a hand and said "Cut!" for the last time, and then the magic words, "It's a wrap, folks." A cheer went up on the soundstage they were working on, and everyone danced around. Champagne was poured, and people hugged and kissed. Jean and Ned were still an item, but there were bets on the set that they wouldn't be for long. He was going to his next movie in May, and would be shooting in South Africa for six months. Douglas was working on another project, and so was Max. And Tanya wanted to go home. She hadn't seen Peter for two weeks, and he hadn't been able to come down.

She had two weeks off, which coincided perfectly with the girls' spring vacation. And then Tanya had to come back for six to eight weeks of postproduction. She would be all through in late May or early June, just in time for the girls to graduate. She had missed the entire year with them. The only consolation was that she'd be home when the girls got their college acceptances. At least there was that.

"Are you going to miss us, Tanny?" Max asked, sipping champagne, as he held a second glass for the dog. Douglas was shaking hands with everyone. There was an atmosphere of New Year's celebration all around them. The cruise was over for the cast. Only the editors and production people would be around for the next two months, working closely with Max, while he and Douglas meticulously looked over the final results. There would be some dubbing, looping, some voices they'd have to add, a lot of scenes they'd cut. The art of movie making was about to be exercised in minute detail, but first Tanya was going home.

By the time she got back to the bungalow to pack, it was too late to catch a flight, so she went home in the morning. She could hardly wait for two weeks at home with Peter and the girls. It was the longest span of time she'd been home since Christmas, which had been disastrous. And she'd worked like a dog ever since. She felt as though she'd been through the wars. She dreaded going back to L.A. for the last two months. She felt as though she had really earned her keep. All she wanted was to go home to Peter and the girls.

The house looked fine when she walked into the kitchen. It looked better than fine, it looked like home. She smiled broadly to herself, and loved being there when the girls got home. Even Megan seemed happy to see her there. She bought groceries, and cooked their favorite dinner. She had the table set and candles lit that night when Peter got home. It was hard to believe she hadn't seen him in more than a month. He smiled as he came through the door and saw what she'd done.

"It looks beautiful, Tan. That was nice of you." He put an arm around her and hugged her, and when they went upstairs that night, she was hoping they'd make love. Peter was exhausted, and was sound asleep before she could take off her clothes. She was disappointed but there was no rush. She had two whole weeks ahead of her at home.

He was up when she woke up on Saturday, and already downstairs in the kitchen. He had made breakfast for her, the girls had gone out, and after she cleared the table, he suggested they take a walk. It was a beautiful, warm spring day. They drove to the base of Mount Tam and started walking. The way he looked at her made her uneasy, and she suddenly felt panic ripple through her again. They walked for the first ten minutes in silence, and when he saw a bench, he suggested they sit down. He looked as though he had something to say to her, and before he said a word, Tanya knew what it was. She wanted to run away and hide. But she couldn't. She had to at least pretend to be grown up. She was scared, and felt about five years old.

"Why is it that I have the feeling I'm not going to like what you're about to say?" Tanya said with a knot in her stomach. Peter looked down at his feet as he leaned over and played with some pebbles on the ground, and when he sat up again, she saw that he looked pained.

"I don't know what to say to you. I think you know anyway. I never thought this would happen. I still don't know how it did or why. But it did, Tan." He was trying to make it fast and as painless as he could, but as he started, he realized that there was no way. It was going to be awful, whatever he did or said. "Alice and I got back together when she was sick, while she had radiation. I know it sounds crazy, but I think I want to marry her. I love you, it's not even about your

being in L.A., or your not coming home for the past month. I think
this would have happened anyway. I have the feeling it was meant to
be." She felt as though he had hit her with an ax. Her guts felt sliced
in two. Her head was spinning, and her heart was somewhere in her
shoes. She stared at him in disbelief.

"That simple? It's over? I haven't seen you in five weeks, and you
decide that you and Alice were meant to be? How the hell did you
come to that conclusion?" She was almost as angry as she was hurt.

"I realized how much I love her when she was sick. She needs me,
Tan. I'm not sure you do. You're a strong woman. She isn't, and she's
been through a lot of shit. She needs someone to take care of her."

"Oh God . . ." Tanya leaned back against the bench, and closed her
eyes. She couldn't even cry this time. Her body and mind hurt too
much to even produce tears. She felt as though she were in shock.
With all her suspicions, she had worried that he was sleeping with
her, not that he was going to marry her, or decide it was "meant to
be." Tanya couldn't get her mind around the concept yet and wondered if she ever would. "I wrote a segment of a soap like this once.
The producer thought it was too cheesy, so he made me cut the
scene. Little did I know I'd be living it one day. Life imitating art, or
some shit like that." She stared at him in disbelief. "What's all that
crap about my being so strong, and Alice needing you? Alice is a lot
tougher than I. I think she set you up, Peter. She decided she wanted
you, and she set out to get you the minute my back was turned. I
think she's a lot stronger than you think." He was so goddamned
naïve, and they were both such shits. It was all Tanya could think.
The fact that her life, such as she had known it for twenty years, was
about to go out the window seemed much less important now than
the fact that she had been totally betrayed by two people she loved,
especially Peter. She felt set up, lied to, and betrayed by both of

them. For the second time in three months. Maybe that was what he meant by "meant to be." She felt "meant to be" screwed over by both of them. They had done a hell of a good job.

"So that's it?" Tanya asked as tears finally sprang to her eyes. They were long overdue. "It's over. You want out. You're going to marry her? What are you planning to tell our kids? That you're just moving next door, a simple change of address? How convenient for you." She sounded bitter, and she had reason to be.

"She loves our kids," he said, hating the way Tanya looked. He had watched the blood drain out of her face. He had been waiting to tell her for two weeks. Once he and Alice got back together, they were sure, especially while he took her to her radiation treatments every day. He hadn't said anything about it to Tanya on the phone. He knew what she had thought. And she had been right once again.

"Yes, she does love our kids," Tanya agreed, wiping her eyes on the corner of her shirt. She didn't care how she looked. It didn't matter anymore. "And apparently you love her, and she loves you. How sweet. And what about me? What am I supposed to do? What does the spurned woman do in these instances, Peter? Step aside graciously and wish you the best? Do we go on being neighbors, and share the kids like one big happy family? What do you want from me?"

"Alice is going to sell her house, and we're going to move to Mill Valley. But it may take a while. I don't think I should move in next door. It might be confusing for the kids."

"Nice of you to figure that out, not to mention confusing for me. When were you planning to tell the kids?" She thought of something then. Her head was spinning and her mind was going in a thousand directions at once, trying to make sense of what he'd said. "I think we should wait to tell them until after graduation in June. It's less than three months away. I'll be back at the end of May, after we finish postproduction, which means we'll only have to live together for a couple of weeks." He had already figured out the same timing as she. "I also have no idea what we're going to do for the next two weeks. You can't move in with Alice, and I don't want to share a room with you." She was looking at him like a stranger. She had come home looking forward to two weeks with him, and he had given her this news. It was shocking beyond belief.

"I can stay in Jason's room, if you want," he said quietly.

"How will you explain that to the girls?" She had a point. He wasn't quite sure how to do that. "Maybe we'll just have to suck it up and sleep in the same room." She wasn't looking forward to it, knowing what she did now. He belonged to another woman. Twenty years of her life were over. She had been canceled, like a TV show with bad ratings. Off the air forever. She tried not to think about the fact that she still loved him. If she did, she might have lain on the ground at the foot of Mount Tam and started to wail. She suddenly wondered if she'd have a nervous breakdown. But it was a luxury she couldn't afford. She'd just have to be grown-up about it, even if it killed her. For a moment, she thought it might. He might as well have shot her. She played his words over in her mind again, but they sounded just as crazy in her head as they had coming out of his mouth. He was leaving her and wanted to marry Alice. Maybe they were all crazy. It made no sense to Tanya. It never had. Everything that was happening seemed insane.

"I'll sleep on the floor," Peter said quietly, reviewing their sleeping arrangements, which were the least of their problems. She nodded. It seemed suitable punishment for him.

"And we'll tell them after graduation," Tanya said, and he nodded in confirmation. "Well, that's simple then. Anything else we need to discuss? Do I have to sell the house?" There was an edge of despair in her voice, and a load of bricks on her heart.

"Not if you don't want to," he said grimly. She looked normal but was sounding crazy, or maybe the reverse. She was trying to mentally walk through all the details so she knew what she was facing. It was a way of staying busy so she didn't fall apart.

"I don't need alimony. I think you should pay for college. I guess that sums it up then. When's the wedding?"

"Tan, don't be like this. I know it's a shock. I don't want to drag this out. We could have waited to be sure it's the right thing, but I didn't want to mislead you. Alice and I need time to figure this out and make sure it works. But I'd rather do that living with her than living with you and pretending, or lying to you any more than we already have."

"Of course. No, lying isn't a good thing," she said, as tears rolled down her cheeks. "I definitely think you should move in with Alice. But actually, I don't want to go to the wedding." In spite of herself, she was sobbing. He tried to put an arm around her to comfort her, but she pulled away from him and stood up. She wanted to preserve what dignity she had left. It was horrifying to realize they'd have to pretend to be married for the next two weeks during the girls' spring vacation. They were no longer married, as far as Tanya was concerned. He now belonged to Alice, and had for several months.

They drove back to the house in silence, with Tanya wiping the tears off her cheeks, and staring out the window. She kept saying the words in her head again and again. Peter was leaving her. He was going to live with Alice . . . with Alice . . . not with her anymore. She was going to live alone now with her children, except that they would be gone, too. She was going to be totally alone in September. No Peter, no children. All she had wanted all winter was to come home, and now there was no one to come home to. In this case, the story had a very bad ending. She would never have written it this way, but Peter and Alice had. In essence Peter had fired her. And all Tanya could think of as they drove back to the house and she got out of the car was that she wanted to die.

# Chapter 14

The two weeks Tanya spent in Marin were agony from start to finish. She tried to put up a good front for the girls, and Peter was extremely civilized and humiliatingly sympathetic. In the five weeks she hadn't seen him, his entire life had turned around, and he now belonged to Alice. Tanya felt as though she was dazed all the time. She kept trying to figure it out, and how it had happened. She blamed herself for going to L.A. and working on the movie. And when she didn't blame herself, she blamed Peter. And of course Alice. She was relieved when she finally left for L.A., to start postproduction. She had lost more weight and had a hard look to her, which was really fear. She was hanging on by a thread by the time she got to the office to work with Max and Douglas. It was a relief to have something to do other than try to guess what her life would be like after Peter left her. For the two weeks in Marin, she kept asking him painful questions, like how much of their furniture he was taking. With the girls turning eighteen in June, the custody issues would be simple. They didn't even need visitation schedules. The kids could visit whomever they wanted. It was all so agonizingly simple. She

still looked shell-shocked as she worked with Douglas and Max the
next day. Max had noticed immediately that she looked terrible, and
asked her about it at the end of the day, as she stuffed papers back
into her briefcase. She had been distracted all day.

"Do I want to know how your break went?" he asked gently. He
had already guessed. She looked about the same as she had after
Christmas, only slightly worse. He could guess the outcome.

"No, you don't." And then she decided to tell him. "He's moving in
with the other woman, after the girls graduate in June. He thinks
they're getting married. Apparently, it was 'meant to be.' My very
own real-life soap. How cheesy does it get? You have to ask yourself
that question."

"Life is cheesy," Max said sympathetically. He noticed that she
seemed angrier than she had in December. And underneath the
anger, heartbroken. He could see it. "It's amazing how tacky life is
sometimes, even among allegedly civilized people. I guess we all behave like shows about people in trailer parks sometimes, whether we
want to or not. It's why those agony shows work so well on TV."

"I guess so," she said, smiling wistfully at him. "I'll be okay. It just
takes some adjustment." He knew her kids were going to college at
the end of the summer. She would be alone, which he suspected
wouldn't be easy for her. Her family had been all she talked about all
year. And now her husband was leaving. She was about to lose
everyone she loved, in one way or another. And the husband, fool
that he was, in Max's opinion, was going off with her best friend.
Max couldn't help agreeing with her. It was tacky. And sad for her. He
felt genuinely sorry for her.

"Sometimes the worst shit that happens to us turns out to be a
blessing. We just don't see it at the time. One day you may look back
and feel that way. On the other hand, one day you may look back and

decide that this time in your life was truly fucked." She smiled in spite of herself at what he said.

"I think that might be the case. I'm not enjoying this much."

"At least we know you're sane. I think the only decent advice I have for you is that your salvation will be work. Mine has always been. When the love of my life died of breast cancer, the only thing that saved my ass and kept me sane was work. It's the only way to go." Tanya nodded. She hadn't thought of that. She'd been thinking about their summer plans and what it would be like to go to Tahoe without Peter, after they told the girls the news, of course. And she had thought about taking them to college. They had gotten their college acceptances while she was home on vacation. The excitement of it had been totally obscured for her by her broken heart. At least the girls had been thrilled. Both girls had gotten into their first-choice schools. Megan was going to UCSB with her brother, and Molly was going to film school at USC. But Tanya had absolutely no idea what she would do after they left. She had thought she would finally have the chance to spend more time with Peter, but he would be doing that with Alice now. Tanya felt like a marble in a shoebox, rolling around aimlessly, with no anchor to keep her in place. All her anchors were about to leave. It was a terrifying thought. Max was right. The only thing she had left was work, and holidays with her kids.

She went home every weekend during postproduction. Their schedule was far more civilized now. She did her best to avoid Peter, who was spending a lot of time next door with Alice. And the girls asked her no questions. It was as though there were a minefield all around them and they knew it, and were being careful not to set anything off. She wondered what they thought. They would all know soon enough. She was dreading telling them and Jason in June. In the meantime she kept to herself, spent time with the girls on the weekends, and started writing extremely depressing short stories at night, an unusual number of them about death. In a sense, their marriage had died, and the only way she knew to mourn it was to write about it. Peter saw one of them on her computer one afternoon, read it, and cringed. She was in a very bleak state of mind.

Douglas met with her in the last week of postproduction in May and made an interesting suggestion. They had had easy dinners several times, to discuss work. He had invited her to his pool again, but she was gone every weekend save one, and that weekend she didn't accept either. She was too depressed. He was planning to produce another movie, with a different director this time, a well-known woman, who had also won many Oscars. It was an extremely depressing story about a woman who committed suicide, and he wanted Tanya to do the script. It suited her mood at the moment, but she had no desire to come back to L.A. In her heart of hearts, she thought her marriage had ended as a result of her working there on the film. It had left a bad taste in her mouth. All she wanted now was to go back to Marin. She told Douglas that over dinner, and he laughed.

"Oh, not that again, Tanya. For God's sake, you don't belong there. Go write short stories there for a while, and come back. Your days in Marin are over, or should be. You wrote a hell of a screenplay on this one, it might even win you an Oscar. And if it doesn't, the next one will. You can't escape your fate. Your husband will get over it. He made it through this year," he said confidently. "He'll make it through the next."

"Actually, he didn't," Tanya said quietly. "We're getting divorced." For once, Douglas looked stunned.

"You? The perfect wife? I can't believe it. When did that happen? You said you were having some problems after Christmas. I just assumed everything worked out. I have to admit I'm shocked."

"Me too." Tanya said, looking devastated. "He told me in March. He's moving in with my best friend."

"How trite. See what I mean?" Douglas didn't miss a beat. "You don't belong there. People in Marin show no imagination. I want to start shooting this picture in October. Give it some thought. I'll call your agent and make a proposal." Douglas was even nicer than usual to her after that and called her agent. Walt called her the next day, stunned over the money. They had offered her even more than before. Douglas wanted her on the picture, no matter what. But she was adamant. She had done L.A. and had no desire to come back. She didn't mind the work, but the fallout had broken her heart. She wanted to go home now and lick her wounds.

"You have to do this, Tan," her agent said. "You can't turn down a deal like that."

"Yes, I can. I'm going home." The trouble was, she had no real home to go to now. She had a house, but there would be no one in it. When she went back to Marin the following weekend, she thought about it and realized how agonizing the house would be without her children. Once the girls left for college in late August, with Peter gone, she'd be totally alone. For the first time in her life. She called Walt on Monday and told him to accept Douglas's deal. She had nothing else to do. She signed the deal the following week. And when she told him, Peter was smug about it.

"I told you you'd go back." But it didn't make him right. She would never have gone back if he weren't leaving her for Alice. In a sense, he had driven her back to L.A. She talked to Max about it, and he congratulated her for the right decision, and she knew he was right. However much she hated Hollywood, once Peter and the girls were gone, she knew that work would save her life.

The rest of the summer was one nightmare after another. She finished postproduction in the last week of May and went home to Marin. The girls graduated a week later, with all the usual pomp and ceremony and tenderness. Peter had the good taste not to bring Alice to the graduation. And the next day they told the children they were getting divorced. Everyone cried, including Peter and Tanya. Megan said she was happy about Alice, though sorry for her mother. She actually put her arms around her and gave her a hug. Molly was crushed about the divorce, and Jason looked shocked, although he was close to James, Alice's son, and was happy about that. The kids were all upset about it, though not as much as Tanya would have thought. They all loved Alice, and although they were sorry for their mother, in some ways it made sense to them. They secretly thought Peter and Alice were a better match, although they didn't say that to their mother.

She told them she was making another movie in October, and none of them was surprised about that either. They asked about Tahoe, and she said she'd go with them. Peter and Alice were going to Maine that week, to visit relatives of hers. It was all very civilized and well organized, and the children had the option to visit whichever house they wanted, Tanya's or the one where their father would live with Alice. It was going to be an easier transition for them than it might have been if he had married someone else. And the day after they told them, Peter moved out, to the house Alice had bought in Mill Valley. She had already been there for a month. Hers next door was in escrow, and he said it had sold to a family they'd like, with kids the same age. All was right in their world, almost. It was a time of transition. Only Tanya looked as though her life had disintegrated and caved in. She could hardly wait to get back to work to keep her mind off everything else. She hated every aspect of her life now, except her children. She knew she wasn't much fun for them, she was too depressed. But she finally seemed more like her old self again when they went to Tahoe. In spite of everything that had happened that spring, when they got there, they all had fun. Even Tanya, who was already working on the new script at night. It was a depressing story, but she loved it, and it suited her black mood at the moment. Douglas called her about it from time to time. She faxed him pages, and he loved the direction she was going. He thought this one would win her an Oscar for sure, if not the last one. This one was called *Gone*.

Peter and Alice both came when they dropped Jason and Megan off in Santa Barbara in late August. Tanya went in her own car. It was the first time she had seen Alice in months, and it was painful, but she got through it. They never spoke to each other. Peter looked far more uncomfortable than Tanya felt.

They took Molly to USC the week after. Tanya loved the idea that Molly would be in L.A., since Tanya was going to be living in Bungalow 2 at the Beverly Hills Hotel again. She moved in the day she dropped Molly off at her dorm. Molly came over to have dinner with her at the bungalow that night. They ordered room service and giggled like two kids. The bungalow felt like home to Tanya now. Tanya was surprised she had survived the last five months, they had been the hardest of her life, since Peter told her he was leaving her. And yet as impossible to believe as it had seemed at the time, she had survived it. And now she could get lost in another movie. Work was the lifeline she clung to. It was the salvation Max had talked about. He was right.

She saw Douglas at his office the next day, to talk about the film. She met the female director he had raved about. Tanya liked her, too. They were exactly the same age and discovered they had a lot in common. They had gone to UC Berkeley at the same time, although they had never met. Tanya was going to enjoy working with her. She felt like a pro now, after the previous year of her innocence. This was going to be a hard picture to shoot, but a lot of fun to write.

After the meeting, Douglas invited them both to lunch at Spago, and he drove Tanya back to the hotel afteward and asked her what she thought.

"I think she's a very interesting woman," Tanya said honestly. "She's incredibly bright." She wondered if Douglas had the hots for her, she was very attractive, but she didn't want to ask. It was none of her business, and he was discreet about the women he went out with. She knew he liked important women, who looked good on his arm. Trophies of sorts, though not the usual kind. He liked women with bright minds. Adele Michaels certainly fit that bill. They talked about her all the way back to the hotel.

"I'm glad you like her," Douglas said comfortably. "How was your summer, by the way? I never asked."

"Interesting," she said honestly. She was more at ease with him than she'd been the year before. Everything had been new then, and she had felt intimidated by him. He was impressive certainly, but he didn't scare her anymore. They were almost like old friends. "Peter moved out. And in with his new girlfriend. The girls left for college. My nest is empty finally. Everybody flew the coop, including Peter and me." She smiled ruefully, thinking of how times had changed in the last year. Now she was back here again. And Bungalow 2 was her home, for the making of another film. "I guess you were right. My days in Marin are over, for now anyway." And possibly for good.

"That's a good thing," he said confidently. "I could never see you there." It had been perfect for her for twenty years, and for her family. Now she had to find her way and make a new life for herself. She was still adjusting to the concept. It still seemed shocking to her at times. "How about a day at the pool again this Sunday? Same rules apply. Conversation not required. We can both relax." She knew life would get crazy on the new picture soon, and it sounded appealing. She had enjoyed it before, particularly when he played the piano. She hoped he would again.

"I'll try not to snore this time," she laughed. "Thanks for the invitation."

"Eleven o'clock Sunday. And sushi one of these nights. Maybe next week, before the insanity begins." They had preproduction meetings coming up. Tanya was looking forward to them now that she had met Adele. It was going to be fun working with her.

She waved as Douglas drove away in his new Bentley, and then she went back to the bungalow. She worked on the script all afternoon, inspired by their meeting, and sat at her computer late into the night. She tried not to think of Peter when she finished work. It was odd being back in the bungalow, and no longer his wife. They had filed the divorce in June, it would be final in December. Twenty years gone, except for the kids, and a house she no longer wanted to go home to. He belonged to Alice now. And the bungalow at the Beverly Hills Hotel felt more like home. It was strange how life changed. And sad.

Tanya saw Molly on Saturday afternoon and took her out to dinner. Afterward she took her back to her dorm. They had had a nice time, and talked to Megan and Jason on Tanya's cell phone. It was nice knowing they were all close by, particularly Molly, whom she felt so close to. They had talked about the divorce over dinner. Molly admitted that she was still shocked about her father moving in with Alice and leaving her mother. It was hard to explain or understand. Molly told her mother she had to move on, no matter how hard it was. She asked her mother if she had any interest in dating, and Tanya told her honestly that she didn't. She couldn't even imagine going out or, worse yet, sleeping with someone else. She had been involved with Peter for twenty-two years in all. It seemed unthinkable to her to go out with another man.

"You'll have to one of these days, Mom," Molly encouraged her.

"I'm not worried about it. I'd rather work." After that they discussed the hot boys at USC. Molly had already met two she liked.

And after Tanya went back to the hotel, she lay in her bed that night, thinking about her conversation with Molly. The prospect of dating anyone seemed horrifying. Even though Peter was living with someone else, she still felt like his wife. She couldn't conceive of being involved with someone else. She had no desire to date anyone. All she wanted was to see her kids and work on the new film. As for dating, she told herself, maybe one day, but surely not yet. And maybe never.

The following morning, Tanya took a cab to Douglas's house, for their promised quiet Sunday at his pool. He was as hospitable as he had been before, the day was as relaxed, the weather was even more beautiful, and this time when he served her lunch, they chatted for a few minutes about the new picture, and then went on to other subjects. She managed not to sleep this time and swam in the pool. It was an easy, pleasant day. As tense as he was sometimes, on the set and in production meetings, she was surprised again by how easygoing he was at home, particularly on lazy Sundays at his pool.

"How are you doing with all these changes in your life?" he asked her in the early afternoon, as they sat in lounge chairs side by side. He was good company and had given her several words for the *New York Times* crossword puzzle. She was impressed by how proficient he was at it. He knew it had to be a big adjustment for her to be getting divorced, and an enormous disappointment after how staunchly she had defended her marriage. He had never expected it to happen to her, and he suspected she had expected it even less. He had no real idea what had happened, but he was sure it had been a major heartbreak for her. She looked thin to him, and sad sometimes, but she seemed to be doing remarkably well, and he admired her for it. He had invited her to the pool that day to cheer her up.

"Honestly?" she said, answering him. "I don't even know. I think I'm in shock. A year ago I thought I was happily married, with the most wonderful husband in the world. Nine months ago I discovered that he had cheated on me. Six months ago he told me he wanted a divorce to live with what was previously my best friend, and the woman he cheated on me with. And three months from now I'll be divorced. My head is spinning," she said to Douglas as he nodded. It was quite a recital. The disintegration of her marriage had moved with the speed of sound. It seemed dizzying even to him and must have been agonizing for her.

"It's pretty amazing," he agreed, "but you look like you're doing all right. Are you?" he asked with a look of concern. Sometimes, he could be a very nice man, especially on home turf. Out in the world, at a conference table or on a movie set, he could be tough as nails.

"I think I am. I'm not sure what the operating standard is here. How nuts am I supposed to feel? Because sometimes I feel pretty nuts. I wake up and think I dreamed it, and then the wrecking ball hits my gut again, and I remember that it's real. It's a pretty nasty way to wake up."

"I've had times like that myself," he confessed. "We all do. The trick is to get through them with a minimum of bitterness and damage. That's not as easy as it sounds. I'm still bitter about some of the bad experiences in my life, and scared to death as a result. I imagine you must feel the same. It sounds like all of it came as a big surprise."

"It did. I thought I was happily married. Shows what I know. Don't ever ask me for relationship advice. I still think my husband . . . my *ex*-husband," she said with effort, "went a little nuts. Not to mention my best friend, who demonstrated a total lack of integrity. As you put it, it was very disappointing."

"Have you been out with anyone since?" He was always curious about her, and intrigued. He loved how bright she was. And how well she wrote.

She laughed. "That would be like asking Hiroshima survivors if they've been to any good bombings lately. I'm not exactly anxious to try again. This may have cured me forever. My daughter was telling me last night that I need to start dating. I don't think so," she said, staring at the pool and looking dazed, thinking back over the past few months. It was mind-blowing when she really thought about it. She tried not to most of the time. "At my age I don't need to get married again. I don't want more kids. And I'm not even sure I want to date. In fact, I'm almost positive I don't. I don't want to take the risk of getting my heart broken again. What's the point?"

"You can't go into religious orders either. And I don't imagine you want to be alone for the rest of your life." He smiled gently at her. "It would be a terrible waste. You'll have to get brave again one of these days."

"Why?"

"Why not?" She stared at the water again and didn't answer.

"I can't think of a good answer in either case."

"That means you're not ready," he said practically, and she nodded. It was weird discussing her dating life with him, or lack of one.

"That would be a major understatement, that I'm not ready. I was feeling like a candidate for the Special Olympics for a while." Peter had knocked her squarely on her ass. She had been feeling winded ever since, none of which was surprising. "Dating doesn't look like all that much fun anyway. Just a lot of people getting dressed up and dicking each other around. I didn't even like dating when I was in college. People were always breaking promises, canceling dates, or standing me up. I hated it until I met Peter." And in the end he had turned out to be the promise-breaker of all time, and along with his promises, he broke her heart.

"It's nice going out with the right person from time to time," he encouraged her. He didn't want constant companionship either. Just the company of intelligent women once in a while, and occasionally extremely glamorous ones. He loved showing them off, as sort of accessories for him. Tanya thought of him more as a solitary man, after knowing him to some degree for the past year. She liked their sushi and Chinese takeout dinners best of all, where they discussed problems with the script and various aspects of their work.

"Look at people like Jean Amber and Ned Bright. They got all excited on the set, had a hot romance, and then wound up in a big fight in the press in July. How much fun is that?" Douglas laughed at her assessment of it. Admittedly, they had made a mess, but they were both famous for it, and they were hot young stars.

"I don't suggest you date boys that age," he laughed at her, "or actors of any age. They're all slightly nuts. And incredibly self-centered. And well known for sloppy behavior. I was thinking of someone more respectable, of a more reasonable age."

"Are men ever reasonable?" she said sadly. "I thought Peter was, and look what he did. How reasonable was that?"

"People go crazy sometimes. It probably destabilized him when you came to work down here. Not that that's an excuse."

"She lived next door, and she helped him with the kids while I was gone. He wound up thinking they had more in common because she was there and I wasn't. He was afraid I would want all this as a permanent way of life. He was convinced I would come back here to do another film. And the stupid thing is that I did, but only because he dumped me for someone else, and now I have nothing else to do, so I came back."

"I thought it was because you were so impressed by the picture we wanted to make," he chided her gently, and she looked embarrassed as they both laughed.

"Well, that too. But I wouldn't have done another picture if I were still married. I wanted to go home."

"I know you did. I think he did you a big favor, Tanya. I hope you'll see it as that one day. You don't belong there. You belong here. You're much too sophisticated to be stuck up there in the wilds of Marin."

"It was nice when the kids were growing up," she said wistfully. "I have to admit that now I'd be a little bored there. But it's a great place to be married and raise kids."

"Since you're doing neither these days, I think you're much better off here. It's a far more interesting life for you. And we're going to get you an Oscar one of these days."

"From your mouth to God's ears," she laughed. It was an expression she had learned from Max. He had called her that week and invited her to lunch. "Winning an Oscar would really be fun," she said, and he laughed.

"Now that's a vast understatement. It's fantastic. Major ego food to be recognized by your peers and acknowledged as the best in your field. You deserve one for *Mantra*, but the competition may be too stiff this year. If so, I think *Gone* ought to do it for you. I'm counting on it."

"Thank you, Douglas," she said quietly, "for the opportunities you've given me. I really appreciate it. I'm glad I came back to work on another picture with you." They both knew this one was going to be special, even more than the previous one.

"I can hardly wait to start shooting. And I'm glad you're on this one, too. I think it's going to be an extraordinary movie, in great part thanks to your script." He had been very impressed by what she'd done so far. The director had been extremely excited about it, too. Tanya had learned a lot in the past year, and honed her screenwriting skills to a remarkable degree. "We make a very good team," he said, glancing admiringly at her. "In fact," he said, so quietly she almost didn't hear him, "I've been thinking that we might make a very good team in other ways as well." For a moment, she had no idea what he meant, but his gaze never wavered from hers as they sat next to his pool. She was in his private world, behind the walls he used to keep everyone out. "Tanya, you're an amazing woman. I think we have a lot to bring each other. I was wondering if you'd like to go out with me sometime, for more than just a sushi dinner. I go to some events I believe you might enjoy. Would you do me the honor of going with me sometime?" She was startled by what he was asking her. He was inquiring in a very proper way if she would consider dating him. She sat staring at him, somewhat stunned, and had no idea what to say. "I promise, I'll take very good care of you."

"I . . . I don't know what to say . . . I'd never thought about you that way. It might be fun sometime," she said cautiously. But she was also worried about getting into an awkward situation with him, if they got involved personally as well as professionally. She didn't want to get in a mess like Jean Amber and Ned Bright, who had become a scandal in the tabloids. She couldn't imagine Douglas behaving that way. She had never thought about herself as an option for him, especially since she had been married during the time they worked together. "I think I'd enjoy it very much," she said quietly, still shocked that he'd asked her, and then with a gentle pat on her arm, he got up and went to his music room. He sat down at the piano and started to play. He played Chopin this time, and Debussy. She lay by the pool with her eyes closed, listening to the music drifting out to her. He played beautifully, and as she pondered everything he'd said to her, she smiled and drifted slowly off to sleep. He found her there, fast asleep when he finally finished, and stood looking at her for a long time. This was exactly what he'd had in mind the first time he met her. It had taken longer than he thought, but the time had finally come.

It was late afternoon, when he woke her gently, chatted with her for a few minutes, and took her back to the hotel. He promised to call her in a few days.

# Chapter 15

The first time Douglas took Tanya to dinner turned out to be a much more elaborate evening than she had expected, but a surprisingly enjoyable one. She wore the black cocktail dress she had brought with her the year before, with black satin sandals, diamond earrings, a little fur jacket, and a small black satin clutch. She wore her long blond hair in a bun. She looked sleek and elegant as she got into his new Bentley next to him, and he seemed pleased as soon as he saw her. She appeared very sophisticated, and she was impressed to see him in black tie. He was more dashing than ever, and they made a very understated glamorous pair. They went to the party of a very well-known actor, who was part of the old guard of Hollywood, an elder statesman who was known for the fabulous parties he gave. The house was as beautiful as Douglas's, though the art was not quite as spectacular. The guests were every important name in the movie business. Tanya met people she'd only heard of, and Douglas saw that she was introduced to everyone and raved about her scripts for *Mantra* and now *Gone*. He made her feel comfortable and was attentive to her from the moment they walked in.

The dinner was excellent, and she danced with him on a Lucite dance floor over the pool, to the strains of a band brought in from New York for the occasion. It was a fabulous evening. They stayed until after midnight and had a drink at the Polo Lounge when they got back. She was looking relaxed and happy, as she told him she'd had a wonderful time. He said he had, too.

"It's usually an interesting crowd at his parties," Douglas commented. "Not just the showy types but the smart ones. I always find people there I like to talk to." Tanya nodded, she had had several interesting conversations herself. Douglas had made a point of including her in every group he met. He had been a thoughtful, considerate date, and she had had a lovely evening. She had been surprised at how at ease she was with him. After their drink he thanked her for joining him. He said she had made it a much more enjoyable evening, and she could see that he meant it. "We'll do it again soon," he promised with a warm smile, and then kissed her on the cheek. "Thank you, Tanya. Sleep well. I'll see you tomorrow." They had pre-production meetings scheduled in his offices the next day. She felt a bit like Cinderella. She'd be back to scrubbing the castle floors again tomorrow, but tonight had been a delightful interlude for her, and for him as well.

He walked her to the door of her bungalow and left her there, and then walked away, looking pensive and smiling to himself. The evening had been even better than he'd hoped, for both of them. He drove away in his Bentley as Tanya slowly got undressed, thinking about him. He was a complex, complicated man. She always had a feeling that there was so much more of him hidden behind his walls. It was a strong temptation to try and get behind them, or to look for the key. What she liked best about him was his mind, but he was a handsome man as well. It had never even occurred to her to be attracted to him, but she was surprised to find she was. She had liked dancing with him, talking to him, and discussing the evening with him afterward. He made her laugh as well, as she did for him. In all, the evening had been a success. She slipped into bed after brushing her teeth, thinking about how lucky she was to have been out with him. She didn't think of him that way, but she knew it was a major coup in Hollywood to be on the arm of Douglas Wayne.

He was extremely circumspect the next morning at their meeting. Adele presented her notes on the script, and they discussed them. Douglas deferred to Tanya several times, and he agreed with her in most instances. When he didn't, he was careful to explain why. He was more respectful of her than usual, and particularly thoughtful. He saw to it that her brand of tea was served to her repeatedly, and joined her at lunch afterward with the others. She had the feeling that he was courting her, very quietly and subtly, and in a way that was comfortable for her. It was an odd feeling, but a very pleasant sensation. He walked her out to her car afterward and suggested dinner again the next day. She agreed. And as she drove away, she found herself thinking of him, wondering where this was going. Nowhere probably, but going out with him seemed like a nice thing, particularly in light of the last six months, which had been nightmarish for her.

Her second official date with Douglas was far more relaxed than the first one. He took her to a cozy Italian restaurant, where they sat and talked for hours. He told her about his childhood in Missouri. His father had been a banker, his mother from a very social family. They had died when he was young and left him some money. He had used it to come to California, and tried to be an actor. It had taken him very little time to figure out that for the most part, the money and the excitement were in the production end. He had invested his savings, and had made a little more money. And from then on he had invested and produced until he had an enormous fortune. It was a fascinating story, and he shared it with her with ease.

He had won his first Oscar at twenty-seven, was a legend in Hollywood by the time he was thirty, and was even more so now. By now he was an institution, not just a legend. There were legions of stories about him, and everyone admired his Midas touch. He was the object of envy, jealousy, respect, and admiration. He drove a hard bargain, had integrity, yet never took no for an answer. He readily admitted to her that he liked getting his way, and was a terrible spoiled brat when someone denied him something. They were all good insights into him, and she was intrigued by what he shared with her. He was allowing her to see what he wanted her to see, but she could sense that his walls were still up, and maybe always would be. She had no reason to try to scale them or take them down. It was an interesting challenge to try to discover who he was. Visibly, he was an extremely intelligent, somewhat distant, cautious man with real financial brilliance. He knew a great deal about art, loved music, and said he believed in families, for other people. He didn't hesitate to admit that children made him uncomfortable. He appeared to have a great many quirks and eccentricities and opinions. And at the same time Tanya could sense that he was vulnerable, kind at times, and he was surprisingly unpretentious given who he was. The somewhat sardonic, cold, unnerving side of him she had seen in the beginning, seemed to have softened considerably as they spent time together and she got to know him.

They went home even later this time, as he wended through the traffic in the Bentley. There was something very old-fashioned about him, but she found that appealing. He was fifty-five years old, and hadn't been married in twenty-five years. They were all interesting bits of information he was giving her, and she shared equally with him. She also referred to her children frequently, but he didn't ask her much about them. He said often, apologetically, that children were not his thing.

He kissed her on the cheek again after another very pleasant evening. She felt respected by him, and had a sense that he would not intrude on her in any way. He kept his distance, had well-defined, obvious boundaries, and expected others to do the same. He made it clear that he disliked people crawling all over him. He had an equal distaste for unctuous waiters, snotty restaurant owners, and maître d's. Douglas liked good service, but didn't like to be intruded on by anyone, for any reason. He gave Tanya that message again and again. Douglas preferred to advance toward people, at his own speed, rather than be crowded, invaded, or pursued. It was fine with her. She was perfectly content to let him set the pace. She had no desire to trap him, crowd him, or hunt him down. She was perfectly comfortable with things as they were, and she expected nothing from him. The relationship they shared currently seemed perfect to her. Despite the pleasant evenings she had spent with him, they were only friends.

Douglas invited her to several more very enjoyable events, one at the Los Angeles County Museum of Art, the other for the opening of a play that was touring from New York. It was very controversial and the people who attended the benefit opening were an eclectic and interesting crowd. They slipped out for dinner afterward by themselves. He took her to L'Orangerie for a late-night supper, and avoided the familiar crowd at Spago, where he would have been standing up and greeting people all night. He wanted to focus on Tanya, and their conversations, not on all the people who would be seeing them and wondering who she was. He ordered the caviar in

eggshells for her. After that they both had lobster, and soufflé for
dessert. It was the perfect meal, a lovely evening, and he was proving
to be a thoroughly enjoyable dinner companion and date. All the un-
easiness she'd felt about him when they first met, his sharp comments to her, his probing cynical view about her life and marriage,
had absolutely nothing to do with the man she was spending time
with now. Douglas was understanding, kind, interesting, interested,
and devoted himself to seeing that she had a good time. He found
unusual things for them to do, which he thought would be of particular interest to her. He was respectful, charming, gracious, poised,
and she had a constant sense that he was protecting her now, even in
meetings or on the set. He made everything easy for her.

Their Sunday afternoons at his pool were becoming a ritual. She
did the crossword puzzle while he played the piano, or she lay in the
sun and slept. It was a perfect counterpoint to their busy weeks once
the filming began. They started a week late, in early October, and
given the content of the film and the rigorous performance demands,
the atmosphere on the set was very tense. Both she and Douglas often needed to get out at night and relax. Sometimes he came over
and they ordered food from room service, or ate at the Polo Lounge,
although it was less peaceful then than in her bungalow. But it was
also nice to see people and get out.

They seemed to have many of the same interests, the same need
for people or not, depending on their mood. And they appeared to
have similar paces and needs and rhythms. Tanya was amazed at
how well they got along. She would never have guessed that being
with him could be so much fun, although she had to admit to herself
late at night, alone in her bungalow, that she still missed Peter terribly at times. It would have been strange if she didn't. You didn't wash
away twenty years overnight. Maybe he had, but it still felt weird to

her not to call him at the end of her day, or to say goodnight. Once or twice, in a moment of agonizing loneliness and missing him, she nearly had. She missed the comfortable and familiar aspects of their relationship, although Douglas was keeping her happy and busy, and kept her mind off how much her life had changed, and how fast. It was hard adjusting to the idea that Peter was gone, for good. She wondered how he was getting along with Alice, if they were happy, or felt they had made a mistake. It was hard to believe that seizing one's happiness, while betraying spouses and friends and breaking hearts, would win them happiness in the end. But maybe it had. The children were careful, when she spoke to them, not to mention Peter and Alice to her, and she was grateful for that. Hearing about them was painful, and she suspected that it would always be to some extent. The divorce was going to be final in two months. She hated knowing that, and tried not to think about it. Douglas provided good distraction from the sorrows in her life.

He asked her about her divorce one Sunday afternoon, at his pool. They had just finished a lunch he had made for her, of endive salad and cracked crab, while Tanya commented on how spoiled she was. This was a far cry from her life in Marin. But everything was now, from dinners at Spago, and the people who recognized her when she went out, to her comfortable life in Bungalow 2 at the Beverly Hills Hotel. Everything about her life had changed, and Douglas was responsible for most of it, if not all.

"When will your divorce be final, Tanya?" he asked casually, sipping a glass of excellent white wine. His wine cellars were extraordinary, and he had introduced Tanya to many wines and vintages she had heard and read about but never tried. He was also an aficionado of Cuban cigars. Tanya loved the smell of them when he smoked them, which he always did outside. He was extremely considerate and polite, and she was surprised by the question about her divorce. Now that she was seeing more of him, and he wasn't trying to provoke her as he had in the beginning, he rarely asked her personal things. He stayed off painful subjects, and kept their exchanges fairly superficial. It was obvious to Tanya that he enjoyed her company, but intimacy was something he shunned.

"At the end of December," she said quietly. She didn't like being reminded of it. It brought to mind a painful time, which was not yet over and might not be for a long time. She couldn't imagine that a day would come when thinking of Peter, and his leaving her for Alice, didn't hurt. It still did. A lot. But Douglas helped, mostly by distracting her. And he was very kind to her. She was grateful for the good times they shared. It added another dimension to the working relationship they had.

"Did you settle all your property?" he asked with interest. The business side of everything intrigued him most. Emotional issues were of less consequence to him. That was her bailiwick, not his.

"There wasn't much to settle. A small stock portfolio we divided equally, and our house. We both own it, but he agreed to let me and the children live in it, for now. Eventually, we'll probably have to sell it. And it won't make sense to keep it once the kids are out of college. Now we can all go back for holidays and summers. And I guess I'll be living there between pictures, if I keep doing this." She smiled at him. "If not, I'll go back to Marin and write. Fortunately Peter's not anxious for the money, he said he can wait to sell. Peter makes a healthy living as an attorney, but kids are expensive, and so are three tuitions in college, so sooner or later, we'll get rid of the house." The kids' college tuitions were a hefty bite. And the money she had made from the two movies she'd written in the past year, she had invested with a stockbroker in San Francisco, and it was her own. Peter had made no claim to that money, and had wanted nothing from her, although they were married under community property, had had nothing when they married, and had no prenup. He hadn't been greedy or financially demanding, he just wanted out, as soon as possible, so he could be with Alice. She had no idea if they were planning to get married, or if so, when. "What made you ask?" Tanya said out loud, wondering why he had inquired about their divorce.

"Just curious," he said, looking relaxed, as he sipped his wine and lit a cigar. Tanya loved the pungent smell of the smoke. It was a Romeo y Julieta from Havana, which someone brought in for him. "Divorce always seems like such a mess to me. People beating each other up over money. Like beggars in the street over a can of pennies, scrambling for each one, and trying to cut the couch and the piano in half. It seems to turn the most civilized people into hooligans." He had had a few run-ins of that kind himself, from women who wanted to extort money from him, or set him up for palimony. His two divorces had been easy and clean when he was young. Since then he had never been tempted to try again. "Would you marry again, Tanya?" he asked with interest, as she hesitated, thinking about it. They talked about every imaginable subject as they lay next to his pool on Sunday afternoons, and sometimes they didn't talk at all, or swam in the pool together, doing synchonized laps. She had never been as comfortable with anyone except Peter. Much to her own surprise, she was getting used to Douglas. It was the Sunday afternoons of just being there together that brought them closest. She wasn't in love with him, but she thoroughly enjoyed his company and the time they shared.

"I don't know," she said honestly, in answer to his question. "I doubt it. I don't know why I would. I don't want more children. I know people have them later than this, but I feel too old to start again, and I'm happy with the kids I have. I can't imagine finding someone again whom I'd be that serious about. I think for me it was a once-in-a-lifetime thing. I was with Peter half my life. I don't think I have the heart to start over, and risk getting disappointed or hurt again." Her eyes were sad as she said it, as he blew careful smoke rings in the air, listening and thinking about what she was saying.

"If your expectations were different, you might not get disappointed, Tanya," he said sensibly. "You believed in the fairy tale, so when the glass slipper broke, all was lost. Some people marry more practically than that, or they're more realistic about the arrangement they make. It leaves less opportunity for heartbreak and disappointment. Personally, if I ever married again, I'd prefer to do that. Romance and passion are much less my style, and I think they're a guarantee of disaster. The only person I could imagine marrying would be a beloved friend, someone I get along with supremely well, who offers companionship and understanding, and a sense of humor about life. The rest seems untrustworthy to me." What he said made sense but wasn't romantic. She could see why he thought that way. She couldn't imagine Douglas falling head over heels in love, but she could see him forming a partnership with a woman he loved and respected, or even one he liked. Douglas wasn't ruled by his emotions, but by his head. Although it was hard to imagine him in partnership with any woman. He seemed perfectly content living alone.

"Can you see yourself marrying again, Douglas?" she asked, curious about him. He seemed the consummately happy bachelor. He didn't appear to need companionship a lot of the time. And when he wanted it, he knew how to organize it and find it. He enjoyed Tanya's company immensely, but she had no sense that he was wooing her or in love with her. He enjoyed the time he spent with her, and his own life as well. It worked perfectly for both of them for now. He didn't press her, didn't make her uncomfortable, didn't want sexual favors from her. They were business associates who, by a stroke of good fortune, and some effort on his part and goodwill on hers, had become friends. It was perfect for Tanya at this point in her life. A man hotly pursuing her would have frightened her, and Douglas knew that. He could easily sense that she wasn't over Peter yet, and might not be for a while, even a long time. She had genuinely loved the man, no matter how unworthy he had proven himself to be in the end.

Douglas answered her question with caution and careful thought. He had asked himself the same question several times, always with the same answer. Like Tanya, he saw no real reason to marry again. Now and then it had momentary appeal, but never for long. He considered himself at low risk for marriage. "I don't know," he said to her, watching his smoke rings dissolve in the air. "I think you're right. There's no real reason to at our age. Although you're considerably younger than I am. Twelve years, if I'm not mistaken. At my age, there's a different perspective. I find myself thinking at times that I'll be alone one day. I don't think I want to end my life alone. Nor do I want the burden of some demanding young woman on my hands now, pestering me to pay for a face-lift and implants, a new sports car, diamonds, and furs. I'd be perfectly willing to give all that to her, but I don't want some high-maintenance annoying woman around for the next thirty years as an insurance policy for my old age. What if I get hit by a bus when I'm sixty? Then I'll have put up with all that nonsense for nothing." He smiled at Tanya, puffing on his cigar again and exhaling languidly. "Actually, I don't think I'm old enough to get married yet. I ought to wait until I'm seventy-five or eighty, and falling apart. Though I might not find a good one then. It's actually quite a challenging dilemma at any age. I don't lose a lot of sleep over it, but I've never found the perfect solution to the problem, nor the person I'd want to spend my life with in the meantime, so I stay as I am. I imagine though in your case, Tanya, you must be very afraid to get hurt again. With good reason. You got a rotten deal on the last one." He had felt very sorry for her about it, although she seemed to be doing well, and he hoped he was helping her. He liked her, and enjoyed her company immensely, more than he had ever expected to when they first met, although he liked her even then. He liked getting to know her better. She never disappointed him. "What would you want in marriage if you did get married again?" he asked her, looking pensive. It was a funny conversation, for two people who really didn't want to get married, to each other, or anyone else.

She hesitated before she answered. "I'd want what I had before, or thought I did. Someone I can love and trust, whose company I enjoy, with the same interests, or similar ones. Someone I respect and admire, and who feels the same about me. Basically, a best friend with a wedding ring," she said quietly, looking at him with sad eyes. It had reminded her of all she lost. Her best friend as well as her husband. It had been a major loss for her, and in truth she hadn't lost him, she'd been robbed.

"What you're saying doesn't sound very romantic," he said carefully. "Actually, I like that. All that hot young romance lasts for about five minutes, and then turns into a disaster. I hate mess in my life. I like order." She smiled, listening to him. She could see that about him. He never had a hair out of place, every inch of him was immaculate and impeccable, his house always looked as though the architect and designer had finished it that morning and they were waiting for *Architectural Digest* to shoot it. Some might have found his obsessive tidiness irritating, but she found it pleasant to be around, and comforting somehow. It implied that all was in good order and nothing would get out of hand. A life in good control. Tanya wasn't a person who found disorder and mess charming, and neither was Douglas. He loved meticulous surroundings, and an orderly life at all times, which he said was one of the reasons he had never wanted children.

According to him, people with children seemed to be dealing with chaos at all times. He had never found that appealing, no matter how much they said they loved them or wouldn't give up parenting for a minute. The thought of a child in rehab, crashing a car, crying all night, or getting finger paint on the couch, or even cookie dough or peanut butter, made him hyperventilate. He was definitely not a candidate for that kind of hysteria in his life, and with children there always was. He admired people who took that on, but he had never had any desire whatsoever to volunteer for that program, and he felt the same way now. He would never have married a woman, or even spent a great deal of time with one, who wanted children. He had enough headaches and responsibilities in his life without that, a bunch of unruly childlike actors among them.

"It doesn't sound like either of us is about to run out and get married, does it, Tanya?" He smiled as he put out his cigar.

"I certainly wasn't considering it," she laughed. "I'm not even divorced yet," although she was sad to realize she would be in ten weeks. Douglas didn't seem to have any pressing desire or need to marry again either. They were the perfect companions for each other, particularly on Sundays. In a funny way, it was a bit like being married, without the sex or the cuddly part. He never kissed her or held her, or even put an arm around her. They just relaxed side by side, contemplating life, from their perspective, and the state of the world as they saw it. They were intelligent observers, casually linked, enjoying a front-row seat on life. It was all she wanted at the moment, nothing more.

After that, Douglas played the piano, as he always did, for two hours. Tanya lay by the pool, listening to him, awake this time. The music was beautiful, and the day was warm and perfect. Life seemed easy and comfortable whenever she was with him. And for some unspoken reason, she felt safe with him, which was what Tanya needed. Peace and safety. Her life had been dangerous and frightening enough for a while. The feeling of safe haven that Douglas gave her was priceless to her and deeply appreciated for now. And the intelligent companionship she offered him, with no emotional demands put on him, was all Douglas had ever wanted.

# Chapter 16

The shooting of the movie *Gone* went well all through November. There was a compelling but steady pace established, the director kept the tension high, and the actors gave the best performances everyone on the set had seen for a long time. Douglas was thrilled, particularly with Tanya's script, which she honed and polished constantly. It was brilliant. He praised her about it lavishly, as did Adele.

The week before Thanksgiving Douglas took her to the premiere of the movie they'd made before, *Mantra*. She wanted her kids to come, but all three of them had midterms and couldn't attend. Jean Amber and Ned Bright were there, not speaking to each other, despite their hot romance of the year before, which illustrated everything Douglas had said pejoratively about Hollywood quicksilver love affairs, which vanished almost as soon as they began. Tanya wasn't a fan of those affairs either. They seemed exhausting and pointless and way too short-lived.

The premiere itself was very glamorous, and there was a party afterward at the Regent Beverly Wilshire. It was one of those movie events where everyone on the planet was there. Tanya had bought a beautiful black satin evening gown, and she looked stunning as she walked in on Douglas's arm. Photographers snapped their picture, and he looked very proud. Max was there looking rumpled in a rented tux, and solitary without Harry. He and Tanya enjoyed a warm conversation, and he said he was hearing great things about the movie she was working on now. Douglas was hoping for an Oscar for *Mantra,* but was almost sure of one for *Gone.*

"Maybe you'll get one too, Tanya," Max said with a warm smile, as Douglas appeared, having posed for photographs with both stars.

"Jesus, those two are going to kill each other one of these days." Ned and Jean had spat insults at each other through clenched teeth, firing rockets past Douglas, while smiling broadly for the photographers who couldn't hear what they were saying.

"Ahhh, young love, it'll do you in every time," Max said wisely with a broad grin.

"How's Harry?" Tanya inquired, and Max looked pleased.

"His tux was at the cleaner so he couldn't make it. It's his bowling night tonight anyway." The dog was his alter ego, and truly his best friend. Anyone who asked about him, and liked him, was Max's friend for life.

"Tell him I said hi, and that I miss him." Tanya smiled.

"Going home for Thanksgiving?" he asked her, and she nodded. She hadn't seen any of her children in weeks, even Molly. She'd been too busy working on the film, even on Saturday nights. And she was usually with Douglas on Sundays now. Their Sundays had become a weekly event, which neither of them wanted to sacrifice. Molly was busy with her friends anyway. Tanya was looking forward to catching up with all of them in Marin, although she was sharing them with Peter and Alice this time. She had Thanksgiving, and he had them on

Friday night at Alice's new house, where they were living. The kids wanted to be with their friends on Saturday. She was planning to fly up with Molly on Wednesday night. Megan and Jason were driving up from Santa Barbara together. It was going to be good to be together again, and she was excited about it, although she had scarcely mentioned it to Douglas. His eyes glazed whenever she mentioned her children.

"What about you?" Max asked Douglas, since they were old friends. "Eating small children as usual instead of turkey this year?" In spite of himself, Douglas laughed.

"You're going to give Tanya a terrible impression, if you give away all my secrets," Douglas pretended to chide him, and Max shrugged.

"She might as well know who she's working for." He grinned, and a few minutes later he drifted away to talk to someone else, as Tanya and Douglas chatted, and agreed how much they liked him, and what a good friend he was to all.

"I've known him since I came to Hollywood," Douglas said. "He's never changed. He looked like that as a kid. His work gets better and better, but he's always the same down-to-earth, decent guy."

"He was really sweet to me when my marriage was falling apart," Tanya acknowledged, and a little while later she and Douglas made their way back to the red carpet, and glided gracefully out the door. Douglas said they had done their job. He drove her back to the hotel in the Bentley, and neither of them was in the mood for the Polo Lounge. She asked him if he wanted a drink in the bungalow. It felt like her own house now. He teased her about it sometimes, and said she'd better buy it, because it was obvious she was never going to give it up. She had moved the furniture around to suit her better. She had her own duvet in the second bedroom for her children, and she had photographs of them in silver frames everywhere, and pots of white orchids she had bought at the flower market. It looked cozier than ever now.

"That would be nice," he said in answer to her invitation, and after handing his car keys to the doorman, he followed her down the path to her bungalow. She had a bottle of the wine he liked in the fridge in the kitchen. Neither of them was paying close attention to it, or attributing deep meaning to it, but they were seeing a lot of each other these days, both on the set and at night. They had casual dinners once or twice a week, at least one of them takeout in her room, and he took her to some party or event about twice a week. And they talked on the phone every night, usually about the script. And then there were sacred Sundays at his pool. In fact, they were together almost all the time.

She poured him a glass of wine, and he sat down easily in one of the room's comfortable chairs and stretched his legs out, admiring her.

"You look beautiful tonight, Tanya," he said simply, and she smiled.

"Thank you, Douglas. You look very handsome." She was always proud to be out on his arm, and flattered that he took her with him. She still felt a little like a country bumpkin, particularly among the sea of women who had had plastic surgery, collagen, and Botox, and whose breasts were invariably hanging out, with figures worthy of a chorus line in Las Vegas, in clothes she couldn't imagine wearing. She had a quiet, elegant, natural Grace Kelly look compared to all that, which he much preferred. He had seen enough of the other in his years in Hollywood to have a vast indifference to it. Implants, bleached hair, and nose jobs no longer turned him on.

"What are you doing for Thanksgiving?" she asked him. She knew he no longer had family, and was suddenly worried about him. She didn't like the thought of him being alone over the holidays. But she could easily imagine that inviting him to Marin with her children would have been his worst nightmare. And probably theirs as well.

"I'm spending it with friends in Palm Springs. Not exciting, but peaceful. That's really all I need." They had both been so busy on the picture, they were exhausted, as was the cast, but neither Douglas nor Tanya looked it that night. She looked radiant, and he was obviously in good spirits, and enjoying being with her.

"I was thinking about asking you to Marin, but I figured that to you that would be a fate worse than death." She smiled, and he laughed.

"Indeed it would. Although I'm sure they're very nice kids." Then he mentioned something to her that he'd been thinking about for a while. He wasn't sure how she'd feel about it, or what her plans were for her kids. "Do you suppose you and the children would like to come on my boat sometime? It'll be in the Caribbean over Christmas, and you could all meet me in St. Bart's. How do you think they'd like that?" He looked as though he meant it, and she stared at him with wide eyes.

"Are you serious?"

"I think so. Unless you tell me they all get seasick and hate boats, or you do. We have stabilizers, so it's a pretty steady ride, and we don't have to go far. If they prefer, we can come into port at night."

"Douglas, that's an incredible offer." She looked stunned. She had been thinking of taking them to Tahoe to go skiing. Spending time on his yacht in St. Bart's was an incredible gift to her, and to them. "Thank you. Do you mean it?" she asked with a look of awe.

"Of course I do. I'd love to have you on the boat. And I think they'd enjoy it, too." From everything she'd heard about it, she knew her children would think they had died and gone to Heaven. She didn't know what Peter's plans for them were, but she was sure they could work something out. "I'm going down a few days before Christmas, and you'll probably want to be together over the holiday. I can send the plane for you whenever you want." Douglas never flew commercial, he had his own jet. Being anywhere near him, or spending time with him, was a lesson in living well.

"I would absolutely love it," she said honestly. "Let me talk to the kids over Thanksgiving and see what their plans are. I don't know what arrangements they've made with their father."

"There's no rush," he said quietly, setting his glass down on the table. "I'm not inviting anyone else. I figure we'll all be so exhausted by then, I'd just go down, make script notes, and relax."

"That sounds fabulous to me." She beamed at him, grateful to him for offering her children an extraordinary opportunity. Douglas might eat small children for Thanksgiving, as Max suggested, but he had been nothing but kind to her, and now to her kids as well.

They chatted for a few minutes, and he got up to leave. She walked him to the door of the bungalow living room, and thanked him again for his incredibly generous invitation to the boat. He turned and smiled down at her. She looked tiny next to him, but he knew her well enough now to know that her spirit was ten feet tall.

"I'd like to have you on board with me," he said honestly. "The boat is a wonderful part of my life. I hope you enjoy it, Tanya. We could take some wonderful trips on it together." She was mildly surprised by what he'd said. Their friendship had deepened and expanded over the past several months, particularly since she'd come back to do *Gone,* but traveling together was another dimension. She was surprised and touched by his invitation, and his wanting to share his yacht with them.

"I'd love that," she said softly, feeling unexpectedly shy with him. He was so good to her, she had no way to reciprocate or even thank him, and as her eyes met his, he bent toward her slowly, and kissed her gently on the mouth. He had never done that before. She didn't know what to say, and before she could, he kissed her again, harder this time, pulling her into his arms gently, and exploring her mouth with his tongue. She had never expected him to do that, and felt breathless and startled in his arms, but she had no desire to pull away, and found herself kissing him back, with unexpected passion. Everything that was happening between them left her feeling stunned and a little overwhelmed. She had never thought of Douglas in a sexual way before, or as a potential man in her life.

When he finally stopped kissing her, she looked at him with wide eyes that searched his for the meaning of what he'd just done.

"I've been wanting to do that for a long time," he whispered. "I didn't want to frighten you, or do it too soon. I'm in love with you, Tanya," he told her, and she nearly gasped as the force of what he was saying hit her like a wave. She had no idea what she felt for him in that vein. This was all new to her, but she knew she liked him very much, and felt more comfortable with him than she ever had with anyone else, except Peter. She respected and admired him, liked him. But she didn't know if she could love him, or already did. She was totally unsure what she felt.

She didn't know what to say, as he put a finger to her lips. "Don't say anything yet. You don't need to. Get used to the idea first. We'll figure it out in time." He kissed her again, and she melted into his arms. It was hard to believe this was happening to her. She didn't know if this was a Hollywood romance or a real one for him, and she knew even less what it was for her. He had taken her totally by surprise.

"Goodnight," he said then, and before she could answer him or comment, he had slipped through the door of the bungalow, and left, as Tanya stood staring after him, and could hear the rapid beating of her heart. She couldn't decide if what she felt was fear, desire, or love.

# Chapter 17

Molly and Tanya met at LAX on Wednesday afternoon. Tanya had barely left the set in time and had been running, so as not to miss the flight. She had felt scattered on the set all day, and only glimpsed Douglas for a few minutes. He looked at her with a slow smile, as he stood surrounded by a group of people, and with a shy look, she had smiled back. Suddenly everything had changed between them, and she hadn't talked to him since the night before. She had thought about him for hours all night, trying to sort out what she felt in her head. He was a dazzling man, and she liked him, but she had never thought of him as a potential man for her. He still wasn't yet. But his saying he was in love with her turned her whole world upside down, in a very pleasant way. It was exciting and scary all at once.

Molly was waiting for her at Starbucks in the terminal, as promised, and they ran to catch the plane. They just made it, and were the last ones on. Tanya's cell phone rang just as she sat down on the plane. They hadn't made the announcement to turn cell phones off yet, so she answered it and was surprised to hear Douglas's voice.

"I'm sorry we didn't get a chance to talk today," he said in the smooth, familiar voice that had new meaning. "I didn't want you to forget what I said last night, or to think it was the wine. I love you, Tanya. I have for a long time. Since last year in fact, but I knew you wouldn't be open to it. I didn't think this time would ever come for us. I think now it has."

"I . . . I don't know what to say . . . I'm stunned . . ." And more than a little frightened. She didn't know if she was in love with him, but she felt very close to him. The thought of being involved with him had never crossed her mind. She'd had no idea whatsoever that he cared for her, and had never thought of him in that light.

"Don't be afraid, Tanya," he said calmly, and she was aware of feeling safe with him again. "I think this could be the kind of marriage we both want. A powerful alliance between two interesting people who care about each other. Best friends with wedding rings, as you put it, when we talked about it a while back, in more general terms. That's what I want. I'd never wanted to marry again until I met you." He was coming on fast and strong. "Give yourself time to get used to the idea."

"I think I have to do that," she said cautiously, feeling anxious again. She felt awkward talking to him, with her daughter in the next seat. She didn't want Molly to know what was going on. She needed time to get used to the idea herself first, before she said anything to them. She wasn't over Peter yet. But she felt drawn to Douglas more powerfully than she would have thought possible. And although it frightened her more than a little, she liked what he said. It did much to soothe her wounds of the past year.

"I'll call you over the weekend," he promised. "Don't forget to ask the kids about the boat."

"I won't . . . and Douglas . . . thank you for everything . . . I mean that . . . I just need a little time . . ." She said as they made the announcement to turn cell phones off. They were getting ready to pull away from the gate.

"I know you do. You can have all the time you need," he said, sounding calm and in control.

"Thank you," she said softly, wondering what incredible stroke of fate had dropped him into her lap. Maybe it would prove to be the greatest blessing of her life. She didn't know yet, but she suddenly hoped it would be. It would turn a tragic ending into a happy one after all. How perfect would that be? She said goodbye to Douglas and turned off her phone as Molly watched her.

"Who was that?" Molly asked with interest. She had been watching her mother's face.

"My boss," Tanya laughed. "Douglas Wayne. He was calling about the script."

"You looked weird. Do you like him a lot? Like a guy, I mean?" Out of the mouths of babes, Tanya thought, but didn't tell her what had happened, or what he'd said.

"Don't be silly. We're just friends." She leaned her head against the seat then and closed her eyes. She held Molly's hand on the flight, and fell asleep thinking of Douglas and the amazing things he had said. It was all like a dream.

They took a cab to Marin from the airport in San Francisco, and the house looked tired and dusty to Tanya when she walked in and turned on the lights. No one had been in it since September, and to her it had the look of a house no one loved anymore. It seemed sad to her. She fluffed up the cushions, turned all the lights on, and made a run to Safeway while Molly called her friends. By the time she got back, Jason and Megan had arrived, and there was chaos in the kitchen. Half a dozen of their friends had already shown up, and everyone was talking about boyfriends, girlfriends, parties, school. The noise was deafening, the music was on, and Tanya beamed. These were the scenes she loved and missed so terribly now in L.A. She was glad they had come home, instead of having Thanksgiving in L.A. at the hotel, which would have been a huge mistake. The kids had wanted Thanksgiving and Christmas here, at their home, and so did she.

She made hamburgers and pizza for them, a big tossed salad, and french fries in the microwave. By midnight, the friends had left, the kitchen was clean, her children were upstairs, and she had set the table for Thanksgiving. It was nice being home again, and sad to think how much their lives had changed. The children were all away at college, nearly grown up, and off to their own lives. Peter was living with Alice. Their divorce was almost final, and she was living in a hotel in L.A. Being in Ross again was like a time warp somehow, but one that was dear to her, and that she knew she would always love. Sadly, she was aware that she still loved Peter, too. She realized that she wasn't over him yet, and wondered if she ever would be. Here in Ross, where they had shared their lives, missing him was more acute.

She got up, as she did every year, at five A.M. to start the turkey. It had been hard sleeping in her bed alone. The Thanksgiving before was when she had first suspected Peter's affair with Alice, even before it had begun, and now the tides had swept them all away, to other shores. She stuffed the turkey and put it in the oven, as she thought of Douglas and wondered if he would enjoy it here. It seemed unlikely that he would. This was too down home for him, but he offered other pleasures and blessings. She could hardly wait to ask the children about going on his boat after Christmas. She hoped they'd say yes. She would love to do that with him and have all her children with her. It seemed like an amazing adventure for all of them to share.

Once the turkey was in the oven, she lay on her bed and dreamed. Trying to forget Peter, she made herself think of what her life might be like with Douglas, in the spectacular house in L.A., listening to him play the piano and sharing his life with him. It was a very exciting prospect, even though unfamiliar to her. But it meant a lot that she felt safe and was so comfortable with him. It wasn't romance or passion, but it was friendship, and hopefully in time love. She was open to the idea, although it was still confusing and very new. His sharing his feelings with her had come as a huge surprise to her. She let her mind drift, examining the possibilities of what life could be like with him.

As they always did, the children dressed for the Thanksgiving meal. Both girls wore dresses, as did Tanya, and Jason wore a suit.

They took their places at the table, and Tanya said the blessing as she always did, for the food, for the gifts of the previous year and the one to come, for bringing their family together, and for the love that they shared. As she said it, her voice caught and her eyes filled with tears. All she could think of were the wrenching changes that their family had been through that year, and the divorce that wasn't even final yet. As she started to cry, Molly reached out and touched her hand, and Tanya finished the prayer with a loving smile at all three of them. In truth, they had much to be thankful for. They had each other, which was still the greatest gift of all.

Jason carved the turkey, in his father's place this year, and did a fine job of it. The meal was delicious, with the exception of the sweet potatoes, which Tanya had slightly burned.

"I'm out of practice," she apologized to her children. "I haven't cooked since last summer." It was hard to believe she'd been living in a hotel for that long.

"Alice makes puree of chestnuts, and stuffing with bourbon in it," Megan announced, and it sounded like a reproach to her mother. Tanya made no comment, and Jason gave his sister an evil look. They were going to Peter's house the following morning, and all of the children were well aware that diplomatic relations between the two houses were somewhat strained. They tried not to mention either parent to the other, or Alice to their mother. It was still too soon, and awkward for them, too. Megan had stayed very close to Alice, all through the turmoil of the divorce. Molly had distanced herself from her, distressed over the affair that had broken up their parents' marriage. And Jason tried to stay out of it, and hoped that eventually the shitstorm would calm down. He had no desire to take sides with either camp, and wanted to visit peacefully in both.

"I have an invitation to share with you guys," Tanya said in the middle of dinner, to try and divert the conversation from Alice's menu choices and cooking skills, which were painful for her to hear about. Megan was still resentful of Tanya's life in L.A., and had told her months before that whatever her father and Alice had done, the divorce was entirely her fault. It had been hard to hear, but was clearly what she felt, and brought up Tanya's own worst guilt and fears about having left for L.A. "We've been invited to the Caribbean on a very fancy yacht during Christmas vacation," Tanya announced grandly, as all eyes turned to her.

"Whose? Some movie star?" Megan asked hopefully.

"The producer I work with. Douglas Wayne. In St. Bart's. He'll fly us down on his plane."

"How did that happen? Are you dating him or something?" Megan asked, instantly suspicious of her mother and the lavish invitation.

"I haven't been. We're just friends, but I think it could lead in that direction at some point." She didn't want to tell them he was talking marriage and had said he loved her. It was too soon, for her, and almost surely for them, too. She wanted them to get to know him first before she handed them a fait accompli. And she needed time to adjust, too. "We could go down right after Christmas, and spend New Year's on the boat," she said cautiously.

"What about Dad?" Megan was quick to defend her father's interests, and time.

"I was going to Squaw with friends," Jason said vaguely, considering the invitation, not sure which would be best. He made his decision quickly. "Actually, I think I'd like to come." He had always loved boats, and a yacht in the Caribbean was too sweet to resist.

"I'll stay with Dad," Megan was quick to add, just to be contrary, even if it "cut off her face to spite her nose," as her brother liked to say when she blew up the bridge, which she did at times, to make a point.

"You can always change your mind later," her mother told her gently, and then turned to her other twin. "Molly? What do you think?"

"I'll go with you." She smiled softly. "It sounds cool to me. Can we bring friends?" Tanya gulped.

"I think it might be rude to ask. Maybe another time, if he asks, but not the first time." They were due to spend Christmas Eve with their father, Christmas Day with her, and she suggested they go to St. Bart's on the twenty-sixth, and come back on New Year's Day, since they had to be back in school on the second. It gave them five days on the boat, which might be enough for Douglas, and it was a wonderful treat for them. Everybody looked pleased, even Megan for not going.

In the end, they had a nice meal and a good Thanksgiving. The kids went to their father's the next day, and the house seemed empty after they left, and better again on Saturday when they returned. They said not a word about Peter, which was a relief to Tanya. Douglas called on Friday, and she told him what the kids had decided about the boat.

"We'll be on hiatus till the eighth," he reminded her. "Why don't I send your kids back on the plane, and you and I stay on the boat for a few more days, till the seventh? It would give us some time alone." He made it sound as though they already had a relationship, and she was wondering if they would by then. As always, he had everything organized and planned. He needed to control his world.

"You're awfully good to us, Douglas," she said, sounding grateful. "This is going to be a fabulous treat for my children. Are you sure you're okay with it?" She knew how he felt about kids.

"They're not four years old," he said blithely. "I'll be fine. I'll enjoy getting to know them, and spending time with you." He sounded more relaxed about her children than he had until that point, and Tanya couldn't help wondering if he had really thought about what being around teenagers would be like. He was totally unaccustomed to kids, and claimed he had an aversion to them. She hoped that hers would be an easy adjustment for him.

"I'm going to enjoy spending time with you, too," she said warmly. It all seemed too good to be true.

"When are you coming home from Marin?" he asked with interest.

"Molly and I are on a four o'clock plane on Sunday. The others are driving down in the morning. I should be back at the hotel by six."

"Why don't I bring over dinner? Maybe I can figure out something more fun than takeout Chinese. Some curry or Thai food. What do you think?"

"Hot dogs would be fine with me." She was excited now to see him. Exciting things were starting to happen in her life. He had kissed her, said he loved her, mentioned marriage, and they were going on his boat with him. A lot had happened in only a few days. Her head was spinning, and she felt as though she was trembling on the brink.

"I'll come over around seven. See you then . . . and Tanya?"

"Yes?"

"I love you," he said softly, and hung up, as she looked around her room, amazed. How life had changed.

# Chapter 18

When Douglas showed up at Bungalow 2 on Sunday night, he was wearing a black cashmere sweater and jeans. He looked relaxed and happy, and had brought several kinds of Indian curry, which smelled delicious when they unpacked them together in the kitchen. Tanya served them on the plates that she had stolen from room service. He kissed her as soon as he walked in, and told her about his weekend. She told him about Marin and the kids, how sad it felt to be there, how empty the house looked when she walked in, like a fallen leaf from a forgotten summer, brittle and dry and faded. It had depressed her to be there, but she loved being with her kids, and it was still home for all of them. And officially for her, too. She admitted to him that she felt homeless now. She no longer knew where she belonged or lived. The bungalow she lived in had become home to her, and she had no painful memories here. It was clean. Peter had only visited her there for two days. The rest of the time it had been entirely hers.

Douglas sat on the couch next to her after dinner, and put an arm around her as they talked. He was far warmer with her than he had ever been before, and it felt like an odd combination between new romance and old friend. There was a lot about it she liked, and it was wonderfully comfortable for her. He was entirely familiar to her, even though they'd never been romantically involved before.

They sat and talked for a long time with his arm around her, and eventually they started to kiss again. His passion for her mounted quickly, and she was surprised to find herself responding to him with equal fire. She had thought all those feelings had died in her when Peter left, and now she was finding they were very much alive. She was slowly discovering that she was powerfully attracted to Douglas. There was something very sensual and male about him that took her breath away now that it was unleashed.

A little while later, they walked into the bedroom, with her bed perfectly turned down. He turned off the lights, and she pulled the bed open, as they both undressed, smiling at each other in the half light. This didn't have the feel of a new love affair, because they knew each other so well. It had more the sense of two people, already comfortable with each other, adding a new facet to what they already shared. She was amazed to find that she was totally at ease with him, and starving for his love and passion. The sex between them was extraordinary, and they made love again before he left at two A.M. It had been an incredible evening, and the relationship that had just begun between them no longer frightened her as it had at first. The sex they shared was powerful and steamy. Douglas was an expert, attentive lover, whose whole focus was on pleasing her. There was something very cerebral about their relationship. She had the feeling that Douglas was always planning and thinking. But everything he planned was to make her happy and pleasure her.

"If I'd known it would be like this," he said gently, as he kissed her before he left, "I'd have done this a long time ago. I'm sorry I waited." She laughed and kissed his neck. But they both knew any sooner would have been wrong. He had been smart to wait. The timing was just right. She was ready for him now, ready to try, and start. And even now, it was a challenge not to think of Peter and the years they'd shared. It seemed so odd to Tanya to be in bed with someone else. But by the end of the night, a deeper bond had formed with Douglas. They had crossed the bridge into a whole new world.

He kissed her passionately again before he left, and called her when he got home to tell her he loved her and missed her already. She kept reminding herself of how lucky she was. But for the tiniest of instants, as she lay alone in her bed again, she found herself missing Peter and had tears in her eyes. The sex had been wonderful with Douglas, and he was a thoughtful caring lover of considerable skill, but for sudden, brief, flashing moments, she missed the familiar feel and smell of Peter. It was hard to let go of twenty years. And yet that night a new chapter in her life had begun. She felt swept away by the tides of what she and Douglas had started that night.

They saw each other often after that. He came over almost every night. They made love, read script notes together, discussed the film, ordered room service, and went out to dinner several times. Tanya was happy and comfortable with him, and they were working like demons on the set. They were trying to conduct their affair discreetly, but once in a while their eyes met, and blind people could have seen what was going on. Things were equalizing slowly and Tanya was falling in love with him. He said constantly what a lucky man he was. The part of her life he did not know yet was her children. And it worried her that he looked nervous whenever one of them called. At least they'd have the time on the boat together, and Tanya knew the rest would take time. The boat would be a great start. But for Douglas and Tanya, as a couple, all was going ex-

tremely well. Douglas had restored her faith in life, and her severely
bruised self-esteem.

The month on the set was insane. She didn't get home to Marin till
the twenty-third of December, the same day the kids arrived. So she
never had time to open, clean, or air the house. A cleaning service
was doing it once a week, but it didn't look the same.

Douglas flew to St. Bart's the same day she went back to Marin. It
was a busy night as the kids arrived, their friends showed up, and the
next day the house was deadly quiet on Christmas Eve when they
went to Peter and Alice. It was hard sharing them. She went to midnight mass alone, and was sad when she got home. It was too late by
then to call Douglas on the boat. She sat alone in the living room for
a long time, thinking of when her children had been little, and the
happy times they'd shared. She had a moment of wanting to call
Peter and wish him a merry Christmas, and then knew that she
couldn't. It was too late for that, or too soon. They were in the no-
man's-land of everything being too fresh, and the wounds not having
yet healed.

It was a relief the next day when the kids came home. They exchanged presents, had lunch, and finished packing for St. Bart's that
night. Molly and Jason were excited, and Megan went back to Peter's
after dinner, as the others were leaving early the next morning.

"Sure you don't want to change your mind?" her mother asked
her, and Megan shook her head. Cutting off her face to spite her
nose, till the end. She had no problem being close to Alice, but still
blamed her mother for the divorce.

The three Caribbean travelers left for the airport at six A.M. They
were there just before seven, and Douglas's jet took off at eight. They
headed for Miami, and landed just after one P.M., four P.M. local time.
They refueled and took off again an hour later, after Tanya and the

children wandered around the airport for half an hour, to stretch their legs. They reached St. Bart's at eight, Miami time, nine P.M. in St. Bart's, after a harrowing landing, which was standard fare for St. Bart's. There were three of Douglas's crew members waiting in the airport for them. They had been traveling for eleven hours by then. They could never have made the connections in one day, were it not for Douglas's plane. The kids looked impressed when they saw the trim nautical uniforms with the yacht's name. *Rêve.* It meant "dream" in French. And Tanya felt as though she were living one. She didn't even know what a two-hundred-foot yacht looked like, although she'd seen photographs of his at his house. It was seventy meters and looked nearly like a cruise ship to them when they saw her. None of them had ever seen a boat that big. *Rêve* was the largest yacht in the port, which was lively and brightly lit. There were little shops all along the quay, and Douglas was standing on deck, waving to them, as they got out of the cab with their bags. He was wearing white jeans, a T-shirt, bare feet, and a deep tan. He beamed the minute he saw them, and Tanya's heart gave a leap. It seemed like a good sign. The children were looking up at the yacht in awe. Tanya would have, too, except her gaze was concentrated on him. They were clearly excited to see each other. This was going to be a fun vacation. She was finally beginning to feel as though she belonged to him. The bonds between them had begun to form and take hold.

The crew members waiting on deck welcomed Tanya and the children to the boat. A stewardess took Molly and Jason to their cabins, which were on a deck below. They disappeared, as Tanya walked up the staircase to the next deck to see him. He instantly put his arms around her and kissed her, and she leaned happily against him. She was becoming deeply attached to him. Her feelings for him had begun to take root, and she was happy to see him, particularly in this exotic, romantic setting, and there was no better place for him to get to know her kids.

"You must be dead after the trip," he said sympathetically, and then poured her a drink and handed it to her. It was a margarita, which seemed just right in the balmy night. The weather was perfect. She had no idea where the kids were, but they were being served club sandwiches in the dining room, unable to believe the luxury of the boat. There was a crew of fifteen, all visibly anxious to make Tanya and her children feel at home.

"I'm hardly tired," Tanya commented as she took a sip of the drink and licked the salt gingerly with her tongue. "Your plane is so comfortable and you spoiled us so much, we all feel like we died and went to Heaven. The boat is gorgeous," she complimented him, and he looked pleased. He had been thinking of her for days and couldn't wait for her to arrive. He was thrilled she was there, although she sensed an invisible tension about him as he smiled at her, as if he wanted to be at ease with her, but something was worrying him. She hoped it wasn't the presence of her children on the boat, and then told herself she was being paranoid. He had been warm and welcoming the moment they arrived. And he was so proud of his boat and of sharing her with Tanya.

"She's pretty, isn't she? I've had her for about ten years and I keep wanting to build a bigger one, but I can't seem to part with this one." By boat standards, ten years was old. She looked brand-new to Tanya and, like everything else he owned, was in exquisite condition. Douglas liked owning the best of everything, whatever it was. *Rêve* was no exception.

Tanya sat on the deck and chatted with him in the balmy tropical breeze, and he seemed to relax as they did. A stewardess had handed her a cashmere shawl, and she was eating sushi made from local fish, when Molly and Jason joined them on deck, looking dazed. It was the first time they had met Douglas. They were extremely polite and too awestruck to do much more than say hello. The moment they appeared, Tanya sensed his tension rise again. He looked almost imperceptibly stressed as he glanced at them and then went on talking to Tanya, paying no attention to them, as though he weren't ready to face them yet, so he ignored them instead. He had absolutely no idea what to say to young people their age, and Tanya could see fear in his eyes. They were too tired to notice, and Tanya hoped it would get better after a few days, when they knew each other better. Her kids were easygoing and friendly, and she was proud of them. Douglas looked terrified.

They eventually all went to their cabins around midnight. Molly and Jason sneaked out of their rooms to talk to the crew in the galley. They were delighted to have young people on board. And in the owner's cabin, as Tanya discovered it was called, she took a shower. When she emerged, Douglas was waiting for her with champagne and strawberries. And as soon as they slipped into his bed, he began making love to her. They shared passionate moments in his cabin until daybreak, when they finally fell asleep. She had never gone to check on her kids, but she was sure they were fine and well protected on the boat. She was certain they were having a ball.

When Tanya awoke, Douglas was already up, and she found him sitting on deck in his bathing trunks, looking strained. He smiled as soon as he saw her. She had been woken up by the boat steaming out of port, on the way to find anchor where they could go swimming and take out the Jet Skis. Molly and Jason were sitting with him in silence, and all three of them looked uncomfortable. The kids looked bored, and she could see panic in Douglas's eyes. Her children began giving her pointed looks the moment she sat down with them. She went down to the cabin to put on a bikini shortly afterward, and both of her children appeared moments later to tell her they thought Douglas was weird.

Jason complained instantly. "Mom, I tried to talk to him a few times, and he didn't even answer. He just kept reading his paper."

"I think he's scared," Tanya said quietly. "Give him a chance. He's never around kids, and I think they make him nervous." Tanya looked worried, too.

"I asked him about the boat," Molly added, "and he told me children should be seen and not heard. And then told Annie the stewardess to take us to the galley and feed us, and not let us mess up the dining room. For chrissake, Mom, he thinks we're six years old."

"Not with that body, sweetheart," she said to her daughter, who was dazzling in a bikini top and a thong. She looked gorgeous. "Give him some time. He was nice to have us down here. You guys have only just met. This is hard for him, too." Tanya wanted so much for it to work, for all of them.

"I think he wants you here, not us. Maybe we should go back," Molly said, feeling awkward and looking hurt.

"Don't be silly. We're all here to have a good time. We will. You can use the Jet Skis after breakfast." But when they did, Douglas got upset. He said he didn't want her children to get hurt, and then he made matters worse by saying he didn't want them to sue him if they did, or break the equipment. He finally agreed to let them use the Jet Skis with a crew member driving and them holding on, on the back, although she had assured him that Jason used the same one every summer in Tahoe. But Douglas was a nervous wreck, as he watched Jason show off.

"I've been sued by guests several times," he explained, looking tense. "Besides, you'd never forgive me if one of your kids got hurt, or worse." He was alternately either overprotective or curt. He seemed unable to find the right balance in his attitude with them. He was either terrified for their safety or annoyed that they were around. It was obvious to Tanya by then that it had been a mistake to bring them on the trip. Douglas seemed unable to adjust to their presence, or welcome them.

At lunchtime he sent the children to the galley to eat with the crew. He asked them not to use the hot tub unless they had showered and had no sunblock on their skin. And he told Jason absolutely not to use his gym. He said the equipment was delicate, and calibrated just for him. They were allowed to swim in the ocean with a crew member watching but not to lie on the sunbeds, because they had sunblock on, which Tanya insisted on in the bright sun. And they ate dinner at six with the crew. Douglas invited her to go out to dinner in St. Bart's, and he couldn't have been more gracious to her, but he was still tense whenever her kids were near.

"Douglas, they're fine," she tried to reassure him, but he looked miserable till they got off the Jet Skis and came back on board. He allowed Molly and Jason to do absolutely nothing except eat, sleep, and stay with the crew. He was stressed beyond belief whenever they were around. Fifteen crew members had been assigned to do all in their power to entertain them and keep them away from Tanya and him, and he obviously wanted her to himself. She finally realized that he was jealous of them. Molly and Jason were miserable by the second day and clamoring to go home. She didn't want to be rude and tried getting Douglas to mellow up a bit, explaining that her "children" were really adults and were not used to being treated like little kids. She did everything she could to be a bridge between both camps, to no avail. He wanted to be alone with her, and they hated him.

That night after dinner two of the crew members took Molly and

Jason to several bars and a disco club to cheer them up. The two kids came home happy as clams at four A.M., staggering and blind drunk. They had a ball and walked right into Douglas and Tanya's cabin to tell them what a great time they'd had. As they stood there, Molly threw up, and Tanya rushed to clean it up, while Douglas sat up in bed and gagged, with a look of horror.

"Hi, Doug," Jason greeted him, swaying on his feet, "great ship. We had a blast tonight."

Douglas was speechless at the sight of them, as Tanya frantically tried to clean the bedroom carpet and made it worse. The smell was awful in the enclosed space. Douglas finally got up and left, and she put her errant children to bed. Douglas spent the night on deck, and an entire crew cleaned his cabin carpet the next day.

"That was an unpleasant little escapade last night, wasn't it?" Douglas commented to her over breakfast. "Do you think children that age should be allowed to drink?" he asked, with obvious disapproval.

"I'm so sorry. They're kids, you know how that is." She assumed he had once been one himself, even if he had none of his own.

"No, I don't know how that is. Do they do that a lot? Drink to excess, I mean."

"Sometimes. They're college kids. Molly isn't used to it, which is why she got sick, I think. Jason usually holds his liquor better."

"Have you thought of putting them in rehab?" he asked, and she realized with horror that he was serious. It was obvious to all by then that he had had no idea what he was doing when he invited them on the trip. Even though his intentions had been good, young people were a terrifying foreign breed to him.

"Of course not," she answered calmly. "They're fine. They don't need rehab. They only do it once in a while, on vacations. And I think they're as uncomfortable as you are." It was the first time either of them had acknowledged how ill at ease they all were, particularly their host. They had all wanted it to work, but clearly it wasn't.

"I'm sorry, Tanya. I guess I wasn't up to this. I thought I was." He looked stiff and stressed, nervous, and disappointed in himself, and Tanya felt sorry for him.

"It was nice of you to try," she said sadly, and he nodded. He didn't know what else to say.

The kids were a mess when they got up. They were both hung over, and Molly threw up again, this time in her own cabin, and wiped out another carpet, much to her mother and the crew's dismay. They managed to keep it from Douglas this time. Molly felt particularly guilty, as she was aware of the tension between Douglas and her mother, and knew that they were causing it. He looked like he hated having them on the boat. She couldn't figure out why he had asked them, except to please their mother. Their mother was a nervous wreck, trying to keep them happy and out of his hair. It had become abundantly obvious by then that he had only invited them as a courtesy to her. He clearly had no intention of getting to know them, and had no idea how to relate to them.

Douglas took her out to dinner again that night, and did not invite her children. He just couldn't cope with them. He didn't know how to speak to them, or what to say, and by then he was too unnerved to try. He felt completely unable to bond with them. Tanya didn't even mention it at dinner, after the fiasco of the night before. The kids were getting on famously with the crew at least, and hanging out with them, but she had barely seen her kids. And it was no vacation for her, worrying about the growing awkwardness and animosity between Douglas and her children. This had not been her plan or his.

The topper came on New Year's Eve, when the kids went ashore with several crew members, all of whom got drunk along with them, and the entire group got brought back by the police, who turned them over to the captain rather than put them in jail. Tanya put her kids to bed, apologizing to Douglas again.

"It is New Year's Eve, after all." She and Douglas had been drinking champagne on the deck and kissing when the police van arrived with everyone singing loudly. Douglas was clearly not amused, at his crew members either.

"Your kids are corrupting my crew," he complained, although his crew had been far more inebriated than her kids. "I think they all got drunk together," she said calmly. She didn't like it either, but the trip was such a disaster by then that there was nothing she could do or say to salvage it. He hadn't had a single meal with them and barely spoke to them, and it was obvious that he regretted inviting them. He was crazy about Tanya, but not her children, and it had been a miserable vacation for her. All she wanted was for all of them to get along. And she knew her kids had hated every minute of the trip, and so had he.

Even their departure from the boat was an unhappy one. Molly and Jason were so hung over they looked grim when they left for his plane the next morning. Douglas observed both of them with a miserable expression and said he hoped they'd have a better trip next time. He mumbled something about not being used to kids, and they thanked him politely and left. Douglas looked enormously relieved as soon as they were gone. Tanya looked heartbroken as he put an arm around her with an apologetic look.

"I'm sorry, darling," he said, kissing her as she looked up at him sadly. "I don't know what to say to you, Tanya. I think I panicked. Having them on the boat was harder than I expected." That much was obvious, but Tanya couldn't imagine how it would get better in the future. He was obviously terrified of children, and had an aversion to them, just as he had warned her from the first. She was so disappointed at how it had turned out, and she knew Molly and Jason were, too. Their vacation on Douglas's yacht had been a nightmare. Tanya was really sorry she'd put them through it. It was going to be nearly impossible now to convince them that Douglas was the man for her. And she had serious questions about it herself. It was essential to her that he get along with her children, which was clearly impossible for him.

"Can you ever forgive me for handling this so badly?" he asked her with a worried look.

"Of course. I just want you all to get to know each other and be friends."

"Maybe we'll do better with that back home. I was terrified they'd get hurt while they were on the boat."

"I understand," Tanya said, wanting to put it behind them, but she knew she'd hear about it from her kids for a long time. The trip had been a disappointment for all concerned.

She tried to relax once the kids left, but it took her two days to stop worrying about the chasm between Douglas and her children. She knew it would take time, maybe a long time, to resolve.

And then finally they had four idyllic days on the boat alone, drifting from island to island, swimming, eating on deck, relaxing, and making love. It was the perfect vacation he had wanted. Theirs was an adult relationship, which left little or no room for her kids, and she had no idea if that would change, unless Douglas warmed up to them. There had been no sign of that while Molly and Jason were on the boat. She had apologized to them again, in several phone calls since, and they said they understood. But even Tanya wasn't sure she did. Douglas was not an easy man to understand.

The rest of the trip went smoothly, and she flew home to Los Angeles with Douglas on his plane. He slept while she worked on the script, and he took her back to the bungalow when they arrived. But she was sad. The attempt to introduce him to her children had been a disaster, even if she had had a nice time on the boat with him afterward. But their time alone wasn't enough for her to make a life with him. Her kids meant everything to her. She was seriously worried about her future with Douglas now. The potential for having a serious relationship with him had drastically diminished, given his behavior toward Jason and Molly on the boat, and his inability to adjust to them.

"I'm going to miss you tonight," he said, kissing her before he left. He seemed oblivious to how upset she was. Unlike Tanya, he had stopped thinking about her children as soon as they left the boat.

"Me too," she said quietly, and after he left the bungalow, she sat down on her bed and burst into tears. There was so much about Douglas she liked, but this piece was crucial to her. For whatever reason, he was impossible with her kids. There was no hiding from it. Just as he had said to her in the beginning, he had a profound aversion to children. Even hers. Or maybe especially hers. The only thing he wanted was to be alone with her. And to Tanya, she and her children were a package deal. They were a package, and a gift, which he was both unwilling and unable to accept, which changed everything for her.

# Chapter 19

For the rest of January, Tanya tried to overlook what had happened on the boat. Her kids had commented on it several times, and she apologized again. She asked them to give him another chance at some point, and she'd talk to him, and try to straighten things out.

Otherwise, the relationship was perfect. He was wonderful to her. He spoiled her, he was attentive, he was thoughtful and kind. He brought her gifts, took her to dinner, was respectful of her work. The only thing that bothered her was that he had a tendency to make decisions for her. He thought she needed an air filter in her room, and had one set up without asking her. She knew he meant well, but the sound it made disturbed her while she was writing. He planned a vacation for the two of them at Easter, on the boat again. He didn't ask her, he just planned it and told her. She explained that she couldn't leave her children then, and they had plans to go to Hawaii. He told her to let them go, and she could come with him on the boat. They didn't exist for him. And when she caught a nasty sinus infection in February, he called his doctor, and got an antibiotic for her, without asking if she wanted one. He meant well, but he was controlling and high-handed, and had declared a cold war on her children. It was not a small problem for her. She felt constantly stressed now, although there were aspects of the relationship she loved, his fine mind, his culture, his profound admiration of her writing. She loved his sensitivity when he played the piano. The way they made love, well and often. He was a deeply caring lover, even more so than Peter, and the sex was fabulous between them. He played her body like a harp. But it was an entirely adult relationship, which in no way included her kids.

And it became more and more obvious to her that it never would. He wanted her to sell the house in Marin, and move in with him in L.A. He wanted to get married that summer, and spend a two-month honeymoon on his boat in France. She asked him what he thought she would do with her children during that time. He looked blank, and suggested she send them to their father. He did not understand that she loved being with them, too, not just him. She was not trading them for him. She needed both.

They wrapped *Gone* at the end of February, and she stayed on for two months of postproduction, as planned. They finished the week of the Academy Awards. Their previous film, *Mantra,* had been nominated in five categories, including Best Film, although she hadn't been nominated for the screenplay. He told her with absolute certainty that her winning film would be *Gone.*

She had promised to go to the awards with him, which was exciting for her. She had bought a dress at Valentino, and he had hair and makeup artists from the set do her face and hair. She looked spectacular when they got out of the limousine. Her dress was a shimmery pale silver, and she looked like a Greek goddess on his arm. She knew her children were watching for her on TV, in their dorms, and she waved. It was a long, tiring night sitting through the awards, and disappointing for him since *Mantra* didn't win for Best Film. His face was stoic, but she could see the muscles working in his jaw when another film was called for the award. He looked angry for the rest of the night. Douglas didn't lose easily.

She could see now what Max had said to her from the beginning. Douglas was all about power and control. He was addicted to both. Being with him would mean that he would always be controlling her, making decisions for her, and excluding her kids. She knew she couldn't do it, no matter how good the rest was. She was thinking about it, her head bowed, as they walked along the red carpet again on the way out.

They were scheduled to attend half a dozen parties that night, but Douglas's heart wasn't in it, since they hadn't won an award. He was programmed for victory and success. Anything less than that was a narcissistic injury he couldn't tolerate. Douglas *had* to win, he had to have the power and control at all times, even over her. It made her sad thinking about it, because there was a lot about him she liked. But not enough. Even if the sex was great, even if he loved her and wanted to marry her, she needed a more normal life than he could ever offer her, and one that included her kids. His life just didn't, and never would. It was clear to her now. And whatever feelings she'd had for him began to die like flowers in snow.

"Depressing, isn't it?" he asked her, as they drove back to the hotel. Before, he had wanted her to go home with him. Now he didn't. With no Oscar in his hand that night, he wanted to be alone. "I hate losing," he said through clenched teeth as they drove to the Beverly Hills Hotel, and got out. He was going to take her to her door and go home alone. He was being an incredibly bad sport.

He walked her to the door of her bungalow, and she looked at him sadly after he kissed her. She could have waited, and she felt cruel adding to tonight's woes. But she knew so clearly now what this was and what it wasn't. In a funny way, he wanted her as a trophy. The star screenwriter whom he thought would win an Oscar next year. And what if she didn't? It was all about that with him, and nothing real. To Douglas, winning was all.

"Douglas, I can't do this anymore," she said in a small, apologetic voice. He looked so angry he almost frightened her. He was so upset they didn't win. She'd seen Max at the Oscars, and he looked disappointed, too. But he had still managed to shrug and grin and give her a warm hug. There was life beyond the movie business for him. But not for Douglas. This was all there was.

"Can't do what?" He looked at her blankly. He didn't understand what she was saying. It had looked so hopeful for a while, to both of them. Now all she wanted was to get away, and go back to Marin, where life was real. "Do what? Lose on Oscar night? Yeah, me too. Don't worry, Tanya. We'll win next year for sure."

"I didn't mean that," she said, looking at him sadly. "I need a relationship that includes my kids. This one never will." Time stood still for a long minute as he stared at her.

"Are you serious? You told me they were adults."

"They're eighteen and nineteen. I'm not ready to let go of them yet. They're going to be around a lot for a few more years, during vacations at least. I like it that way. They'll always be an important part of my life. I can't shut them out to be with you."

"What are you saying to me then?" He looked stunned. It had never occurred to him that she would do something like this. He couldn't help wondering if she would have done it if he'd had the

Oscar in his hand. Probably not, he told himself. Winning was every-thing, and she knew it, too. There was nothing worse than the smell of defeat around a man.

"I'm saying that I can't do this anymore," she said clearly, in a small sad voice. She was shaking, but he didn't see it. This was hard for her. "It doesn't work for me or my kids." He nodded then, backed away from her, swept her a small bow, turned on his heel, and walked away without another word. She stood looking after him, sad for him, and sadder for herself. She knew he really didn't under-stand. Maybe he had loved her, to the best of his ability. But even if he had, he would never have loved her kids. And that was too impor-tant to her to give up for an Oscar, or any man.

She let herself into her bungalow then. Her bags were packed. The movie was over. She had stayed for the Academy Awards for him. Her kids were coming home for the summer in two weeks. For the second time in a year, she was checking out of Bungalow 2 the next day. It was time to fold up the circus tent and go home.

# Chapter 20

The house looked even more depressing than usual when she got back to Marin the next day. The couch looked tired, the carpet was worn. She saw that there had been a couple of leaks around the windows from one of the winter storms. The weather was beautiful, and it was warm at least. She made a list of the things she needed to replace and fix. She wanted to spruce up the house before the kids got home.

She hadn't heard a word from Douglas since the night before, and she knew she never would. What she had said to him was too big for him to deal with, and his own sense of loss over not winning the award the night before was going to paralyze him for a while. He would never have included her children in his life. Whether he admitted it to her or not, they both knew it wouldn't work. Their lives and values were too different and nothing would ever change. She had come home for good this time. She was sure he wouldn't ask her to do another movie. And she didn't want to now. She wanted to go back to her short stories, her quiet life in Marin, and being with her children whenever they came home. She had a book in mind, another anthology of short stories. She was looking forward to being home, staying home, wearing jeans and T-shirts, and rarely combing her hair. It sounded good to her. She had been gone for twenty months, in the madness of Hollywood. It was time to come home and settle down. She was through with L.A.

The children came home two weeks later. They got summer jobs, they saw their friends, they had barbecues. Tanya wrote in the early mornings, and hung out with them when they were in the mood. She and Megan made friends again. Alice had tried to come between her and her father, and Megan felt betrayed. Tanya knew Alice's betrayals well.

Peter and Alice got married that summer, in a ceremony on Mount Tam. Tanya's children were there, and she spent the day alone at Stinson Beach, looking out at the sea, thinking of the years she had spent with Peter, and their own wedding day. She felt as though a part of her had died the day he married Alice. She felt as though she finally buried what had been dead for a long time. In an odd way, it was a relief.

They went to Tahoe in August, and at the end of the summer the children went back to their colleges, and Tanya hunkered down in earnest to work on her book. She'd been at it for a week when her agent called. He said he had a fantastic offer for her, and she laughed.

"Nope," she said, grinning, as she turned her computer off. She had absolutely no interest in whatever he had to say. She was finished with L.A. She'd done two movies, learned some things, had a romance with one of the biggest producers in L.A., and come home again. She wasn't leaving now for anyone or anything, and surely not for a movie offer. She had been there, done that. She was all through. She spelled it out to him in no uncertain terms.

"Don't be like that, Tanya. Let me at least tell you what it is first."

"Nope. Don't care. I'm not doing movies anymore. I did one more than I said I would. I'm done. I'm sitting here working on a book." She sounded peaceful, happy, and pleased with herself.

"Good. That's wonderful. I'm proud of you. Now put it aside for a few minutes and listen to what I have to say. Gordon Hawkins. Maxwell Ernst. Sharon Upton. Shalom Kurtz. Happy Winkler. Tippy Green. Zoe Flane. And Arnold Win. Put that in your pipe and smoke it, baby." He had caught her attention, but she didn't know what he meant. He had rattled off the names of some of the biggest stars in Hollywood.

"So?" She sounded blasé.

"So my ass. Is that the most star-studded cast you ever heard? Those are the names of the actors in the film they want you for. Some nut down there has fallen in love with your work, and says name your price. What's more, it's a comedy. You're good at that shit. It'll be fun to write. And they're doing this one fast and dirty. This is no epic about suicide where they make the actors bleed for eighteen hours onstage. They want to spend two months doing this film. They'll start in December. Preproduction in two weeks. Another month to clean it up afterward. You're done in February, tops. And you have a hell of a good time, make a hell of a lot of money, as I do off your back, thank you very much," he said, and she laughed. "All expenses paid, and they'll give you Bungalow 2. I told them that was part of the deal, and they said fine. Am I good to you or what?"

"Shit, Walt. I don't want to go back to L.A. I'm happy here." Not happy maybe, but peaceful, and doing good work.

"Bullshit. You're depressed. I can hear it in your voice. Your nest is empty. Your husband's gone. Your house is too big for you. You don't have a boyfriend that I know of. You're writing depressing stories. Hell, I'm getting depressed just thinking about it. It'll be good therapy for you to write a comedy in L.A. Besides, no one does funny like you."

"Oh come on, Walt . . ." She hesitated. It was such a stupid thing to do. This was her real life. That wasn't.

"Listen, I need the money. So do you." She laughed at what he said. The only thing that tempted her was the cast, the names were in fact incredible, and comedy was fun to write. It was a short shooting schedule, but still. She hated to go back even to Bungalow 2. It was becoming her second home. But she did have friends in L.A. now, more than she did in Marin. Everyone in Ross acted as though she were from outer space. She had become an alien being as Douglas had predicted she would. No one called her to invite her to anything anymore, they were used to her being gone. They made comments about how fancy she was now, how she had outgrown Marin. Peter and Alice had corralled her entire social life. She was totally isolated now, much more so than in L.A., especially working on a film. At least then she would see people and have some fun. Walt was right about that.

"Oh shit," Tanya said, laughing. "I can't believe you're doing this to me. I said no more films."

"Yeah, I know. Just like I say no more blondes. I married another one last year. Now she's pregnant with twins. Some things don't change."

"I hate you."

"Great. I hate you, too. So go do this movie. You'll have a ball. If nothing else, it's worth it just to meet the cast. I want to visit you on the set on this one."

"What makes you think I'll do it?"

"I reserved Bungalow 2 for you today, just in case. So?"

"Okay, okay, I'll do it . . . when do I get the rough notes for the script?"

"Tomorrow. I FedExed it to you today."

"Don't tell them yes till I see it." She was a pro at this now.

"Of course not," he said, sounding businesslike and official. "What kind of agent do you think I am?"

"A damned pushy one. I'm telling you though, Walt, this is the last movie I'm doing. After this I'm only doing books."

"Okay, okay. At least you'll have a good time doing this one. You'll laugh your ass off all the way back to Marin."

"Thanks," she said, looking around her kitchen. She couldn't believe she was about to agree to do another movie. But as she looked around and listened to the silence in the house, she knew that he was right, and there was nothing for her here anymore. The spirit and purpose of her life in Marin were long gone. Peter was with Alice, and her kids were on their own. There was nothing here for her.

She read the concept the next day, and the rough notes they'd sent her. The story was hysterical, it had her laughing out loud, sitting in her kitchen. And the cast was beyond belief. She called Walt as soon as she finished reading.

"Okay, I'll do it. Last one, though. You got that?"

"Okay, okay, Tan. Last one. Go for it! Have a ball with this!"


She turned up at the Beverly Hills Hotel two weeks later, and checked into Bungalow 2. She felt like a boomerang by now. She kept coming back to the same place. Like a bad penny that kept turning up. She rearranged the furniture the way she liked it, put out the photographs of the children, got in the tub and turned on the Jacuzzi, and then sat smiling to herself. It felt good. It was like coming home.

She was at the studio promptly at nine o'clock the next day, and then the fun began. There didn't seem to be a member of the cast who wasn't utterly insane. They had brought the cast in first for notes on this one. Every major comedian in the business was in it, of every race, sex, shape, and size. They were funny just talking to them. None of them could focus for more than five minutes. They tried out lines on her constantly. She couldn't even imagine trying to get them to learn the ones she wrote. She felt like she had accepted an assignment in an insane asylum, but the inmates were so damned funny and fun to be with, she didn't stop laughing all day. She hadn't had this much fun in years. All but one of the stars had come in to see her that day. The last one was flying in from Europe that night, and coming in to see her the next day. He was their main star, and he was fabulously good-looking as well as funny. She had met him once with Douglas, and he seemed very nice.

It was odd not to be seeing Douglas now that she was back in L.A. She hadn't heard from him in five months, and it would have been awkward if she'd called. So she didn't. It had ended badly and in silence.

She worked on the script that night, and found that the story came easily, the lines were fun to write. She could imagine each of them in their characters. It was going to be one of the funniest movies in years. Who cared if she won an Oscar? She was going to have a ton of fun working on the film. She already was. Two of the actors called her that night, and had her in hysterics. She laughed out loud herself at lines she wrote. She couldn't wait to try them out on them the next day. Her meeting with Gordon Hawkins, their big star, was set for ten o'clock the following morning.

She was sitting in the conference room, drinking tea, with her feet on the table, when he walked in. She'd been talking and laughing and horsing around with one of the other stars. Hawkins walked over to where she was sitting, and sat down next to her.

"I'm glad you're not killing yourself on this," he said seeming sincere, and then took her tea, sipped it and made a face. "You need sugar in that. Look, I just got off a plane from Paris. I'm tired. I'm sick. My hair is a mess. I'm not feeling funny. They're not paying me enough to take meetings when I have jet lag, so I'm going to my hotel. I'll see you tomorrow. I'll be much funnier with some sleep. I'll give you my notes then." He stood up, took another sip of her tea, shook his head, poured it out, and walked out of the room, while she grinned.

"I take it that's our star. Where's he staying?"

"The Beverly Hills. Bungalow 6. He always stays there. It has his name on it."

"We're neighbors," she said to a production assistant. "I'm 2."

"Watch out. He's hell on wheels." There were already bets placed as to which of the other stars he'd sleep with. He got involved with his costars on every movie. And it was easy to see why. He was one of the most beautiful men Tanya had ever seen. He was forty-five years old, had jet-black hair, blue eyes, a gorgeous body, and a smile that just didn't quit.

"I think I'm safe," Tanya said as they all talked about him. "I think the last girl I read about him going out with was twenty-two."

"No woman is safe with Gordon. He gets engaged on every picture. He's never gotten married yet. But he gets a hell of a lot of press out of it, and gives them gorgeous rings."

"Do they have to give them back?"

"Probably. I think he borrows them."

"Damn. I thought maybe I could at least get a ring out of it," Tanya said with a grin, and then looked around. "Shit, he threw out my tea." Someone gave her another cup, and the meeting went on from there. It was a day of banter and joking, figuring out who was comfortable saying what, and then going back to her bungalow and writing. She was still working at midnight, cackling to herself, when she heard a knock on her door. She opened it with a pencil in her hair and another in her teeth. It was Gordon Hawkins. He handed her a cup of tea.

"Try this. It's a brand I always carry with me. I get it in Paris, and it won't jangle your nerves. That stuff you were drinking this morning was shit." She grinned and took a sip as he walked in. "Why is your bungalow bigger than mine?" he asked, looking around. "I'm much more famous than you are."

"That's true. Maybe I have a better agent," she suggested, as he sprawled out on the couch and turned on the TV. He was obviously crazy, but she loved it. He looked like a wild Irishman with his cornflower blue eyes and jet-black hair, as he dangled his feet off the end of the couch. He set the TiVo for two of his favorite shows while she laughed at him. He had a lot of nerve, but he was funny to be around. Just watching him made her laugh. He had a great deadpan face, and a funny expression in his eyes.

"I'll come in and watch my shows with you here," he said comfortably. "I don't have TiVo in my room. I think I have to fire my agent. Who's yours?"

"Walt Drucker."

He nodded. "He's good. I saw a soap you wrote once. It sucked, but it made me cry anyway. I don't want to cry in this movie," he warned her. He looked about thirty-five, and acted about fourteen.

"You won't. I promise. I was working on it when you walked in. Thanks for the tea, by the way." She took another sip. It was good. It tasted of vanilla, and the tag was French.

"Have you had dinner?" She shook her head. "Me neither. I'm on another time zone. I think it's breakfast time for me." He checked his watch. "Yup. Nine-thirty A.M. in Paris. I'm starving. Do you want to have breakfast with me? We can charge it to your room." He reached for the room service menu, called them, and ordered pancakes. He suggested she have French toast or an omelette so they could share. And she found herself doing what he said. She had no idea why, but he had that kind of effect on her. He was so crazy, he made you want to play with him. But she knew he was a very good actor, too. She was excited to be working with him.

They munched their way through pancakes, French toast, and several Danish pastries, fruit salad, and orange juice for two. It was the craziest meal she'd ever had, while he discussed the comparative virtues of Burger King versus McDonald's.

"I eat at McDonald's a lot in Paris," he explained. "They call it Mac Do there. I stay at the Ritz."

"I haven't been to Paris in years."

"You should go. It would do you good." He lay back down on the couch again then, exhausted from their feast, and then he picked his head up and looked at her with interest. "Do you have a boyfriend?" She wondered if he was taking a poll or checking her out for himself.

"No." She didn't elaborate.

"Why not?"

"I'm divorced and have three kids."

"I'm divorced and have five kids, all with different mothers. Long relationships bore me."

"So I hear."

"Ah, so they warned you. What did they say? Probably that I get engaged on every picture. Sometimes I just do it for publicity. You know how that is." She nodded, wondering just how crazy he really was. She was getting sleepy. It was nearly two, and he was going full steam ahead, wide awake, on Paris time. She was on L.A. time, and about to fall asleep. He noticed her yawning and sat up. "Are you tired?"

"Kind of," she admitted. "We have early meetings tomorrow," she reminded him.

"Okay." He stood up, looking like a tall, gangly kid. He couldn't find one shoe, and then finally did. "Get some sleep." He waved at her from the door, and then went back to his own bungalow, while she stood there and grinned. The phone rang almost immediately, It was Gordon again. "Thanks for breakfast," he said politely. "It was delicious, and you're fun to talk to."

"Thank you. So are you. And breakfast was good."

"Next time we can have it in my room," he offered, and she laughed.

"You don't have TiVo."

"Damn. That's right. I'm calling my agent tomorrow to complain. Do me a favor, wake me tomorrow, will you? What time do you get up?"

"Seven."

"Call me when you leave."

"Goodnight, Gordon," she said firmly. He could have called the operator for a wake-up call. She should have made him, but he was so damned charming and flaky, he was hard to resist. She felt as though she had adopted a little kid.

"Goodnight, Tanya. Sleep tight. See you tomorrow." With that, she hung up. She was still smiling about him as she turned off the lights, put on her nightgown, climbed into bed, and went to sleep. She was thinking about him as she drifted off. This movie was going to be fun to do. For once, Walt was right.

# Chapter 21

The set of the movie Tanya was working on was in almost constant bedlam. With a dozen comedians involved, a funny story, and a comedic script, they could hardly keep straight faces to say their lines. There were a million outtakes that were even funnier than the movie. The director was hysterical, the producer was a good guy. The cameramen were funny. And Tanya had a great time writing the script. It almost wrote itself. She loved going to work every day and telling her kids about it. Molly came to visit her once and loved it. She thought Gordon Hawkins was gorgeous, and so did everyone else. He and Tanya were fast friends by the second week of shooting. She could see him checking all the women out, trying to decide which one he wanted. Movie sets were like a supermarket for him. There were no great beauties on this movie. But there were some very nice, smart women who knew better than to get involved with him. He was coming up dry on this one, which was unheard of for him.

He was lying on Tanya's couch, watching TV one night, while she was making script changes. He had just eaten his way through two hamburgers and a milk shake. In spite of that, he was relatively thin.

He was a bottomless pit. He worked it off in the gym. "Do I look older to you, Tanya?" he asked, looking worried.

"Older than what?" She was busy and not paying attention. He talked a lot. And he hung out on her couch constantly. He was bored and lonely, and he liked her.

"Older than I used to look," he explained, changing channels for the fiftieth time in an hour. He channel-surfed constantly. Whenever she saw something she would have liked to watch, it vanished instantly. It was a lot like being married.

"I wouldn't know. I just met you. I don't know how old you used to look."

"That's true. There are no decent women on this picture. It's very depressing. They should have hired one for me."

"From what I've heard, you do fine on your own," she reminded him, and he shook his head vehemently.

"That's bullshit. I always get involved with the women I work with. I can never meet women outside work."

"You may have to make a supreme effort and try this time," she told him, and turned her computer off. It was too distracting to work with him in the room. Besides, he was fun to talk to.

"That sucks," he said in answer to what she'd just told him. "What about you? You're a damned fine-looking woman."

"Thank you." She took what he said with a grain of salt. She told him regularly that he was full of shit, which he readily admitted was true.

"Do you like me?" he asked her with a look of innocence, and she laughed at him. They were rapidly becoming friends, hopefully for longer than just this movie. She really liked him. He was a nice guy, and fun to be around, even if silly. He was harmless, and underneath the craziness was a nice person. And he seemed to love his kids, and even his ex-wives and ex-girlfriends. And more important, they loved him.

"I like you very much," she said honestly. "Are you having some kind of insecurity crisis? Should I call your shrink?"

"No, he's in Mexico on vacation. I must pay him too much. I like you, too. Maybe you and I should go out during this picture."

"Are you nuts? I'm twice the age of the women you go out with. Besides, I don't want to get engaged unless I can keep the ring."

"That's annoying," he said, looking thoughtful. "We could go out and not get engaged. That's a better deal for me."

"Or not go out, and say we did," she teased him, as he sat up on the couch suddenly, looking like he'd been struck by lightning.

"Christ, I think I have the hots for you, Tanya. I mean it. It just occurred to me."

"You're probably just hungry. Call room service."

"No, I'm serious. You turn me on. I just realized it. You're very funny. You're smart, and you're sexy as hell."

"No, I'm not."

"Yes, you are. I think smart women are very sexy."

"I'm not your type," she reminded him, unimpressed by his discovery. He was just shooting off his mouth, but it was fun listening to him. She enjoyed him. And looking at him was certainly a treat.

"No, you're not my type," he agreed. "I usually go for dumber women with bigger boobs. Am I your type?" he asked with interest.

"Not at all," she reassured him. "I like them older and more serious. Kind of preppy. My husband was an attorney."

"I'm definitely not your type," he said, appearing both thunderstruck and delighted. "Do you know what that means?" he said, visibly thrilled.

"Yes, that we won't be dating," she laughed at him. "I can figure that much out."

"No, when people aren't each other's type, they get married. When they're each other's type, they have a hot affair and fuck it up just like they always did. It's the ones who aren't your type that you're supposed to marry. None of my wives were my type," he said, as though to prove the point.

"And you're not married to them anymore. So much for that idea."

"Yeah, but I still love them, and they love me. I think they're terrific."

"You've finally convinced me, Gordon. You're certifiably crazy. Maybe you should go out on disability."

"No, I mean it. I want to date you. We don't have to get engaged or married, if you don't want to. Let's just try it and see what happens."

"My children would kill me if I married you," she said, laughing. Actually Molly had thought he was fantastic and the funniest man she'd ever met. Tanya was inclined to agree. But that didn't make him dating material, just amusing to be with.

"My children would love you," he said seriously. "So what do you think?"

"I think it's time for you to go back to your room. It must be time for your medication or something. Or mine, if you hang around here much longer with crazy ideas like that." With that, he got up off the couch, walked to where she was sitting, and kissed her, gently, on the mouth, like a real kiss. She looked at him in astonishment, as though he had done something truly outrageous, which he had. But he was so persistent, and so insanely sexy, that she found herself kissing him back, and wondering why she did. And then he kissed her again. He was a hell of a good kisser.

"See what I mean? You're not my type, but you turn me on like crazy, Tanya."

"You turn me on, too," she admitted, looking dazed. "Look, Gordon, this is not a good idea. Let's not do something really stupid. Let's be friends."

"Let's fall in love. It's more fun," he suggested.

"It'll be a mess if we do."

"No, it won't. I'm telling you, we could end up getting married."

"No, we *won't!*" she said emphatically.

"Okay, okay. Sorry. I won't mention marriage. Let's go to bed with each other," he said, as he put an arm around her and continued to kiss her. But it was too much fun to stop. They were both loving it. He was the sexiest man Tanya had ever met, as well as the funniest. It was an unbeatable combination, and nearly impossible to resist, although she was trying, and not getting anywhere. He wouldn't stop kissing her.

"I *won't* go to bed with you either," she said, sounding outraged.

He didn't argue with her, but half an hour later, they did. Tanya was horrified afterward and couldn't believe she'd done it.

"You're a lunatic, Gordon Hawkins," she said, lying in bed with their arms around each other. They'd had fun, and he was sweet, and he said he loved her body. He was fabulous in bed.

"You're gorgeous, Tanya," he said, nuzzling her like a big puppy. He was so gentle and affectionate, it was delicious. She loved being with him, and making love with him had been extremely nice.

"Go to your room, Gordon," she said, and tried to sound as though she meant it, but she didn't, and he didn't move an inch. He stayed in her bed, holding her all night. They made love two more times and slept like children. They woke up the next day with the sun streaming into the room, and took a shower together. They had breakfast in her room, and then he went back to his to get dressed. They left for the studio together, as Tanya looked at him in amazement. She couldn't believe she had slept with him, but she wasn't unhappy about it, even if she thought she should be.

"So what is this?" she asked him as they drove to the studio. "Your affair for the movie? How crazy is that?"

"Maybe it could be forever," he said hopefully. "You never know. I'd like it to be. I like you a lot, Tanya."

"I like you, too, Gordon," she said softly, wondering to herself what she was doing. She had no idea. But whatever it was, it wasn't hurting anyone and she was having a good time. How bad could that be?

# Chapter 22

Tanya's affair with Gordon Hawkins while they worked on the movie together was possibly one of the craziest things she'd ever done. It felt like it, it looked like it, and it seemed like it. But she'd never had so much fun in her life. And the script was like silk to write.

He sat in her bungalow at night, watching television, while she tried out ideas on him. Some he thought were funny, some he didn't. But he always came up with great suggestions for her. She was thrilled with what was happening with the script, and even more so with what was happening with him. She could see why he had been married so often, and had so many girlfriends. Gordon was wonderful to women and genuinely liked them. He had no chip on his shoulder, no ax to grind. He was just a truly nice person, who loved being with her. And when Megan and Jason came down from Santa Barbara to visit her on the set, he was wonderful to them, and they fell in love with him. They begged her to invite Gordon to Marin over the break.

"I'm sure he has better things to do." Tanya tried to discourage them. There was nothing serious about what was happening. She didn't want them getting too attached to him. But when she finally got up the guts to suggest it to him, he thought it was a terrific idea. He suggested they stay for a few days, and then all go skiing together. He said he'd like nothing better than spending a week with her and her kids.

She couldn't believe her eyes the day he arrived in Marin. His hair was sticking up straight, he was wearing jeans and a turtleneck, and he had four giant suitcases with him, loaded with his gear. He was beaming from ear to ear and swung her around her kitchen as the kids watched with amusement. He looked like he was moving in, which would have delighted them.

He took all of them out to dinner that night, Tanya, her kids, and half a dozen of their friends. He made popcorn for everyone afterward, and finally after everyone else had gone to bed, he helped Tanya clean up, and followed her upstairs to bed.

"I love this house," he said happily, "and your kids are so great." She was beginning to wonder if she had finally lucked out, and found the man of her dreams, or if he came from another planet. Maybe both.

The next morning she went grocery shopping with him, and they both laughed as people stopped to stare when they recognized him.

"My God, I think that's Gordon Hawkins," one woman whispered to another at the checkout counter, as he continued to juggle cans of chili she had bought for Jason. He enjoyed whatever he was doing, and whoever he was with. He was the easiest person to be with she had ever met in her life. And by the time they got to Tahoe to go skiing, she was really beginning to wonder if she was in love with him. It was impossible not to be. There was nothing about him you couldn't love, and he was incredibly kind to Tanya and her children.

He was also a nearly Olympic-class skier. He and Jason made end-less runs down the mountain, on all the hardest trails. He showed the girls some new techniques, and then skied sedately for a while with Tanya. There seemed to be nothing he couldn't do. And he caused a sensation in the restaurants they went to at night. Every-body recognized him, wanted autographs, stopped to talk to him, and felt as though they'd made a new friend when they walked away. Tanya knew what a big star he was, but she didn't get a sense of it until people begged him constantly to pose for photographs with them.

"Good lord, Gordon, everybody on the planet knows you."

"I hope so." He grinned at her happily. Tanya looked just as happy as he did, and so did her kids. "If they didn't, I'd be out of a job. They would never have hired me for the picture we're working on, and I would never have met you, or your kids. So it's a damned good thing they all know me." It made sense.

They all hated to leave Tahoe after five days, especially her kids. It was a far cry from the vacation she, Molly, and Jason had taken the year before on Douglas's yacht. What a misery that had been for them. And what a joy this was for them all. It was particularly fun because Gordon had such a good time himself. He was always in a good mood, loved everyone he met, and enjoyed everything he did. It was hard to beat. And Tanya didn't try. She no longer asked herself what the relationship was about, what it meant, or where it was go-ing. She was enjoying the hell out of it, and she let it go at that. So did Gordon. He had even stopped saying that she wasn't his type. They were all sorry when the vacation came to an end, and they had to close the house in Marin again and head south.

She and Gordon looked sad when they were back in her bungalow that night.

"I miss your kids," he said miserably. "They're so great."

"I miss them, too." They called them all after that, and some of his. She hadn't met any of his children yet, but he was promising to introduce her soon. His were younger than hers, and ranged from twelve to five. He'd been busy, since he had five, all with different women, as he had told her in the beginning. But he was on good terms with all of his children's mothers. Everyone loved Gordon, even after their romances with him were over. He didn't have a mean bone in his body.

The movie they were working on ended in February, as planned. Gordon had no set plans after that, and he stayed in her bungalow with her till the end of March, while she worked on postproduction, and he hung around and visited friends.

She stayed on after that for another week, at her own expense, into early April, so they could go to the Academy Awards together. She was nominated for the script for *Gone,* just as Douglas had predicted she would be. The film was nominated for nine Academy Awards. Gordon had never won any, but he was thrilled for her and excited to be going with her. She got seats for her kids, and the five of them were going together. It was a major event for her. Gordon went shopping with her to buy a dress, and talked her into a half-naked incredibly sexy pale pink Valentino. She looked like a movie star in it. Both girls came to L.A. to shop for the event.

On the night of the Academy Awards, Tanya put on the pale pink Valentino. She had her hair and makeup done, and wore towering silver Manolo Blahnik sandals. The girls looked beautiful, too, in fairy-princess gauzy pastel dresses they had found at Marc Jacobs, and Gordon and Jason looked handsome in their tuxes. They were a striking-looking group as they started their odyssey on the red carpet. Tanya had her hand tucked into Gordon's arm, and a wall of photographers stopped them immediately to take pictures. For the first time in her life, Tanya felt like a star. She turned and grinned sheepishly at her children, as they beamed at her, obviously and justifiably proud, even Megan. She was over Alice, and back on board with her mother. Alice had proven herself to be less of an ally and friend than they once thought. They had since decided that she had used them to get to Peter. Their relationship with him was suffering as a result. And Molly had confided that Peter didn't look too happy. Tanya couldn't help wondering if he had regrets about what he'd done, but it was too late for that.

The walk down the red carpet took forever. Photographers stopped them, TV cameras shone bright lights in their faces, and interviewers wanted to know what Gordon thought, and how Tanya felt.

"How good do you think your chances are?" was their favorite question.

"How are you going to feel if you win? . . . or lose?"

"How do you feel about never having won an Oscar?" That to Gordon.

It went on forever, until they finally got into the auditorium and took their seats. And then it took even longer. Gordon yawned frequently, and cameras caught him. And then he waved. He kissed Tanya several times, joked with the kids, applauded when people won. And then finally the moment came. The five screenwriters were shown on a giant screen, as they squirmed in the audience, trying to look calm and failing dismally to do so. They showed clips from the films, and then Steve Martin and Sharon Stone came out to open the envelope and read the winning name. Tanya sat in her seat squeezing Gordon's hand. She felt stupid, but suddenly it really mattered to her. She had never wanted anything so much in her life. She had noticed Douglas several rows ahead of her. He hadn't acknowledged her when she walked in. It had been exactly a year since she'd last seen him. They had broken up the night of the last Academy Awards. She had mentioned in passing to Gordon that she had gone out with him. It didn't bother him at all. He had dated half of Hollywood.

Steve handed the envelope to Sharon. She was wearing a vintage Chanel dress and looked incredible. And then she said the name. Tanya listened, and it didn't sound familiar. It was just words that hit her ears like a blur, and then she heard Megan scream.

"Mom! You *won!*" Gordon was looking at her and smiling, and she didn't understand. He lifted her gently out of her chair, and then she realized what had happened. The words they had said had been her name. Tanya Harris. She had won an Oscar for Best Screenplay for the movie *Gone.* She stood up, looking dazed, and stumbled past Gordon into the aisle, and an usher got her up to the stage, where she actually managed to walk to the podium, and stand there staring into the lights. She wanted to see her children, but she couldn't, and Gordon, but it was all a blur in the lights. All she could do was stand there, shaking from head to foot, clutching the gold statue everyone else in the room wanted so badly. She was startled by how heavy it was in her hand. And then she adjusted the microphone as Sharon and Steve disappeared.

"I . . . I don't know what to say . . . I didn't think I'd win . . . I can't remember everyone I want to thank . . . my agent, Walt Drucker for talking me into it . . . Douglas Wayne for giving me the chance . . . Adele Michaels, who is an incredible director and made the movie what it is . . . everyone in it . . . all of you who worked so hard, and put up with all my script changes every day . . . thank you for doing it with me, and teaching me so much. And most of all, I want to thank my wonderful children for supporting me"—tears sprang to her eyes as she said it—"for letting me do it, and giving up so much themselves so I could come to L.A. and work. Thank you, I love you so much." Tears were rolling down her cheeks by then. ". . . and thank you, Gordon . . . I love you, too!" With that, she held the Oscar high, and walked off the stage. A moment later she was walking back down the aisle to where Gordon and her children were sitting, and as she walked past him, this time Douglas stood up. He kissed her cheek and squeezed her hand as she walked by.

"Congratulations, Tanya," he said with a smile.

"Thank you, Douglas," she said, looking him right in the eye. She meant it. He had given her the chance, on both pictures she'd made for him. She reached up then and kissed his cheek. And then she went back to Gordon and her children. Both girls were crying, and all three of them kissed her, and then Gordon kissed her hard on the mouth. He looked gorgeous and as though he were going to burst with pride.

"I'm so proud of you . . . I love you . . . ," he said, and kissed her again. And then the rest of the names were called. The evening didn't seem so long anymore.

*Gone* won everything. Best Actor, Best Actress, Best Picture, Best Screenplay, and Best Director. It was a major statement about suicide and an important film. Tanya smiled when she saw Douglas go up. He looked ecstatic. She remembered how unhappy he had been the year before when he didn't win. This year more than made up for it, although Douglas wanted to win every year. He made a very serious and moving speech, which she could tell he had prepared just in case.

There were a million interviews afterward, with Tanya tightly clutching her Oscar. Afterward they went to the *Vanity Fair* party, and several others. It was three in the morning before they all got back to her bungalow. It had been an incredible evening. They were all sleeping there that night, Jason on a roll-away bed in the girls' room, and Gordon in bed with her.

They were one big happy family, and Tanya was still grinning when she and Gordon went to bed. She set the Oscar on the night table next to her.

"What a night!" Gordon said, holding her close. She was so glad it had happened this year, and not last. It meant more to her to be celebrating with Gordon and her children than if Douglas had still been in her life.

She was sound asleep within minutes, as Gordon smiled at her, kissed her neck, and turned off the light.

# Chapter 23

The days after Tanya won the Oscar seemed anticlimactic. The kids had to finish school, and neither she nor Gordon had jobs to do, so he suggested that he and Tanya go to Paris.

They stayed at the Ritz and had a ball. They spent a week eating, playing, and shopping. The weather was gorgeous, the city had never looked more beautiful, and both of them were happy. They went to London for a few days after that, and then stopped in New York on the way home. She had no plans, and Gordon didn't have another film to do until August. She invited him to Marin for the rest of April, May, June, and July. She was afraid he'd be bored there, but he was delighted. He had a studio apartment in New York, but he had no desire to stay there. And he was delighted to move in with Tanya and her children in Marin until he had to go back to work. He was going to be filming in L.A.

The children loved seeing him there when they came home from college. Tanya did some writing, and Gordon loved puttering in the garden. They went into the city, and rented a house in Stinson Beach for the weekend, which he thought was gorgeous.

"You know, I could get used to a life like this," he told Tanya one night, as he was stretched out on the couch and she ran her fingers through his hair. He looked relaxed and happy, and she was the happiest she'd been in years.

"I think you'd get bored eventually," she said, trying not to be sad about it. She had kept her promise to herself to live this with him day by day. They had been together by then for seven months. It was the longest he had been in a relationship in years, and by the time he went back to work in L.A. in August, it would be nearly a year.

"I think this could work," he said, thinking about it. "This is a nice place to come home to. And you're a good woman, Tanya," he said, and meant it. "Your husband was a jerk to go off with someone else." He had met Peter and Alice once and wasn't impressed with either of them. "But I'm glad he did, by the way."

"So am I," she said, and meant it. She was happy with Gordon. He was crazy at times, but always nice, and so loving.

They spent June and July in Marin, and he went with them for the first week in Tahoe. And then he had to go to L.A. to work. He was the star of another film, with another dazzling cast. And a beautiful costar this time. He said for once he didn't care. He had finally, after all these years, found what he wanted. He said he had the perfect life with her.

Tanya stayed in Tahoe with the children until the end of August. They came back and she got them organized to go back to college. She had had several offers by then, to do screenplays for important films, but nothing she wanted. She wasn't even sure she wanted to do it again. She'd done three movies now, and maybe that was enough. She still wanted to finish her book of short stories, and she was thinking about writing a novel. She was enjoying drifting for a while. And as soon as the kids left for school, she had promised to meet Gordon in

L.A. He had requested Bungalow 2 at the Beverly Hills Hotel, and she was going to stay there with him.

She saw Megan and Jason off in the morning, and flew to LAX with Molly. She dropped her off at school, and then went to the hotel to see Gordon. It was Sunday, and she was surprising him. He wasn't expecting her till the next day. But she had gotten everything done in Marin, so she had flown down with Molly a day earlier than planned.

She got to the hotel, and walked the familiar path to her bungalow. They had given her the key at the desk, and welcomed her back, as they always did. She was smiling to herself when she let herself into the room. He was out, and the place was a mess. He had obviously ordered a huge breakfast, and they hadn't picked up the trays yet. The "do not disturb" sign was on the door. He hated being bothered by the maid and people checking the minibar, and it was his day off from shooting.

She put her bag down quietly in the hall, and walked into the bedroom to take a shower. Her first reaction was to smile while she saw him sound asleep on the bed. He looked, as he always did, like a giant boy, and then she felt as though someone had shot her. There was a woman lying next to him, sound asleep, tangled up in the sheets, with long blond hair and a gorgeous body. They both awoke simultaneously as she let out a gasp. The girl sat up first, not sure what to say, and then Gordon turned and saw her. Tanya was standing in the middle of the room, staring at them, not sure which way to turn.

"Oh my God . . . I'm sorry . . ." Tanya gasped.

Gordon leaped out of bed in a single bound and looked at her in dismay. For once in his life, he couldn't think of anything funny to say. The girl disappeared into the bathroom, and came out in a bathrobe. Her clothes were in the living room, and she was discreetly trying to get past them, so she could get the hell out. Tanya saw immediately that she was the star of his new movie.

"Some things don't change, I guess," Tanya said sadly, as Gordon grabbed his jeans and put them on.

"Look, Tan . . . it doesn't mean anything . . . it was stupid . . . we had a lot to drink last night, and got a little crazy."

"You always do that . . . sleep with the star, I mean . . . if they hadn't been so ugly on our picture, you'd have wound up with one of them and not with me." They both heard the door to the bungalow close behind his costar. She had no desire to be part of a domestic scene.

"That's bullshit. I love you." He didn't know what else to say. They had been together for almost a year. It was an eternity for him, and just long enough for both of them to think it was for real. Just long enough for Tanya to think they might get married, and for her to want to.

"I love you, too," she said sadly, and sat down. She wanted to run out the door, but she couldn't. She couldn't move. She just sat there, looking at him, feeling stupid as tears ran down her face. "You're always going to do this, Gordon. Every goddamned time you work on a movie."

"I'm not. I've changed. I love your life in Marin. I love you . . . and I love your kids."

"We love you, too." She got up then and looked around the room, knowing she'd never want to see this bungalow again. Too much had happened. She'd been there with too many men. Peter, Douglas, and now Gordon.

"Where are you going?" he asked her, looking panicked.

"Home. I don't belong here. I never did. I want a real life, with someone who wants the same things I do, not someone who sleeps with every star he works with." Gordon looked at her and said nothing. He had been sleeping with his costar since the second week of the movie. There was no point lying to Tanya. They both knew it would happen again. For him, it was an occupational hazard.

She didn't say a word to him. She walked to the door and picked up her bag. And he didn't stop her. She turned to look at him, and he said nothing. He didn't tell her he loved her. They both knew he did. But loving her didn't change anything. This was just the way he was. She walked out of Bungalow 2 and closed the door softly behind her, leaving Gordon where and as he was.

# Chapter 24

Molly called Tanya in Marin two days later. She had called her at the hotel, and was surprised when Gordon told her that her mother had gone back to Ross.

"Is something wrong?" Molly asked her when she called her mother. "He sounded funny. Or actually not so funny. He sounded sad. Did you two have a fight?"

"Sort of." Tanya didn't want to talk to her about it, just as she hadn't told her when Peter had the affair with Alice. "Actually," she said, choking on the words, "it's over." He hadn't called her. He was doing what he always did and having a hot romance with his costar. She was his type. Tanya wasn't. Maybe that's why it had lasted longer. They'd had a good run, and she was philosophical about it, but sad that it was over. It was just the way things went in L.A.

"I'm sorry, Mom," Molly said, genuinely sad for her. They all loved Gordon. "Maybe he'll come back."

"No. I'm okay. He's not the kind of guy to stick around, or get domestic."

"At least you had nine great months with him." Molly tried to cheer her up. It seemed pathetic to Tanya that the best that grown-ups who loved each other could do was last nine months. She and Peter had lasted for twenty years, and even that meant nothing once he got involved with Alice. Nothing lasted anymore. Promises were no longer kept, and always broken. To Tanya, it seemed a sad state-ment about people. No one knew what they wanted. And when they claimed they did, they screwed it up anyway. The thought of it de-pressed her.

She talked to Molly for a while, and eventually the others called her. They had heard the news from Molly. They were all sorry about Gordon. She didn't explain what had happened.

She spent a week mourning him, and then went back to writing short stories, living in the empty house in Ross. It seemed like a barn now without her children.

She worked for months relentlessly, saw no one, rarely went out, and finished the book of short stories just before Thanksgiving. It was a long, lonely autumn. It was the day the kids were due home for Thanksgiving that Walt called her. He was happy to hear she'd fin-ished the book. He had a publisher for it, and took a breath before he told her he had a movie for her, too. He knew before he said it what her reaction would be. She'd already told him in no uncertain terms, months before, not to call her again for a screenplay. She said she'd done the L.A. thing, and under no circumstances would she go back and do it again. She'd done three films, won an Oscar, and spent a to-tal of nearly two years down there. It was enough. From now on, she only wanted to do books. And she was determined now to start a novel. And live in Ross.

"Tell them I'm not interested," Tanya told him bluntly. She was never going back to L.A. She didn't like how people lived down there, or what they believed in. She liked even less the way they behaved.

She had no life in Marin, but she didn't care. She no longer saw her old friends. They belonged to Peter and Alice now. All she was interested in was her writing, and her children when they came to visit. Her agent didn't like the way she lived, but he had to admit, her current writing was terrific. Richer, stronger, deeper. It was easy to see how much she had suffered. But at forty-four, he thought she deserved more of a life.

"Can I at least tell you what this picture is about?" Walt sounded exasperated. He knew how stubborn she was. She had closed the door on the movie business, and she wasn't even willing to hear him out. She never was. Since her Oscar, he had called her at least a dozen times.

"Nope. I don't care what it's about. I'm not doing movies, and I'm never going back to L.A."

"You don't have to. The producer/director in this case is an independent. He wants to make a movie in San Francisco, and the story is right up your alley."

"Nope. Tell him to find someone else. I want to start a novel."

"Oh, for chrissake, Tanya. You won an Oscar. Everybody wants you. This guy has a great idea. He's won all kinds of awards, though not an Oscar. You could write the script for him with your eyes closed."

"I don't want to write another screenplay," she said bluntly. "I hate the people who make movies. They have no integrity and no morals. They're a pain in the ass to work for, and every time I go near them, it screws up my life."

"And your life is so great now? You've turned into a recluse up there, and the stuff you're writing is so depressing, I have to take mood elevators when I read it." She smiled at his comment. She knew what he said was true, but the work was good, and he knew it. He just didn't like it.

"Then get a new prescription. Because the novel I want to write is no joyride either."

"Stop writing such depressing shit. Besides, the movie this guy wants to make is serious stuff, too. You could win another Oscar." He was trying to entice her and getting nowhere.

"I have one. I don't need another one."

"Sure you do. You could use them as bookends. For all the depressing books you're going to write holed up in your castle." She laughed at what he said.

"I hate you."

"I love it when you say that," he said. "It means I'm getting to you. The producer in this case is English, and he wants to meet you. He'll only be in San Francisco this week."

"Oh, for chrissake, Walt. I don't know why I listen to you."

"Because I'm right and you know it. I only call you for the good ones. This is a good one. I can feel it. I met him in New York before he went out there. He's a nice guy. And he makes good movies. His list of credits is excellent. He's very respected in England."

"Okay, okay, I'll meet him."

"Thank you. Don't forget to let the drawbridge down over the moat." She chuckled, and Phillip Cornwall called her late that afternoon. He told her how grateful he was that she was willing to listen to him. He didn't tell her, but her agent had warned him that the likelihood of her seeing him was slim to none.

She met him for coffee at Starbucks in Mill Valley. Her hair had gotten longer, and she hadn't worn makeup in six months. Her year with Gordon had brought her joy and fun, but losing him had taken a toll. In the last few years she'd been disappointed too often, and lost too many men. She had no desire to try again. And when he met with her, Phillip could see that bad things had happened to her. There were rivers of pain in her eyes. He had read it in her writing.

He described the story to her, while she drank tea and he drank cappuccino. She found his accent soothing. And she liked the fact that he wanted to make the movie in San Francisco. The story was about a woman who died while traveling, and traced her back to where it all began, what had led her to the place where she ended, and why she had died, as the result of her late husband leading a secretly bisexual life and contracting AIDS. It was a complicated story, yet the themes were simple. She liked everything about it, and was intrigued by what he said. She paid no attention to how he looked. She liked his creative spirit and the complex workings of his mind. But although he was young and good-looking, she had no interest in him as a man. That part of her was completely numb. Or dead, she thought.

"Why me?" she asked him quietly, sipping her tea. She knew from his biography that he was forty-one years old, had made half a dozen movies, and won a number of awards. She liked how straightforward he was when he talked to her. He didn't try to butter her up, or win her over. He was well aware that she was unlikely to do it. He wanted to convince her based on the merit of the material, not on charm. She liked all that about him. She was long past wanting to be vulnerable to charm. And if nothing else, he wanted her opinion and advice.

"I saw the movie that won you the Oscar. I knew I had to work with you as soon as I saw *Gone*. It's an incredible film." With a powerful message, like the screenplay he wanted her to write.

"Thank you," she said simply. "So what will you do now?" She wanted to know his plan.

"I'll go back to England." He smiled at her, and she saw that he looked tired. He looked both young and old at the same time. Wise, yet still able to smile. In some ways, they were a lot alike. They both looked tired, and somewhat worn by life, yet neither of them was old. "Eventually, I hope to gather up my pennies, bring my children, and come to live here for a year. And make my movie, if I'm lucky . . . I'll be very lucky if you write it." It was the only charm he had allowed himself and she smiled. He had deep, warm brown eyes that looked as though they'd seen a lot of life, and some hard times.

"I don't want to write screenplays anymore," she said honestly.

She didn't tell him why, and he didn't ask. He respected her boundaries as well as her skill. She was something of an icon to him, and he thought she had enormous talent. It didn't bother him that she was distant and chilly with him. He accepted her as she was.

"That's what your agent told me. I was hoping to convince you otherwise."

"I don't think you can," she said honestly, although she loved his story.

"So he said." He had almost given up hope of her writing the script for him. But it had been worth a try.

"Why are you bringing your children here? Wouldn't it be easier to leave them in England while you work?" It was a detail, but she was curious about him. He had dark hair, fair skin, and those soft brown eyes that bored into hers, with a thousand questions he didn't dare ask. She was braver than he.

He answered her question as simply as he could, without offering details. "I'm bringing my children because my wife died two years ago. In a riding accident. She was crazy about horses, and very headstrong. She went over a bush and broke her neck. It was rough terrain. She grew up riding to hounds. So I have to bring my kids. I have no one to leave them with at home." He sounded matter of fact and not sorry for himself, which touched her more than she showed.

"Besides, I'd be miserable here alone. I've never left them since their mother died, until this trip. I only came over for a few days, to meet you." It was hard not to be flattered, or touched.

"How old are they?" she asked with interest. It explained what she saw in his eyes and on his face. There was pain and strength. She liked the mixture of both, and what he'd said about his kids. There was nothing Hollywood about him. Everything about Phillip seemed real.

"Seven and nine. A girl and a boy. Isabelle and Rupert."

"Very English," she said, and he smiled.

"I need to rent a place, if you know of anything dirt cheap."

"I might," she said quietly, glancing at her watch. Her kids were coming home, but it was still early. She had given herself plenty of time when she agreed to meet with him. She hesitated, and then decided to stick her neck out, and wasn't sure why, except that she felt sorry for him. He had a lot on his plate, and he wasn't whining about what had happened to him. He was making the best of it, keeping his kids with him, and trying to do his work. You had to give him credit for that. "You can stay with me until you find a place. I have a comfortable old house, and my kids are away at school. They're coming home tonight. But normally, they're only here over Christmas and in the summer. So you can stay for a while, and the schools are good here."

"Thank you." He looked moved and didn't speak for a minute, touched by her offer. "They're good kids. They're used to traveling with me, so they're pretty well behaved." It was the kind of thing all parents said, but if they were English, Tanya suspected it was true, and it would put a little life back in her house until he found a place to rent. She wanted to do something to help him, even though she wouldn't write his script. He'd have to find someone else to do that. But she didn't mind their staying at her house until he found his feet.

"When are you coming back?" she asked with a look of concern.

"January. After they finish their term. Around the tenth."

"That's perfect. My kids will be back at school by then. They won't be home again till spring break. When do you leave?"

"Tonight." He had the material on the table between them, and she picked it up while he held his breath. She held it in her hands for an interminable moment and their eyes met.

"I'll read your stuff and let you know. You can stay with me either way. Don't get your hopes up. I'm not going to write another script. But I'll tell you what I think." She was impressed by what she'd heard so far and by him. She stood up then, holding the folder in her arms. "I'll call you after I read it. But don't count on anything. It would take a lot to make me do another movie. I'm about to write a novel. I'm through with films, no matter how good your story is."

"I hope this is the one that changes your mind," he said, as he stood up, too. He was very tall, and thin. There was barely a smile between them. He had left her his UK cell number, and his home number was on the papers. She thanked him then for coming from England to see her. It was a slightly crazy thing to do, but he said he was glad he had, even if she didn't do the script. They shook hands then, and he left.

He got in his rented car and drove away, and she drove home, and put the folder on her desk. She didn't know when she'd get to it, but she knew she would at some point. And two hours later her kids were home, and the house came alive again. It was so good to have them home, she forgot all about his folder until after the Thanksgiving weekend. She saw it on her desk and sighed. She didn't want to read it, but had said she would. She felt she owed him at least that.

She read it on Sunday night after the kids left, and finished it at midnight. It was eight in the morning in England for him. He was making breakfast for his children when she called him. She wanted to hate him for it, but she couldn't. She knew this was one screenplay she had to write, and this would be the last one. But it was a piece of work she was suddenly longing to do. She had made copious notes as she read it, and already had a million ideas. The story he had outlined was brilliant. Clean, clear, pure, simple, powerful, and at the same time complex and fascinatingly intricate. She had to write it.

"I'll do it," she said, as she could hear children's voices in the background. There was all the noise and chatter that happened over breakfast with children. They were the sounds she missed so much. It would be nice to have them stay with her, even if only for a few days, or however long it took him to find a place. She could hardly wait to start work on the script.

"I'm sorry . . . what did you say?" Rupert had shouted at the dog just as she had spoken. And now it was barking again. "I didn't hear you. I've got a noisy lot here." She smiled as she listened.

"I said I'd do it." She spoke softly, but this time he heard her. There was a long silence while the dog barked and the kids were squealing.

"Shit. Do you mean it?"

"Yes, I do. And I swear this will be my last one. But I think it's going to be a beautiful movie. I fell in love with your idea. The outline made me cry."

"I wrote it for my wife," he explained. "She was an interesting woman. She was a physician."

"I suspected it was about her," in some altered form, since she had died in a riding accident, and not of AIDS. "I'll start working on it now. I was going to start a novel, but it can wait. I'll fax you what I've got, as soon as it starts to make sense."

"Tanya," he said in a choked voice, "thank you."

"Thank *you*," she said. And the two people who hadn't smiled enough in a long time were both suddenly beaming. There was no doubt in her mind. It was going to be a very, very good picture. And hopefully, a terrific script. She was going to give it her all.

She started working on it the day after Thanksgiving. It took her three weeks to get a handle on it as she sketched out scenes, and laid out the flow of the picture. It was Christmas week before she faxed some material to him. He read it in one night, and called her in his morning. It was midnight for her, and she was sitting at her desk, working on it, when he called her.

"I love what you did," he said, sounding jubilant. "It's absolutely perfect." It was even better than he had hoped. She was making his dream come true.

"I like it, too," she said, smiling, as she looked out the window into the darkness. "I think it works." She had cried several times as she wrote it, which was always a good sign. And so had he when he read it.

"I think it's brilliant!" he said to her.

They talked for nearly an hour, as she discussed some problems with him. There were rough spots in the material, things she hadn't figured out how to handle yet. It was all still in its early stages. But together they batted ideas back and forth and solved the problems one by one. She was surprised to find afterward that they had talked for two hours.

He was still coming on the tenth of January. He wanted to hire local actors. He knew a cameraman in San Francisco he said was very good, a South African he had gone to school with. Phillip was going to be making his movie on a shoestring. He had offered Tanya all he could to write the screenplay. She thought about it and called him back afterward. She told him she'd take a percentage at the back end. She didn't want anything from him up front. She thought the project was worth investing in. She was more interested in making it with him than in making money.

She started to get a real grip on it shortly before Christmas, and the screenplay was almost writing itself. It felt like destiny at work. She was writing everything he had felt, and he was thrilled with what she wrote.

Her kids came home, and they had a wonderful Christmas vacation. Jason went skiing with friends. Megan had a new boyfriend at UCSB, and Molly was talking about going to Florence to study for junior year. Tanya told them all about the independent movie she had started to work on. They were intrigued by what she told them. She told them little about Phillip Cornwall, because he was the least of it. What had gripped her was the story. She had been working on it since Thanksgiving and was haunted by it. Phillip had been the catalyst, but by now she loved the story itself. It had a life of its own, as all good stories did.

Phillip arrived on schedule on the tenth of January, with Isabelle and Rupert. He had already started putting out feelers for an apartment, and promised not to stay with her for too long. She put him in Molly's room, and the children in Megan's. She put a roll-away bed in the room, so they could be close together. The children were adorable, and totally, incredibly English. Rupert was nine, and Isabelle was seven. They were extremely polite and well behaved, and looked like children in a movie. They were beautiful and sweet, with big blue eyes and blond hair. Phillip said they were the image of their mother. And as they walked into the house with him, they looked up at her with their huge eyes, as he stood over them proudly. She could see in the first five minutes that he was a very good father, and they adored him, and he them. They were a tightly woven loving unit.

It was British teatime when they came in, exhausted from the long flight. She had made little sandwiches for them, hot chocolate with whipped cream. And she'd gone to the English grocery store to buy scones and clotted cream. She had sliced strawberries and jam to go with it, and both children screamed when they saw what she had prepared. They loved the scones, and Isabelle dove in so vigorously that she got clotted cream on her nose. Phillip laughed as he wiped it off.

"You're a little piggy, Miss Izzy. We'll have to throw you in the bath."

It was wonderful hearing the sound of children's voices again. Tanya could hear them laughing in their room, talking to their father. And she heard him reading a bedtime story to them when she walked by their room that night. It was at least an hour later when he came downstairs to the kitchen. She was working on the screenplay, and he said they were sound asleep.

"They're nackered from the trip," he said, and she looked up and smiled.

"You must be, too." The deep brown eyes looked tired, but happy. He was dying to get to work.

"Not really." He smiled at her. "I'm excited to be here." He was planning to enroll them in school the next day, and then wanted to meet with his cameraman later that week. They had a million plans and things to talk about. In some ways, it was easier to have him right in the house, so they could work. They talked for hours, over several cups of tea, and finally the jet lag got him and he went to bed.

She made breakfast for them the next morning, and told him how to get to the school. She lent him her car to get there. He was back two hours later, the children were settled, and he was ready to get to work. They worked relentlessly on the screenplay together all through the week. The project was well in control, and moving ahead by leaps, faster and better than either of them had expected. They were turning out to be a powerful team, as they played ideas off each other, which enriched the script and the story day by day.

She spent the weekend with him and the children, showing them around. She babysat for Isabelle and Rupert while he looked for apartments. She made cupcakes with them, and they made papier-mâché puppets with her, as she had done with her own children years before. When he got back, the whole kitchen was a mess, but his children were beaming at their new friend. They had made little animals and puppets, and Isabelle had made a mask.

"Good lord, what have you all been up to? What a dreadful mess!" He laughed, and noticed that Tanya had papier-mâché all over her chin. He pointed, and she brushed it off.

"We've had a very good time," she confirmed with a smile.

"I hope so. It'll take you a week to clean it up." After they put the children's creations aside to dry, he helped her clean up and put everything away. The children were playing on the swings outside, which were still there after all these years. Tanya said it was nice to see them used again. Isabelle and Rupert were bringing the house back to life, and so was he. He was bringing something different and new to her work. She was learning a lot from him, and he from her.

He said he had found an apartment in Mill Valley, and she was sorry to hear it. She liked having them there. He apologized that it wouldn't be available for another week.

"That's fine with me." She smiled at him. "I'll be sorry when you go. It's so nice having the children here." She was tempted to ask them to stay, but he needed to have a life and place of his own. They couldn't live in her children's rooms for six months, although it would have been nice. "I hope you come to visit often," she said to him. "They're such sweet kids." They had mentioned their mother to

her, and looking very solemn, Rupert explained that she had died
when she fell off a horse.

"I know," Tanya said seriously. "I was very sad to hear about it."

"She was very pretty," Isabelle added, as Tanya nodded.

"I'm sure she was."

She distracted them then with pads of paper and colored pencils
and suggested they make drawings for their father. He had been delighted to get them when he got back. He was touched that Tanya
was so nice to his children. She took all of them out to dinner that
night. The children ate hamburgers and french fries, and she and
Phillip had steak. And she felt like a family again, when she got back
to the house, with Phillip driving, and the two little ones chatting animatedly in the backseat. They told Tanya they liked their new
school, but they told her they'd be going back to England next summer, after their dad finished making his movie.

"I know," she said, as they walked into the house. "I'm going to
work on it with him."

"Are you an actress?" Rupert asked with interest.

"No, I'm a writer," Tanya explained, as she helped Isabelle take off
her coat. The little girl looked up at her with a smile that melted
Tanya's heart. It wasn't hard to do.

Phillip and Tanya continued to work on the script together for the
next week. What they were doing was essentially preproduction on a
modest scale. They were getting all their ducks lined up. And the following weekend he and the children moved out. She hated to see
them go, and made him promise to bring them back to visit soon. As
it turned out, he brought them to her house often. He brought them
after school, to play in the kitchen and do homework, while he and
Tanya worked on the script.

Phillip hired several local actors, and a young girl from L.A. They started shooting the movie in April. They finished at the end of June, and by then he and Tanya had worked together for six months night and day. Isabelle and Rupert were totally comfortable with her. She had them over to dinner often, and bought them familiar things to eat from the English grocery store in the city. It was fun doing things with them. One Saturday when they weren't filming, she took them to the zoo. She brought them back to Phillip at dinnertime, with cotton candy all over their faces, and they had stopped at the carousel on the way. And in the summer, she and Phillip took them to the beach. It was like a reprieve for Tanya, who said her children were much too grown up, and busy with their own lives now.

Having Tanya nearby was a relief for Phillip. He brought the children over more than he intended to, but she insisted she loved it, and his children begged to visit her in Ross. They liked her rambling old house that her children had loved, too. And over their many months of intense work, she and Phillip had become friends. They had shared many confidences by then, about their past lives, their children, and their spouses, even about their childhoods. She said it helped her writing. Insights into other people always gave her work more depth.

The children were staying with her for the weekend, and her own children were home from school, when they finally finished the movie on the last day in June. Molly and Megan thought Isabelle and Rupert were absolutely adorable, and took them out with them sometimes when they had errands to do. Isabelle was particularly serious, and Rupert had a funny little sense of humor. They were sweet children, and Tanya felt a pang to realize how attached to them she had gotten. When Phillip said they were going back in July, she wanted to beg him not to go. She couldn't imagine what it would be like once the children were gone and her house was silent again. She couldn't bear the thought. He was touched when she said it to him one night over dinner. They were doing postproduction now, and Tanya was relieved that it was moving slowly. They had been remarkably diligent about every aspect of the film. Phillip was very proud of it, and Tanya was proud of him. He had done a fantastic job, and he was thrilled with the script.

Their relationship had been entirely professional so far. Phillip was a relatively formal person, and very English. The only time he let his hair down with her was when he saw her with his children. Each time he did, she touched his heart.

"I think you should stay another year," she teased him at dinner one night, with her children and his.

"Only if you do another movie with me," he teased back.

"God forbid," Tanya said, and rolled her eyes. She kept swearing this was her last film forever. It had been an enormous amount of work, more than either of them had expected or planned, but they were both convinced the results were good. Phillip was planning to edit it himself when he went back to England. He had rented a studio from a friend.

By the end of July, he had done everything he wanted to in the States. Tanya wasn't sharing the final editing process with him, but she did as much as possible before they left. He was planning to spend the last two weeks of his trip traveling around California, and surprised Tanya by asking her to go with them. Isabelle and Rupert begged her to. She had just enough time to do it with them before taking her own children to Tahoe, and then she had an idea.

"Why don't you come to Tahoe with us, after your trip? We'd love it. And then you can go back after that." He had already let go his apartment, and she told him he could stay in the house again. It would only make the summer livelier, and once he agreed to go to

Tahoe, she agreed to join them on their trip around the state. It was something to do, and Molly and Megan thought it sounded like fun for her. It worried them that all she did now was work, and she had looked so grim all year, ever since her romance with Gordon had broken up. Finding him in bed with his costar had hit her hard. It was nice seeing her more relaxed again, and they could see that she and Phillip were friends. Even Megan approved, and had mellowed a lot that year.

Tanya, Phillip, and his children started their trip in Monterey. They went to the aquarium, and then wandered around Carmel. They went to Santa Barbara, where they visited Jason at summer school at UCSB, and from there they went to L.A. They spent two days at Disneyland, which Isabelle and Rupert loved. Tanya took them on all the rides, while Phillip took photographs of all three of them. They were exhausted but happy as they watched the parade and light show on the last night, and she turned and looked at Phillip as Isabelle held her hand. She saw him smiling at her. He wanted to thank her, but didn't know how, and then they took the train back to their hotel. He put an arm around her shoulders as they walked in. Isabelle was sleeping with Tanya and Rupert with him. Isabelle had asked to sleep with Tanya, and she was thrilled. He came in to kiss her goodnight and tuck her in, and then he turned to Tanya with a warm look.

"Thank you for being so good to my children," he whispered as Isabelle fell asleep. She was smiling happily with an arm around the Minnie Mouse doll Tanya had bought her. Rupert had been obsessed with the Pirates of the Caribbean and gone on the ride twice with her.

"I love them," she said simply. "I don't know what I'll do when you go away," she said with a look of sorrow in her eyes, which was suddenly mirrored in his.

"Neither do I," he said softly. He started to leave the room and then turned back to her, as though he were about to say something, but hesitated. "Tanya . . . these have been the best months of my life in years, you know . . ." He knew they had been happy months for his children, too, the happiest since their mother's death.

"Me too," she whispered. It was the children that had been the greatest gift. They owned her heart. Writing the film had been icing on the cake. He nodded, and then took a step closer to her, and without thinking, he reached out and smoothed down her hair. She hadn't looked in the mirror since that morning, and didn't really care. She had concentrated on Isabelle and Rupert, and doing everything they wanted to do, running from one ride to another, standing on line, seeing Mickey and Goofy, and getting them fed. It was the most fun she'd had in years, and she loved sharing it with him, just as she had the film. It was strange to think of a life without him now, and agonizing to think of life without them. They had become her precious little friends. And she had gotten used to all three of them. Watching them leave for England in a few weeks was going to be a major loss for her. Phillip was looking at her as she thought of it, and he could see the pain in her eyes. It was the same pain he felt leaving her. He didn't say a word to her, and wouldn't have known what to say. It was so long since he had done anything like it. He pulled her close and kissed her, and time stood still for both of them while he did. When he pulled away at last, he wasn't sure what to do or say or if he'd made a terrible mistake.

"Do you hate me?" he asked her softly. He had thought of it before, but told himself he was insane. He didn't want to confuse things while they were working together. And now it was too late. They were about to leave. But he had shared his most important piece of work with her. And he treasured her as a friend.

Tanya slowly shook her head. "I don't hate you. I already miss you, and you haven't even left." Life was so strange sometimes. People came into your life and left again, sometimes kindly, sometimes cruelly, and always with regret. She was going to miss them terribly. She looked into Phillip's eyes, wondering what the kiss meant.

"I don't want to leave," he said softly. The emotions he had held back for months were spilling over him, and nearly drowning him, now that the walls were down.

"Then don't," she whispered back.

"Come with us." His eyes begged her, and she shook her head.

"I can't. What would I do there?"

"The same thing we did here. We could make another movie together."

"And then what, when the movie ends? I'd still have to come back. My children are here, Phillip."

"They're almost grown up. We need you, Tanya . . . I need you," he said with tears in his eyes. He didn't know what to say to her, but he didn't want this to end. This trip. This time. The life he had shared with her, that was about to end forever when they left.

"Are you serious?" she asked as he nodded and kissed her again. "Now what are we going to do?" she asked, looking distressed. Why had this happened now, so close to the end? It seemed too late. They had to leave, and she had to stay here. But her life would seem empty now without them.

"I'm very serious," he said somberly, pulling her tighter into his arms. "I fell in love with you the day we met. I didn't want to screw things up by saying anything while we were working together." It was the opposite of what Gordon did, playing on every movie he made. Phillip had been professional till the last. Perhaps too much so. They had wasted months that they could have spent together. She had felt something, too, but had chosen to ignore it until now. She had poured her heart into Isabelle and Rupert, and his film. But now she couldn't ignore what she felt for Phillip. All he wanted to do was hold her, and stop time from moving forward. They were down to their final days together, and then would go their separate ways.

"Let's talk about this tomorrow," she said softly, and he nodded. There was a smile in his eyes now, a spark of life. Some part of him was coming alive again, and he could see it in her eyes, too. "Are we completely crazy?" she asked him, looking worried.

"Yes. But I'm not sure we have a choice here. I don't think I can do otherwise." She wasn't sure that she could either. She was feeling swept away on the tides of what he was saying to her and what they were feeling for each other. Everything between them was changing. She wanted to stop and be sensible, to make reasonable decisions. But the decisions seemed to be making themselves. She felt as though she were losing control over her destiny as she looked at him.

He kissed her again and left, and she lay awake all night, next to Isabelle in the bed beside her. She held the little girl close to her, and thought of him. What strange fate had brought them all together? And why, if they were going to have to leave each other again? She didn't want to love one more person she couldn't have, or one more person who would leave. They were leaving in three weeks. And yet, she realized now, she was falling in love with him, or had been all along. Not only him but his children. And there was no way she could go with him and live in England. There had to be some other way. The secret was to find it. If it was meant to be, she told herself, they would find a solution. If not, they wouldn't. All they had to do was be brave enough to look. And braver still if they dared to trust life again.

# Chapter 25

The rest of their trip to southern California was a strange journey for Phillip and Tanya. They spent most of it looking at each other over his children's heads and smiling. They had found something magical on the trip. Something they'd had all along and didn't even know. But now that it was out of the closet, it was impossible to resist, and neither of them wanted to. Now there was no putting it back or hiding what they'd found and finally admitted. It was out in the bright sunlight, blinding them with its light.

They took long walks on the beach in San Diego, walking behind the children, watching them as they got their feet wet in the surf, and picked up shells to give the children.

"I love you, Tanya," he said softly in the accent that was so familiar now. She had been firmly convinced she would never hear those words again from a man, nor wanted to.

"I love you, too." But she had no idea what to do about it. They both thought about it quietly on the long drive home.

The girls seemed not to notice the transformation that had

happened on their travels. Jason came home, and they all went to Lake Tahoe. It was only once they were there that the older children became aware of something different happening between their mother and Phillip. Until then, they had been firmly convinced that all their mother and Phillip shared was work. They liked him, although their situation seemed complicated even to them. He was leaving for England with his children in two weeks. He asked her one night if she would move to England with him, and she said again that she couldn't. She said that she had children and a life here.

"I can't leave my kids." And he couldn't stay in the States either. He had no permit to work, except on this film. And it was finished. He had to go back. They were going to be six thousand miles apart. It seemed a cruel turn of fate to both of them.

And then as Molly talked about spending a semester in Florence, Phillip and Tanya looked at each other across the table at dinner one night, and their eyes met. They had the same idea at the same time. He waited until the children had gone to bed to ask her. She knew what he was going to say before he said the words.

"Would you be willing to live in Italy with me for a year while we figure this out?" One or both of them was going to have to move, and it was too soon to make any decisions yet. They knew each other well after six months of working together, but there was much they didn't know, and needed to find out. Things they had both forgotten and thought they wanted to forget, until now.

"My kids won't be home again until Thanksgiving," Tanya explained to him. "I suppose I could come to England and stay with you after they leave for school in September, and I could stay for a couple of months. Maybe while I'm there we could look for a house somewhere near Florence. If Molly goes to school there for the se-

mester after Christmas, we'd be close to her. She could even stay
with us. Maybe Megan would want to come, too." Jason was far less
interested in studying in Europe, but he was also less dependent on
her and he could come over to visit for vacations, which would be
less disruptive for him. "Could you and the children come here for
Christmas, Phillip?"

"I don't see why not. I've got some free air miles floating around
somewhere." His eyes lit up as he said it. They were finding solutions.
It was like fitting the pieces of a puzzle together. It seemed miraculous
that the bits of sky and trees were beginning to fit, when only days ago
they made no sense. "If you come to England in September until
Thanksgiving . . . and we go to Italy and look for a house . . . then I
come back with you for Thanksgiving and Christmas . . . we go to
Italy in January when Molly starts her term there . . . we stay until the
summer, or even for the rest of the year, if we love it. It's a bit of a
patchwork, isn't it? But I think it could work. It gives us a year to see
what happens. By then we'll know what we want to do . . . won't we?"
He looked at her cautiously, and she laughed.

"I think we've just pretty well squared away the next year of our
lives. Maybe we'll think of another movie to work on together.
Maybe a lot of things will happen in the next year, Phillip. Something
very big just did happen to us. We fell in love, or let ourselves acknowledge what must have happened months ago when we were so
busy working. Now we just figured out how to spend the next year
together, or maybe year and a half. I'd say that's very creative problem solving." There were a few holes in the theory that remained to
be solved, finding a house in Italy . . . visiting Megan in Santa
Barbara if she didn't want to do a semester in Europe with Molly. It
was less than perfect, but it just might work. It was fraught with risk,

as all things in life were. But what if it worked? What more could one ask? There were no certainties in life, of how things would happen. No guarantees that disaster or tragedy wouldn't befall them. But hand in hand, there was a good chance they could make it work. With love and patience and courage, there was nothing they couldn't do. Particularly if they were both willing to try, which they were. Phillip put his arms around her then and held her. She felt warm in his arms, as she always did.

"I can't believe this is happening to us, Tanya. I never thought I'd fall in love again."

"Neither did I," Tanya said softly. "I don't think I wanted to," she said honestly. "I didn't want to risk my heart again."

"And now?" he asked, sounding worried, as he looked tenderly at her.

"I don't really think we have a choice. I think this time the decision reached out to us. All we can do is follow it and trust. Sometimes you can't see the end of the path at the beginning. You just have to follow where it goes." They were both doing that this time, and taking the risks together. Solving the problems, facing the obstacles, meeting the challenges, one day at a time.

"It feels right to me, Tanya." And it did to her, too. She couldn't even explain it or justify it. But everything felt so incredibly right to her, for the first time in years. It all made sense, to both of them.

There was no solid evidence to the contrary. No guarantees. All they could really do was trust. They had each decided to do that at exactly the same time. The synchronicity of it seemed amazing that they had fallen in love, told each other, come up with a plan, and found a solution all at the same time. It would have been easier to land a 747 on the head of a pin. But they had done it, or started to.

The rest would have to unfold as time went on. All they needed now was the courage to follow through on what they'd started, and a little luck along the way. Nothing was impossible. Anything could be done, if you wanted it badly enough. The movie they had just made was proof of that. And so was almost everything in their life. They had survived tragedies and disappointments. The demise of Tanya's marriage, the death of Phillip's wife. They had been through it and survived. The rest would be easy now compared to all that.

They told the children about their plans the next day, and everyone thought it an amazing plan. Megan liked the idea of going to Italy with Molly. Better yet if Tanya and Phillip had a house somewhere nearby. Jason didn't mind them going. He said he'd come over for spring vacation, and in the summer. He had been wanting to travel around Europe with friends. Everyone was thrilled, although a little startled to hear about the budding relationship between Phillip and Tanya. But the more they thought about it, the more they liked it. And all of Tanya's children thought he was a great guy.

Isabelle summed up the situation when she heard that Tanya was coming to England to visit them until Thanksgiving.

"Good," she said practically. "Then you can do my hair for school properly just like my mum. My dad can't do hair at all."

"I'll do my best," Tanya promised, as all seven of them looked at each other, chatted animatedly about their plans, and sat down to dinner, talking all at once about the house in Italy they hoped to find . . . Megan and Molly's plans for school . . . Isabelle's hair . . . and the movie Phillip and Tanya were going to make . . . Rupert sidled up to Jason then, with a grin. Jason was the closest thing he'd ever had to a brother, and he liked the idea of spending more time with him.

"It all sounds a bit mad, doesn't it?" Rupert looked philosophical about it, and more than a little pleased. "But I think it might work."

"So do I," Jason agreed, smiling at him. He was a cute boy, and he was right. There was no reason why it wouldn't. In fact, with enough love and luck, there was every reason why it would.

# Chapter 26

In the end Tanya and Phillip delayed leaving for Italy until the end of January. Molly and Megan didn't begin their term in Florence until then. They had found a house just outside Florence in October. It was furnished, big enough for all of them, and it was waiting in perfect order. All they had to do was arrive, and turn the key. Phillip, Rupert, and Isabelle had spent Christmas with Tanya and her family in Marin. Isabelle and Rupert still believed in Santa Claus, so Christmas had new meaning for all of them. The girls had helped them put out cookies and milk for Santa Claus, and carrots and salt for the reindeer. And at the last minute, Rupert had decided to add a beer.

Their school in England had very kindly allowed them to take a month off, as long as they took their assignments to California with them, and did their homework while they were away. Jason went back to UCSB in January, and the girls had the month at home to get ready for their semester in Florence. Tanya had them take a course in Italian at Berlitz, so they would be able to manage a little better once they were there. And she took several lessons, too. Phillip preferred to wing it.

But the real reason for the delay was so that they could attend the Golden Globes. It was the award given by the foreign press, both for television and feature films. And although one couldn't always rely on it, in many instances, the film that won the Golden Globes went on to win an Oscar three months later. The film Phillip and Tanya had made, honoring his late wife, had been released at the end of December, and had been nominated for an award for best feature film. Phillip and Tanya wanted to be there. And all of their children were going to attend.

Unlike the Oscars, it was set up like a benefit, with tables, and a dozen people at each table, rather than in a theater. It was always a fun event, and seeing who won the prestigious awards was always exciting. Neither Phillip nor Tanya had ever been. It was incredibly momentous for them when they found out that their film had been nominated. It was the high point of Phillip's career, more than for Tanya, who had won an Oscar the year before, but she was just as excited as he was, and she was thrilled for him.

They flew to L.A. with Phillip's children and the girls the morning of the awards. Jason was driving down from Santa Barbara and meeting them there. And as she always did, they were staying at the Beverly Hills Hotel. Phillip, Tanya, and all the children were wildly excited. They had bought dresses in San Francisco, and Phillip bought a dinner jacket for the event. Tanya got Rupert a suit at Brooks Brothers, and a black velvet dress for Isabelle, which she loved. She had tried it on a hundred times, with black patent-leather Mary Janes she had brought from England.

Tanya had requested two bungalows, one for the children and another for them. She had specifically asked them not to give them Bungalow 2. But as it turned out, there had been a mix-up in their reservation. The children were given the presidential suite, and

Phillip and Tanya were in Bungalow 2. They acted as though they were doing her a favor. It wasn't big enough to give to the children, since there were five of them, and the bungalow would have been too crowded. She wanted to give the children three rooms, so they wouldn't be crawling all over each other while trying to get ready, and Isabelle liked sharing a room with Rupert. Jason preferred to be alone.

Tanya walked into the bungalow with trepidation. All she could think of was the last time she had been there, when she walked in on Gordon with his costar in his bed, and the unhappy scene that had followed. Before that her relationship with Douglas had ended on the doorstep, and her marriage had gone downhill with Peter, when he came down to L.A. to visit, or possibly before that. But she still remembered all too clearly when he had looked around the bungalow miserably and predicted she would never come home after the life she led in L.A. In the end, he was wrong, and he was the one who had left her. She had gone home, and now she was finally leaving again. Maybe this time for good. But to a different life, the one she hoped to share with Phillip in Italy, and maybe one day in England. They hadn't decided yet where they wanted to live. And they had yet to try their wings. Although so far, after two months with him in England, and three months since in Marin, everything seemed to be going extremely well. And they had rented the house in Florence for a year. Their journey had begun.

Tanya hadn't wanted to stay in the bungalow with him, because she had been there with too many men. She had written three movies there, cried over Peter, backed away from Douglas, and cavorted with Gordon, for a while at least. They had had fun, but it didn't last long. She didn't want to stay with Phillip in a room she had shared with three other men at different times. And she looked unhappy as she walked into the bedroom. She felt instantly attacked by ghosts. She had been through too many stages of her life in these rooms. But the hotel insisted they had no other suite or bungalow to give them. It was their only choice. And Phillip instantly saw the expression on her face. She looked first wistful, and then troubled as soon as the bellman set their bags down in the room.

"Have you stayed here before?" he asked, as he looked around and then at her. He could sense her reluctance to be there, when only minutes before she had been elated at the evening that lay ahead and the possible outcome. She desperately wanted him to win the award.

"Yes, I have," she said quietly, not bothering to push the furniture around this time to the way she liked it. She didn't feel possessive about the rooms anymore, she had no proprietary interest in the bungalow, and it no longer felt like home.

"I lived here off and on for two years, writing my first three movies."

"Alone?" he inquired cautiously. He could see shadows in her eyes. They were shadows of old ghosts.

"Most of the time. I was married when I first came here. I mourned my marriage to Peter in this room."

"And others?" She nodded. She had not gone into detail about the other men in her life. She didn't think he needed to know, only that she had gone out with a producer and an actor, and that the relationships had ended before he came along. Phillip suddenly felt as though there were a crowd of people in the room with them. There hardly seemed like there was room for the two of them. "Does it bother you to stay?"

"It's the only room they've got." She shrugged and then kissed him. "It's all right. I feel as though these are old chapters of my life, in a very old book. It's time to put it away." She already had. Maybe it was right that she came here with him and exorcised the past. Their future was bright, and they had a long stretch of open road ahead of them. This was the last gasp of her old life. The days of disappointments, broken promises, and lost dreams. Theirs was the dawning of new hope, for both of them. She felt silly suddenly for being upset about the bungalow. All that mattered now was that she was there with him. The past no longer mattered.

The girls dressed in their room late that afternoon, and helped Rupert and Isabelle to get dressed. Jason had arrived from Santa Barbara and put on his tux. And then all five of them went to the bungalow to find their respective parents. Phillip was putting on his shoes, and Tanya was almost dressed. She had on her underwear and high heels, her jewelry, and her makeup and hair were done. She put on her dress, and the girls arrived just in time to zip her up.

"Wow, Mom, you look gorgeous," Megan said admiringly, as Phillip smiled at her and whistled. She was wearing a long, sexy, red dress that showed off her figure and was a knockout.

"You look pretty wow yourself," she said to all of them, and then turned to Phillip and kissed him. A long look passed between them, with all the love she felt for him in her eyes. Her life had finally come to a peaceful place, and everything around them felt right.

All seven of them got into the limousine shortly after. When they got to the Beverly Hilton, where the Golden Globes were held, they had to go through the obstacle course of the red carpet. Hundreds of photographers stopped them, flashed their picture, and called her name, while sticking microphones in their faces. It was just like the Academy Awards. Phillip had never been to any of the awards ceremonies before, and he looked dazzled as they finally made it to the other side, when Tanya was stopped and asked to comment. She smiled and said something inane, and then joined the others again.

"They don't kid around, do they?" Phillip commented as they picked up their escort cards and began the search for their table. It was another half hour before they had waded through people, many of whom she knew and who greeted her enthusiastically, and found their table, and sat down. And it was another hour after that, as dinner was served, before the ceremony started. They began with awards for television first.

Their children were fascinated to watch, and excited to see stars everywhere around them. Tanya's children had seen enough of it in the past two years to be slightly more jaded. Phillip's children were young and so new to this that they didn't know who they were seeing or where to look first. Tanya put Isabelle's napkin on her lap, and helped her cut her chicken, while talking to Phillip and telling him in undertones who people were as they drifted by, chatting from table to table. She introduced him to everyone who stopped to say hello, including Max, who hugged her warmly and said he missed her. He was with a very attractive older woman.

It seemed an eternity before they got to the meat of the matter with feature films. Tanya had not been nominated for the screenplay, but Phillip had been nominated as the producer for Best Picture. Tanya squeezed his hand and held her breath, as they called off the names of the nominees for Best Picture. And as they always did, they showed a brief clip of each film. The one of Phillip's movie riveted people to their chairs, and stopped just as the female lead was about to die. There was a gasp as the clip came to an end. And then Gwyneth Paltrow held the envelope, tore it open, smiled, paused for an agonizing minute, and read off Phillip's name. As she had when she won the Oscar the year before, for an instant Tanya felt dazed. But it hit her faster this time, and she looked at him with wide eyes as he stared at her, unable to believe what he had just heard. He stood up unsteadily out of his chair, bent to kiss her, kissed each of his kids, and hurried toward the stage.

"I'm afraid I'm going to be terribly incoherent," he said, sounding very British, as Tanya wiped tears off her cheeks. "I can't even imagine what I did to deserve this, other than make a movie that meant a great deal to me." He thanked his cameraman, all his actors, the production crew as a whole, his children, and then there was a pause as his voice began to break. "I also want to thank the woman who inspired this film, and whom it's dedicated to, an extraordinary person . . . my late wife, Laura . . . and the woman who has loved and supported me since, Tanya Harris, who wrote the screenplay, which is brilliant. She should be getting this, and not me . . . I love you . . . thank you . . ." He brandished the Golden Globe in his hand, and wiping tears from his eyes, he ran smiling off the stage and back to his table, where everyone embraced him, and Rupert and Isabelle were hopping up and down. Tanya kissed him as soon as he sat down.

"I'm so proud of you . . . Congratulations . . ." She beamed at him.

"You did it . . . I didn't . . ." he kept insisting, as she shook her head and smiled.

"No. *You* did it . . . you made this movie. You talked me into it. You're brilliant . . . now you're going to win an Oscar," she predicted. She was convinced of it. They would just have to come back from Florence for the Oscars in April. Phillip looked ecstatic and completely overwhelmed.

At the end of the evening, all the reporters crowded around him. He was interviewed, photographed, manhandled, and congratulated, as Tanya walked beside him, slightly in the background, looking proud.

They finally got back to the hotel and walked the children to their suite. They were proud of him, too. Jason was carrying Isabelle, who had fallen asleep, and Rupert looked like he was sleepwalking as they got him into his room, undressed him, and put him to bed. Tanya did the same for Isabelle, and then all of her children hugged Phillip again.

"Congratulations," they said in unison, and then kissed their mother goodnight, and a few minutes later Tanya and Phillip went back to their bungalow, where she poured him a last glass of champagne, and he collapsed on the couch.

"I never thought this would happen, you know. I thought they were crazy when we were nominated, and I never expected to win anything tonight." He loosened his tie and took off his shoes as he grinned at her. She sat down next to him and kissed him and reminded him that "they" hadn't done it, "*he*" had.

"This is your victory, sweetheart. Savor it, enjoy the night. You should be very proud of yourself. I sure am."

"I'm proud of you," he said quietly, "for the movie you turned this into, and the extraordinary woman you are."

They sat talking quietly for half an hour, reminiscing about the evening, and then they brushed their teeth, undressed, and went to bed.

He made love to her that night, and she forgot she'd ever been in the bed before. Everything was new now. The past had vanished, they had been born again as new people with new lives.

They woke up in the morning, and she ordered him breakfast. The room service waiter looked familiar, but he didn't say anything to her.

She didn't acknowledge she had ever been there before. Bungalow 2 was no longer her home or her room. She was no longer the same person she had been when she first stayed there during *Mantra* or even the second time while she dated Douglas and wrote *Gone*. Her days with Gordon were behind her. He had gone on to a lifetime of other movies, and all the stars he was going to sleep with every time he was in a picture. And Peter was with Alice. They had all gone on to other lives, and so had she now. It was time.

Bungalow 2 was just a hotel room to her now, not a home. Other people would stay there. Happy things and sad ones would happen to them, and disappointments would crush them, just as Gordon had done. And dreams would come true for them, just as they had for her and Phillip.

They were checking out of the hotel at noon and met the children in the lobby. All but Jason were flying back to San Francisco, and in two days they were going to Florence. A whole new life had begun.

Phillip stood next to her, smiling at her proudly, grateful for all she'd done for him. She smiled at him, and then turned back to the front desk to hand over her key to Bungalow 2. She looked at it for an instant, and then handed it to the manager.

"We're checking out of Bungalow 2," she told him. She had been there too often, and for too long. She didn't mourn it or regret it. She took Phillip's hand as they shepherded their children out of the lobby, kissed Jason goodbye, and got into the waiting limousine. Jason would be joining them in Florence for spring vacation. The others would be with them. And somewhere in the world they would make their home, wherever that would turn out to be. But for now and forever, as she smiled at Phillip, sitting in the car beside her, she knew she would never see Bungalow 2 again.

It had served its purpose in her life, and been home to her for longer than she'd expected. She no longer needed it. Her home was with Phillip and their children now, wherever they wound up, in England, Italy, or back in Marin one day. Neither of them was quite sure what the map of their life would look like, or where it would lead them. But wherever it would be, they knew it would be the right place as long as they were together. As familiar landmarks slipped away, a bright new world awaited all of them. And as they drove away, like a blessing, the California winter sun shone down on them. For Tanya and Phillip, it was only the beginning of the story, not the end.